WHEN
Dreams
BECOME
REALITY

ANNE BEEDLES

When Dreams Become Reality

Copyright © 2018 by Anne Beedles

No part of this publication may be reproduced, distributed, or transmitted in any form or by any means, including photocopying, recording, or other electronic or mechanical methods, without the prior written permission of the author, except in the case of brief quotations embodied in critical reviews and certain other non-commercial uses permitted by copyright law.

Tellwell Talent

www.tellwell.ca

ISBN

978-1-77370-791-4 (Hardcover)

978-1-77370-790-7 (Paperback)

978-1-77370-792-1 (eBook)

Table of Contents

Acknowledgements

I WOULD LIKE TO thank Paula my daughter for being there when I needed her throughout this journey. Also, many thanks to my son Andrew and my daughter-in-law Stacey for their love and support.

Dedication

I dedicate this book to Roger my husband. Without his love and encouragement it may never have been written.

CHAPTER ONE

Tea With Friends

MARY ARRIVED AT the tearoom that she had been coming to for the last five years. As always, she was first to arrive. As soon as she sat down, June arrived. As always, she was rushing with a hundred things to do. They sat and waited for Shirley to arrive before they ordered. It was the same order every week: three teas and three toasted teacakes—buttered.

"It's not like Shirley to be late," Mary said. Shirley's husband Jim passed away only six months ago, and she was having a hard time coping. Jim had done everything. He paid the bills and ran the house and made all the major decisions. June and Mary were a little worried about her.

Molly came across to chat to them. She owned the tearoom and reserved the same table in the corner for the three friends for every Wednesday at 10:00 AM.

The tearoom was now filling up with all the regulars, who were catching up on all the gossip that went on in a village like Brookdale.

The village of Brookdale was set in the English countryside. It was a thriving village with a very active community. Everyone took great pride in their homes and gardens.

There were a number of pubs, inns and hotels in and around the area. It was a large village but not big enough to be a town. The local bakery made the best bread, pies, and cakes for miles around. The community centre, which was run entirely by volunteers, had a well-stocked library with an excellent selection of books.

What put Brookdale on the map were the two golf clubs. The one was just your average golf course where all the local budding golfers got their first taste of golf. Now, when you were ready to progress, Fairview Golf Club was another story.

Fairview Golf Club had a very good reputation in the golfing world. It was expensive to be a member, but well worth it. Many a business deal had been done over a game of golf at the Fairview. It had a golf professional who offered coaching lessons; as well, it boasted a very popular social club.

The tearoom was filling up. In one area a group was discussing the community centre. From the raised voices, it seemed not everyone was in agreement. There was another group chatting about the village school and the upcoming parent meeting.

Mary and June looked at their watches and started to worry about Shirley. By now she was thirty minutes late. This was not like Shirley at all. Molly came across to them and said that Shirley had phoned to say she was on her way and that she would be another five minutes.

Both Mary and June were pleased to see the door to the tearoom open and Shirley walk in. She sat down, and so they placed their order.

Shirley then proceeded to tell the two friends what had kept her. Her daughter Heather had phoned and wanted her to sell her house and go and live with her and her family. Mary and June looked at one another; they knew what Shirley's daughter Heather was like.

They listened as Shirley said that Heather had decided it would be the best thing for everyone.

So, after listening, Mary asked her what she thought about the idea. She knew there was more to this idea than Shirley was saying.

Shirley then proceeded to tell them that if she went to live with Heather she could look after her granddaughter while Heather was working and also get supper ready each night. June, who was not one to mince her words, said, "Heather has it all worked out, Shirley. We have all been friends for a long time, and so I want you to tell us that you're happy with this arrangement. Also, what do your sons think of this idea?"

Shirley looked at them and started to cry. "They want me to do whatever makes me happy."

Mary said she should tell Heather that she was not ready to make any decision about moving yet. "Give yourself time to think it through."

"Enough about me," said Shirley. "June, what have you been up to this week and who have you been helping?" June was always doing someone's shopping, or visiting at the hospital, or volunteering.

"Well, I went to help out at the seniors home at the edge of the village. I helped with the gardening group. We did the planters with spring pansies. We're all so lucky to be in our own homes, so, Shirley, think very carefully before you make a decision about giving up your own yours."

"What about you, Mary?"

"Well, you know me, shopping. Oh, and Stan booked me into that new spa that has just opened. I had a massage, manicure and pedicure. I highly recommend it."

June rolled her eyes. "What a waste of money."

"June, don't say that when you've never been to the spa. You should give it a try. We should all go and make a day of it. Give it some thought, then I can get it booked."

Shirley and June looked at one another and rolled their eyes and smiled.

The tearoom was very busy as always. Molly had a good business. If you wanted to know anything, this was the place to come to. Everything was baked fresh every day. As soon as the weather started to get colder, Molly offered her famous soups that everyone loved. June very often came in and took the soup home for her supper, as she was on her own.

Just then, the vicar came in to drop off leaflets for the up-and-coming Harvest Supper. He came over to June, Mary, and Shirley's table. "I would like to ask if any of you ladies would be interested in helping out with Harvest Supper. We're having a meeting in the village hall next week, and I would love to see you all there."

Once he left, June said: "Well, what about it? Who is coming to the meeting? I think it would be good to get involved."

Mary quickly said she was far too busy with all her activities and did not have the time. Shirley said she would like to get involved but had never done anything like that before. June quickly said she would pick her up and that they could go together to the meeting. "When I see the vicar on Sunday, I'll let him know that we'll be there. When you get there, Shirley, I'm sure you will know most of the people there as they are all from the village."

Before long it was time to go. "Shirley," June said. "Promise us you won't make any decision before we meet next Wednesday, and if you want to chat before then, call us and we'll meet. Remember, We're here for one another through thick and thin."

Mary

Mary was very stylish, tall and slim. She took great pride in herself. June and Shirley would say she was "high maintenance." She had her nails and hair done every week.

Mary had been married to Stan for forty years and wanted for nothing. She had a gardener, a cleaner, and an odd-job man. They lived in a nice house in a very upscale part of Brookdale.

She had two children. Her son Clive was blond, tall and handsome, "just like his dad," everyone said, and he was the apple of her eye. He had had the best education at the best schools money could buy, but he still couldn't hold down a job. According to Mary, it was never his fault. He was still living at home but moved in and out on a regular basis, all at a cost to Mary. If Stan only knew what she had spent on Clive over the years he would not be happy.

They also had a daughter Susan, who was a carbon copy of Mary. Susan could twist Stan around her little finger. Susan was a popular girl and everyone loved her; she would help anyone. She was married and had their only grandchild, a little girl called Emma. What a beauty! The only disappointment was that Susan and Emma now lived three hours away, and so they didn't see her as much as they would have liked.

Stan and Mary both belonged to the golf club and both played regularly. Mary loved being quite the social butterfly. Her passion was flowers, and she often got called upon to help at weddings and any large gatherings in the village.

Stan was an accountant and worked for himself, which meant long hours when it came to the year-end taxes. Most of the business people called him for advice at that time of the year.

They enjoyed many exotic holidays over the years. Of course, Mary liked to stay at the best hotels, and she expected the best treatment. Susan often said to her: "Mum, you're a snob." Of course, Mary disagreed with her; Stan just laughed. Christmas time at Mary's house was not to be missed. Everyone who was anyone got an invite. Mind you, it was not Mary doing the food. She brought in the caterers, but she did all the Christmas decorating herself both inside and outside the house. This was a party not to be missed.

Stan was a golfer and was a member at the Fairview Golf Club. Mary was also a member. She did not play much golf, but she liked the social side of the club. She had been called upon many times to head the entertainment committee for social events. You could say that was her calling. She loved to be the centre of attention. But at the end of the day, she was very good at putting an event together.

June

June was small and neat in her appearance. Her hair had been in the same style

for years—a no-nonsense short bob. Mary had offered to take her shopping many times, but has since given up trying to get her to change.

June had been a widow for many years. She met Gordon in school and fell in love with him. They were inseparable from the moment they met. She was married by nineteen and could not have been happier. First they lived in the flat over the bread shop on the main street. The smell of freshly-baked bread filtering into the flat was something they looked forward to. June and Gordon were in that flat for five years until they saved enough money to put a down payment on a small house, which they turned into a palace.

Their plan was to have children, but things did not work out that way. After three miscarriages the doctor said it was unwise to try again as it could put her health at risk.

They had a good-sized garden where Gordon grew most of their vegetables and where June grew her beloved flowers.

Gordon worked in the local factory with heavy machinery, which he loved. He was doing well. One day the boss came to him and said he wanted to send him on a three-day course. He told him to talk it over with June, but he needed to know by the next day. He pointed out that it would mean he would be moving up to management and that there would also be a pay raise.

After talking it over with June, he told the boss he would like to go and thanked him for putting him forward.

June got his bag packed and ready. She had never been on her own before, and so she was a little nervous. She kept telling herself it was only for three days.

He was due back on the Friday night. She was so excited to see him, but time was going on and there was no sign of him. She started to get worried. She phoned the boss of the company to see if he had heard anything. He knew nothing. This was not like Gordon, as he knew June would worry and he always kept in touch if plans changed.

Then it was dark. Still no sign of him. The next thing: a knock on the door. It was the police. Her heart sank. The policeman asked if he could come in. He told her there had been a car accident and that Gordon had been taken to the hospital. He did not say more than that.

She raced to the hospital, but she was too late. Gordon had just passed away from his injuries. She went in to see him. There was not a mark on him. The injuries were all internal.

Their family all came around and were a great help. The next few days were one big blur. There was so much to do, but the support was amazing. Mary and Shirley were by her side through it all and, as Shirley had gone through it with Jim, she could relate.

She did not remember much about the funeral. She thought she was in a dream and would wake up and Gordon would be there by her side.

She went back to work and got busy filling her days with whatever she could do. That was how she started volunteering anywhere she was needed. The church was a great help to her and a big comfort to her when she needed it most.

She did not drive but had a car outside the house. Then, one day there was a knock on the door. A man from down the road wanted to know if he could buy the car. And so she decided she would learn to drive. She did not want anyone else driving Gordon's car.

The next day she went to the driving school and got some lessons. Before long she had passed the driving test. Much to her surprise, she enjoyed driving.

Life was never the same, but you can either feel sorry for yourself on get on with it. So many people are worse off than me, she thought.

Shirley and Mary were very proud of her. And June was amazed at what she was capable of doing. She knew how much Gordon loved the garden, and so she set about learning how to grow vegetables, knowing he would have been very proud of her. The first year she had so many tomatoes and green beans she was giving them away.

Shirley told her she could set up a business, but June was not interested. It was too much work, she said.

Shirley

Shirley was always had a smile on her round face. She has lovely curly hair, even if it was a little unruly. She was taller than June and a little heavier, and not very fashion conscious.

Shirley was a true homemaker. When she left school she went to work in the local council office, a job she loved. She never wanted to do anything else. She got on with her work and kept herself to herself. She was not a great mixer. If she could get out of going to the work socials like the Christmas party she would, or to any other parties for that matter.

Then, one day Jim came to work in her office. Much to everyone's surprise, Shirley and Jim got on from day one. Eventually, Jim plucked up the courage to ask Shirley out and that was the start of the relationship.

Things moved along slowly, but in a good way. She started to attend company gatherings with Jim by her side. Everyone in her office was pleased to see her come out of her shell. Then, one day, they announced they were getting married, which came as a surprise to everyone. Her family could not have been happier. They had always been good at saving money, and so they were able to put a deposit down on a nice house on the outskirts of the village. The house needed some work, which Jim and Shirley enjoyed doing. They knocked down walls, rebuilt and painted the house until it looked like a brand-new home. Both families were so proud of them.

Shirley liked nothing better than to drive out into the countryside with her sketchpad, but there was never enough time. By the time the work was completed on their house, she was expecting a baby, and so the sketch pad was put away.

Over the years they had three children, who were now all married. Their one son Alex was slim and of average height. He followed Jim with a few health problems. Jim and Shirley were always helping him out financially as he had two children. Jim would get fed-up with this from time to times, given that it was a drain on their finances, but Shirley would always take Alex's side. Alex's wife Linda wanted everything. Once she got them into severe financial problems, and that was when Jim and Shirley bailed them out.

They also had a son John and daughter Heather. They were no problem at all. Heather would say: "You must put a stop to helping Alex or you will have no money left for yourselves in your retirement."

Heather took after Shirley in build. Her long, curly hair was her crowning glory. She could be a bit overbearing and would run their lives if Jim and Shirley let her. Jim had to put his foot down a few times after yet another heated discussion. Both Alex and John lived in Brookdale. When Heather married Dave she moved away. Although Shirley and Jim were sad to see her go, it made for a much more peaceful life.

John was very much like Jim in his ways but was taller and heavier set; they got on very well. He even worked in the council offices. Much to John and Jill's disappointment, they could not have children. However, they made up for that in other ways. They were involved in all kinds of sports, but their favourite had to be cycling. They belonged to the cycling club and went on many cycling holidays. They were a popular couple who were very involved in the community.

Their grandchildren were the apple of their eyes. After Shirley retired she liked nothing better than to go and pick the grandchildren up from school and bring them home with her. Jim would work on a project in the garden while Shirley got the meal ready. Alex would come and pick them up by seven. By that time, everyone was exhausted.

Both Jim and Shirley had good health, as they looked after themselves with regular visits to the doctor. Shirley made sure they ate all the right things.

They kept an eye on Dan, the elderly man who lived next door. Whenever Shirley was baking there was always an extra pie or cake for Dan next door. When his family came to visit him from out of town they would always come around to see Jim and Shirley and thank them for their kindness. If it wasn't for them, Dan would have to go and live in a home, which he would hate.

Jim cut Dan's grass and kept his garden tidy and Shirley kept his house clean and did his shopping. The only time he would come in for a meal was at Christmas time, and only if they were on their own, as he did not want to intrude.

Jim and Shirley were very content with their life and considered themselves very lucky. So it came as a big shock when Jim had a heart attack and died. Shirley was a complete mess and could not get her head around the fact that Jim had died. She was angry with the world.

CHAPTER TWO

Village Life

IT WAS THE Summer Fete in the village and everyone was out and enjoying themselves. There were animals, children's entertainers, and fruit and vegetable tents where everyone brought their prize offerings. In the cake tent, people were fussing around making sure everything was perfect.

June was as busy as she could be, rushing and helping out. She thought it was time she went for a sit down and a welcome cup of tea. She made her way to the refreshment area. Just as she entered the tent, she fell down. The next thing she knew she was being helped up by Shirley, who also was on her way for a welcome cup of tea. They looked at one another and laughed; they were having so much fun.

Ever since Shirley had attended the meeting that the vicar had arranged over a year ago now to help out with the Harvest Supper she had not looked back. She would always say Jim would be so proud of her getting out and being part of the village.

As June and Shirley sat there enjoying their tea and cakes, they both said they wished that Mary would come and join them. June said: "Mary is out of touch with everyday people, but we're not giving up on her."

The day went very well. The sun shone and a good time was had by all. Now it was time to start help clearing away. There were lots of helpers and lots of young men to do the heavy work.

When it was finished, Shirley asked June if she would like to come back to her house and have some supper with her. "That sounds like a great idea!" June replied.

On their way to Shirley's house, Mary passed them in her car, and so she stopped to see what they were doing. Shirley asked Mary if she also wanted to join them for a little supper, adding: "We're only having soup and a sandwich, so don't get too excited!"

As they made themselves comfortable, Shirley got the supper ready. Then, both June and Shirley noticed the Mary did not seem herself, and so they asked if she were okay, and if anything was worrying her.

Mary was worried about Stan. He was working longer hours than usual and when he was home he seemed very worried and was also not sleeping at night. "I don't like to nag him, but I'm worried. What do you think I should do?"

After a lot of discussion, it was decided it might be a good idea if Mary suggested taking Stan out for a meal to that nice hotel in the village. That way they could chat away from the house.

After they finished supper Mary said she would drive June home. "It is so nice to have good friends you can count on to talk things over with"

They said goodnight to Shirley and were on their way. "We'll see one another on Wednesday morning, as always. We look forward to hearing how your dinner date with Stan went," they said.

Wednesday morning June arrived first followed by Shirley then Mary. June asked what Shirley had told her daughter, as she had wanted her to sell her house and go and live with her. Shirley said she had told her she would not be selling her house or moving in with her.

Since that phone conversation Shirley had heard nothing from Heather, which upset her, but she knew it was the right decision for her. Both John and Alex were happy she was staying in her own home if that was what she wanted.

They waited for Mary to tell them how her supper went with Stan, but she did not bring it up. They chatted about everything and all the village news until it was nearly time to go.

Mary told them how she had asked Stan to come for a meal, but he said he was far too busy and could not make time. In fact, he got quite annoyed with Mary for even suggesting such a thing.

June and Shirley could see that Mary was very upset and were at a loss to know what to say next. Mary said she was going to phone Susan, her daughter, and see if she could go and stay with her for a few days. She thought a few days away might bring Stan to his senses.

"I think that sounds a good idea," said June, "but have you thought that Stan could be unwell and does not want to worry you?"

Mary was very quick to reply, saying he was a very fit man, that he played golf and went to the gym on a regular basis.

Shirley said she had to leave as she was helping out with arranging a fundraiser to raise money towards repairing the heating in the church before winter set in.

June smiled at her. "I can't believe how you have changed, Shirley. I'm so proud of you. If you need any more help, please call me, as I'm a willing helper."

"Thank you, June. I'll see how the meeting goes today and let you know."

Shirley and June both gave Mary a special hug and told her to phone them any time while she was at Susan's, which Mary agreed to do. They said their goodbyes and all went their separate ways.

By the time Shirley got to the meeting there was quite a crowd in the church hall.

Everyone put their ideas forward. Before long it was all arranged what they were going to do. The fundraiser was to be held in the village hall on the first week in September where there would be a cake sale and a book sale. "We could get the ladies in the village to knit scarfs and mitts, so that would be a good start," Shirley said.

The men in the group were going to put leaflets up asking for books to be donated and also asking for ladies to bake their favourite cake recipes. Someone in the group was going to organize children's face painting—that always went down well.

One of the men was a golfer, and so he would be going to Fairview Golf Club to see if they would give a round of golf for four. Everyone would buy tickets, given that it was very expensive to play a round of golf at Fairview.

There was also a group that would be making tea and coffee. "I think June would like to be involved in that, and so Shirley will phone June as soon as she gets home," Mary said.

June said she would be happy to help and that she would come to the next meeting. "I'm sure there will be a few meeting before the event."

Before long, the whole village was involved one way or another and everyone was happy that the heating in the church would be repaired before the winter.

Shirley did phone Mary to see if she wanted to get involved. She thought it may take her mind off Stan, but when she spoke to Mary she learned that she was leaving the next day to go to Susan's. She said she would see her on Wednesday morning as usual as she would only be away three days. Shirley wished her well and a safe journey.

The fundraiser went very well. Everyone came out to support the event; even the local businesses got involved by donating towards the grand draw. The tickets to play a round of golf at Fairview were a big hit.

All the volunteers went back to the vicarage for a glass of wine, there the money raised was counted. To everyone's delight, enough money was raised so the heating could be repaired.

June and Shirley were sitting in the tearoom waiting for Mary to arrive. They were both feeling anxious to see if things were better for Mary after her stay with Susan. Susan was down- -to-earth and level-headed, and so they kept their fingers crossed that it was beneficial.

Just then, Mary arrived. June and Shirley gave her a big hug as they were so pleased to see her. She had had a good visit with her daughter, but she didn't think Susan understood the situation between her and Stan. Basically, her daughter told her it was all in her imagination.

Mary said she was very pleased to be home and meeting up with her friends. Although Mary had many acquaintances at the golf club and the bridge club they were not close friends like June and Shirley. One thing she did say was that the lawyer had called and left a message on the phone for Stan, who was to call as soon as possible. When she told Stan, he said the lawyer had him mixed up with another one of his clients, which was very odd. She knew something was not right but could not make it out. She said she had not ruled out that Stan was having an affair. June and Shirley both said that that did not sound like Stan, and that he always made such a fuss of Mary. They changed the subject and told Mary about the successful fundraiser and how everyone had worked so hard.

They said their goodbyes as always. Over the next few days it was quiet in Brookdale. Sunday morning there was a loud knock on June's front door. She looked at the clock; it was only 8:00 AM.

Who could be at the door at this time on a Sunday morning? she wondered. She opened the door to find Mary standing there with tears in her eyes. She looked like she had been up all night.

She brought her in and told her to calm down. "Now, tell me what's wrong?"

"I've been at the hospital all night long and couldn't face going home to an empty house. I came home yesterday after my bridge club only to find Stan's car in the driveway, but I couldn't find Stan. He wasn't in the house. I went outside and found Stan collapsed on the floor of the wood shed. I called for an ambulance and Stan is now in the hospital. He's comfortable at the moment, but he had a massive stroke. I've been in touch with the children. They're on their way to the hospital, and so I'm going to freshen up, then go back to the hospital as soon as possible.

Mary asked June if she would go with her to the house. "I thought we could also phone Shirley. I feel I want my closest friends with me."

June gave Mary a cup of sweet tea then went to phone Shirley. "We'll pick Shirley up on our way to your house, and then we'll go with you to the hospital," June told Mary.

They arrived at Mary's house and opened the door to hear the phone ringing. Shirley answered it. It was the hospital. Shirley handed it to Mary. They told her to get back to the hospital as soon as she could. When they arrived back at the hospital Clive was there and Susan was on her way. Mary looked terrible. The nurse came out as soon as they saw her and took her in to see Stan. Clive was in with Stan. Things did not look good.

June and Shirley went and got a coffee and waited. Within no time Susan arrived with her husband, but then Stan suffered another stroke. This time he did not recover. It was decided that, after they had time to say their goodbyes, the machine would be switched off. He was pronounced dead at 2:00 PM. Mary and the family were inconsolable. It was such a shock to them.

The next few days were a blur. June and Shirley had been through it when their husbands died, and they knew what Mary was going through.

As Stan was such a well-known accountant in the area he had many clients. He was also very well-known and respected at the golf club. The arrangements for the funeral were overwhelming. They were trying to keep it as private as possible. Clive and Susan were a great support to Mary. Then it all came out that Stan had been seeing the doctor for the last few months and had been told he had to slow down as his health was suffering. Mary felt so guilty, as she had not recognized any of the symptoms.

On one occasion June and Shirley called in to see Mary. She was having a hard time. She blamed herself. She said she should have known Stan was unwell.

"Stan was a very private person and he didn't want you to know as he knew you would worry, and so you must not blame yourself," June told Mary.

Clive and Susan continued to be a great support to Mary. As soon as the funeral was over, Mary, Clive, and Susan made an appointment with the lawyer to go over the will. He said there was paperwork to go over. They also had to think about the business. Mary said to the children: "We'll go through it all with the lawyer when we meet."

They decided on a day that worked for everyone. They arrived at the lawyer's office. He was a friend, which made it easier. He started to speak. They could not understand what they were hearing. Stan was an accountant and very clever man. How could this be happening? Mary, Clive and Susan sat and listened to the lawyer in disbelief.

Apparently, Stan had become involved in a business venture with three business men. They had bought a large parcel of land with large buildings on it. The plan had been to demolish the buildings and build houses that were needed in the area. After they bought the land they found out the buildings could not be pulled down. Also, they could not get permission to build on the land.

Clive got up and said: "This can't be true. Dad would never agree to do anything like this. He was much too careful."

The lawyer then said, "One of the business men in the group turned out to be a real crook. He was the one that said all the paperwork was in order and swore that he had checked it out. It turned out he had done this before and was wanted by the police for another similar case. He met Stan and Ken at a golf tournament. He knew they were successful businessmen and managed to pull the wool over their eyes. By the time Stan and Ken came to me they had signed all the legal documents, so there was no going back. To make matters worse, they handed over money."

Clive asked, "Why did Dad not bring the paperwork to you to look over?"

"I only wish I could answer that question for you. The police were informed. All I can say is that Stan was beside himself. He put the house up as collateral to raise the money needed for the business venture."

Mary asked: "How long has this been going on? The house is in my name as well as Stan's so how could money be raised without my signature?"

"That's a good question. You're not going to like the answer: Stan forged your signature on the legal documents. By the time Stan came to see me, the crook in the group was long gone, along with the money. The police are now involved here and abroad as they have reason to believe he has left the country."

Susan could not speak. This was so out of character that she was convinced Stan must have been blackmailed.

The lawyer suggested he get all the outstanding loans paid first.

"Do you mean Stan borrowed money to buy this land?" said Mary.

"Yes, I'm afraid he did. We need to take one step at a time so we don't miss anything."

Mary said she felt that she was in a bad dream. Mary then told the lawyer that Ken had phoned her. "He would like to come and see me. Clive said he would also like to meet Ken. I'll call him when I get home and arrange a meeting. I'm sure he is as devastated as we are."

The lawyer thought it was a good idea to meet. "You never know what might come up in conversation. I think he would like to bring his wife Carol with him. She's having a hard time understanding how this sort of thing can happen."

The lawyer was busy over the next few weeks gathering all the paperwork together and putting it in order. He paid Mary a few house calls, as he wanted this to be as painless as possible.

June and Shirley were a great comfort to Mary through all this. She would always say if it was not for them she could not have coped.

Mary agreed to meet Ken and Carol. They came to see her at the house one afternoon. She wanted to meet with them on her own, much to Clive's disapproval.

The meet went well. Carol could not stop crying, which made Mary feel worse. Carol settled down after a glass of wine. They were a very nice couple who owned a large company that manufactured furniture. They promised to keep in touch as they had so much in common.

Mary got a call from the lawyer to say he was now ready to have another meeting with the family. So Mary got Clive and Susan together and arranged another meeting. They were all nervous going into the lawyer's office.

They all sat there not knowing what was coming next. He gave them all a copy of the outstanding loans that had to be paid. Mary was sick to her stomach as she read down the list. They were all in shock at the amount of money owed.

The lawyer went through it one by one, but the main questions were: Would there be any money left? Also, was there enough to pay these loans? Mary said she would have to sell the house. "I just can't believe Stan would get into this sort of financial mess," she said.

Both Clive and Susan were in shock. "Mum, I don't want you to get upset. We'll get this mess sorted out if it means the house has to be sold, so be it. I know you love the house, but it is much too big for you on your own. We'll help you look for something a bit smaller and it will still be our family home as you will be in it."

"Thank you for that, but I'm just in shock. I feel we're not talking about your dad but a stranger."

"The lawyer said when you sell the house there will be enough money to buy a smaller house. Also there's the business to think about. We'll be selling the business so that should raise a good amount."

It was agreed to get the loans paid and the business valued, and then put up for sale.

They all left the lawyer's office with very heavy hearts. Mary suggested they go and have lunch and talk things over.

"Good idea," Clive said. "Let's go to the hotel it will not be busy as the lunch rush hour will be over now."

As they walked into the hotel, Mary asked the host for the table in a quiet area. Over lunch they all came to terms with the situation they found themselves in.

Clive really stepped up to the mark and was a great support to Mary. Susan did not live as near to Mary. Also she had a husband and daughter Emma to look after.

It was agreed that whatever Mary wanted, Clive and Susan would go along with it. But all of them were going to be sad to see the house go. Mary said, "Let's not jump too fast. I want to take it one step at a time. As long as we have one another we'll cop."

Even Mary was pleased at how calm she was.

Susan had to get back home, and so she was first to leave, followed by Clive. Mary was going to call June and Shirley before she went home.

Shirley was already at June's house, as she had thought Mary would call in after the visit to the lawyer's office. They could not believe what Mary was saying. She said again she was so lucky to have such good friends to discuss things with and know it would not be repeated around the village. "I know everyone will know in time, but I'm not ready for that yet," she added.

She told her friends that the house would have to be sold to help pay the outstanding debt. Mary wished Stan had been able to share the worry with her, but she understood that he would not have wanted her to worry.

Over the next few weeks Mary and Clive were in meetings with the bank, estate agents and lawyers. Everyone was very helpful, but it did not make things any easier. The debt was greater than they had first thought. No wonder Stan was in such a state.

The bank suggested getting the business on the market first. One step at a time. Stan had a secretary, and so Mary was going to see her first and tell her what the plan was.

To Mary's surprise, Pat the secretary showed interest in buying the accounting business as her brother was an accountant and wanted to move back to the village.

"Oh, Pat, that would be so nice. I'm sure Stan would want that. I'm waiting for the estate agent to get back to me with a price. As soon as I hear, I'll let you know.

When Mary got home she phoned Clive and Susan to tell them that Pat was interested in buying the business. All agreed that that was what Stan would have wanted; he had great respect for Pat and always spoke highly of her.

Within a few days the estate agent got back to Mary with a price they wanted put the business on the market for. She was very surprised, but then again she had had no idea what the business was worth.

She called Pat and asked her to come to the house to discuss the business. Pat said she would like to get in touch with her brother and bring him to the meeting.

Mary was kept so busy, and this helped her with the grief at losing Stan, but she still had many down times when she was sitting in the house on her own.

Pat and her brother came around the following afternoon and went through the figures. Now that they were interested, she called the estate agent, as she wanted them to deal with the agent, not with her. Pat was very respectful, as she knew Mary was very vulnerable. As they left she said she would keep in touch.

It was not long before a price for the business was agreed upon. After that things moved along quickly. It was not good to have a business closed for too long.

With the lawyer, Mary signed the final papers to sell the business, which was one load off her mind. Clive and Susan were both pleased that Pat and her brother were buying the business.

The following Wednesday, Mary said she would meet June and Shirley in the usual place. June and Shirley were both in the tearoom when Mary arrived. They were so proud of her. Mary got the friends up to date and told them what the next move was going to be. "Now I've to get the house sorted out and ready to go up for sale."

Susan was going to come and stay with her and bring Emma, which made Mary very happy. They were going to look for what was available in the area that would suite Mary. She did not want anything too big, but she wanted a small garden.

Susan arrived with Emma. Clive came as well and started going around the house to see if they needed to do much before it went on the market. Apart for a few things that needed to be packed away, it was all very good. Stan always kept everything up to date in the house. They would call the estate agent in the morning to see if they could come and start the ball rolling to get the house on the market. Also, they would head out tomorrow to see what was on the market for sale at a price that would suit Mary.

It was hard, but they were all very positive about the next stage for Mary.

The next morning Susan was getting Emma breakfast when the estate agent arrived. He was so helpful and was very impressed with the house. "This won't take long to sell," he said.

The price was more than Mary and Susan thought, but they wanted to call Clive, as it was going to be a family decision.

Clive came over to the house, and they all agreed on a sale price for the house. The next day the police called to bring Mary up to date with their investigations. It turned out that the man was part of a larger group. This was so well planned. Stan and Ken had been the picked as they were both successful business men. They first met on the golf tournament and had become very close friends. The man they befriended was known to the police and had done a similar offense some years ago; that time he was found guilty and did a spell in jail.

Mary could not understand how Stan could be taken in by this crook, but the one policeman said: "When you're dealing with a professional group of crooks like this they are very convincing, so please don't think too badly of Stan."

"Have you any idea where he is? And do you think you will catch them?"

"All we know at this time is that we believe he has left the country. But We're actively working on it. As soon as we know more we'll be in touch."

Mary told the police that she was going to be selling the house to pay all the debts that she found herself with. They nodded in sympathy.

Mary then called Clive and Susan to let them know what the police said. They both asked about Ken and Carol. "Ken is putting on a brave face for the sake of Carol, who is having a hard time of it," Mary said. "I know time is a great healer. We plan on meeting within the next week." Mary kept in touch with Ken and Carol. It did help in a funny way, as they understood what she was going through.

CHAPTER THREE

A New Start

THE PHOTOS WERE taken and the brochure was done. So the house was now up for sale. It was bittersweet, but it had to be done. June and Shirley had been a great help in getting the house ready for sale. There was so much to do. Mary could not believe how much stuff they had collected over the years. Now it was time to start looking for a new home for Mary. June and Shirley had arranged to pick her up, and then they were going to drive around the areas that she might be interested in moving to.

The following week Mary had just finished her supper when the phone rang. It was Ken who said they would like to come around to see her.

When Ken and Carol arrived it was a little strained at first, but Mary made some tea then she showed them the sale brochure for the house. She could tell that Carol was having a hard time with all this. Mary had quite a few questions she wanted to ask Ken, who answered as much as he could. He was feeling very frustrated with himself about the whole thing and as to how they had both been taken in, and just how they had believed everything they were told. Carol also realized how fortunate they were compared to Mary. All they had had to do was sell some of their properties to cover the money they had lost.

Ken said: "The worst thing of all in this terrible mess is that Stan lost his life. That will live with me always. The one thing that has come out of this is that I'll never play another game of golf as long as I live."

Before Ken and Carol left they agreed to keep in touch. Ken said that if there were anything he could do to help during the selling of the house and moving to let him know. Mary really liked both of them and would be keeping in touch.

The interest in the house was very good, but the one thing she did not like was all the viewing. She phoned Susan one day and said, "I'm sure a lot of the people were just plain nosy." It did not take long before they had a call from the agent to say she was coming around to discuss an offer. Mary phoned Clive so that he could be there with her when the agent arrived. The offer was good, and so they decided to accept it.

By now everyone in the village knew about the situation Mary was in. Everyone
was supportive and pleased to see Mary being so positive about it all. She surprised herself at
the strength she found within herself.

She went to see a few nice bungalows. One she really liked, ad so she asked June and
Shirley if they would go with her to have a second look. All three of them loved it. It had three bedrooms that were not large but big enough for when Susan came to stay. The garden was just the right size for her to manage. And there was a garage.

The agent suggested she put an offer in on the bungalow, as the sale on her house was looking good. For the first time she was getting excited about moving.

The following week the offer on her house was accepted. At the same time, the offer she had put on the bungalow was also been accepted. Things were looking a bit more positive. She could not wait to tell June and Shirley her news. Clive and Susan had been so helpful during the selling of her house and the buying of the bungalow. Mary had detached herself from her house, but Susan was having a hard time accepting everything.

The following Wednesday in the tearoom, Mary, June, and Shirley were getting the move all planned out. They were making lists as to who was doing what. There were boxes to be collected and packing to do. It was so nice to see Mary laughing again.

The packing was in full swing when Clive called around to the house. He was just amazed as to how much they had done. June had brought lunch that day so they were all organized. There were a few boxes that Mary had put aside to be taken to the charity shop in the village, and so Clive loaded them into his car. "I'll be back with some more empty boxes," he said.

Moving day arrived. Mary had arranged to move over two days, which worked out well. June, Shirley, Susan and Clive were busy, and then Ken and Carol turned up to help as well. The bungalow looked beautiful with Mary's furniture in it. Susan came with the biggest bunch of flowers you ever saw. It was a sunny day. Mary said she felt Stan was with her all day. "I know he would approve of the move," she said.

Clive came around and said he had booked a table at the hotel for a meal. All the ladies said they looked a mess, but Clive would not take no for an answer. "So comb your hair and get your lipstick on or whatever you ladies do."

June, Shirley, Susan and Mary just laughed.

He made a point of including Ken and Carol. They were pleased to have been able to help.

Clive ordered a nice bottle of wine to have with the meal and made a toast to Mary and said: "We're so proud of you," he said. After the end of the meal and the second bottle of wine he ordered a taxi to take them all home. It was the end of a perfect day and the beginning of a new one.

Susan slept the first night in the bungalow with Mary and then went home the next day.

Mary was sorting through a few more boxes and thinking about how her life had changed. She was also thinking of all those friends, or so-called friends at the golf club. It seemed a lifetime away now. Not one of them had offered to help or ask how she was.

As she made another cup of coffee she thought she would phone the police station and let them know that she had moved. If, or when, they had more information for her it was important they would know where to find her. Also, she had to go to the bank to go through more paperwork. The bank manager had been so helpful and so reassuring that things would be sorted out when the business and house was sold.

When she arrived at the bank, she felt good for the first time in a very long time. The manager came out to see her and take her into his office. "Well, everything is looking much better," he said. This was true. Now that she was in the bungalow, which was smaller than her large house, she was mortgage free and still there was enough money for her to live on. Stan had provided well for her after his death, which came as a nice surprise as she knew nothing about the life insurance he had taken out years ago.

From the bank, she went to the florist's and got some flowers for June and Shirley for being so helpful and supportive over the last few months. June and Shirley were thrilled with the flowers but both said there was no need. "Yes, there is a need," Mary said, "and it is just a small appreciation for being there for me when I needed you both so much.

They both said: "See you Wednesday as usual!"

When she got home, Ken and Carol called around to see how she was getting settled in. Mary felt comfortable with them both. Carol was the sweetest lady. She had been feeling sorry for herself until she met Mary. Then she realized that, compared to Mary, she had nothing to feel sorry about.

She admired Mary for selling the house and buying the bungalow, and all without Stan.

They loved Mary's bungalow. Ken helped move some things around in the garage so that Mary could get her car in the garage. Mary had a thing about her car. It had to be in the garage. Carol helped Mary in the garden, not that there was much she wanted to change.

By the time they left Mary was exhausted and went for a lie down.

She could not believe how she had settled in, and how she had not given her big house that she had loved so much a second thought. I guess this is home now, she thought.

Wednesday morning Mary was first to arrive at the tearoom. Molly was pleased to see her looking so much better. Mary was telling her all about the bungalow when June and Shirley arrived. "Well, I'll leave you ladies to it. The usual order?"

They all nodded. At another table in the tearoom there was a group of ladies that Mary recognized from the golf club. She looked at Shirley and June and shook her head and said, "Just ignore them. How shallow are they!"

Shirley had started art classes at the community centre on Thursday. She was enjoying the classes very much. She was telling them all about the class and wanted to know if Mary would like to come along.

"Well, I've never done anything like that before. I don't think I'd be any good," Mary said.

Shirley said it had been years since she picked up a brush "Why don't you come and give it a try?" she pressed.

"Well, I could give it a try. What do I've to bring with me?

"You don't have to bring anything with you in the beginning. Just come along to see if you like it."

June was so pleased that Mary was willing to give it a try. Shirley said: "You never know, Mary, we may be able to persuade June to come."

"Now, Shirley," June laughed. "Don't go on. You know I just can't draw or paint. I'm just not arty."

Mary smiled, and said she had to agree with June.

Shirley was saying that Heather was coming to see her, and that she had not seen much of Heather lately. Things were a bit strained between them ever since Heather had asked if Shirley would go and live with her.

June told her to try and get along with her.

"I'll do my best," Shirley sighed. "But I'm not having her rule my life for me."

June said she had to go as she was helping out at the senior's home that afternoon.

Shirley said she would see Mary on Thursday for the art class. "It's at two thirty in the community centre."

Mary arrived at the community centre the same time as Shirley so they could go in together. When they went in Mary realized she knew a few people there. She was made to feel very welcome. The teacher was called Gary. He was very nice. You could see he was very passionate about the class and had plenty of patience with everyone.

They all got set up, and the class began. Mary found it very interesting and really enjoyed it. Gary was giving her a few tips, which made her fit in. He told her to do whatever she wanted to do.

Halfway through the class they all stopped for coffee and what Shirley called 'a good old fashioned gossip.' Some of the members had been coming for quite some time and were very good. On the other hand, some had not progressed much from their first lesson, but were still enjoying themselves.

They were telling Mary that at the end of term they always have an art exhibition. Mary looked at Shirley and said: "I'd better get my act together as I've a lot to do if I'm to have anything good enough to go in an art exhibition!"

Gary rang a bell. That meant it was time for the coffee break. As soon as the coffee break was over everyone went back to their artwork and were soon deeply absorbed.

Shirley liked sketching better than painting, and so she was concentrating on a bowl of fruit. There were two other ladies also sketching the bowl of fruit. It was so peaceful. Gary asked Mary what she would like to try her hand at. Thinking about it, she decided that she would like to start off sketching first and see how it went.

By the end of the class, Mary was learning a few basic details and slowly getting the hang of it. Gary said he hoped she would come again next week. She said she would.

On the way to their cars Mary thanked Shirley for asking her to join as she had really enjoyed herself. Everyone said good night and all shouted: "See you next week!"

Things went on as usual over the next few weeks. June was helping everyone and anyone. Shirley was also involved in the community. And Mary was settling into her new home and now she had the art class.

The following week Ken and Carol called around to see how Mary was getting on. "We have something we want to ask you."

"Well, you had better come in this sounds very mysterious. I'll put the coffee on and we can chat."

Ken and Carol had a cottage in Devon by the beach and wondered if Mary, along with June and Shirley, would like to go and have a holiday. Mary was a little taken aback, but the more she thought about it the more she thought it would be so nice to get away and have some sea air.

Carol said it was only a small, three-bedroom cottage but that the bedrooms were charming. "We want you at least to think about it. We only keep it for ourselves and our family, and so all you have to do is speak to June and Shirley and let us know when you would like to go. The weather would be nice any time from early June onwards. You can go for at least two weeks. It'd be something for you to look forward to. We thought it would do you some good."

Mary promised she would speak to June and Shirley on Wednesday when they met. "This is so kind of you both to do this. Thank you both very much!"

When she met with June and Shirley she was so excited and was hoping they would be, too. She sat there, waiting for them to arrive. How times have changed, she thought. They were always waiting for me. Now I'm the first to arrive.

Then June came in. She took one look at Mary and asked what was going on. "I can't say anything until Shirley arrives." At last Shirley came through the café door.

"Come on, Shirley." June said. "Mary has something she wants to talk to us about." Mary gave them all the details. They were very quiet at first, and then all three of them started to laugh at the same time. June was first to say, "Yes, let's go," followed by Shirley.

"I'm so pleased you said 'yes.' We'll have the best time," Mary promised. "We have a lot of planning to do. First of all, when shall we go? What about the first two weeks in June. Do you both agree?"

"I think that sounds good with us," June said.

"I'll phone Ken and Carol as soon as I get home and check that the cottage is free, and then I'll phone you both back so we can start planning our very first holiday together," Mary said.

After speaking to Carol she said the cottage was free the first two weeks in June. Mary spoke to June and Shirley, who were so excited.

"We only have six weeks before we go so we have a lot to do to get organized," Mary said.

It was agreed they would go in Mary's car to take all their luggage, as Mary's car was larger. Shirley told John and Alex, who were thrilled for her, and then she called Heather and told her about the trip. She made no comment.

John and Alex said they would look after the house for her, so she was to go and enjoy herself. "You three are going to have so much fun together," Alex said.

Clive and Susan were also thrilled to hear about the trip. "Mum, this is just what you need. This is so kind of Ken and Carol to offer their cottage to you all."

June rang Shirley and Mary and invited them around to her house for supper to make a start on the planning. Mary came with the address of the cottage and a road map and before long the route was planned. It would take a good six hours, and so they worked it out to start at 9:00 AM. They could make a stop for lunch and should be there by 4:30

They were enjoying the planning as much as the holiday. They decided to do some shopping first, as they all wanted a few new clothes. Mary said she was going to phone the spa she used to go to and get a little pampering. Much to Mary's surprise, June and Shirley said: "Book us in as well."

The planning and shopping was done, and now it was time for the spa day. Mary had booked the spa for a massage, manicure, and pedicure. June and Shirley had never been to the spa before, and so they were very excited about it.

On the day of the spa appointment, Mary picked June and Shirley up at 8:30 AM, as they were all booked in for 9:00 AM. They were very excited as they crowded into Mary's car. June said she felt like a teenager. She could not stop smiling.

They arrived at the spa and were taken into a nice room. Each met the masseuse and were given a nice, warm fluffy robe to change into. That was followed by the best massage they had ever had. And this was the first time June and Shirley had ever had a massage!

Mary laughed at them. They were then taken into a beautiful lounge and were given a choice of herbal tea and were told to put their feet up and relax. There was a selection of magazines. Soft music played. "This is living!" said Shirley, who by now was relaxed and enjoying every minute. All three were soaking up the experience. After about thirty minutes another lady came in and escorted them into another area of the spa to have their pedicure followed by a manicure.

After this was all this was finished they decided to go for lunch. All through lunch they could not stop talking about the experience at the spa. "I think we should treat ourselves to a spa day every now and again. What do you all think?" June said.

Mary looked at June and Shirley. "I never thought I'd see the day that you two would talk about a second trip to the spa.

Chapter Four

First Trip

Only a few days to go until they went on their first adventure. They were all so excited. Bags were getting packed. It was Shirley and Mary's last art class before they went. Mary was really getting quite good. Gary was very impressed with her. She was more interested in learning watercolours, but as she said, it was a lot to learn.

Everyone in the class knew about their trip and Shirley could not stop talking about the day at the spa. By the end of the class everyone wish them well and could not wait to hear all about it upon their return.

Gary was tall and well-dressed in an arty kind of way. He had grey hair, which he wore on the longer side. He also had a well-trimmed moustache. Shirley often commented to Mary about how distinguished he looked.

As Shirley was getting into her car Gary shouted: "Make sure you take your sketch pad with you!"

The day before the trip they met up to go over all the final details. They had everything planned: what they were taking, etc. Mary was going to pick them up around 8:30 in the morning at Shirley's and then on to pick June up after; so they could be on their way by 9:00. Mary filled the car up with petrol so she would be ready.

The alarm went off in Mary's bedroom. She could not believe how her life had changed and what her and her greatest friends were about to do. She jumped out of bed, ran downstairs to make a quick cup of tea to drink while she got herself ready.

She was at Shirley's house at 8:30. They put her bags in the car, and then drove on to pick June up. June was waiting, all ready to go. "I can't believe how excited I'm," she said.

At 9:00 they were on the road. Mary handed the road map to Shirley, who was sitting in the front passenger's seat. "Now, Shirley, don't get us lost," Mary teased.

They all smiled at one another, and then June said, "Can you believe we're really going?"

The roads were good, no traffic. And the weather was kind to them. They were in no hurry, and so they decided to stop for a cup of coffee. It was 11:00. After fifteen minutes it was back in the car. The next stop would be for a lunch break.

They stopped for lunch in a small café. Sitting at the next table was a couple. They started to talk to them. The couple were also going away on holiday. It was their wedding anniversary. They were excited, as they had not been able to get away together for such a long time.

June said they were also going to Devon for a two-week holiday. She did not go into details. She just said that a friend had given them use of their cottage for two weeks, and that they were also in need of a break. Shirley and Mary smiled at June.

After lunch it was back on the road. They decided to keep going, no more stops until they got into Devon. At the first road sign that said *Welcome to Devon,* they all gave out a squeal of delight. The cottage was in a small town called Clifton. "According to the map we're only ten miles away from the cottage," Mary said. "The cottage is located on the South Shore road, so look for the signs."

June spotted the sign to South Shore road.

"Now all we have to do is look for number 541. Carol gave me a photo of the cottage so it should be easy to find. Look there it is! It looks just like a picture postcard."

Mary pulled up in the small driveway of the cottage. They could not wait to get out of the car and unlock the front door of the cottage. Once inside they found the most charming little cottage you could imagine.

There was a note on the table from Vera, the lady who looked after the cottage for Ken and Carol. It said: *I've put tea, coffee, milk and a few things in the fridge. Have a nice holiday.* Also she left her number and to call her if they needed to know anything as she lived nearby. The cottage was very sunny with lots of windows and decorated so beautifully. There was a front porch with six very comfortable chairs overlooking the beach.

"Let's do a tour of the cottage!" Shirley said.

There was a living room with a dining area that led to an open-plan kitchen. There was also a powder room. Upstairs there were three double-sized bedrooms and a good-sized bathroom.

They each picked a bedroom and went downstairs to the car to get their cases. It took a while to get all the boxes unpacked as they had brought plenty of groceries with them. After they were all unpacked, Shirley made a pot of tea, put it on a tray on the front porch and shouted to the others. They all sat on the front porch drinking their tea and soaking up the late afternoon sun. "This is so perfect. Can you believe we're so lucky?" Shirley said.

Mary called her children on the phone and Shirley called her children. Now they were all going to enjoy themselves.

By now all three of them were tired, and so it was an early night. "Tomorrow we can go for a walk on the beach and explore the area," Mary suggested.

They all hugged and said goodnight. The beds were very comfortable, and so they were soon all fast asleep.

June was first downstairs. She opened the curtains. The sun was starting to break through. She put the kettle on and started to make a pot of tea. Just then Mary came down. "I think Shirley is still sleeping," June said. "I'm going to take mine out on the front porch."

"Me, too," said Mary.

June opened the front door. To her surprise a little dog walked in and sat on the carpet in front of the fireplace. June and Mary looked at one another. "What a cute little dog and very well looked after. I wonder were he lives?" Mary said. He did not want to move, that was for sure. They gave him a drink of water. "We have to find out who owns him," Mary said.

Shirley came down the stairs to see their new little friend making himself at home in the living room.

June said she would go and get dressed and then go next door to see if the dog belonged to anyone.

Nobody seemed to know who owned the cute little dog. He had no collar, but he had obviously been cared for. "I'm going to phone Vera. She may know something or may be able to suggest what we can do with him." June said.

Vera, it turned out, had no idea who owned him. She had never seen him before.

After breakfast they decided to go for a walk down onto the beach. They found some string in the garage that they could use as a lead. Just as they were closing the door, Mary said: "We had better take an empty bag. We don't want him to mess on the beach."

Shirley was not really into dogs, but June and Mary were quite taken with their new friend.

They walked along the beach. All took their shoes off and paddled in the sea. Their new little friend was enjoying himself and was friendly to everyone he met.

After a while they sat down and decided to go to the local police station to see if anyone had reported a missing dog. Back at the cottage they cleaned up after the walk, ready to go to the police station.

The police officer took all their details, but no one had reported a missing dog. The police officer gave them the name of a vet and said the vet would check if the dog had a chip in him with his details. "What a good idea! We never thought of that, as we're not dog owners," Mary said.

They were back in the car now and off to find the vet. The little dog was quite enjoying himself. Mary said: "We had better stop and get some dog food. What do you think?"

"I think we should go to the vet first, and then go and get some food. The vet will tell us what food we need to buy," June said.

"Good idea," Mary said.

Shirley didn't say much. She was not too impressed with their new, four-legged friend. Mary was driving, and the dog was on June's knee on the front seat.

At the vet, the receptionist took their details and was very helpful. She told them to take a seat in the waiting room and that the vet would be with them as soon as possible.

Mary had the dog on her knee. June and Shirley sat next to her. After a few minutes the vet came to talk to them. He asked them to bring the dog to his room. He lifted the dog up onto the table to take a look at him.

"This dog has been very well looked after and is used to coming to the vets. He is so good and does what he is told."

After the vet examined him, he told them he did have a little chip, and so he would scan it for his information.

When the vet came back he told them that the dog's name was Toby and that he was three years old.

"Does it tell you where he lives?" June asked.

"Yes, " said the vet. "He must have been down here with his owners as he lives about two hours away. Do you want me to phone them for you?"

"Yes, I think that would be a good idea," Mary put in.

Off he went to the other room to call the owners. When he came back into the room he told them the owner was so happy that Toby was all right. "The owner is a lady called Janice and she had been down with her son and family for a few days. When they were packing up ready to go home they thought Toby was in the back of the car, as he loves the car and always sleeps, and so they never hear him. When they got home they discovered Toby was nowhere to be found. They started to panic. Janice has been very upset as Toby is her sole companion."

The vet suggested they phone Janice and arrange to get Toby back home as soon as possible.

Mary spoke to Janice. She was so pleased to hear Toby was fine. She asked them if they could keep him until tomorrow afternoon. So it was agreed that Toby would stay with them the night. Mary gave Janice the address and arranged a time to come and pick Toby up. "Could you tell us what food he has as we don't want to give him something that's going to upset him," Mary said.

By the time they got back to the cottage everyone was hungry and tired. Within no time at all the meal was ready and they were sitting down to enjoy it. Toby ate, too.

Later that evening as they sat on the front porch with a nice glass of wine they went over their first day. "I wonder what will happen tomorrow. It has been a very interesting first day," Mary said.

They made Toby a bed, and he was sleeping in no time.

Mary was awake earlier than normal, as she could not stop thinking about Toby and how she was going to miss him. She decided to go downstairs and make herself a cup of coffee. It was the start of another nice day. The sky was clear and the sun was just coming up.

Toby was still in the little bed they had made for him. By the time Mary had her coffee made Toby was by the door waiting to go out. She went and sat on the front porch with her coffee and Toby came and sat by her.

June heard Mary moving about so she came and joined her on the porch with her coffee. "Oh, June, I wish we could keep Toby," Mary said. "I didn't know you could get so attached to a dog in such a short time. What do you think about me having a little dog like Toby?"

"Well, I think it could be good for you, but it is a commitment, that's what you have to think about. I'll have a chat to Janice when she comes to pick Toby up later today."

"That sounds like a good idea!"

Shirley was not impressed with Mary's idea of having a dog. "Are you sure you want to be tied to having a dog?"

"I really think I would like it. I've never had a dog. Stan would not hear of us having one. The children wanted one when they were growing up though."

Janice arrived about 1:30. Toby and Janice were so pleased to see one another. He jumped all over her and would not leave her side. Janice could not stop thanking them for looking after Toby so well. "I live alone and didn't realize how much I depended on him until he wasn't there."

They all decided to go for a walk as Janice had been sitting in the car driving for two hours. Mary asked Janice all about having a dog and what it entailed. Janice said Toby was the first dog she had ever had and that she could not imagine her life without Toby.

Mary told Janice about her situation and how, now that she was on her own, she thought having a dog would be good for her.

"Well, you have to remember it is a commitment, but the rewards are well worth it. If you're interested, my neighbour breeds Scottie dogs like Toby. I could speak to him if you like. I think he has a litter of pups at the moment, but I'm not sure if they are all spoken for."

Mary had a chat with June and Shirley to get their opinion about her having a dog. They both said as long as she was prepared for the work involved it could be good company for her.

"That settles it, I'm getting a little dog!"

Mary then told Janice she had decided to get a little dog like Toby. Janice said she would go and see Ted her neighbour when she go home and let Mary know.

Back at the cottage they had a meal before it was time for Janice to be on her way home. "Well, I hope you have a great holiday. I first came down to Clifton with my husband, and then we brought the children down every year. Since my husband passed away a few years ago I now come down with my children and grandchildren."

Janice made sure Toby was safely in the car. Mary gave Janice her phone number. "I'm going to keep my fingers crossed for you," Janice said.

After Janice left they all sat on the front porch with a glass of wine and enjoyed the views. "I could get use to this. I feel we have been here ages and it's only the first day."

"What are we going to do tomorrow?"

"I suggest we go into town and explore the shops and anything else that takes our fancy."

Next morning after breakfast they set off to walk into the town. It was not a large town. Janice had told them about the town square, and said it was not to be missed. She was correct. It was made up of beautiful gardens with seats everywhere.

They decided to sit on one bench and admire the gardens. Just then a car pulled up and out got three ladies with gardening tools. The one lady shouted "good morning" to June, Shirley and Mary and explained that they tended the gardens once a week. They went on to say that volunteers maintained all the gardens in the town.

"What a great idea! We should do that in Brookdale where we live," Mary said.

The ladies introduced themselves and asked how long they were you staying in the Clifton. June said two weeks. "We're staying in a cottage on South Shore."

Amy, the one lady, said: "What number South Shore?"

"Five forty one," said June.

"Oh, you must be staying at Ken and Carol's cottage. They're members of our gardening club. Whenever they're down, Carol comes to our meetings. That is the most charming cottage. I hope you're enjoying your stay."

"Well, it has been eventful since arriving," Shirley said and told them about Toby.

"We have a garden meeting tomorrow night at the community centre if you're interested. We could give you some ideas as to how to get a garden group together for your village."

Mary said that would be nice and they all agreed to go. Amy told them where the community centre was and that they met at 7:00 PM.

"We better let you get on with your gardening. We're off to look at the shops and to do some shopping," June said.

They found a great little cheese shop. "Come on," said June. There were two ladies behind the counter who offered them some samples. June was very impressed; before long she was sampling the cheese and the chutneys. "Shirley, come and taste this, the flavour of the chutney compliments the cheese so well."

By the time they finished, they had bought cheese with red wine, cheese with chilli and a standard cheddars, along with three different chutneys.

Mary asked, "Would we be able to buy some ham and bread?"

Shirley told the ladies they would be back for more.

From there they went into a gift shop that seemed to sell everything. It was a high-end gift shop. Bill, the owner, introduced himself to Mary first and was soon busy telling her his life story. June said to Shirley, "I think he fancies our Mary. Look at him looking at her."

Bill's shop went from room to room; it was the kind of shop that had something for everyone. Shirley called June, "Come take a look at the selection of silk scarfs. Look, June, they're made locally."

Shirley bought one for Heather; it was blue with splashes of green going through it.

They all bought something. As they left the shop, Mary said, "We'll be back before we go home next week."

"I look forward to that," said Bill.

Outside the shop, June and Shirley smiled at Mary. "You look like the cat that has just found the cream," Shirley said.

"I think it's time to look for somewhere we could get lunch," Mary said as she touched her hair. "What about that little pub next to the cheese shop?"

The pub was full, and so they went and sat on the patio at the back of the pub overlooking the gardens. You can't beat a pub lunch on such a nice summer day. After looking at the menu they decided on a glass of wine and chicken salad. "That was the best chicken salad ever," said June. "So tasty. Now back to shopping and exploring Clifton."

June noticed a sign pointing up a side entrance between two shops it read: *Whatever you're looking for, we have it.* "Let's go and have a look," June said.

It was an old barn that looked very interesting. They went inside. There was a lady sitting by the door. She told them to come in and have a look around. The barn went on forever, or so it seemed.

They looked all around the ground floor first and could not believe the things they were finding.

Shirley found some old postcards dating back to the end of the war. The lady at the barn said they do a lot of house clearing, so that is where the postcards came from.

She agreed on a price, and so Shirley bought them. Mary came across a small jewellery cabinet. She also picked out the most beautiful necklace with emerald stones, and so she bought that.

They then made their way up the rickety old stairs. June was first up there and called the others to join her. "I've never seen so much stuff," she said. In the far corner there was a chair with teddy bears stacked on it. June went over to it. She could not resist the little one that was perched on the arm of the chair. She picked the bear up and took it downstairs with her. After she had paid for it they left feeling very pleased with themselves.

The lady was still sitting by the door as they left. She told them the barn had been in her family for many years. She was pleased they had enjoyed themselves.

It was decided to make their way back to the cottage. Back at the cottage June made some coffee and they sat on the front porch and put their feet up. No one would own up to it, but they all fell asleep. Later June said that it must be the sea air.

Shirley prepared supper. The cheeses and chutney along with the crusty bread rolls and ham did not disappoint.

After supper they took a walk on the beach. With their shoes off they walked and walked. Quite a few people were also strolling along the beach.

A group of teenagers were laughing, just enjoying an evening on the beach. Shirley suggested, "Lets make our way back and see the sunset from the torch of the cottage."

Mary was lost in her thoughts. June asked her if she was feeling okay. For the first time she started to talk about Stan. She got teary as she said, "You know, sometimes I get so angry with him. I can't understand how he could have got himself mixed up with that man and lose all that money.

"You know Stan never took a risk on anything like that in his life," Shirley said and told her not to think of the bad things. "Think of all the good times you had with Stan instead and think, too, of the children."

"Yes, I know. You're right but sometimes when I'm on my own I can't help but think about it."

June poured them all another glass of wine, and before long they were chatting about other things.

Next morning Mary's phone rang. It was Janice to say her neighbour had one puppy left out of the litter. She asked Mary if she was still interested. "You can think about it and phone me back when you've decided. Remember it's a big decision."

Janice told her it was a female puppy, all white and that she was a little beauty. However, she would not be able to have her for another two weeks. Mary decided she would call her back the following morning.

She came off the phone and told June and Shirley she had already made her mind up to take her. "Now, what am I going to call her!?" Mary was so excited. "Let's all make a list of names we like. I want you all to help in picking a name. I think this is exactly what I need. I've never had a dog, and so it will take a get a bit of getting used to. I wonder what Clive and Susan will think?"

"Let's have a lazy day today," said June. "Since we're going to the meeting tonight in the community centre at seven."

"That sounds good to me," said Shirley. "I'm going down to the beach and see if it's warm enough for a swim."

Mary went for a walk down to the little shop at the end of the road to get a paper, and that was pretty much all they did that day.

They set off in plenty of time to get to the community centre by 7:00 PM. When they got there it was busy, but they were made very welcome. As they sat down, Amy and the other ladies came across and said it was nice to see them.

Before long, the meeting started. Tonight concentrated on the community gardens and in making sure they had enough volunteers to go around. The president then spoke and introduced June, Mary, and Shirley. June then spoke up. "We are interested in finding out how to go about organizing community gardens."

It was very interesting, and they were given good information on how to get started. The main thing was to get the local garden centres involved. "You will be amazed how helpful local companies will be when you get started," the president said.

Before long June, Shirley and Mary were interacting with the group and making new friends. Everyone was interested in hearing about what they did in Brookdale.

Then it was time for a coffee break. June tapped Shirley on the shoulder as they spotted Bill from the gift shop coming over or, it should be said, coming over to talk to Mary.

Bill was medium height, slim, very well dressed. You could see his clothes were expensive and well tailored. He had a navy blazer with a silk handkerchief in the top pocket. He looked very dashing, Mary thought.

The evening turned out to be very interesting all round. Mary and Bill were engrossed with one another for the entire second half of the meeting. At the end of the meeting the president came across and invited them to come along to a BBQ that one of the members was throwing next week. They took the details. All agreed it would be lovely to go. "We have local artists that like to show their artwork. If you want to buy any of the art work, I'm sure the artists would be delighted to sell," the president then said.

Mary told Bill she would pop into the shop and see him. On the way home in the car June and Shirley were very discreet and did not ask Mary too many questions about Bill. Mary did say he was a very charming man and very lonely, as his wife had died two years ago.

The next morning Mary phoned Janice to say 'yes' she did want the puppy. Janice gave Mary all the information and suggested they call in to see her on their journey home. She could meet Ted and also see her new puppy and get all the information on her. "Now, come on, girls, what am I going to call her?"

June came up with Poppy or Polly. Shirley came up with Sky or Molly. And Mary came up with Lucky or Daisy. After going over the names they decided on Polly. "I really like that. It sounds cute," Mary agreed.

Mary's phone rang again. "My, I'm popular today," she said as she went off to answer it. She came back outside where June and Shirley were enjoying the morning sun. They looked at Mary when she told them it had been Bill on the phone.

Shirley said, "That was nice. Did he want anything important?

"He invited me to have supper with him tonight."

"What did you say?" asked June.

"I said I would call him back in an hour as we were in the middle of something. I didn't know what else to say. What do you think? Should I go or what?"

"It's entirely up to you," Shirley said. "Bill is a charming man and you always have such a lot to talk about."

June agreed. "It's only supper, for heaven's sake! It's not as if you're going to jump into bed at the first available moment."

Mary looked horrified at June, and then they all saw the funny side of it.

Mary called Bill back and arranged to meet at the restaurant in the town square. He wanted to come and pick her up, but Mary said she would drive herself and meet him at the restaurant. "I really don't know what Clive and Susan will think. First I've decided to have a dog, and now I'm having supper with a man I've only just met! It must be the sea air."

The three friends then decided to make a picnic lunch and take it down on the beach. June spotted a perfect cove in the rocks. It did not take long before they were ready to go. Carol had told them there were blankets for the beach, and so Shirley grabbed one and off they set.

"This is the best location ever," Shirley said. "See, how it's shaded from the full sun."

Mary and June had their books and Shirley had her sketching pad. They then opened the picnic basket that had lunch. Over lunch Mary started to talk about Bill. "You know I feel like a teenager going on a first date. I can't remember when I felt like this. It's certainly been a long time. Whatever would Stan think?"

June and Shirley looked up at the same time and declared: "He would be proud of you."

Soon it was time to pack everything away and walk back to the cottage. Mary said she had better start getting ready for her supper date with Bill. "What time did you say you're meeting Bill," asked June

"Six thirty at the restaurant," Mary said. "And so I had better get a move on."

Shirley and June were busy putting everything away and cleaning around the cottage. "I guess it will be just the two of us for wine this evening," June said with a smile.

"I think we can manage that," Shirley said.

CHAPTER FIVE

Everything Changes

W<small>HEN</small> M<small>ARY</small> <small>CAME</small> out onto the front porch June and Shirley stared. "You look amazing!" they chorused.

"Do you think I've overdone it?"

"Heaven's no!" June said. "You look very classy. We're thrilled for that you're having supper with such a nice man like Bill."

"Now go and enjoy yourself," Shirley put in. "Mind you, we'll be waiting up and will want all the details."

They hugged as Mary got in the car and set off for the restaurant.

When Mary arrived at the restaurant, Bill was already there. He did look very handsome. As Mary approached the table he got up to greet her. "You look so beautiful, Mary."

"Now, don't make me blush," Mary said.

Bill ordered some Chablis. They started chatting about everything and anything all evening. He went on to tell Mary all about his wife Olive of twenty-five years and how she became sick, only to find out she had cancer. They were childhood sweethearts and lived a happy life until the day she died. "We couldn't believe what we were hearing when the doctor told us about the cancer. It was as if he was talking about someone else. Our world fell apart."

Mary could see the pain in his eyes. "It must have been a terrible shock for you both."

"It was, and a terrible terrible time. And then I had to tell the girls that their mother had cancer and that the outlook was not good. They were both devastated. At first they wouldn't accept it, but they became my biggest support. We helped one another through the good days and the bad. From the time Olive started her treatments to the time she died was only lived eighteen months. She suffered quite a lot, but at least we were able to have her at home most of the time. Family and friends all came together and were so supportive. The back-up from the hospital was first class." Bill took a sip of his wine and sighed. "Olive's wish was that I carried on with our gift shop. We had worked so hard in building together. But when I was ready to sell the business, I could do it with her blessing."

Mary had tears in her eyes hearing all this. Bill changed the subject, saying he did not want to spoil the evening. "But do you know? I've not talked like this ever since Olive died. I feel so comfortable talking to you. I do believe I could tell you anything."

Mary just smiled back at him. "Now, I want you to tell me about your twin daughters. Where are they living? Are they married or not?"

Bill went on to tell Mary about the twins. They were both married, but had no children. "They both live in Scotland so they have each other," he added.

"Do you see much of them?" Mary asked. "I'm sure you all must miss one another."

"Well, yes, I'd love to see them more often, but they both lead busy lives working, and they have busy social lives, too. They don't even get to see one another as often as they'd like, but that's life."

During the rest of the meal they just talked and laughed.

"The gift shop keeps me busy, but it can also be lonely," Bill admitted.

Mary told Bill she understood about being lonely, that's why she decided to have the puppy.

"That sounds like a good idea. When do you get her? And what are you going to call her?"

"Polly. I'm going to call her Polly. On our way home we're going to call in and meet Ted the breeder and also meet my Polly. I'm very excited, but I've a lot to learn about owning a dog."

Supper was wonderful and so was the company. Both Bill and Mary did not want the evening to end, but it was time to go. Outside the restaurant Bill walked Mary to her car and kissed her good night.

June and Shirley were waiting to hear all about her evening, just as if they were her parents. Mary walked in through the door.

"Well how did it go? Did you have a nice time?" June asked.

"Let me get in through the door first and I'll tell you. It really was a wonderful night. The restaurant, the food, the wine, and, the icing on the cake? The company. I think we'll definitely be doing this again. We both felt we could talk about anything. The evening flew by."

"We're both so happy for you, Mary," Shirley said. "This holiday is definitely a turning point in your life."

All three of them talked and talked. In the end, June said she was going to bed and that she would see them in the morning. Shirley and Mary were not long behind her. As they went to bed, Shirley said to Mary: "Be happy, Mary, and don't feel guilty about feeling happy."

"I'm so lucky having such good friends as you and June," Mary replied. "I know I've told you before, but it is so true."

Over the next few days they walked, talked and just enjoyed themselves. They went back to their favourite place on the beach where they had picnics, read books, and went swimming in the sea since the weather was so beautiful.

Bill called Mary and chatted for hours. They had so much in common. Mary invited Bill to come for a drink after he closed the shop tonight. June and Shirley were also getting to know Bill and soon realized what Mary saw in him.

Bill and Mary would go for long walks on the beach and sit and watch the sun set.

June was usually up first, but this morning she came down as normal and put the kettle on. Then she saw that the front door was open, and so she went out onto the front porch. Mary was sitting there with a cup of coffee with a faraway look. She was lost in her thoughts. She didn't even hear June come out. June heard the kettle boil, and so she went back in and made herself a cup of tea. Then she went back out onto the porch with her tea. This time Mary heard her. "June, I hope I didn't disturb you, but I couldn't sleep."

June asked her if something was worrying her.

"I'm not really worrying, but I do have a concern."

"Well, what is it?"

"As you know, we'll be going home at the end of the week and the thought of not seeing Bill is tearing me apart inside. I think I'm falling in love with him. Do you think that is possible in such a short time?"

"I don't think there is a time limit to fall in love with someone, Mary. How does Bill feel? Do you think he feels the same about you as you feel about him?"

When Shirley got up they made breakfast and Mary told Shirley how she was feeling about Bill. Mary said she felt silly. "Do you think it's just a holiday romance? You do hear about people getting carried away on holiday, don't you?"

"Let's see what happens. We're here for another four days," Shirley put in. "Bill could always come to Brookdale to see you. It's not the other end of the world."

"Shirley, you're always the logical one and the voice of reason," Mary said.

Shirley smiled, and then snapped her fingers. "Remember, tonight we have the BBQ to go to. June do you have the address?"

"I wonder if Bill will be going," said Mary. "I'll call him as soon as we've finished breakfast."

Mary called Bill. He said he was going and was pleased they were all going also. Shirley suggested they get some flowers for Lucy, who was hosting the BBQ.

"Yes, that's a great idea," said June.

"I did see a florist on the main street," Mary put in. "It was near the restaurant Bill took me to the other night. We could buy the flowers on our way to the BBQ."

"Let's go down to our spot on the beach and enjoy the day," June suggested.

"Good idea," said Shirley, who had never done so much swimming in her life—Jim was never much for the beach.

The BBQ starts at six, but we must not be late," said Mary. "We must give ourselves plenty of time to get ready and pick up the flowers on our way."

The flower shop had a great selection. They settled for basket full of daisies. Bill had given Mary the instructions on how to get to Lucy's house.

They drove down a winding road that went on forever. "This must be wrong," said June. Then, all of a sudden, the road opened up to show a set of gates leading to a house in the distance. June frowned. "I hope this is right. We're going to look pretty silly if we're wrong!"

"Oh, stop worrying, June, and relax," said Mary.

Once they went a little further they came upon an area with all the parked cars. Their jaws dropped as they got out of the car. "This is like a stately home!" June said. "Look at the gardens. They're magnificent."

Shirley said she was pleased they went for the basket of daisies and not just a bunch of flowers.

Lucy came out to greet them and welcomed them to the BBQ. "Now," Lucy said. "I want you all to feel at home and enjoy yourselves." She took the daisies, delighted. They were her favourite flowers, she declared.

They walked around the side of the house to the rear garden. The views took their breath away. "Wow, this is just lovely," said June. Rolling hills stretched as far as you could see. Off to the right, gleaming horses grazed in a bright green field.

They recognized some familiar faces from the meeting in the community centre. Lucy introduced them to Joe, her husband, who quickly offered them a glass of wine or whatever they wanted to drink. Everyone was walking around the garden with a glass of wine in hand.

June said to Mary, "Pinch me. I feel as if I'm in a dream, or on a movie set."

While everyone was chatting to one another and enjoying the gardens. Mary spotted Bill in the distance he had just arrived. She waved and over he came. "Bill, you never said it was such a magnificent house. We feel as if we're on a film set"

"Yes, I suppose it is pretty grand. Now relax and enjoy yourselves," Bill said. "By the way, have you been in the orangery yet?"

"No, but point us in the right direction," June said.

"Come on, I'll show you around," Bill said. "Now, the orangery was built onto the sunny side of the house and dates back to Victorian times. Oranges were grown there for the ladies of the house."

They stepped inside the orangery. People were sipping their wine, chatting and soaking up the late afternoon sun.

Amy came over to see them and said she was so pleased that they had decided to come. "So, what do you think of Lucy and Joe's house?"

June said she was speechless.

Amy laughed. "Please don't think we all live in houses like this, because we don't.

This house has been in Joe's family for centuries. They do rent the grounds out for lots of local events. Even weddings have been held on the grounds. Also, it has been featured in quite a few films over the years. It costs a lot of money to run a place like this, even though the family is very wealthy. Now, I think we had better be getting back to the patio as the BBQ will be ready soon and Lucy likes us all to be eating at the same time. We'll have time later to enjoy the garden and the sunset from the orangery."

Bill and Mary were engrossed with one another.

"They make a handsome couple, don't they?" June said.

"Well, I just don't want her to get hurt," Shirley sighed.

The four of them sat at a table to eat. June said, "This is the most delicious BBQ I've ever had. Not that I've been to many." Joe kept their wine glasses topped up. Everyone was laughing and having a great time.

The dinner flew by and then it was time for them to make their way towards the orangery, ready to see the sunset. Lucy said the sunset would be spectacular as it was such a clear night. There must have been be at least forty people at the party and everyone was so friendly. Joe and Lucy were the perfect hosts. You could see they were used to doing this.

The sunset did not disappoint. The three friends had been enjoying amazing sunsets from the cottage every night, but this sunset was something else.

After the sunset everyone made their way back to the patio for coffee and deserts before going home. They all thanked Joe and Lucy for such a wonderful evening, then got into their cars.

Mary came over to June and Shirley and said Bill wanted her to go back to his house for a nightcap, and so they could drive back to the cottage. "Bill will drive me home later," she assured them.

June and Shirley had no problem, and so they said goodnight to Bill and Mary.

Mary had not been to Bill's house and was not sure where he lived, and so you can imagine her surprise to find out he also lived in a grand house by the beach. "Bill, this is beautiful. You never said you had such a grand house!"

"Well, you never asked. Anyway, this is not grand compared to Joe and Lucy's house."

He took her inside and he poured them both a drink. Then Bill put on some music on and asked her to dance. "You know, Mary, you look so beautiful tonight. I didn't want to tell you at the BBQ as I didn't want to embarrass you."

Mary smiled as they waltzed. And then they danced and danced until the music ended. They kissed. The next thing they were upstairs in bed. And so you could say, the rest is history. Making love to Bill was the most natural thing that could have happened.

Mary woke up next morning. Bill was not in bed. She looked around. Just then he came in with breakfast on a tray. "Mary, I don't want you to think I make a habit of doing this, because I don't."

"Bill, I don't think that at all, but I also don't want you to think I jump into bed with any Tom, Dick or Harry." They both laughed and tucked into breakfast.

Mary asked what time it was. She was surprised when he said it was 9:00 AM. "I never sleep that late. What about your shop? What time do you open?"

"Whenever I please. Remember I'm the boss, so it doesn't matter."

Later Bill dropped Mary off at the cottage. June and Shirley were sitting on the front porch. Mary went into the house to get changed, then turned to her friends and said, "Don't say a thing."

Within no time at all Mary came back out with a coffee in hand and sat with June and Shirley on the porch. "I think I've lost my mind. That was the most incredible night of my life. What am I going to do now?"

June and Shirley looked at one another and laughed. "Well, We're just jealous," June said. "And we want to know all the details, so don't miss out anything."

Mary was proceeding to tell June and Shirley about how she felt about Bill when her phone rang. She went inside to take the call. She talked on the phone for quite a while before coming back out onto the porch.

"Come on, girls. What am I going to do? We're leaving on Saturday and it's Thursday today. Bill is picking me up at six to go for dinner and talk to me. I really don't want to lose him.

June said, "You don't have to lose him. We all live in the same country, remember. And you both drive."

"Yes, but what are my children going to think when they find out their mother is sleeping with another man within months of them losing their father?"

"For one," Shirley said. "I think they will be pleased to see you happy after what you have been going through. It will come as a surprise in the beginning. You will have to tell them if you intend to carry on the relationship with Bill."

"For what it's worth, I agree with Shirley," June put in. "Also, remember we're here for you."

The rest of the day was spent walking on the beach and swimming. "Let's make the most of today and tomorrow before we set of for home," Mary suggested.

June wanted to finish her book then go swimming. Shirley was doing yet another sketch. "When I take all these sketches to the art class I think Gary will be impressed," she said.

Mary was also soaking up the sun and taking a swim.

Back from the beach, Shirley and June decide to go for an evening drive and call into yet another country pub. June said she could get used to this. "The food is so good!"

Mary was busy getting ready for Bill to collect her. All three of them were sitting on the front porch when Bill arrived in his open-top red convertible. He called it his summer fun car. "See me when you see me," Mary said to the girls as she was leaving, and then gave a wink as she got into Bill's car.

Shirley and June set off, not knowing where they were going to end up. As they were driving along the coastal road enjoying the scenery they spotted the perfect country pub with tables outside. June was driving, and so she pulled into the parking lot.

They got themselves a table and started to look at the menu. A nice young lady came up and took their drinks order while they were deciding what to eat.

She came back and they ordered their meal and then sat back to enjoy the evening.

They went over the two-week holiday in Clifton in the cottage by the beach, June said. "Who would have thought so much could happen? First, finding Toby the dog, then meeting up with the Amy with her friends, and doing the gardens in the town square."

"Let's not forget Mary meeting Bill," Shirley put in. "And getting invited to the garden club meeting in the community centre, which also got us invited to that unforgettable BBQ."

June leaned forward. "Oh, and remember Janice who owned Toby and that we'll be calling to meet Janice's neighbour on our way home as Mary will be buying one of his puppies. This holiday is not over yet."

Shirley looked at June and said, "You know Jim would never go anywhere, and so this trip has been such an eye opener to me. It has made me realise that this is the start of more holidays to come. I want to try new things and go to more places. Let's explore together. What do you think?"

"I think that is the best idea, and I agree one hundred percent. Where are we going next?" June asked as they clinked their glasses.

June then asked Shirley what she thought of Mary and Bill. "You know something? I think it will turn out to be a serious relationship."

"I agree," said Shirley. "I just don't want her to get hurt. I know I've said that before, but it troubles me."

They were both pleased to see the young lady come back with their meal as the sea air made them hungry. Most of the tables were full by now, and then the couple at the next table started to talk to them, and asked if they were staying for the music that would be starting soon.

June said they were not aware there was music on tonight, and so they decided to stay.

After they had ordered some more drinks the music duo arrived and started to set up. The couple on the next table were great fans of the duo as they had seen them before. "You're in for a treat," they told Shirley and June.

The music was great. Before long the place was packed and people were dancing on the patio and having a great time. Even June and Shirley were asked to dance and enjoyed every minute of it. They ended up staying to the very end. What a great way to end the holiday.

Mike and Ann, who were on the next table, were such good company and they all laughed and sang along with the group, all night. They asked June and Shirley if they lived in the area or if they were on a holiday as there was another music night next week.

June told them they would be going home tomorrow but hoped to come back at another time as they had had such a good time.

They wished them well at the end of the night and a safe journey home. June and Shirley arrived back at the cottage and saw there were no lights. Mary must have stayed over at Bill's house, the realized.

June put the kettle on. "I need a cup of tea after all that dancing and singing."

"Great idea. I'll go and get changed," Shirley said. By the time they got to bed it was after midnight. "I think we'll both sleep well tonight," June said to Shirley as she shut her bedroom door.

Mary arrived back in the morning, just as June and Shirley were getting up. "You two are late this morning. Where did you go last night?"

"We were dancing and singing till late," June told her. "We went out to a country pub on the coastal road for a drink and a meal, only to find out they had a music duo, and so we stayed and had a great time. By the time we got back and made a drink it was after midnight."

"I think we should contact Vera to let her know we're leaving," suggested Mary.

"What was your evening like, Mary?" Shirley asked.

"Well, we also went for a drive along the coast road stopped for a meal, and then went for a walk on the beach. We talked and walked and then sat on the rocks. It was a perfect night. I've never done anything like this before. Bill is a true romantic. I've got some big discussions ahead of me."

After breakfast, they phoned Vera. She was happy to hear from them. She said she would come around to say goodbye before they left.

"Let's spend the last morning on the beach," June suggested. "We can pack a picnic, swim, read, and just laze around.

"That sounds great to me," said Shirley. "We want to leave no later than two in the afternoon though."

Before long they were ready and walking down to their favourite place on the beach. "This really is the best-kept secret, as it is never packed and the sea is so clear and the sand is clean," Mary said.

Shirley and June told Mary about their plans to do some more traveling. June said: "This trip has made us realise that we want to explore new things. I think that is a great idea. We only live once, and so we must make the most of it while we can."

Mary told them that she had made her mind up: she was going to tell Clive and Susan about Bill. "I really don't want this to end. We do have something special."

"I think that it is so romantic," said June, who had never been the most romantic person around. She gave Mary a big hug then and even had a tear in her eye.

They all went for a swim and just enjoyed a good old-fashioned day at the beach, watching children playing and the boats sailing out to sea.

Back at the cottage they started to pack the last few things up, but very reluctantly. Mary called Janice to ask what was the best time for them to call in to meet Mary's new puppy, Polly.

Janice said if they arrived by four she would have a meal ready for them.

They all agreed that was a good idea. Mary was so excited to finally see Polly and find out when she would be able to take her home with her. Bill called and wanted them to stop by the shop on their way home.

"We had better get ourselves organized," Mary said.

Shirley and June were ready first, and so they went to sit on the porch in the afternoon sun to wait for Mary.

Just then, Vera called in to see them before they left for home.

Mary looked radiant; she was glowing. All three of them had a nice suntan and were looking healthy, but Mary had a twinkle in her eye as well.

They set off to drive through the main street and stopped outside Bill's shop. He came out to make sure they had all they needed for the journey home. Mary was a little teary, but June and Shirley said to her: "You have so much to look forward to."

They were soon on their way. In no time at all they were pulling up outside Janice's house. Janice was so pleased to see them. As soon as they got out of the car, Mary wanted to go and see Polly.

Janice shouted to Ted, who lived next door, to see if it would be all right for them to come and see the puppies. Ted came out. He looked a little eccentric, but he was devoted to his dogs. "Yes, come on," Ted said. "They're all doing very well, but they're a bit noisy. She had four pups in the litter. One went yesterday."

Ted went over to the pups and picked out the one for Mary. "What are you going to call her?" he asked.

"She is going to be called Polly." She was adorable. Mary fell instantly in love with her. She explained to Ted she had never had a dog before. "And so I want all the advice you can give me!"

Ted proceeded to make a list of things Mary should get ready for when she took her home.

"How long do you think it will be before I can have her?"

"I would think another two weeks," Ted said.

She was beautiful, a Scotty, just like a ball of white wool. June and Shirley were taken with her almost as much.

"I can see she is going to be well loved by all three of you," said Ted. "I've nothing to worry about. They like company, and so she will be a great companion for you. A dog has so much love to give."

After they had eaten, they were back on the road. Next stop: Brookdale.

"It feels as if we have been away for ages and not just two weeks," June said.

They stopped at the supermarket to get a few things. Mary dropped June off first, then Shirley. By the time she got home she was feeling very tired and she missed Bill very much.

They all started to settle back to normal, everyday living, but they all knew things were never going to be the same again. June and Shirley were already starting to think about their next trip.

June said, "What about a walking holiday? We both like the outdoors and meeting new people."

Shirley suggested they both make a list of the trips they would like to do and then meet up for lunch and go through the list.

The following week, as always, they met for coffee in their favourite cafe. Molly was so pleased to see them. She had missed them and wanted to know all about the holiday.

Mary could not stop talking about Bill. They had been talking on the phone a few times every day since she came back. Mary told them she had Clive and Susan coming for supper tonight, as she wanted to tell them both about Bill at the same time. "I feel a bit nervous and unsure what I'm going to say."

June and Shirley told her not to worry as they were sure they would be very happy for her.

"Also, I'll be telling them about Polly. I think they'll think I've lost my mind!"

Molly could not believe they found so much to do in such a small town in Devon. "You three amaze me."

June and Shirley told Mary about their plans and said she was also included, but Mary quickly said she had so many plans of her own. "Firstly, I've been to the pet shop as I need to get ready for

Polly. The man in the pet shop was so helpful and wants me to take Polly in to see him as soon as I get her. I can't wait."

June and Shirley wished Mary good luck in telling Clive and Susan and reassured her everything would be just fine. "Don't forget, call us later to let us know how you got on," Shirley said.

As soon as Mary got home she started to prepare supper. She could not believe how nervous she was. The table was set and the house looked great. Supper was ready. Clive and Susan both arrived at the same time. Susan took one look at Mary and said, "Mum, you're looking radiant. The holiday did you good. Even Clive, never the most observant guy, complimented her. She poured them a glass of wine. "Supper is ready, and so you can come to the table."

They wanted to know all about the holiday, of course, and so Mary told them. She also told them she would be having a little dog and how that came about.

Susan said she thought it was meant to be. "Emma will be so pleased you're getting a little dog."

Clive said it would be good company for her as she was on her own. "One thing you have to remember when you have a dog is that it can tie you down, but I don't say that to put you off as I think it's a great idea. Have you got a name for her yet?"

"Yes, I'm going to call her Polly, and I will be picking her up next week. We did lots of walking and swimming as the cottage was so near the beach."

Susan asked what the area and shops were like. "Did you buy anything? I know you love to shop."

There was a good selection of small local shops, she explained, and then she went on to tell them about Bill's shop. Susan saw her mum light up as soon as she spoke about Bill and so picked up straight away. "Well, I can see this Bill made quite an impression on you, Mum."

Clive quickly said, "Don't talk such nonsense, Susan."

Mary then went on to tell them that she had been out for lunch with him and that they got on so well. "I know this may sound silly, but Bill has put the light back in my life."

Both Clive and Susan stared at her for a moment and said nothing, Susan got up from her seat and came over to her mother and gave her a big hug and told her she was so happy for her. "Now, when are we going to meet this Bill!"

Clive just sat there a while longer before he came over and also hugged her.

"I can't tell you how happy this makes me feel," Mary sighed. "I've been a bag of nerves all day. I know it's not that long since your dad died, but I really think he would want me to move on with my life."

The rest of the evening went well. They talked about everything. Susan brought Mary some photos of Emma. "As soon as Polly arrives, I want you to come and bring Emma over to meet her," Mary said.

"Mum, I won't be able to keep her away!"

Clive told Mary that the police had been in touch with him but only to say that, though they had thought they had a lead on the man who was responsible for Stan losing money in his business deal, it turned out to be another false alarm.

Susan left first as she had a longer drive home. Mary wanted to make sure Clive was happy about Bill, and that he would be happy to meet him. Although Clive said it seemed quick, he was pleased she was moving on.

After they left, she could not wait to phone Bill and tell him how it went. They talked for quite a while. "Now it's your turn to tell the twins," she said.

"I'll get on it tomorrow," he said. "Fingers crossed it goes as well for me. I'm sure it will."

Mary phoned June and Shirley the next day as they were both waiting to hear. Ted phoned Mary to say she could come and pick Polly up whenever she wanted to now. "Oh, I can't wait," Mary cried. "I'll speak to June and Shirley and get back to you."

After speaking to June and Shirley she called Ted back and said they would pick Polly up on Sunday. They were all so excited and could not wait to see Polly again.

Mary then phoned Janice to tell her they were coming down and would pop in to see her. Janice said she had been in to see Polly and that she was growing fast. "She is the cutest puppy you ever saw." she said.

Mary was up early doing the last check on everything she had bought for Polly. By the time she had the cage in the car it was time to go and pick up June and Shirley. The traffic was busy. It was such a nice Sunday, and so everyone was taking advantage of the beautiful weather and enjoying the day.

They were soon at Janice's and were eager to go and pick up Polly. Ted had her all ready, as well as a few last bits of advice for Mary. He told her that she could phone him any time if she had any questions, as he was always willing to help.

Janice got her dog Toby and then suggested they take both Polly and Toby to the park. Polly looked so stylish with her new pink lead. Mary was so proud of her.

The park was very busy on such a beautiful Sunday afternoon. They walked all around the park then stopped for coffee. Polly did not leave Mary's side. She had to carry her in the end, as she was not used to long walks. Janice had a meal all ready for them in the garden. Toby and Polly were both tired and fell asleep together. They looked so cute.

When it was time to go, Mary put Polly into the cage in the back of the car on her new fluffy blanket together with a toy for her to play with. By the time they got to the end of the road she was fast asleep.

Mary dropped June and Shirley off. When she got home, Polly woke up. Mary carried her into the house. She sniffed everything and ran from room to room before she settled on the rug in front of the fire. She looked so contented. Mary looked at her and smiled.

Susan called to see how Polly was doing. "Can you take a photo and send it to Emma tomorrow? I think we'll be over to see you next weekend if that works for you."

"Yes, I look so forward to showing Polly to Emma," Mary said.

CHAPTER SIX

Meeting the Children

LIFE IN BROOKDALE was never quite the same. Mary had Bill. And June and Shirley had so many plans spinning around in their heads.

Shirley's sons, Alex and John, were so pleased that their mum had had such a good time and also that she was thinking of other places she wanted to visit with June. They both told her this was her time. Now she must go out and enjoy herself. They said she should make a bucket list and that June should also make a bucket list, and then see what they come up with.

Shirley was quite surprised as to how open they both were. "I wonder what your sister Heather will say."

"Don't take any notice of her, Mum," Alex said. "You know what she's like. She just wants to be in control."

The following day Shirley called Heather and, as always, it was all about her. She never asked if her mum if she had had a nice time; all she did was complain that she needed help with her daughter and that all her friends' mothers helped to look after their grandchildren.

Shirley let her carry on, where as before she would have been in tears and so upset. Not anymore. She felt very proud of herself.

"Are you still there?" Heather asked.

"Yes, I'm listening to you going on and on."

"I don't know what has happened to you. I think you must be going through a midlife crisis. Do you think you should see a doctor?"

"Heather, nothing is wrong with me. I've just decided that June and I will be doing more traveling in the future, and so I suggest you get used to it."

Heather asked her how she was going to pay for all this traveling.

"Well, as a matter of fact, your father left me in a very comfortable position, and so you don't have to worry about that. Alex and John are very happy for me and ready to help in any way they can. They are both pleased that I'll be enjoying my life and not just sitting at home watching TV."

"I see. Well, Mum, I've nothing else to say on the subject until you come to your senses."

Shirley put the phone down, and then she called June and asked her if she could come around and have a glass of wine. This took June by surprise, and so she said she was on her way.

When June arrived, Shirley had the wine open and two glasses ready. "What is all this about?" asked June.

Shirley was still shaking after her phone call to Heather. "I spoke to Alex and John. They were so pleased for me and offered to help in any way. Then I phoned Heather. Well, that was another story." Shirley proceeded to tell June what Heather had said. June could not believe this of Heather, although she was not totally surprised. She was a princess and always wanted her own way. "I hope Heather has not changed your mind about us doing a bit of traveling."

"Absolutely not, June, I'm more determined than ever. We're going to spread our wings."

"I'll toast to that!"

The rest of the evening was spent making the bucket list of where they wanted to go in the future.

June ended up staying the night at Shirley's. It was not a good idea for June to drive home. They had drunk the bottle of wine between them and were not used to drinking.

"On our way to meet Mary we'll go a little earlier and stop off at the travel agent and pick up whatever information they have," Shirley said.

They entered the travel agent's office. They could not believe the selection of options available to them. The lady was so nice and put some literature together for them to take with them. She said to go through what interested them and then come back in and she would help put a trip together for them. She did suggest they think about getting passports because they would need one for most of the trips they had been considering.

Shirley and June were now on their way to meet Mary for coffee. They could not wait to hear to hear how Polly was settling in. Mary was already there when June and Shirley got to the cafe.

Mary could not stop talking about Polly and how she had settled in. "She follows me everywhere I go. I can't imagine her not being there. Clive loves her and Susan is coming at the weekend with Emma to meet her." Mary was upset to hear about Heather's reaction about Shirley wanting travel, but she was not surprised. She said the same as June about Shirley not taking any notice, but to carry on with her plans.

They showed Mary all the information from the travel agent. "We're also going to get ourselves passports when we leave here today," June said. Mary could not stop smiling at them.

That evening Bill phoned. He told Mary that both the girls were happy for him and wanted them to go up to Scotland, but that he said he would like them to come down to Brookdale, that way Wendy and Amy could meet Clive and Susan. He thought it would be nice to all meet at the same time.

"What do you both think of that?" Mary said to Shirley and June.

Both Shirley and June thought that was a great idea.

They all chatted and before long it was time to go. Mary had to go and buy yet more things for Polly. As Shirley and June walked to their cars, they made arrangements to get the forms for passports, and then meet up the following afternoon at June's to plan their next vacation.

Bill called Mary, and it was all settled. Wendy and Amy were coming down the following weekend. "I've booked them into the hotel, so can you check with Clive and Susan? I'll book a table for us all to have a meal together." Bill reassured her she had nothing to worry about, as the girls were very excited to meet everyone. Clive and Susan were also excited for Mary and Bill, plus about meeting Wendy and Amy.

Mary went to the hotel to make sure the rooms and table were all booked, as she wanted this to go well. 'I'm not taking any chances,' she said to herself. She went to get her hair and pedicure appointment booked.

Shirley and June both called Mary to wish her well.

Bill was first to arrive, as he knew Mary was nervous. He came to the house, as he wanted to take Mary to the hotel so they could be first there. Also he wanted to meet Polly, who was a big hit with everyone she saw.

Bill and Mary arrived at the hotel just as Clive and Susan were also arriving. Mary introduced them as they walked into the hotel. Bill said he would go and see if the girls had arrived.

Clive got Mary and Susan a drink. Susan said, "Mum, he's very handsome."

"I hope you and Clive are going to like him. He means a lot to me."

Susan told her to stop worrying and relax.

Just then Bill walked in with Wendy and Amy. Mary went straight over to the girls and gave them a hug. After everyone was introduced they all chatted. The rest of the evening could not have gone better.

Bill gave Mary a wink and said again how beautiful she looked. Susan was staying over at Clive's so they all arranged to meet the following day before Susan had to get back. Wendy and Amy were staying a couple of days. Emma was coming but she had a tummy upset, and so Susan did not want her to travel. She was very unhappy, as she wanted to see Polly. "If she is better by next weekend we'll be back," Susan said.

Bill decided to stay at Mary's, who had invited them all for coffee the next day. She wanted them to meet Polly.

Bill told Mary that Amy was not very happy in her marriage, which was very upsetting. "I don't think things have been good with them for quite some time. This is when I'm not sure what I should do."

Mary told Bill. "You have to let them sort things out on their own. Just make sure she knows you're always there for her."

Bill said he was pleased Susan was staying with Clive, as they could have the house to themselves. Things could not have gone better. Susan and Clive told Mary they really liked Bill as well as both Wendy and Amy. Clive also told Mary: "Dad would have liked Bill and would be happy for you." This made Mary cry. Also Polly was a big hit with everyone.

Susan and Wendy got on like a house on fire, as they had the same interests. Clive seemed to be talking to Amy quite a lot. Mary wished he could find someone and settle down, but Susan said that would never happen. He had his own house, a nice car, and a good job he enjoyed (at last), but Mary still worried about him. Susan was first to leave for home since Wendy and Amy were staying another night. Clive offered to take them out the following evening, an offer which they quickly accepted.

Bill and Mary had a nice evening together. It was the perfect way to end such a perfect weekend. Bill cracked open a special bottle of wine, which they ended up drinking in bed. Mary could not have been happier when Bill told her he loved everything about her and wanted to spend the rest of his life with her.

They made love, drank wine, and talked most of the night.

The next morning at breakfast, Mary told Bill she was going to talk things over with Clive and Susan, as there were many things to consider. Bill asked Mary if she would like to come down to Clifton and bring Polly. "Just let me know when."

"As I said, I'd like to talk it over with Clive and Susan first. I hope you agree to that.

"I'm happy with whatever you decide to do. You know how I feel about you. Take your time."

Next thing, Clive, Wendy, and Amy were strolling down the path. Clive said they had had a great evening, but that Wendy and Amy were ready to set off back to Scotland.

They all had coffee. Mary could not believe how Clive had taken to the girls, as he was a bit of a loner and did not mix that well. But she did notice he was particularly taken with Amy. They never stopped chatting and laughing. Even Bill noticed.

They all went outside to see the girls off. Bill and Mary promised the girls they would take a trip up to Scotland later in the year. Clive was quick to add he would keep in touch.

As soon as the girls had gone, Clive shook Bill's hand and said he was so pleased he was making his mum happy. That meant so much to Mary. He then gave Mary a hug before he left. Bill and Mary took Polly for a walk; then, after lunch, it was time for Bill to be on his way. Mary told him to call her as soon as he got home. Mary had been down to stay with Bill, along with Polly, which she had enjoyed. Clive and Susan just wanted her to be happy, but not to rush into making any big decisions like selling her house yet. Clive said she could go and spend as much time as she liked in Clifton, as he would keep an eye on her house.

One day Bill called and asked Mary if Clive had said anything about Amy.

"No, why do you ask? But I'll just say, he has been going around with a grin on his face and seems to be very happy. I just thought things were going well at work."

Bill said Wendy had called him to say that Clive had met up with Amy, as she had now moved out and was now living on her own.

"I'm seeing Clive tomorrow, and so I'll ask him."

"Well, I'm going to call Amy to see if she is all right. I know she has not been happy for a while. I just want her to be happy."

When Mary asked Clive the following day about Amy he said he was falling in love with her and she felt the same. "Mum, she wasn't happy and had moved out and was living on her own. We met up the other weekend and had a great time. We have so much in common. I've never felt like this before."

"Have you spoken to Susan about you and Amy?"

"We have spoken. She just wants me to be happy, but doesn't want me to get hurt. Amy and her husband haven't been living together for a long time. They seem to want different things, I need you to know that I'm not the cause of them breaking up."

"Susan is coming at the week end with Emma, and so I think it would be a good idea for us to have supper together," Mary said.

"Sounds good to me," said Clive.

"Also, I've made my decision about moving to live with Bill in Clifton, and so we do have a lot to discuss."

June had arranged for Mary and Shirley to have supper at her house that night. With Mary going down to Bill's, it seemed ages since they had a girls' night to catch up. She also wanted to tell Mary about their travel plans.

June was ready when Shirley and Mary arrived. Mary started by telling them she had made her decision to move down to live with Bill in Clifton. "I'll be telling Clive and Susan at the weekend," she added.

They were both pleased for her and said they would help in any way with the move.

"I wanted to tell you two first and then Clive and Susan. I then plan on going back down to Clifton next week to tell Bill. I don't want to tell him over the phone."

"I think that's a good idea. He will be thrilled," June said.

"What will you do about the house?" Shirley asked.

"Well, that is what I want to discuss with Clive and Susan. I don't want to live my life without Bill, and it is too far to keep travelling back and forth. He did say he was prepared to sell his business and move to Brookdale, but he loves the business, and I must say I've come to feel so at home in Clifton. We'll make some changes on the house, but really it would be decorating and changing furniture around, as I'll want to take some of my furniture."

Shirley said, "Well, you do realize we'll be coming down to stay with you."

June said, "Yes, we'll be putting that on our list of places to visit."

"I would be very disappointed if you didn't come and stay," Mary said. "There will always be a welcome for you any time."

After supper June and Shirley got their brochures out to show Mary. "We thought we would do a six-day bus trip to France," June said. "We have filled in the forms and sent them off for our passports, which will take a few weeks."

"When are you thinking of going?" said Mary.

"We thought about September. The girl at the travel agent's said this was a popular trip and that she always had good feedback from couples who had done it. The quality of the hotels is top notch. She did say it gets booked up quickly, so we're going tomorrow to book it and pay our deposit."

"John and Alex are thrilled for us, but Heather is a different story," Shirley put in. "I just don't understand why she is so bitter."

Mary asked Shirley if Heather was happy in her marriage, because it is not natural to be like this. "She's not easy to talk to, but I could ask John and Alex if they know anything. I don't like us not talking to one another." Shirley said she had been back to her art class and that Gary was very impressed with the sketches she had done when they were in Clifton. "Gary is working on putting a trip together to go to Scotland later in the year. It would only be four days, and so I would like June to come with me."

June quickly said she wanted to but was not sure, as she was not 'arty.' Shirley smiled at Mary and said she had not given up yet.

Mary told them that the police were no further ahead in finding the guy that ripped Stan and Ken off. "I really have a hard time in accepting the fact that they have no leads and that he seems to have vanished into thin air. The problem is that these sort of criminals are so clever. They are always one step ahead. Also, they don't have a conscience about taking things that do not belong to them."

June asked if she was going to tell Ken and Carol about her moving to Clifton.

"Yes, I'll invite them to come for supper next time Bill comes to stay. I think you should both come as well."

"That sounds like a plan," June said.

Mary was waiting for Clive and Susan to arrive and was putting the final touches to the meal. Polly had been out for her walk also. She was happy to be sleeping. Then she heard the door go. It was Susan with Emma, followed by Clive. Emma went straight over to Polly, and so that was the end of her nap. She always brought Polly a new toy. "We'll have more than the pet shop soon," Mary said.

"Mum, you know we can't come without one. If only you knew how long it took her to choose one."

Susan took their overnight things into the bedroom. Mary said supper was ready. They waited until after supper and Emma was in bed before they discussed Clive and Amy or Mary's move.

Clive told them that him and Amy were very serious about one another, but that he did not want to talk about it anymore at this time. He did promise to keep them up to date if anything changed.

"I also want to tell you both that I've made a decision about Bill," Mary said. "I've decided to move down to Clifton and live with him. Clive and Susan looked at one another, and then hugged Mary and said they were both happy for her. What does Bill think about this? I've not told him yet, as I wanted to tell you two, and then I'll tell Bill. I've told June and Shirley and they are thrilled. I plan on going to see Bill next week as I do not want to tell him over the phone.

Clive asked if she would be selling the house or keeping it.

"I've decided to sell the house, as it does not make any sense in keeping it."

Susan agreed with that. "Do you like Bill's house or will you be buying one together?"

I see no reason in buying another house as I love Bill's house, but we'll do some redecorating. I told June and Shirley I want to take some of my furniture, which Bill agrees with. He wants me to make it our house. He is very concerned about that."

The rest of the weekend was so much fun for Emma. All she wanted to do was take Polly to the park and play with her. When it was time for Susan and Emma to leave, Polly was exhausted.

Mary was more excited than usual to make this trip to Clifton. She set off, as always bright and early, with bags packed and Polly in the back. Polly was a very good traveler. She just went to sleep.

She made a couple of stops and called Bill each time. The plan was she would arrive as he was closing he shop. All went accordingly.

As Mary pulled up outside the shop, Bill came out with a big smile to welcome her. She got Polly out of the car and they went into the shop, just as Bill was getting ready to close up for the day.

He suggested that on their way home they pick up some Chinese food, which they both enjoyed. The house looked welcoming with fresh flowers. Mary commented on the house; she knew Bill wanted her to feel at home.

After they finished supper, they took Polly for a walk. The area that Bill lived in was very nice. You could walk to the beach or walk along the cliffs. Back at the house, Bill helped Mary bring her things into the house. He was smiling at all the bags.

Next morning Bill was getting ready to go to the shop and Mary was pottering around the house. "Why don't you make yourself at home and when you're ready come down to the shop."

"That sounds good," Mary said. Mary really did like the house. It had a good feel to it. The more she was in it, the better she liked it.

She got Polly and they went for a walk down onto the beach. It was a beautiful morning. The sun was beginning to break through the clouds. As they walked along the path to the beach she realized there was someone behind her.

She turned around. There was a lady walking her dog. She stopped and said good morning. "It looks like we're both going in the same direction."

Mary introduced herself and that was how she met Liz and her Yorkshire terrier, Pepper,

It turned out that Liz lived in the house next to Bill. She was very friendly and had known Bill and his wife for many years. She said she was so pleased he had found someone with whom to share his life. They walked along the beach and back up the path. Polly and Pepper got on so well together that by the time they got back Polly was exhausted.

They arranged to meet the following morning at the same time to go for a walk. Liz told Mary to call her anytime Mary wanted to know anything about the area.

When she got down to the shop she told Bill about Liz and their walk with the dogs. He said Liz and Olive were great friends. "She is a very nice person." He was pleased Mary was making friends.

"This really is a nice place, Bill. I can see why you wouldn't want to move from here."

"I don't want to put any pressure on you at all. I want you to take your time. You and Polly have all the time in the world."

She gave Bill a kiss. "You really are a nice person, and I do love you so much."

During the next few days it became quite a regular thing. Every morning, Mary and Liz along with the dogs, went for a walk, either to the beach or along the cliffs. Mary told Liz she could get used to this. "Well, to be honest. It has been a long time since we have seen Bill so happy. The smile on his face says it all."

As the time was going on, Bill asked Mary if she would like to redecorate and change the furniture around. "You know, if you do decide to move down here you will want to bring some of your furniture. We'll work it out together, yours and mine. You know, there is a meeting at the community centre tonight with the garden club. Would you like to go? I'm sure they will make you welcome as you will see quite a few familiar faces from when you were down with June and Shirley."

"I think that would be a good idea," Mary said.

The meeting was very interesting as they were deciding on the community flowerbeds around the town, as well as on flowers, colours, and design. It got a bit heated a couple of times, but the outcome was good in the end. They made Mary very welcome and quite a few remembered her and also asked about June and Shirley.

As they were driving back to Bill's she turned to Bill and said she could settle into life in Clifton very nicely. Meeting Liz has made a big impact on her. As far as Polly was concerned she just loved her walks with Pepper.

They went in and Bill made them a nightcap. Mary said she had something to tell him. She told Bill she had decided to move to Clifton. "You have made me so happy," he said.

They clinked their glasses and Bill said: "We now have a lot of plans to make."

Mary said she would need his help in deciding what to bring, and also to help with the move.

The first thing Bill asked her was had she told Clive and Susan. As soon as she told him they were both happy with the move, he said, "I'll be telling the twins tomorrow, and I can tell you now, they will be thrilled."

The following evening the phone rang. Bill answered. It was Amy. They chatted for quite a while, and went he hung up the phone he told Mary, "She wants to come down for the weekend and Clive is coming with her."

Mary asked Bill if he was still okay about it.

He said, "If she is happy that's all I'm concerned about. She did say that Clive would be calling tomorrow night to speak to you.

I'm sure he just wants to make sure we're both okay about them coming together."

"Susan had phoned and said Clive and Amy were spending a lot of time together, and so I'm not really surprised."

"They will be our first visitors," Bill said to Mary.

"I promise not to let you down," Mary said as she smiled at Bill. "It will be strange for Amy. This was her home when her mother was alive, and so I'll be very careful."

Clive called the next night and said they would arrive around 9:00 PM on Friday and would be staying until Monday morning.

"I can't wait to see you both, drive carefully," Mary said.

Clive told Mary he had been spending a lot of time with Amy. They were having a great time together as their interests were so similar.

When they were on their walk, Mary told Liz that Amy was coming down. "I've always liked those girls," she said and was not surprised when Mary told her that Amy and her husband had parted. Then Mary told her how Amy had gotten friendly with Clive since they all met that first time.

"Well, let me tell you," Liz said. "I never liked her husband. He always seemed odd to me, but don't tell Bill I said that."

The rest of the week Mary spent getting the house ready, as it needed a woman's touch around the place. She had bought flowers and put nice touches around the place. Bill told her which room was for Amy, and so she made a special effort, but was also very careful not to remove anything.

When Bill came home on Friday after work he was so impressed with the house. Mary was in anguish for Bill to see Amy's room.

"I've not seen this room look like this since Olive used to get it ready for her," he said as he hugged Mary with a tear in his eyes and then added: "You're one special lady."

Clive called around 7:00 PM to let them know everything was going according to plan and that they would be arriving by 9:00

PM. Bill and Mary were both a little uptight, as they so wanted the weekend to go well.

On the dot of 9:00 they heard the car pull up. Both Bill and Mary went to greet them. They were tired, as they had worked until lunch time and been driving ever since.

Amy was first to come in while Clive got their bags out of the car. Bill was so pleased to see Amy. His face lit up when he saw her. He was close to both his girls. Clive took the bags up to Amy's room and settled in. Bill got a bottle of wine and glasses and also some snacks out. They had stopped for a meal on their journey and weren't hungry for dinner.

When Amy came down, she walked straight over to Mary and gave her a hug and thanked her for making her room so pretty.

"That means so much to me as I don't want to overstep the mark. I'm pleased you like it."

"I love it. Wendy and I've not seen Dad look this happy since Mum died. It's time he moved on. We could not be happier, like we told you when we met for dinner in Brookdale."

Bill opened the wine and said he wanted to make a toast. "Mary has decided to move down to Clifton. I did say we could sell this house and buy one together, but Mary loves this house, although we'll be making a few changes."

Mary was quick to respond: "We'll only be doing a bit of redecorating. I do want to bring a few items of furniture."

Clive and Amy were delighted with the news. Amy said: "I'm delighted that they'll be living in the same house."

Polly was, of course, the centre of attention as always.

Mary told Amy and Clive about her meeting Liz and their walks with the dogs. Amy said she really liked Liz. "I'll be popping around to see her tomorrow," Amy said. "And, of course, I want to introduce Clive to her. I don't think she will be surprised that I'm now on my own. Liz was a great help when Mum died. She was there for all of us. She was a tower of strength, and so I'm so pleased you like her."

Next morning Bill went to open the shop as Mary was busy waiting for Clive and Amy to come down for breakfast. Polly was a bit put out, as she was not getting her walk that morning.

After breakfast Clive and Amy had plans for their day. Bill had booked a table for supper at 7:00 PM, and so she gave them the information. Again Amy told Mary that she had never seen her room so nice. Clive gave Mary a peck on the cheek and also thanked her.

"So where are you two going today?" Mary asked.

"I plan on showing Clive the sights. Also, we plan on dropping in to see Dad's shop. After that I'm not sure."

Mary was busy around the house. She was now looking at each room and thinking of what she would like to do. She always had a good eye for décor. The more she went around the house, the more she worked out what she would like to change and where her furniture would fit in.

Later she called Liz to see if she wanted to take the dogs for a walk. So, before long they were walking down to the beach and Polly and Pepper were running on ahead as they knew the walk so well.

Mary told Liz that Amy was going to come and see her and introduce them to Clive. Liz suggested they all come for drinks on Sunday evening. "And then you can meet Fred. I know he is dying to meet you as Bill has told him all about you."

"That sounds like a nice idea, I'll let Bill, Amy and Clive know," Mary said.

When she got back from the walk she found that Amy and Clive had also just arrived back. Amy was making a pot of tea and Clive was sitting in the living room admiring the view. "Mum, this is such a beautiful area. I can see why you love being here."

Mary sat beside him. "Clive, I want to ask you about my house. I'll be selling it, as I don't see the point of keeping it. What do you think?"

"I think that's the best way to go. When you come back we'll get an agent and go from there. I know Susan will agree. This is a great place to live, and I know you will be happy."

"We'll talk about it with Susan when go back home."

"That sounds like a good idea to me. I had no idea Clifton was such a nice area. Amy took me all over the place today."

Amy brought the tea in and Mary told her that Liz had invited them over for drinks tomorrow evening to meet Fred. "You'll really like Fred," Amy said. "Dad and Fred have been friends forever."

"It will soon be time for Bill to come home, and so we had better get ourselves ready to go out for supper," Mary said.

Clive was first to make a move, and so Amy and Mary cleared the tea away. Amy came into the kitchen and told Mary that she must do whatever changes she wants to in the house. "I know I can also speak for Wendy."

Amy told Mary that she had put in for a transfer and had received an email to say that there was a position available for her in the bank in Brookdale if she wanted it.

Mary asked her what Clive thought about it.

"I've not told him yet. I'll tell him over supper tonight. He will be thrilled, I can tell you that."

All four of them arrived at the hotel restaurant for supper. It was Saturday night, and so the restaurant was busy. The food was very good, as always. Halfway through supper Amy said she had some good news she wanted to share with everyone. She said she had received an email to say there was a position in the bank in Brookdale if she wanted it. "I've to let them know as soon as possible, as they have someone else interested."

Clive could not contain himself. He leapt up and gave her a big hug.

Bill asked her if she was going to accept it. She smiled at Clive and said, "Yes. I can't wait. I'm so excited. I called Wendy first and she was thrilled for me." Amy then looked at Mary and said, "It looks like we're all going to be moving."

Mary looked at Bill and smiled. The rest of the evening was spent chatting about everything and anything.

Later that evening when Clive and Amy had gone to bed and Bill and Mary were snuggled up in their own bed, Bill turned to Mary and said how happy he was. "Next week we'll go through the house together and we can decide what changes you would like to do."

Sunday was always a typical lazy morning. Bill went for the papers. He had a lady that looked after the shop on Sundays during the summer season. He closed in the winter season. By the time he came back with the papers Clive and Amy were getting up.

They sat outside for breakfast and discussed the day. Amy wanted to go down to her favourite beach, as the weather was beautiful. Mary said she would make them a picnic. "I could get used to this spoiling," Amy said and smiled. "What are you two going to be doing?"

Bill said he was taking Mary for a drive and that they'd stop for lunch. "Don't forget we're invited for drinks next door with Liz and Fred's tonight," he said.

Amy said she was looking forward to seeing them, then turned to Mary. "Have you told Liz you've decided to move down here?"

Mary said she had not said anything, as she wanted to tell her when Bill was with her, and so tonight would be perfect timing.

The day was perfect. They drove in the convertible along the coastal road where the scenery was breathtaking. Bill had lived in this area for many years, and so he knew the best places to go. They went to a little restaurant on the edge of the cliffs and had lunch. It seemed to be only locals there. They chatted to another couple at the next table and agreed that it was the best-kept secret.

Clive and Amy arrived back about the same time as Bill and Mary. They both had quite the suntan. "I think we should be ready to go to Liz and Fred's by seven," Amy said.

Mary had bought Liz a beautiful bunch of yellow roses, as she had said many times they are her favourite.

When they arrived, Liz and Fred were already sitting out on the rear deck enjoying the evening sun. Liz loved the flowers. Bill introduced Mary to Fred and Amy introduced Clive to Liz and Fred. Fred then said, "Let me get you all some drinks. Bill, do you want to come and help me?"

When they all had their drinks, Bill announced that Mary was going to move to Clifton to live with him. Liz was so excited. She gave them both a big hug. Fred toasted to friends.

CHAPTER SEVEN

Packing Again

Monday morning Bill left for work after saying goodbye to Amy and Clive. They said they would be leaving about 10:30. Amy had replied to say she was going to accept the job in the bank in Brookdale, and so she had lots to do. Mary asked when she would have to start the new job. "I've got to be in the Brookdale branch in two weeks." She added that she needed to give one week's notice at her rented flat and move to Brookdale, ready to start work. "I don't have much furniture to move. Still, it will be so hectic."

"Don't worry," Clive said. "I'll be helping. I'll take a week off. They owe me so much time off."

Mary told Clive she would be coming back up to Brookdale the following week. "I've boxes still packed from when I moved in." Mary saw Amy and Clive all packed and ready to go. Call me when you get home. They all hugged and away they went.

Polly was sitting there, thumping her tail, clearly thinking 'I hope I'll be going for a walk now.' Mary called Liz and arranged to meet in five minutes. Polly could not get her lead on fast enough.

Pepper and Polly, now off their leads, had a great time, dashing about and chasing each other.

Liz was so happy that Mary was going to move in with Bill. Mary told her she wanted to do some decorating. Liz and Mary had the same taste, and so they were bouncing ideas off one another. Liz also said she was pleased to see Amy so happy.

"I'll be going back to Brookdale next week to get my house on the market. Now I've made my mind up I feel so much better. It's so nice that Clive, Susan, Wendy and Amy are all happy for us. I don't know what I would do if they weren't," Mary said.

The rest of the week was busy. Bill and Mary were making plans and Liz was a great help to Mary. By the end of the week the furniture they would not be using was moved into the garage, kept safe in case they changed their minds.

Mary had called June and Shirley and told them she would see them next week. June said they had a few things to tell her as the trip to France was now booked. Mary also told them about Clive and Amy. "I can see we have a lot to talk about," Mary said.

Mary arrived back at her house by late afternoon. June and Shirley had arranged to bring supper, and so they could have the evening together catching up. Polly ran all around the house checking it all out, not sure what she was looking for.

Mary opened all the windows to let the fresh air in. Before long June and Shirley arrived with supper. There was enough food to last Mary the week. She was not sure just whom they thought they were feeding!

After supper they got the brochure out all about their trip to France. The tour they were going on came highly recommended from Suzi, the travel agent. "We get on the bus in Brookdale. That takes us down to the boat to cross into France," June said.

Shirley was nervous about the boat crossing, and so Mary suggested she go to see the doctor. "I'm sure he can give you something," Mary said.

"I'll call him tomorrow. That's a wise idea."

"The hotels look very nice," June put in. "All our meals are taken care of, and so we have no added cost for food. We have sent off for passports, and they will be back in a couple of weeks. We're so excited. Also, we have decided to go to the spa a few days before the trip.

Mary thought that was a great idea. "The spa will put you in the mood."

Shirley said that they were not going on the trip to Scotland with the art group. "June was not too happy about it, and so we decided that whatever trips we do go on, we have to both be on board."

"I'm so pleased for you both," Mary said.

"Now tell us about Clive and Amy," Shirley said.

And so Mary told them about Amy getting a job offer in the bank in Brookdale. "They are so happy together. We'll see what happens. Clive's house is big enough for the two of them for the time being. It is early days."

"What about your next move?" asked June.

"Well as you know, I've made my mind up to move and live in Clifton to be with Bill."

"We're both so happy for you," June and Shirley chimed.

"I never thought I would meet anyone else. All I know is I've never felt so happy in a long time." Mary then told them all about Liz who lived next door and how she had become a very good friend. "Clive is getting in touch with the estate agent, who will be coming to see me, then get this house on the market. I hope it doesn't take too long to sell."

"Well, you can count on us to help with packing or whatever you need doing," June said. Shirley nodded.

"I'm going to phone Ken and Carol. I thought I would ask them to come for a drink one evening just to let them know what I'm doing."

June thought that was a nice idea. Shirley asked if she had heard anything from the police.

Mary shook her head. "I've not heard one word from them in weeks. That is another reason I'd like to speak to Ken and Carol."

Mary was getting tired, as it had been a long day. She thanked June and Shirley then said she would see them both on Wednesday morning as usual. She reminded Shirley to call the doctor in the morning about tablets for the boat crossing.

By the time they met on Wednesday, Shirley had been to see the doctor. He had given her some tablets to take for the boat. June said that their passports had come. "You should see our photos. We both look dreadful."

Shirley was looking as though she had the world on her shoulders. June asked her what was worrying her.

"Alex came over to see me. Things are not going well between him and Linda, but as you know one can't interfere. One can only just be there for him. I'll phone John when I get home to see if he knows any more than me."

Mary asked if they had finalized their trip and when they were going.

Shirley said, "It's all booked. We're going in four weeks."

"I'm so excited for you both. Have you got to do much to get ready for the trip?"

"Apart from a few items, we're ready to go," June said. "But we'll have plenty of time before we go to help you with the move or whatever you need. Now tell us what is happening with your house. When will it be going on the market?"

"The agent came to see me with Clive and is now coming later in the week to take photos for the brochure, and then it will be for sale. Oh, also, Ken and Carol are coming on Friday for lunch. I do hope you're both available to come."

"Yes, we'll be there."

"I like them and Carol is the sweetest lady ever. I'm anxious to speak to Ken to see if he has heard anything from the police. Do you think they will ever catch this guy?"

June looked at Shirley. They both shrugged. "We thought we would go to the spa before our trip," June said. "Will you have time to join us?"

"Yes, I'd love to come. I feel I need pampering."

"Will Bill be coming up to Brookdale before you move?" Shirley asked.

"Yes, he plans on coming, but I'm not sure of the date yet."

Mary was ready when Ken and Carol arrived. Mary thought it was so nice to see them. Carol had come a long way since the first time they met. June and Shirley arrived shortly after them. It was a warm and sunny afternoon, and so they all had a glass of wine outside before lunch.

They were so pleased to hear she had decided to move to Clifton. "We'll see you when we come down to the cottage," Carol said.

Ken turned to June and Shirley and told them they would be more that welcome to use the cottage if they were not using it. Shirley was quick to respond with a smile on her face.

Mary asked Ken if he had heard anything from the police, as she had not heard a word in weeks. Ken said he had also heard nothing. "To be honest, the longer it goes the more I can't see them finding him. He sounds a slippery character that knows exactly what he's doing."

"I think you could be right," Mary sighed. "Well, lunch is ready so if you would like to come into the dining room."

Polly was not impressed, as she had to go into the other room while they were eating. Carol was very taken with Polly. She said her and Ken had never had a dog. "But I've got to confess I'd love one like Polly."

At that, Mary wrote down Ted's information, the breeder she had gotten Polly from. "Give him a call. Then on your next visit to Clifton you can drop in to see him."

June and Shirley were telling Ken and Carol how having that holiday in Clifton had opened their eyes about taking other trips. "We're going on a bus tour to France in a few weeks." June said. "We had no idea of the options open to us. Suzi at the travel agent office in the main street has been so helpful."

Mary said they were going to be quite the jet-setters. She turned to Ken and Carol. "The next time Bill comes I'll phone you. If you're available I'd like you to come meet him."

"I think I've been in his store," Ken added.

It turned out to be a very pleasant afternoon. Mary said she would be in touch and Carol thanked her for Ted's information.

After Ken and Carol had gone, June and Shirley stayed to help Mary clear away as the estate agent had said she already had a viewing for the weekend. Mary also told June and Shirley that Amy was starting her new job at the bank in Brookdale on Monday.

Bill phoned later to see how everything was going. He said he would be coming up the next weekend as he had arranged help for the shop. Amy would have had a week in her new job, and he was anxious to hear all about it. He had started to clear out the things they had talked about to make room for Mary's furniture. He had also cleared out the closets for her clothes. After Olive had died, he had spread his things all over the house, and so it really was in need of clearing out. Also, the garage was in a terrible state. Fred was helping him do the garage and garden shed. He could not believe the amount of junk he had accumulated. But he now had a good incentive to get it cleared out.

Gary called Shirley. He wanted her to put some of her sketches in the art exhibition. Shirley was not sure they were good enough, but Gary persuaded her to bring them to the art class and he would go through them with her. She told him she was going away, but the exhibition was when she came back, so no more excuses!

June and Mary were so pleased for her. She had come a long way and was now doing some very good work. When she first went to the art class she had never sketched anything in her life other than a few doodles many years ago.

June was busy helping with the preparation for the Summer Fete. Mary was busy with the selling of her house, which was getting a lot of interest, and Shirley was busy with the upcoming art exhibition.

Gary went through the sketches with Shirley and picked out six for the exhibition. "We need to get them framed. Also, we have to discuss a price for each one."

Shirley laughed. "Do you mean to tell me I could sell them?"

"Of course you can sell them. They're wonderful."

That night she phoned both John and Alex and told them about the art exhibition. She also told them about her trip to France with June. She gave them the dates. Both the boys were thrilled for her. They both asked if she had phoned Heather yet. "I'm about to," she told them.

Heather was not as enthusiastic as John and Alex and could not understand that she could possibly have artwork good enough for an exhibition. When she told her she was going on a trip to France with June, Heather just went quiet. At this stage Shirley asked her if she would like to come home for a couple of days so they could spend some time together.

"Hmm, I'll have to see what we're doing at the weekend. I'll get back to you, Mum," Heather said.

"We could go out for a meal or whatever you would like to do. Let me know what you decide."

When June and Shirley met Mary for coffee, Mary said she had had an offer on the house but that it was a bit low. "And so we're going back and forward, although it sounds good. The only stipulation is they would want me out in six weeks, and so I'll have to get moving."

"Remember we'll help, and so keep us up to date," June put in, and Shirley nodded.

June told them about the Summer Fete. "Shirley is also helping. It seems to get bigger every year, but we do have a lot of helpers. We have collected a lot of big prizes for the draw, and so I think we could make a lot of money this year. The businesses in the area have pulled out all the stops, and so the vicar is very pleased."

Shirley told them about the art exhibition and her six sketches that had been accepted. "I met with Gary as they have to be framed, and also priced out. The sketches that have been accepted were the ones I did in Clifton."

"You're becoming quite the art expert," Mary said and smiled. "Once I've moved, Bill and I'll be coming to support you. You never know, we may buy one of your sketches. Let me know the date of the exhibition when you get it."

Shirley told them she had asked Heather if she would like to come home for a couple of days. "I do feel there is something going on I don't know about. She is so down all the time and just seems unhappy."

Mary called June and Shirley the next day to let them know her house was now sold. "I can't believe it happened so quickly. Bill is coming at the weekend, and so we can really get organized. As I've not been in this house that long, I still have a few boxes that have not been unpacked."

Mary called Liz in Clifton to tell her. "She was thrilled for me. She said they had been helping Bill clean out the garage and the garden shed. Liz said Bill is so happy, and I'm looking forward to having a walking partner with the dogs. Ken and Carol came and met Bill. Carol recognized Bill as she had been in the shop and purchased many items over the years. "If I remember correctly you sell those famous silk scarfs."

"We'll keep in touch when I've moved, and you can come over to see us when you're down in Clifton," Mary put in.

They said they would love to. Carol also said she had called Ted and they had arranged to call in and see him on their way to Clifton. "We're going down next week so and, you never know. We could have a little dog like Polly when we next see you," Carol said.

Shirley was pleasantly surprised to have a call from Heather, who was going to come down on Friday and stay until Sunday. Although she was nervous, she was looking forward to be able to spend some time together. Shirley told John and Alex that Heather was coming but made it clear she wanted to have time with Heather on her own to try and find out what was making her so unhappy all the time.

Both John and Alex thought that was a good idea. "What about us just calling in on Saturday morning for coffee?" John said.

"That sounds great. I had planned on us going out in the afternoon to the new garden centre that just opened. Heather was always interested in flowers and anything new for the garden. If all goes well we'll have a meal out, but I'm going to take it as it goes."

Shirley had the house looking very cheerful with flowers inside and out in the garden. "I don't know what happened, but my garden looks beautiful this year," she told June. June was the one that, whatever she plants, grows. On the other hand, Shirley's plants and flowers never seemed to thrive.

Heather was due to arrive for supper, and so Shirley was ready when she did. She commented on the garden, which Shirley found nice to hear, as things had been very strained lately. By the time Heather had put her things in the bedroom Shirley had supper on the table. "Mum, this is so nice and it smells delicious."

"Well, let's hope it tastes as good as it smells." Shirley suggested they have their coffee on the rear patio overlooking the garden, as it was a warm evening. After a glass of wine and a nice meal Heather seemed very relaxed. Shirley asked her if there was anything worrying her. "You know I'm here for you, so please don't shut me out."

Tears welled up in Heather's eyes and she started to cry. Shirley rushed over and gave her a hug. "I know something is not right." Then Heather started to talk and did not stop. She had found out that Dave her husband was having an affair with a girl he worked with. "To make things worse, I confronted him and he confessed, but he's not willing to give her up. He wants me to accept it and carry on as normal! Mum, I didn't know how to tell you. I've been in such a mess. I know I've been horrible to you and to John and Alex. They've both asked me what the problem is. Dave is a good father to Jenny and he'll do anything for her. He has Jenny this weekend and he takes her everywhere. I think he knows I'll be telling you."

Shirley was so shocked. She asked her if they would consider going to see a counsellor. "I don't know I could ask him. The trouble is, he has is in his mind that this is normal."

Shirley told her that John and Alex were coming for coffee in the morning. "Do you want to tell them? They're worried about you."

Heather decided she wanted John and Alex to know, but wanted Shirley to tell them before they arrived. "I'll do whatever you want. What if I call them this evening and tell them. That way it will not be such a shock. You three have always been so close and they will support you whichever way to want to deal with this."

"Mum, you're the greatest. Now I want to hear more about your trip to France with June. Go and get the details. Have you got a passport?"

"Yes, we have our passports ready. It's quite exciting. I'm a bit concerned about the boat crossing, and so I got some tablets from the doctor."

They spent the rest of the evening going over the itinerary. "I'm so happy that you agree with me taking this trip," Shirley said.

"Mum, I'm thrilled. And I'm so sorry for my behaviour. I was so out of order."

"Well, let's put that all behind us and move on."

"By the way, when I was in Clifton I bought you a little gift." Shirley brought out the silk scarf. The blue with the green going through it looked even better than Shirley remembered. Heather just loved it.

As soon as Heather went to bed Shirley called John and Alex and told them about Dave and his affair. Alex was calm, but John wanted to punch him in the nose. Shirley said there was to be none of that. "We're here to support Heather. She's looking forward to seeing you for coffee in the morning."

Heather was up bright and early and seemed back to her old self. "I can't believe how much better I feel now that I've got your support."

"Don't forget, John and Alex are also looking forward to seeing you and are ready to support you in any way you want."

John arrived first and said Alex would be a little late. He gave Heather a hug, and then they went out in the garden to chat. Before long Alex arrived, and so Shirley made the coffee. They all sat on the patio. Heather had thought about what Shirley said and thought it was a good idea to meet with a counsellor.

Alex told Heather about Shirley having six of her sketches in the upcoming art exhibition. "There's no stopping you. This is wonderful!" Heather said.

"Thank you. They have gone to be framed and ready for the exhibition."

"I didn't know you could sketch, Mum. You must be good."

"Well, I don't think so. I just enjoy it and that's all that matters."

When John and Alex were leaving, they both told Heather she must keep in touch and added that anything they could do, just let them know. Shirley told Heather about the new garden centre. "I thought we could take a look, and then have a meal out somewhere."

Heather suggested she call June and ask her if she would like to join them. "I'll do that right away. I'm sure she would be delighted. I know she has been itching to check out the garden centre."

They had a great afternoon and evening. June was thrilled to be invited. The garden centre did not disappoint. It was packed and the flowers were amazing. They all bought flowers or plants, and so the smell in the car was wonderful.

It was soon time for Heather to leave, but the weekend was a great success. She promised to share any worries she had in the future and call as soon as she got home.

Shirley called Mary, as she was concerned about Heather. They had a good chat. Although it was not good news, at least Heather was not sick.

Mary had been busy with her packing. She had had Clive and Amy around, who had both been a good help.

Gary called Shirley to say the sketches were ready to be collected from the framers. He wanted to know if she would like to go with him to pick them up. Shirley was thrilled and could not wait to see them. Gary said he would pick her up in the morning around 11:00 AM.

The sketches looked so professional. She could not believe she did them.

"I've been telling you how good you are," Gary said. "Now we have to think about a price for each one. Have you any ideas?"

"To think that someone will pay money for my sketches blows my mind," Shirley said.

Everything was moving along with Mary. She was getting excited now that the house was sold. Shirley was happier now that she had spoken to Heather. Her sketches would be ready for the art exhibition when she returned from France.

June was happy the way everything was coming along for the Summer Fete. Carol called Mary to say they had stopped to see Ted and discuss having a puppy. He said as soon as he had another litter he would call them to see about picking a puppy. Carol was so excited. She told Mary she could not stop thinking about Polly and how she might soon have a puppy like her.

When June, Shirley and Mary met for coffee they had to decide when to book the spa. They all wanted to celebrate Mary moving to Clifton and June and Shirley going to France.

June said she could not believe they were off to France. "We're going to have a great time." Mary said she could not believe June was excited to be going to the spa.

Shirley told them her sketches look so professional now they are framed. "And to think they will be for sale! Gary is very pleased with the art exhibition. He said that this year the quality of the art is to an exceptional standard."

CHAPTER EIGHT

Off to France

SHIRLEY CALLED JUNE to check they had all the information they needed for their trip. "We have everything ready. Stop worrying. I'll call Mary to see what time she is picking us up to go to the spa tomorrow, then let you know."

"Sounds good to me," said June.

They entered the spa. It smelled so relaxing, and was decorated in soft pinks and lilacs. Soft music played.

The young lady greeted them and took them through to get changed into the robes. "When you're ready, please come through to the lounge," she said. They were sitting in the lounge when the three ladies entered who were going to give them the massages. Then they were each taken into separate rooms.

After the massage they were taken into another room, which again was exquisitely decorated. They were told to help themselves to a selection of herbal tea and fresh fruit. There was no rushing. "Please relax," the lady said. They all smelt wonderful.

Mary nudged Shirley, "Look at June. I think this is the longest I've ever seen her sitting still."

They chatted for quite a while, and then two other ladies came; they had also had a massage.

Next they had a manicure followed by a pedicure. Then they arranged to go for lunch. While they were having lunch, Mary noticed four ladies sitting a table by the window. June looked at Mary, who seemed uneasy, and so she asked her if there was anything wrong. Apparently they were from the golf club and were once friends of Mary, but when Stan died they stopped having anything to do with Mary.

They ordered a garden salad and a bottle of wine. They told Mary not to worry about them, in fact to just ignore them. The rest of the meal was very enjoyable, but June could see that Mary was not herself. Then one lady came across to Mary as she was leaving and said hello and declared that it was nice to see her. You could see Mary was pleased when they had left.

"That makes me so mad to think what I used to do for the golf club," Mary said. "They are so hypocritical."

Shirley told her to rise above it and think of what she had to look forward to. "I total agree," June said.

"Thank you both so much," Mary said and smiled and added, "You never know, you may come back with a Frenchman each."

June said: "I'll drink to that."

The cases are packed. "Can you believe it? We leave for France tomorrow!" said Shirley. Mary said she would pick them up and take them to catch the bus by 8:00 AM. Heather phoned Shirley to wish her a nice trip, and said she was going to make an appointment to meet with the marriage counsellor.

Mary picked them up right on time. By the time they set off the bus was full and everyone was excited and ready for a vacation. On the way to the port to catch the boat, the bus made a couple of stops. Shirley said she had never seen such a big ship. "This is fantastic!"

June was speechless as she looked up at the ship.

Shirley had taken the medication the doctor gave her so she would not get seasick. They were taking it all in as they set sail. It was not a long crossing. The weather was good. No wind. It was warm but not that sunny. The crossing went without a hitch and before long the ship was docking and it was time to get off the ship.

June looked at Shirley. "We're in France!"

Back on the bus, and then they were heading to their first hotel, which was only an hour away. By the time they got to the hotel everyone was tired and ready for a shower and a meal. The hotel was a country hotel and as Shirley said, "very French." Their room was perfect. There was time for a rest, and then down to the dining room for supper.

The group were all so friendly. There were quite a few who were budding artists as the main attraction on the trip was the visit to Monet's gardens and his house. Shirley had her sketchpad ready. She could not wait. Many had done this trip before, and so they were telling June and Shirley the things not to be missed. After the evening meal, everyone was pleased to get to their rooms for an early night.

The bus driver said they would be leaving at nine sharp in the morning, "So make sure you allow time for breakfast, it is not to be missed."

Everyone was on the bus and ready to go by 9:00 AM. They headed through the French countryside, through vineyards and rolling hills. This was very much wine country. At lunch time they stopped in a small town with a bustling market. And so they all had time to explore.

There was the smell of freshly-baked bread, as well as pastries and the largest selection of cheeses they had ever seen.

They bought some fruit, bread, cheese, and coffee, and then found a beautiful park, which they sat in with other people from the group and soaked up the afternoon sun. The old historical buildings were magnificent. Everyone was so friendly and made them welcome.

They had time to visit one of the churches in the town. The church was so historical. As they entered they got the shivers. They took many photos, could not get over the gardens and flowers. They were all so manicured. You could see that the local people took great pride in keeping everywhere in pristine condition.

Soon it was time to get back on the bus and off to their next hotel. That night they were staying in a larger hotel. They would be staying there for three nights. After they got unpacked they decided to go for a walk and explore. They wandered around, up the cobble streets and again admired the old buildings.

During the evening meal they were all excited, as tomorrow was a visit to Monet's gardens. June said she could not wait to see the Japanese water gardens, and Shirley wanted to see Monet's house and famous bridges. They were so pleased they had plenty of time so they would not be rushed.

After their meal they took their coffee out on the terrace at the hotel.

One couple came and joined them. They had been to France the year before and enjoyed it so much they had returned. "One word of advice. Make sure you have comfortable shoes on." They were keen artists, and so Shirley told them she had brought her sketchpad and could not wait to see Monet's house and garden.

The next morning everyone was ready for their visit Claude Monet's house and gardens.

June said to Shirley: "Can you believe what we're doing? This is a wonderful experience."

The weather was perfect, not too hot, just perfect. June was making sure Shirley had her sketch pad and pencils or whatever she needed. Shirley was smiling at June. "I've never seen you so excited about anything."

Claude Monet's gardens are set in Giverny, which is a tiny village with about 500 inhabitants. It is a place of outstanding beauty.

Getting off the bus and entering the gardens was an experience they could not describe. They had decided to go to the gardens first. There was so much to see, and the colours were out of this world. Shirley wanted to stop by some seats and do a sketch. "That works," said June. "I think I could sit here all day. There is so much to take in."

It was decided to go to the water gardens after lunch. Shirley was sketching along with many other people. They noticed an art class taking place one location. It was the most peaceful feeling. The garden were as nice, if not better that you could imagine; it exceeded their expectations.

Lunch was spent on the terrace of the café in the gardens. Shirley was still sketching. "I hope you brought more than one sketch pad," said June.

"Don't worry, I came well prepared," Shirley replied.

June had her notebook and was taking notes on all the different varieties of flowers and way they grouped the flowers together.

Lunch consisted of fresh coffee along with fresh bread, cheese, and fruit. What more could you ask for?

From where they were sitting having lunch Shirley said, "Everywhere you look is a vignette. I feel that we're sitting in one of Claude Monet's paintings."

After lunch they headed for the Japanese-inspired water gardens and famous Japanese bridges. "The lily ponds are exactly as I pictured," Shirley said. "Look, June, every lily is out perfectly, and the colours are outstanding."

They found a spot to sit and Shirley starting sketching. June was happy to sit and take it all in. The couple they talked to last night at the hotel came by, and so they chatted for a while. Shirley didn't look up once from her sketchpad.

Later they went to see the Japanese bridges. As they walked around the pond they passed a sign that read: *this wisteria arbour was planted by Monet himself.* The way he painted the bridges over the lily pond made a wonderful statement.

"Just wait till Gary sees all these sketches, I think he'll be impressed," Shirley said.

"You know, Shirley, you're very talented."

"Why don't you try, June? You never know, you could come to like it."

"No it's not for me, but I love watching you do it."

Towards the end of the day they met up with a group from our trip who decided to walk into the village of Giverny.

Walking into the village they saw many interesting old houses with walls around them. Flowers cascaded over all the walls. The vibrant pinks mixed with reds were a sight to be seen.

At the end of the village was an interesting old church. This was where Monet was buried. It was the most peaceful place. They went further and came across a British Commonwealth War Cemetery.

The rest of the day was as perfect as it could be. The bus picked them up. By the time they got back to the hotel it was time for the evening meal. Everyone was talking and swapping stories about the day. "Just think, we get to do it again tomorrow," June said.

Next morning they were all ready. They set off on time and were soon at the gardens. Quite a few of them were heading towards the house. Again it did not disappoint in any way. The architectural detail on the house was breathtaking. "To think Claude Monet lived here!" June said.

The house was beautifully preserved and painted in pastel-pink and flanked by fabulous gardens.

Shirley did her sketching as June wandered around, soaking up the atmosphere. People were so friendly. June found herself talking to people from all over the world and, of course, happy to be in the Monet gardens.

They ended up at the same place for lunch. After lunch, they went back to the gardens and spent the rest of the day taking photos of the flowers. Shirley wanted to get one more sketch of the Japanese bridge, the one with the wisteria climbing all over it.

Sadly it was time to walk towards the area where they had to get back on the bus to take them back to the hotel. As they got on the bus they realized that everyone had bought something from the gift shop to remind them of the gardens. Shirley bought a painting of the Japanese Bridge and June bought one of the lily pond.

After dinner, everyone had coffee on the terrace of the hotel and shared their thoughts of the last two days. It really was an unforgettable experience. "I think Bill and Mary should do this trip," June said.

The next day they headed for one of the vineyards. The drive was through the most breathtaking scenery you ever could imagine. They arrived at the vineyard in time for lunch. After lunch they were taken on a wine tour, and then a wine tasting, which they had to say was a great success.

June and Shirley found it was so interesting to learn all about winemaking and to realize that when you buy a bottle of wine in the store and take it home, you don't realize how much goes into making the wine and bottling it.

It was only a short journey on the bus before they arrived at the hotel. This hotel was much smaller than the previous one, and it was surrounded by countryside that was dotted with little villages. This charming place was owned by a British couple who had bought it ten years ago. Their room was overlooking the vineyards and was decorated in blue and white. It was so fresh.

After unpacking they had time to go for a walk, but they were too tired to walk far. All that wine had tired them out, and so they decided to go back to the hotel for a sleep before the evening meal.

The next day they were free to do as they pleased and so, along with quite a few out of their group, they caught the local bus to the next village. This village had a fruit market that also sold local crafts. After breakfast they all set off. When they arrived at the market, they found it was packed. They all went their separate ways and planned to meet at the bus stop at 4:30 to go back to the hotel.

They had so much fun trying to buy gifts to take home. Their French was not the best. Shirley came upon a local artist who was selling his paintings. He was also very interested in what Shirley was doing with her art. He lived in the next town, but he said this market was the best around and was always busy.

Both June and Shirley bought one of his paintings. Shirley took one of his cards and said she was going to check out his website when she got home. They then went on to check out the pottery. They were most surprised again that they were all local artists. The young lady who did the pottery said it was a shame they didn't have an art centre to display everyone's art.

Shirley was busy collecting cards from as many artists as she could. "At this rate you will need another case to take all this art back with you," June teased. They stopped for lunch at a small café and sat on the terrace overlooking the market.

Back at the market June wanted to see some of the needlework on display. She bought the most beautiful tablecloth, complete with napkins. She said to Shirley: "I don't know when I'll ever use it, but I just love the attention to detail."

They had both taken many photos around the market and the market stands.

By 4:30 everyone was ready to catch the local bus back to the hotel. "How on earth are we going to get all this into our cases?" Shirley asked.

"We're having so much fun, Shirley. Let's think about that later," June replied.

Back at the hotel they decided to order a tray of tea on the terrace before they went up to their room. The owner brought it out to them. Her name was Gladys. Shirley said she could understand why she would want to come and live here.

"We were on a holiday, just like you two," Gladys explained. "And before we went home we knew that we would be back. It was hard work for the first year as our French was not good, but after the first year, we never looked back. As soon as we walked into The Hotel Charlemagne, we knew it was ours. It needed some love and tender care, but the location was right. The rest is history."

Shirley said she had been talking to a few of the local artists and explained how they said they needed an art centre as there were so many artists in this area and nowhere to display their work. "To be honest, what is needed apart from an art centre is somewhere where artists can hold lectures and classes," Gladys said. Gladys went on to say that people come to this area from all over the world throughout the year. "Well, I had better get on. Enjoy your tea, ladies, and I'll see you later."

June and Shirley sat and had their tea, not saying a word. Then June said: "Are you thinking what I'm thinking?"

"You know, I think I am. Do you think we could do it?"

"Well, how is your French?"

"Not good."

Over their evening meal they began to think of it more seriously. "Do you really think we could do this?" June wondered aloud.

"Let's make a list of questions to ask Gladys," Shirley said. "What if we buy an old house with some outbuildings that could accommodate an area to hold lectures and also artists to come and display their art work? If we could have two or three letting rooms, that would give us an income."

At the end of the meal Shirley went to find Gladys and asked her if she could spare some of her time for a talk.

"Of course! Take your coffee out onto the terrace, and I'll come and join you in a little while."

In no time, Gladys came out to join them. "How can I help you?"

"We've been thinking about what you said also about what we found out today." They told Gladys of their thoughts and asked if she thought it was at all possible.

"I think it's a splendid idea. I'm sure you would both love it. I do have to point out there will be hard times in the beginning."

"We both own our own houses and have been very good friends for many years," June said. "That will help."

"What I suggest is that I give you the name of a good agent who will help you. I'll explain what you're looking for and get him to call you. I have your details, but if you could write them out then I'll pass them on to the agent, and I'll give you mine."

June thought it would be better if he phoned Shirley.

"Yes, that works, too." Gladys said and went off to get the information for them with Shirley's details in hand. Before long she was back. She smiled at them both. "I would imagine you will need to come back in a few weeks, so give me a call and I'll book you in to stay here. Now, I think you have the morning free as your group is not due to leave until two. Would you like me to drive you around the area in the morning? And if I can arrange for you to meet with the agent, then at least you then can put a face to the voice when he phones you."

"Oh, that would be very helpful if you can spare the time," Shirley said.

"I would love to help. I know what it is like, remember."

That night neither June nor Shirley could sleep. "This is so exciting!" Shirley said.

"I agree. Are we completely mad or what," June said and shook her head. "Neither of us has ever taken a risk in our lives. So it is now or never."

As soon as breakfast was over, Gladys came over to them and said she would be ready to leave shortly. They both had their cameras ready—they wanted to take as many photos as possible.

They got into Gladys' car. She said she would show them the surrounding area. June and Shirley were taking notes and taking photos. The area just outside the town was beautiful, with vines growing everywhere you looked.

Gladys stopped in one area where they went for coffee to discuss what their plans.

She suggested if they were serious after speaking to the agent that they should sign on for French classes. "It will be a great advantage if you can speak French."

Shirley nodded. She could speak a little French, but not enough to run a business.

During their coffee they fired questions at Gladys, who was very helpful. It was soon time to set off back to the hotel since the bus was leaving at two.

"We have a lot of thinking to do," June said, and Shirley agreed.

They had the agent's information and agreed to call him as soon as they arrived home. June asked Gladys to tell the agent what they would be looking for so that when they called him he would have an idea if there was anything available. She added that she should tell him that they were in no hurry.

Everyone was on the bus ready to leave at 2:00. They had one more night before setting sail for home. During the journey to the final hotel, June and Shirley could not stop talking about their new adventure. "What do you think Mary will say?" asked Shirley.

"I think she will be thrilled for us," June said.

"I wonder what John, Alex and Heather will say," Shirley wondered.

When they arrived at the hotel there was just time to freshen up before their evening meal. After the meal everyone was reliving the trip. Of course Shirley and June did not tell anyone of their plans. "You can understand why people do this trip over again and again. It has opened our eyes," June said to one couple, to which they agreed.

Next morning after breakfast it was time to head to the dock and make ready to sail home. Shirley took her medication so she would be okay on the journey home. They both enjoyed sailing and were again amazed at the size of the ship and what it had to offer.

This time they were more comfortable in exploring the ship. They even went into the shops on board. "Look at us! We're hardened travelers now," they said and laughed, and then they went along to the coffee shop, which was set out just like the cafes they had visited during their time in France.

They ordered two pastries and soaked up every last minute of their trip to France.

The loud speaker announced that would be docking in thirty minutes and to collect all personal belongings, ready to disembark.

Before long they were back in Britain and heading for home on the bus. They were still planning what to do next. "We do have to make sure we're still as interested now we're back home," Shirley said.

June said she could not be more committed. Shirley agreed with her one hundred percent.

They arrived back in Brookdale to find Mary there waiting for them. They had decided not to say anything about their plans to Mary that day. June said she would make supper for them all the following night at her house where they could catch up, then added: "As Mary will be moving in a few weeks, I'm sure she will have lots to tell us."

Mary was so pleased to see them. "I've missed you two so much and have so much to tell you both." They all hugged and got into Mary's car along with all their stuff. "Did you buy France while you were there," Mary joked.

"I think we did go a bit over board on the shopping," June said and laughed

"Well, did you both have a good time? I want to hear all about it! Shirley, how did you manage on the ship?" Mary asked.

"That medication from the doctor worked. We enjoyed every minute of the trip and when you see the photos of Monet house and gardens you will understand why."

As Mary was dropping June off, June told her that she would like to cook supper the next night at her house so that they could have a good catch-up. "That works for me. I can't wait," said Mary. Next she dropped Shirley off.

Shirley did ask her if all was going well with the sale of her house, just to make sure there was not going to be any hold-ups.

"Everything is going so well. I've got to keep pinching myself, as it seems that I'm living in a dream. Bill is on the phone all the time. He is the sweetest man ever."

They said goodbye and that they would be at June's for 6:00 the following night. "I love a girl's night in," Mary said.

CHAPTER NINE

More Changes

JUNE WAS BUSY all day shopping and getting the house and meal ready for the evening meal. Shirley called her to say she was not going to say anything to the children until they had talked it over with Mary. June thought that was a good idea.

June was ready when Mary and Shirley arrived. It was a nice summer evening so they had a glass of wine on the patio before the meal. Mary wanted to know all about the trip, but June said they wanted to know her news first. "Not much to say other than the move is scheduled for next week and the packing is all done. Clive and Amy have been helping me as I had furniture that I no longer needed. My house looks very unlived in. Poor Polly is not happy. She seems lost. I've noticed she is very clingy at the moment."

June said, "You should have brought her with you tonight."

"I did think of calling you about bringing her, but I took her for a long walk, and so she was happy to be in her bed sleeping."

"Would you like to come in now, girls, as the meal is ready," June said.

"Now, that is enough about me. I want to see your photos and all the details of the trip." June said it was a wonderful trip from start to finish. "The people on the bus and the bus driver were all so friendly. Many had done the trip before and we could understand why. The scenery took our breath away on more than one occasion—rolling hills and so many beautiful vineyards."

Shirley told about the village markets and the artists they had met. "One of the highlights was our visit Monet house and gardens. You and Bill must do this trip. It is so romantic." she showed Mary the photos she had taken.

"Did you do any sketches?" Mary asked.

"Oh, I did hundreds, but I've to go through them and finish them off."

Then they started to tell Mary about their idea of moving to France and creating a place to hold local artist's work. "We would also like it to have some letting rooms," Shirley said. "There is nowhere for local artists to hold lectures and workshops. We talked to many artists in the local markets to get as much information as possible."

June went on to tell Mary about Gladys and how she helped them. Mary sat there and listened, and then Shirley asked: "Aren't you going to say anything?"

"Well, you two have taken my breath away."

Mary asked Shirley if she had spoken to the children about this idea. "No," Shirley replied. "We wanted to talk it through with you first before we did anything."

June put in that she had made a call about joining a class to learn French, but that was it. "Well?" Shirley said. "What do you think, Mary? Do you think we're completely mad? We're very excited about it, that's for sure."

"I think it sounds great. You know when I met Bill, I thought it was too soon after Stan died, but I thought if you don't take opportunities when they come your way, you lose out. I'm thrilled for you both. You know one another so well and have always got on."

Shirley said she would be more involved with the artists and June would be more involved with the running of the house and letting the rooms. "I'll be telling John and Alex first, and then I'll phone Heather," Shirley said and then sighed. "I'm not sure how they will all take it."

Shirley and June had bought a painting for Mary and she loved it. It was a painting of the Monet gardens. "Bill will also love this painting," Mary declared.

June said they would be calling the agent to start looking for a property. "Also we have to get our own properties valued. We're in no hurry, but we have to start somewhere."

Mary said she would like to make a toast. June topped up the wine.

"Here's to you both," Mary said. "I would like to wish you all the very best in your new venture!" As that, they clinked the glasses.

The following morning Shirley called John and Alex and asked them to come and see her as she had something to discuss with them. She was wondering what they would think. Then she phoned Heather to see how she was and to see if she had convinced Dave to go to see the marriage counsellor.

Heather said Dave would not hear of going to a marriage counsellor, as he said there was nothing wrong with their marriage. He also still thought it was not a problem for him to have a girlfriend. Heather was at her breaking point, and so she made an appointment and was going to go on her own to see if that would help her.

Heather asked her Mum if she had enjoyed her trip. To Shirley's surprise, Heather said she would come and see her for the weekend. "Jenny keeps asking when she can come again."

"That would be great. I look forward to seeing you both. I'll tell you all about my trip at the weekend."

John and Alex came after work and, to Shirley's surprise, after the first shock, they were okay with the news. John said that he wanted to come with her on the next visit to help her, as he spoke French.

"I'm sure June would not mind," he said. "I just want to know what you're getting yourselves into."

"Don't worry so much. And by the way, we're going to take a class to learn to speak French.

Alex and John looked at one another and smiled. "Mum, you never stop surprising us," Alex said.

Shirley told them that Heather was coming for the weekend and she would tell her then. "So please don't discuss it with her until I've talked to her." Shirley added that things were no better with Dave and that he refused to go with her to counselling.

Gary called later in the day and wanted to know if Shirley would have time to help out with the planning of the upcoming art exhibition. She arranged to go the following morning to the community centre.

When she arrived at the community centre, Gary was already there along with a group of other artists. They were busy getting organized. "The art work has to be mounted on the walls and we have to make sure they are grouped correctly. Oh, and they also have to be priced," Gary said. "Although the exhibition is two weeks away there is a lot preparation to be done." Gary then asked if June would be willing to help with the refreshments.

"I'll ask her and let you know," Shirley promised.

Gary was still waiting for some artwork to come back from the framers. "They also rent out tables for suppliers to come and show all the different brushes, paints, pads, etc.," he said. "It gives the students a chance to stock up and see the latest items on offer in the art world."

When they were finished, Gary asked Shirley if she would like to have lunch, and then she could tell him about her trip and all about Monet gardens. "That sounds like a good idea. I'm ready for something to eat.

Over lunch Shirley told Gary about the trip and also about her and June's plan. He was very interested and also very impressed. He wanted to see her sketches, but she said she had to finish them first. "You have become one professional artist. You amaze me," he said.

He thought the art exhibition this year was turning out to be one of their best. "We're getting more art each year and the standard is higher. I've been in touch with the local radio station. They will do some advertising for us." Gary then asked Shirley what the next step was as far as the new venture in France.

"Well, I'm going to call the agent as soon as I've told Heather. She is coming this weekend. I do hope she will be as interested as John and Alex. John even wants to come to France with June and myself when we go to view property."

As they left the café, Gary wished Shirley the very best of luck in the new venture. "I'll be coming out to the art workshops and lectures as soon as you get started."

As soon as she got home she called June to see if she would help with the refreshments at the art exhibition. June was pleased to be asked. "I need to brush up on the art world," June said.

Shirley said, "You only have to help with tea and coffee." She also told June that Gary was very interested and that he would be coming to their art workshops and lectures in France.

June then asked how John and Alex had taken the news about France.

"They were a bit shocked, but they were not against the idea. John would like to come with us when we fly to France to view properties. I hope you don't mind. He speaks fluent French, and so I think it will be a great help."

"I think that's a great idea," June said.

"Heather is coming at the weekend, and so I'll tell her then."

"Are things any better for her?" asked June.

"No change there. I did not want to tell her over the phone though. But I think I'll call the agent in France as soon as I've told Heather."

June said she had registered for French lessons. "I said we're beginners and seniors so she will have a challenge on her hands, but we have to learn." June also said she went into the library and found two very useful books about moving to live in France.

"Mary said this Wednesday morning will be our last coffee together so we have to make the most of it," Shirley said just before they hung up.

It turned out June and Shirley were there before Mary. "I hope you have told Bill that you're coming back in two weeks for the art exhibition. We'll be there, don't worry."

June and Shirley both offered for Mary and Bill to stay with them when they came to Brookdale. "Thank you," Mary said. "But we'll be staying with Clive and Amy. By the way, Amy is very happy in her job at the bank in Brookdale. She said the staff are much friendlier that the bank she was at before."

Mary was pleased that John and Alex were happy with Shirley moving to France. "I'm sure Heather will be happy, too."

"Well, she said she could not imagine us speaking French," Shirley said. "Our class starts next week!"

As they left the café, Molly, the owner of the café, gave Mary a gift, and wished her all the luck in the world. She also told her to make sure she comes to see her when next in Brookdale. Mary was a little teary, but very happy.

June and Shirley said they would be around to help on Friday, the moving day. "That would be nice," Mary said, "although I'm quite organized. I think Polly would love to see you both. She is not happy at the moment. She senses something is going on. I'll be pleased when we're in Clifton."

The move went without a hitch. Mary was very tearful at saying goodbye to everyone. Susan had driven down to Clifton with Emma to be there when she arrived. Bill and Susan had set that up to make her welcome.

It was later in the day by the time Mary arrived at Bill's and she was so tired. The look on her face when Bill, Susan, and Emma opened the front door! It was hard to tell who was the most excited: Mary or Molly. Emma was so happy to see her little playmate, Molly.

The van with her furniture would be coming tomorrow, and so it worked out perfectly. Bill was arranging a Chinese take-away. Mary said she would like a shower first to freshen up. By the time she had her shower, the food was just being delivered.

During supper Susan said she could stay until Monday. Bill had arranged staff at the shop until Monday, and so he could be at home. Mary felt at home straight away, which made Bill happy. All Emma wanted to do was take Polly for a walk.

The furniture arrived right on time and was unloaded by lunch time. Although she did not bring that much, the things she was not sure about went into the garage. Liz came around and said they were doing a BBQ at five. "So you don't have to worry about food. Don't forget to bring Polly with you so Pepper and Polly can play in the garden."

Liz and Fred made them so welcome. Bill announced he was planning on building Emma a playhouse for the garden. Susan said: "She won't want to leave if you make her too welcome."

Emma loved Bill. He was always doing some project with her. You could see he loved children and was so patient with Emma. Nothing was too much trouble.

Sunday morning Mary had arranged with Liz to take Polly and Pepper for a walk. Emma could not wait. It was a little overcast but still warm. Mary called Clive to say everyone was fine and to thank him and Amy for their help.

Mary reminded Clive that they would be coming up to stay with them for the weekend of the art exhibition. "Don't worry. I've it written down. We're looking forward to seeing you both," Clive said.

Back in Brookdale, Heather arrived with Penny. Shirley was so pleased to see them. "Well, come on, Mum. I want to hear all about the trip to France."

Shirley had a present for Penny, and so she was happy. She got the photos out. She also showed her sketches, but she told her they were not quite finished. "Mum, you're really good." She went on to tell her all about Monet house and gardens. "The gardens are out of this world. The whole trip was amazing. We had such a good time."

Later she went on to tell her about the plan that her and June are looking into. Heather did not say anything for a while, which worried Shirley. "Mum, you keep on amazing me. I think you should check it out. We only live once. If I've learned one thing after the situation I find myself in, it is: follow your dreams."

"I thought we would invite June over for supper tonight, and then we can go into more details about out new venture."

Heather asked: "What do John and Alex think about your plan?"

"John wants to come with June and I when we go to see what properties are available."

"That sounds like a good idea. If I remember correctly, John had an old school friend who went to live in France. I'll ask him when I next speak to him."

Shirley called June to invite her for supper to go over ideas with Heather. June was thrilled and also said they should call the agent in the morning. Shirley had a nice day with Heather and Jenny. "It is so nice that we're getting on now," she told June.

Heather did not mention Dave all day. They went to the park that Jenny loved and she played with the other children on the swings. It was a great day.

June was to arrive by 6:00 PM. Shirley had everything ready for supper. Jenny loved June as she always brought her something, and she always played with her. Jenny was waiting at the window. As soon as she saw June's car pull up outside she jumped for joy. June did not disappoint. She had a colouring book and crayons. The colouring book was of cats. Jenny loved cats. "We'll do some colouring after supper," June promised.

Heather was asking about the trip during the meal. "It sounds like you two had yourselves a great time. When Jenny has gone to bed I want to know more about your ideas on the big venture of yours. It sounds so exciting."

After supper June did some colouring with Jenny while Shirley and Heather cleared away the dishes. Jenny was getting tired, and so Heather told Jenny it was time to say goodnight. Shirley said she would make the coffee while Heather was putting Penny to bed.

Heather was very interested in all their plans. "I'll phone John about that old friend who now lives in France. It would be nice to have a contact in France." Heather was also impressed to hear about the French classes they were going to take.

"My French is a little rusty, but I'm sure it will soon come back," Shirley said. "John can speak French, which will be a great help."

They said there were so many artists that have nowhere to show their work. Shirley then said: "We want a property where we can hold lectures and workshops and also have two or three letting rooms."

June said Shirley would be more involved with the artists and that she would be running the house and dealing with the letting accommodation. They also told her about how helpful Gladys was from the hotel where they stayed. "Gladys has many contacts and references for us about getting any work we would need done to the property. It is a great help that she is British, but she did say we need to learn French," June said.

When June left it was arranged that Shirley would be phoning the agent the next morning. Also both June and Shirley would phone an agent to get their houses valued. Heather said she would phone John about his friend in France, as that could be helpful.

As soon as they had finished breakfast, Shirley phoned the agent in France with their list of requirements. The agent's name was Val. Gladys had already been in touch with her and gave her in the picture as to what they were looking for. When Shirley came off the phone, she looked at Heather and told her Val was very helpful. "She said she would be back in touch with me as soon as she had news of properties available for us to view."

Heather then phoned John. He had remembered his old friend and had already spoken to him. He gave John details of where he lived in France and said that he would be pleased to help in any way he could.

Then Shirley phoned the agent to come and value her house. She arranged for her to come next Tuesday. She said she was also going to see June's house on Tuesday. Shirley asked Heather if she would like to see her artwork in the community centre. "We'll drive past to see if it is open," Shirley said.

As they pulled up Shirley could see other artist working on their displays. She could see Gary, too, and so she introduced Heather and Jenny, and then said she wanted to show Heather her sketches. Heather was so impressed. "Mum, you really are good. I had no idea you could draw. John and Alex must be as impressed as I am."

"They've not seen them yet. I've told them to come to the art exhibition."

On their way out, Gary asked Heather what he thought of her talented mother. "I think she is amazing. I had no idea she could sketch. She never stops surprising us and, now, along with June she has a new venture. There's no stopping them."

Gary asked Heather if she would be coming to the art exhibition. He told her, "This is the best one yet. We even have the local radio station involved. The school has even got involved and are organizing art compositions in each year. If you can come, I'm sure Jenny will have a great time as she can enter in her age group."

As they got back in the car, Heather said she would see if they could come to the exhibition. "I think it will be good. Brookdale is moving with the times. I'm impressed."

The rest of the weekend flew by. Before long it was time for Heather and Jenny to pack up and head for home. "Let me know how to get on when the agent values the house. I think you will be surprised," Heather said.

"I hope you're right," Shirley sighed. "I'll need as much as I can, and I know June thinks the same. I'll phone John and Alex and let them know they are both interested. Not sure if I should have it valued by more than one agent. What do you think?"

"That might be a good idea. Let's see what this agent says first," Heather said.

Shirley cleared away the dishes and went directly to bed, as she was exhausted. She was already thinking of things she had to do before the agent came to value the house. She wanted it to look as good as possible.

Chapter Ten

Art Exhibition

June and Shirley were both surprised at the value of their houses. John and Alex had a look at the valuation on both houses and thought they were correct, but they did say if they wanted to get another agent in that it was their decision. They both decided to stay with the agent they had.

They phoned the agent and made an appointment to go into the office and sign the papers to sell the houses, but they wanted to wait until they went to France and saw what was available first. The meeting went well. The agent understood their circumstances and did not want to put any pressure on them. It was agreed that they would keep in touch with one another as things progressed.

This was the final week leading up to the art exhibition and everyone was busy making sure that all the last minute details were taken care of. June was with the group getting all the refreshments ordered.

Mary and Bill arrived on the Friday night before the exhibition. Heather and Jenny also arrived. Jenny had done a painting to enter into the children's competition. Shirley told her they would need to go a little earlier to make sure it was entered. Jenny was so excited. She could not wait.

The morning of the exhibition they were all up early. As soon as they had had breakfast they set off. The community centre was buzzing. Heather went to enter Jenny's painting and hang it on the wall. Jenny was so excited to see her painting on the wall. Heather took a photo with Jenny standing by her painting.

The day went without a hitch and, to Shirley's surprise, all her sketches sold. John, Alex and Heather were so proud of her. It was so nice to see her getting so involved, they agreed. Bill bought one of her sketches. Mary said she had just the spot for it. The radio station was a great success and made so much fuss of all the children who had entered. Jenny came second in her group. She was presented with a gift and a blue ribbon that was attached to her painting.

The photographer from the local paper was there. He collected all the children who had entered and took their photos. Jenny had made friends with another little girl. They were having a great time. She went to see June, who gave her some juice, and she chose herself a cake. Heather was so pleased to see her mixing in. With everything going on at home, Jenny had become a little withdrawn.

All the artwork was to remain on display in the community centre for one week. Gary was getting congratulated on putting on the art exhibition, but he was quick to respond, saying he could not have done it without the help of all the volunteers. They truly made this work.

Heather had to leave the next day, and so it was a short visit this time. Shirley told Jenny that they were the "artists in the family."

Mary had arranged with June and Shirley to meet for lunch. Bill was spending time with Amy so the three ladies could catch up. Mary could not wait to tell them about her move and how she was settling in. Also, she wanted to know how things were doing with them.

Lunch went by so fast. Before long it was time to go. Mary was so happy with Bill. She had no regrets at all. Liz, next door, had also helped her settle in. She also said Bill was building Emma a playhouse in the garden. "I had no idea he was so clever," Mary said. "We're not telling Emma. Susan is coming down to stay in a week's time as her husband is working away, and so it will be a surprise when they see the playhouse. When Bill is home, Polly follows him everywhere. Considering he has never had a dog before, he has bonded very strongly with Polly."

Shirley asked about Clive and Amy. "Was it working out for them? Also did Amy like living in Brookdale?"

Mary said they were so happy together. "It's so nice that Clive has someone to share his life. They are always planning what to do next. Amy is getting a divorce, but I don't say too much as I don't want to pry."

June and Shirley said they would go and stay with Bill and Mary after the Summer Fete, but before the summer ended. "We'll also be going to France to view properties. We'll have to see what the agent comes up with," June said.

June asked Shirley how things were between Alex and Linda.

"To be honest, June, I've not asked since we come back from France," Shirley said and sighed.

On Tuesday Val, the agent, phoned from France to say she had some interesting properties that could be suitable. She gave Shirley the addresses and told her to look them up on the computer. As soon as she put the phone down, she phoned June and John. John said he would call in on his way home from work so he could look at them. He asked her to get June to come around, that way they could view them together.

June and Shirley were ready when John arrived. They checked out the properties, only to find three that were of interest. They wanted the main property to be liveable, with two or three bedrooms if possible. John thought all three were worth viewing. Also the price was workable.

Before John left he suggested they go next weekend. He was going to check on flights, and so Shirley needed to speak to Val to arrange the viewings. "Now before we go I want to make sure this is what you both want," John said.

"Absolutely!" June and Shirley chimed.

"That's all I wanted to hear," said John. "I'll leave you to ladies to discuss it further."

The agent booked the appointments to view the three properties. Shirley spoke to Gladys and booked two nights at the hotel for her and June. John was going to stay with his friend, as it was quite near to where he lived. They printed off the details for each property so they could study them. June looked up the location on the map. All three were in the area they had stayed in.

Shirley phoned Heather and gave her the details on the properties. Also, June phoned Mary to give her the details. Both Heather and Mary were going to print them off the computer.

John picked up June and Shirley and they were off to the airport. He managed to get an early flight. "It's only two hours. We'll be there in no time." The first appointment was Saturday afternoon and the other two were on Sunday morning.

John had arranged to hire a car for the two days. He picked it up at the airport. Everything was on time; they were landing in France before they knew it. John took them straight to the hotel to freshen up. Shirley introduced John to Gladys, who was so pleased to see them again.

Then Val came to the hotel to pick them up. She was very helpful and spoke English, which was a great help. As they drove to the property she gave them lots of information on the area and property.

The drive to the property was just how Shirley and June remembered it. John commented on how breathtaking the views were. The agent stopped the car and asked them to get out, as she wanted to show them the property from a distance. As they looked over, they could see the property. It took their breath away.

"That is the property we're viewing. So tell me what do you think?" Val asked.

John did not know what to say, it was that amazing. Shirley and June just smiled at one another.

The property had a nice kitchen/dinette and a large living room with wood burner. Upstairs there were two large bedrooms and a large bathroom. Outside there were two outbuildings. The one could be converted to make two letting accommodations and the other, the barn, could be converted into the art centre. The property was located a long way from any village, which John thought was a concern.

The agent took them back to the hotel. John suggested they go for a drive and have a look around the village and the area they had told him about. He loved the village. It was a good size with plenty to offer. They found a café where they had a meal to discuss the first property.

June was a little worried that it would require too much work to get it to how they would want it. Both Shirley and John agreed with her. "But remember that was only the first property," John said.

After their meal John drove them back to the hotel. Then he was going to meet Tom, his friend. "I've not seen Tom in ten years, and so we have a lot of catching up to do. I'm not sure what brought him to live in France. I'll see you both in the morning."

Next morning John arrived and was sitting in the lounge of the hotel talking to Gladys and her husband when Shirley and June came down. "We're looking forward to today. We like the look of both of these properties we're viewing," June said.

The agent arrived and said they should get going. They got into the car and off they went. The next property was just outside the village and was again surrounded by vineyards. The agent said. "You will not have to do anything to move into this property."

The approach was good, right from the start, with well-maintained gardens.

On entering, they went straight into the farmhouse kitchen/dinette, which they loved, and then onto the living room. It boasted an open fireplace with beams. Straight away June said she loved it. "What do you think, Shirley?"

"I agree."

Upstairs were three bedrooms—two large and one single. The bathroom was a good size, too. Outside there were three *gites*, which were ready to rent out. A *gite* was a rural, holiday rental accommodation. Originally they were developed as cheap, no-frills accommodation, but in recent years the concept of the *gite* had gone up market. These *gites* were fully furnished and included in the sale price. The agent then took them to see the barn. It had a new roof and had all services. They would just need to finish it off. It also had a wood-burning stove installed, which would heat the place in the winter. John said he thought this was in the perfect location without too much work for them to do.

Shirley agreed. They all liked this property. She asked the agent how long it had been on the market. The agent told them it had been on the market about three months, but no offers as yet. "Let's go and see the next property, and then we'll go get a coffee to discuss all three properties," she said.

The next property was a converted barn. The agent said it has been converted to a very high standard. As they entered they saw that it was outstanding, with high-beamed ceilings, and a large kitchen/dinette. It was all very modern. The fireplace in the living room was spectacular. The property had two bedrooms, two bathrooms, and an office on the second floor.

Outside there were two letting accommodations, which were done, again, to a very high standard.

Shirley asked the agent: "Why would anyone do all this work and now want to sell it?" The agent replied that there had been bereavement in the family and they were now unable to move to France.

"The only thing with this property is that, although you have the land, you would have to build a building for the art centre. I hope that has given you a good idea as to what you could expect in France.

WHEN DREAMS BECOME REALITY

I think it would be a good idea to find a cafe so we can get a coffee and discuss all three of the properties."

John had not said much at all at the final property, and so Shirley wondered if he saw something they had not noticed. During coffee it was clear that June and Shirley had fallen in love with property number two. John also thought that was the best option for them. Shirley told the agent they would be getting their houses on the market with view to be calling her on Monday with an offer on property number two.

When she dropped them off at the hotel, Gladys was waiting to see how they got on. They told her that the first property was too isolated, and also would require a lot of money from day one. But the sale price was much lower than for the other two.

"Property two? We loved it," June said. "Great location. We loved the house. There was no work to do. Also the three letting accommodation were fully furnished and ready to rent out. There is a great barn with all the services. We would just have to complete it to make it into the art centre. Now, property three was outstanding, but not what we're looking for. It would make an amazing home for someone."

Gladys suggested they call the agent before they leave to ask her to check if you could convert the barn into an art centre on property two. John thought that was a great idea.

Before long it was time to drive to the airport. Shirley asked John to drive pass the second house on the way to the airport as she wanted to take some photos. John said he also wanted to take photos of property two and the converted barn to show Jill and Alex.

When they went back on their own, June and Shirley walked all around. They could imagine living there, as well as building the art centre. "With the three *gites* we would have an income from day one," Shirley said. Just then John called them, as it was time to go.

They arrived at the airport as their flight was being called. The flight was good and so quick. Next thing, they were landing in Britain.

During the drive from the airport, Shirley and June wanted to know what John thought they should offer on the property. First of all: "Make sure that you can convert the barn to the art centre." And then he told them what he thought was a good offer to start with.

The agent phoned Shirley later in the day on Monday and told her the council said there were no objections to them converting the barn. In fact, there was a grant available towards the work as they were trying to encourage artists to the area.

Shirley thanked her, and then she phoned June, who was delighted that there was a grant available. They decided to put the offer forward and see what happened. She also phoned John to tell him about the grant. He was amazed.

Shirley phoned the agent back and made the offer, who said she would get back to her as soon as she had any news.

Heather phoned to see how things were going. Shirley told her they had put an offer forward. "John had suggested we start with a low offer and see what reaction we get. I'll keep my fingers crossed that the offer is accepted."

June and Shirley had now put their houses up for sale. The decision to sell got a mixed response from some people, as they thought they were having a midlife crisis. Shirley went to help clear away after the art exhibition, and so she told Gary about the properties. He could not be happier for them both.

"I want to book a week in one of the *gites* as soon as you move."

"We would welcome you. You can help us design the art centre. First we have to get the offer accepted, though, and our houses sold, so keep your fingers crossed."

Gary said he was still getting letters and phone calls about the art exhibition. "This is the first year that I managed to get the local school involved and already they are thinking of what they can do for next year."

The following day Val phoned to say the owners would not accept their offer but signed it back a little higher. Shirley asked June to come around, as she wanted to discuss the sign back price, and then phone Val back as soon as possible.

They phoned Val back and before long the sale was agreed. The agent wanted the lawyer's details so she could send the paperwork. The completion date was in three months. Shirley also asked the agent if she could give her the number as to whom she could contact in the council about the grant that would be available.

Heather was so pleased for them. Shirley asked Heather how the situation was with Dave, but there was no change. "I've come to the conclusion that I either accept it or leave. All I know is I do not want to live my life this way."

"Would you like John or Alex to talk to him?"

"Not really. My friends have spoken to him, but it did no good."

Shirley had the information from some of the artists they met at the country market, and so she contacted them to let them know what she and June were doing. To her surprise, she had a response from everyone she contacted. They all thought it was a great idea and knew the property she and June were interested in buying.

Gladys was a great help. She gave them the name of a good lawyer in the area that they could use. Gladys, along with her husband Frank, went to see the property and thought it was in a perfect location.

John phoned to say Jill was very interested in the converted barn. "And so we have made an appointment to go and see it next week. We both have some holidays due to us, and so we're going to check it out. You never know, we could be neighbours."

"I had no idea you were thinking of moving," Shirley said.

"We didn't, but seeing that property made us think. I can do my work from wherever. I would have to fly back twice a month, that's all. We can both speak French, which helps. Once Jill saw the photos she could not stop talking about it. We're just checking it out. She also loved the property you and June are buying and thinks you will do well."

"When you go to see the converted barn, why don't you ask the agent if you could view the one we have the offer on. We would value Jill's opinion, as she has a good eye for design," Shirley said.

John phoned back to say that they had made the appointment to view the barn. "Also, the agent is taking us to your property. I've never seen Jill so excited. I think she is so fed up with her job and she wants a change."

"Tell her to phone me as soon as you're back to tell me what she thinks."

Mary phoned to ask June and Shirley to come and stay for a few days. "If you don't come soon you will be off to France, and I want to see you both before you go."

They decided to get back to Mary by the end of the week.

"Tonight is our first French class. Are we ready?" Shirley asked. June said she was as ready as she would ever be. "I bought myself a French dictionary that translates into English. I'm not sure if it will help. All I know is we have to learn French."

The French class was held at the tutor's house. They were pleased to find there was only four in the class. The tutor was very nice and explained everything well. She made it sound so simple. "We're doing all the basics tonight and then move on from there."

She then told them that after tonight's class they would only be speaking in French. "That way, you will find it easier to pick up," she continued. "I want you all to be relaxed during the class. If at any time I'm moving on too quickly, please tell me."

The other couple in the class already owned a house in France and had been putting off learning French for some time. At the end of the class she gave them some work to do at home. "Try to look over what we did today and, remember, we all have to start somewhere."

The rest of the week was busy, what with keeping their houses ready at all times for prospected buyers to view. Both June and Shirley were doing a big sort-out and taking things to the charities every day.

"I never put myself down as a hoarder," said Shirley. "But I'm not so sure now."

June agreed. "I've found things I've not seen in years. Yesterday I came across work clothes belonging to Gordon, and you know how long ago he died."

Shirley phoned Mary and said they would be going to see her, but they had to get everything in order with references for their houses first. Mary agreed and said just to let her know when they were ready.

John and Jill were planning to fly to France for a few days next week to view the converted barn, and also to look at the property. "The agent will be giving the paperwork for us to sign as well as the forms from the local council about the grant that is available," they told June.

Heather phoned Shirley early one morning. "Dave seems to have come to his senses," she said. "He wants to take me away for a holiday."

Shirley was pleased; Heather sounded so happy. She did not want to ask too many questions.

Shirley also told her that John and Jill were going to France next week to view a property. Heather said she would be getting in touch with John and Alex to let them know things were getting better between her and Dave. Shirley offered to have Jenny if they wanted to go away on their own. Heather said she would discuss it with Dave then get back to her later.

June was pleased to hear about Heather. June was always very fond of Heather and she just loved Jenny. She told Shirley it had made her day.

Heather phoned back that evening to say she would like to take her offer up to have Jenny for a week so that they could get away on their own. "Just let me know," Shirley said. "I would love to have Jenny to myself for a week and I know June will be thrilled to see her."

Two days later, it was all settled. Heather would drop Jenny off next week. Heather and Dave were going to go to Scotland for a week. They both enjoyed the outdoors—walking and horse riding—and they had found the perfect place up in the Highlands.

When Heather dropped Jenny off she was so excited and wanted Heather to leave straight away as she wanted to be a big girl and be on her own with Gran. Shirley was happy to see Heather back to her old self. Heather did say they were taking things slowly. She was not sure who or what turned this situation around with Dave, but as long as it worked it was fine with her.

It was so much fun to have Jenny staying. June phoned to say she would call around later in the day to see Jenny. Jenny was a happy little girl, busy all day long. She asked if they could go to the park when June came. "We could get some ice cream on our way home if you like," June said.

John phoned to say Jill loved the barn, and they would like to come around this evening to bring the paperwork from the agent for her to sign. Shirley said that would be great. They knew Jenny was staying, and so they would be coming before she went to bed.

When they arrived, Jenny was playing in the garden. The couple next door had taken a shine to her. They were an older couple, who had so much time on their hands and Jenny was filling that time. From baking to helping in the garden, by the time it was bedtime, Shirley was not sure who was more tired: Jenny or the neighbours. Jenny certainly slept like a log.

Both John and Jill loved the barn and told Shirley all about it. Jill liked the idea of the two letting accommodations and could not get over the quality of workmanship. Shirley asked if they are serious about moving to France.

John said that Tom, his friend, was in the same line of work that he was. "We had a really good look around all the area." Jill thought that Shirley and June would be very successful at opening an art centre. "The property is in the perfect location," Jill said. "I can see why you both fell in love with it. You two are going to have a very good life in France."

"We're very interested and are phoning the agent as soon as our houses have been valued. John and Jill have a beautiful home. Everything is so organised. Jill has good taste and is a great home-maker, and so their house will not take long to sell."

When Heather came to pick Jenny up, Shirley was so pleased to see her so happy. Jenny was so excited to see her Mummy. Shirley told her about John and Jill. Heather was not surprised, as she knew Jill had not been happy at work.

June phoned Shirley to say her agent said she has a couple wanting to come and view her house and asked if they could they come that afternoon. "I don't want to be here when the agent is showing the house, and so I'll come to see you."

Jill phoned Shirley and asked if she could be any help with the French lessons. Shirley thought it would be great to have some extra help. "I'll speak to June and arrange a time for us to get together. June was pleased to get some extra help as we really do have to learn French if we're living there."

Both June and Shirley were getting viewings on their houses but no offers yet. They were off to spend a few days with Mary and Bill. The agent had the keys to do viewing while they were away, as well as the contact information if any offers came through.

"The agent might have more luck if we're not here. Besides, we need to get away for a few days," June told Shirley.

CHAPTER ELEVEN

Moving to France

MARY AND BILL made them so welcome when they arrived. June and Shirley thought it was nice to see Mary so happy and contented. The house looked beautiful. Mary had a wonderful eye for décor. Bill had gone out of his way to help Mary settle in and Polly ruled them both.

Shirley and June got Mary up to date on what was happening in their venture in moving to France. They had lots of photos to show her. She was very impressed about them learning French. Liz called around to see them and invited them all around for drinks after they had supper.

Bill proudly showed Shirley and June the playhouse he was building for Emma. June said she could move in. He had done a wonderful job, right down to the last detail. The house even had a front porch with two chairs and a small table. Shirley said it was every little girl's dream to have a playhouse like this.

The following day June had a message from the agent with an offer on her house. It was a little low, and so she wanted to talk it over with Mary and Shirley, then she would get back to the agent. After they had chatted about the offer it was suggested she phone the agent back and tell her what she would accept. Within no time, the agent came back and the final offer was accepted. She came off the phone and said her house was sold and would close around the same time as the property in France.

"Now all we need is for my house to sell," said Shirley. Mary said, "With all the viewings you will be getting an offer soon, I'm sure."

Bill called and said, "We should celebrate! I'll book a table for this evening."

Mary asked Bill to book it early as they were going to Liz and Fred's for drinks after. It was all arranged. Bill would meet them at the restaurant as he was coming as soon as he closed the shop.

The evening went without a hitch and, before long they were sitting on Liz and Fred's patio having drinks. June said she could understand why Mary loved living in Clifton. Liz and Fred were very interested in hearing all about France and the art centre they were planning on opening.

The following afternoon, Shirley had a message from the agent with an offer on her house. Again it was low, and so she said she would phone the agent back later. She phoned the agent back with a price she would accept. "So we have to wait to see if it will be accepted," Shirley told June.

It was late in the evening before the agent phoned. "They accept," she said. "But they want you out in a month." Shirley thought about it and finally agreed. She came off the phone and told them she was not sure where she was going to live until they moved to France.

Shirley said she would speak to John and Jill when she got back. "They have the room so I don't think it will be a problem. Alex only has a small house. Also, she is not that close to Linda, her daughter-in law."

It was soon time to head back to Brookdale. Mary and Bill said: "The next time we see you it will be in France."

"We want you to be our first visitors," June said. Bill agreed and said he would hold them to that. The journey back went well and, before long, they were home.

Shirley phoned John as soon as she got in the house to tell him about the offer and ask if she could stay with them until she moved to France. There was no hesitation. He said 'yes' but she wanted him to speak to Jill first. "I'll get Jill to speak to you if that makes you feel better."

Jill phoned back within no time at all. "So that's settled, you'll come and stay with us until you leave for France," she said.

"Thank you both so much for all your help," said Shirley.

June came around to help Shirley pack. Shirley arranged with the moving company that would be moving June and Shirley to France. They would store Shirley's furniture until it was time to move.

John called in on his way home from work to tell Shirley he had spoken to his boss and was told it would be no problem if he moved to France. He would need to fly back twice a month. The rest of the time he could work from home in France.

John could not wait to tell Jill, and so now they had a decision to make. Jill would be very happy, as she was ready for a change. He told Shirley that Jill would phone her later.

Shirley phoned Gladys to let her know how excited they were to be starting this new venture in France. She also told Gladys that John and Jill were hoping to buy the barn.

The packing went well. Alex came around and helped with the garage and shed. He also took a few pieces of furniture and whatever else Shirley did not want.

The movers came bright and early and packed everything into the container, ready to store for two months. Shirley had lots of helpers. As the last few things were taken out, it suddenly hit her that she was moving. This had been the house she had lived in with Jim and had raised their children in for so many years. Heather and Jill were there to reassure her that Jim would be so proud of her and that she was making the right decision.

Jill said she had prepared supper before she left. "It should be ready when we get home," she said. "June, you're invited to join us for supper."

"Well, I won't say no," said June. "I'm starving."

At John and Jill's, Shirley was getting settled into her room. The rest were freshening up. Heather said, "Whatever you have prepared, Jill, it smells delicious."

"It's just a chicken dish that has been cooking all day in the slow cook. Where would we be without the slow cook at times like this?"

John was the perfect host and opened the wine as everyone got seated at the table. "We have to make a toast to the end of a busy day and to Shirley. I'm so proud of you, Mum, you have achieved so much. So here is to the next chapter in your life. I want to include June in this toast. She has been Mum's stalwart friend!"

Jill went on to tell them that their house would be going on the market given that they also were also moving to France. They had put an offer on the barn and it had been accepted.

Heather said they would have plenty of choice when they come to stay in France. Both June and Shirley told her that she would love the barn that John and Jill were moving into.

Over the next two weeks, life was busy for Shirley and June, what with learning French and planning the art centre. Gary was turning out to be a great help with ideas and contacts. The artists in the area were excited and very interested in the art centre. The main question was: when will it be ready to open?

Shirley and June were receiving so much support from everyone in Brookdale. They all wished them good luck. There were a few that thought they were completely mad taking a big risk at their time of life, but June and Shirley couldn't are less.

Moving day went well. Shirley and June wanted to take their own cars and so they drove. Jill drove with June and John drove with Shirley. They wanted to finalize things with the agent on the barn, and then fly back.

It was so nice to have company on the journey, June thought. Everything went without a hitch. The journey was long, but they took many stops on the way to make it enjoyable.

Arriving at the property they found the agent was there to give them the keys. It was a beautiful day, which helped no end. Shirley and June had booked in at Gladys' hotel. John and Jill were staying at Tom's. Their furniture was due to arrive the next day.

Gladys welcomed them with open arms. She was so pleased to see them. After a good night's rest they felt refreshed and ready to tackle the day ahead. They drove over to the property after breakfast, opened all the windows and, before long, the furniture arrived.

John and Jill arrived shortly with Tom and his wife Barb, who wanted to see the property and meet Shirley and June. The movers started unloading the furniture. Shirley and June got busy telling them which rooms the furniture was to go in.

In no time at all things took shape. John and Jill were showing Tom and Barb the barn that was to be converted into the art centre. John told Tom that they were getting a grant and, although not large, it would be a great help.

Barb's hobby was stained glass, and so she was very interested and said she would lend a hand in the conversions. Shirley said Gladys had recommended someone that could do the work for them, and so she would be phoning him tomorrow when they got a bit more settled.

June had found a board and had written on it *Holiday Accommodation for Let.* "I'm putting this up on the gate to see what happens," she said.

John and Tom were laughing. "I don't think we have anything to worry about with these two," Tom said.

Before long it was time for Tom and Barb to take John and Jill to the airport to fly home. They had to meet with the agent about the barn on their way to the airport.

Barb said she would drive over tomorrow when she finished work. Tom and Barb only lived about thirty minutes away. They had a six-year-old son called Michael. "I know Michael would love to come and meet you both," Barb said.

When they had left, Shirley looked at June and said: "Well, now, it's up to us to make this work." They were both looking forward to meeting Michael. Jill had been to the local shop and bought them some groceries and so they had plenty of food to last them.

They had made their beds. Both bedrooms looked beautiful, with views over the vineyards. They were admiring the views when the doorbell rang. June went down to open the door, Shirley close behind.

It was a couple who had seen the sign about the accommodation to let. June got the key to show them. They were looking to rent for three days if possible. When they saw the *gîte* they were very impressed, and so they agreed to rent it.

June would be dealing with the renting of the accommodation. She had all the paperwork ready. Shirley thought she was very professional. Shirley found the kettle and made them a cup of tea. "Well, we have our first paying guests and we have only just arrived."

The rest of the day and evening was spent unpacking and putting things away. Before they finally went to bed they sat outside on the patio outside the living room. The evening sun was just setting. Gladys phoned to see if they were settling in. She said she would call around to see them sometime the next day.

When June woke up next morning she went down stairs to see Shirley in the little room that would soon be the office. She was looking over the plans for the barn. "You're bright and early this morning."

"Yes, I think I'll phone the builder to see when he would have time to come and look around."

"The couple that rented the *gîte* are driving to the Monet gardens today and were just getting ready to leave. Can you believe we could have so many boxes? I thought we had got rid of so much stuff." The sun was already quite warm. June rolled up her sleeves. " I just love it here," she said.

Midmorning they had another couple inquiring about accommodation, and so now they had two let. "I think I need to work on a better sign," said June.

Shirley told her there was no hurry. "But that one does looks a bit amateur, and as we're going to be opening an art centre…" She trailed off and smiled.

Barb came by later with Michael. He was a cutie. Off he went to explore the barn. June asked Barb if she knew anyone that could do her a nice sign to advertise the rental accommodation. Barb said she knew just the person. "I'll get her to come by tomorrow and see you."

Shirley had phoned the builder. He would be coming tomorrow. Shirley asked Barb if she would like to see the plans. "I welcome any suggestion you might have."

"Sure. Let's take them over to the barn. I think Michael must be still in there."

Michael was wandering around the barn. "I've never been in a barn this big," he told his mum. Barb thought it was a great location. "This is what is needed in this area. I was telling the guy that teaches me stained glass this. I would not be surprised if he comes by to see you. Now, these plans look good to me. It's very important to have good washrooms and a kitchen, which you have planned for."

Shirley nodded. "I want the main room to be a good size as I want to be able to hold lectures, workshops, and exhibitions. Do you think it would be a good idea to have partition doors down the middle so I could make it into two rooms with the option to open up into one large area? I want to encourage all types of artists to the centre."

Barb suggested a loft area as there was plenty of height and it would be a shame to waste the room.

"That's a good idea. I never thought of that. When the builder comes tomorrow I'll ask him what he thinks."

As Barb was leaving, Shirley said she would phone her when she has spoken to the builder. Michael said he would be back. Barb told him he had to be invited first. Shirley told him he was always welcome to come.

Heather had been in touch to see how they were settling in. She was amazed when Shirley told her that June had two of the *gites* already rented, and that the builder was coming tomorrow to talk about converting the barn.

Gladys called around later with a beautiful bunch of yellow sunflowers as a welcome gift. Shirley found a flower vase. The flowers looked beautiful on the table in the living room. Gladys could not believe how organized they were. "It looks like you have been here for years!"

"We have to say the place was spotless, and so it made it so easy," June said. "All we had to do was put our furniture in the rooms. I think we'll be moving a few things around. Do you by any chance want any boxes? If not we'll put them in the barn."

They took Gladys around the house and showed her the bedrooms. She was very impressed. The views from the bedrooms were breathtaking.

Next morning the phone rang. It was Gary, calling to see how we were. He wanted to know if he could book to come next week for a week if they had accommodation vacant. Shirley called June as she dealt with the accommodation. June spoke to Gary and made the reservation for next week. "Perfect, see you both next week," he said.

Jacque the builder arrived the next morning. He introduced himself to Shirley and June, who went over the plans with him, and then they took him to the barn. He made a few suggestions, but thought their plan would work very well. As they were going around he made notes, which impressed Shirley and gave her confidence that he would do a good job.

Jacque was a typical French man. He was a big man and wore a flat cap. His skin was tanned from outdoor work, and his smile warm. His English was very good.

Jacque was excited to be involved in their project. He told them news was getting around in the area about the new art centre. "Everyone is getting excited about it. There are many up-and-coming artists in France, so get prepared to be busy."

Jacque was a local man who was very well known in the trade for doing excellent building work. He also had a group of men who helped him, and so this conversion would not take too long. Shirley and June left Jacque in the barn, since he wanted to make a start by checking things out.

Another good thing about Jacque, they learned, was that he knew the local council, and so he would go in to let them know what was going on and make sure the paperwork was in order for Shirley and June to get the grant that was available for them.

Barb phoned later in the day to see how they had got on with the builder. Shirley said that Jacque had made a few suggestion. "But on the whole, he went with our plan. He thought doing a loft area was a good idea, and so we're going with that. He has gone away to price it out. Oh, and he'll also be going to the council."

Shirley and June decided to go to the market where they had met many of the local artists. "It will be so nice to get some fresh produce," Shirley said.

"Oh, and remember that cheese, bread, and the olives. They were unforgettable!" June put in.

When they arrived at the market it was busy and redolent with the amazing smell of the fresh bread. They bought the vegetables, cheese, and bread and then decided they would take them back to the car before going to see all the artists.

The funny thing was as they walked along the street everyone spoke to them. In the bakery, which was family run, they knew all about them. You could say 'news travels fast in a village.'

They were delighted to see some of the artists they had chatted to before. They realized that these conversations had started this whole venture. As they got talking, Shirley gave out a few flyers she had made to let people know about the art centre. By the time they had walked around, all the artists had given them their details so that Shirley could contact them went she was ready to open.

By the time Shirley and June returned to their new home they were exhausted. They unloaded the car. June put the kettle on and

Shirley got the fresh bread, butter, local cheese and fruit on the table. They sat out on the patio and enjoyed themselves. "We love this outdoor living, don't we?" Shirley observed and laughed.

Shirley got all the information from the artists together. "I don't want to miss anyone out," she said. "Now, we do have to decide on a name for our art centre."

June suggested *Petit Bijou*, which in English is 'Little Gem.' Shirley said, "That sounds perfect, as a little gem is exactly what it is!"

June said she would go to the printers in the morning and get headed notepaper and business cards ready for when they open.

Jus then, a car pulled up. It was Barb with Michael. "We thought we would come and visit you," she said.

June went and opened a bottle of wine with three glasses and got a juice for Michael. "We have something to celebrate," June announced. "Shirley said we have a name for our art centre. It will be called Petit Bijou Art Centre." They all clinked their glasses, including Michael. Barb loved the name.

June was kept busy with the *gites*. As soon as one came available someone else came to the door. It took all her time with washing sheets and cleaning rooms. "But I've never been happier," she said to Shirley one morning.

Jacque came back with a price, which June and Shirley accepted, and so work started on the barn. He said he would have the barn finished in two months if all went well. Two other men worked with him. June supplied them with coffee, and so that kept them happy. They were so impressed to see the art centre taking shape.

Gary was due to arrive today, and so Shirley went to the airport to pick him up. She could not wait to show him around. His flight was on time. Very quickly, they were on their way home.

Shirley turned into the driveway. Gary was so impressed. "What a fabulous area," he said.

In the courtyard, they got out of the car. June was there to meet Gary. "I'll take you into your *gite,* and then we'll show you around.

He could not believe how beautiful it was, surrounded by the vineyards and lavender fields.

Shirley took him around the house. They had made it so homely and welcoming.

"I just love it," Gary said. "Now I can understand why you moved here."

"Now we'll go over to the barn," Shirley said. "The work men are working, but we can still look around."

Shirley had a copy of the plans so Gary could see the layout. "This is fabulous," Gary said. Shirley introduced Gary to Jacque, and then she just left Gary in the barn. Shirley told him to come over to the house when he was ready to eat.

John, Alex, and Heather were in touch with Shirley all the time and interested to hear how the barn was coming on. Everyone was happy about the name of the art centre. John and Jill had now sold their house, and so were getting ready to move to France.

Gary was working alongside the workmen in the barn. He had become a friend to Jacque as they got on so well. Shirley asked Jacque if he would like to join them for supper on the patio, which he did. It turned into a regular thing. Gary would shower and change in his *gite* and Jacque would shower and change in the house before supper.

Shirley and June felt bad for Gary, as they did not want him to think he had to work every day; he was on holiday after all. He said he could not be happier. Gary came up with some great ideas for when the art centre opened. He suggested they contact the local schools to see if they would like to get involved.

Shirley and June did want to take Gary to the local market and to see the local artists. "I would love to do that," he said.

"Also, we can pick up the new stationary as it should be ready," Shirley said.

Gary loved the market with all the fresh produce and, of course, the local artists. He told them how the art centre was coming along. They were all so interested. He also told them that Shirley had some very good plans and would have a wide selection of lectures, which would appeal to everyone.

Shirley asked Gary if he would help her in organizing the grand opening of the art centre. He was delighted to be involved and could not wait to get started. "I'll get all my contacts together. Make coffee, and then we can sit on the patio and get inspired."

They went through all the contacts Shirley had collected. "We must make sure we don't miss anyone out," she said. Gary was amazed she had so much information. "Barb has been a big help," Shirley added. "I want her to be involved in the opening."

"And I want to visit the wineries and businesses in the area," Gary said, sipping his coffee. "I also think it would be a good idea to visit the local schools. I've started a list of contacts, so let's start by going through that."

Gary thought it would be good to have someone in the art world to be at the grand opening.

Shirley tapped her pencil. "I'll phone Barb to see if she is available to come over this evening. She knows so many people. We need to get an advert in the paper to get the word out about the *Petit Bijou* art centre. I'll draft out something, then when Barb comes we'll go over it with her."

Barb said she would be over later. "Michael will be with me." June was delighted. She and Michael had formed a great bond. She just loved him. The rest of the day was busy. Gary was with Jacque in the barn. It was really taking shape now.

When Barb and Michael arrived as they were finishing supper. Michael went off with June as she had something to show him. Shirley got her folder with all the information she wanted to discuss with Barb.

They went through the contacts first. Barb catalogued them, saying: "That way we know what to focus on first."

"I'm very impressed at the amount you have," Gary said. "There are a wide variety of artists here."

Shirley said she wanted to work on business cards and flyers. Gary asked Barb and George what they thought of the name *Petit Bijou* for the art centre, both loved it. Gary said: "I think it is perfect as it is going to be a Little Gem indeed, a special place for all artists to come display their work and enjoy learning more from other artists."

"We need to think who we can get to be at the grand opening," Shirley said. "Does anyone have any ideas? Barb said she would contact the principle at the art college, which was located in the next town. "It has a very good name in the art world, and I think to get them involved would help us no end."

By the end of the meeting they had accomplished a lot. Shirley suggested that Jacque could take them around the barn to see the progress. June and Michael were already in the barn. Barb had not been in for quite some time and could not believe her eyes. Jacque had done an amazing job with such attention to detail. He chuckled. "Well, as it is to be an art centre, I wanted to make sure it was perfect."

June could not stop praising Jacque. Barb said to Shirley: "I think June is smitten with Jacque." They both smiled at one another then carried on with the tour. Jacque said the painters should be starting next week. "Then we can get the floors down, followed by the washrooms and kitchen."

After they finished the tour, Shirley said she would go and get the business cards and flyers to the printers. Barb was contacting the art college. June said she would start on planning the landscaping around the art centre.

Sadly for all, it was Gary's last day tomorrow. "I've never felt more at home as I do here with you two; it has been a wonderful time. I've got to say I don't really want to go back. I could be back very soon."

Barb agreed. "We need you here, so hurry back. I'll not say goodbye, only see you as soon as you can get yourself back here." She gave him a hug.

Gary was not the greatest company on the drive to the airport, as he really wanted to stay. "All you have to do is phone us as soon as you're ready to come back," Shirley said. She added that she would really like him to come to the opening of *Petit Bijou* art centre.

"I'll be back, just let me know the date of the opening so I can book a flight. Hmm, or I may decide to drive."

They arrived at the airport. Gary got his bags out of the car, and then he gave Shirley a big hug and thanked her once again for making him so welcome. "We're going to miss you, so hurry back," she said. To Shirley's surprise they both had a tear in their eyes.

Driving back, Shirley decided to stop for coffee as she was feeling so upset at Gary leaving. She sat having a coffee and told herself to pull herself together and stop being silly.

CHAPTER TWELVE

"Petit Bijou" Opens

EVERYTHING WAS GOING to plan. The company had put up the sign on the entrance to the art centre. Shirley called June to come and see it. *Petit Bijou* art centre was getting ready for the grand opening. "The sign looks just great, we both love it," Shirley said as Jacque came around the corner. He was very impressed with the company that installed it.

The tables and chairs would be arriving later in the day tomorrow. June had been busy in the kitchen to make sure everything worked. She had been working with Jacque on the finishing touches. Shirley said she would phone Barb to let her know the sign had been installed.

The final touches were being put together for the opening. Heather, Dave and Jenny had arrived for the grand opening. They were staying in one of the *gites*. John and Jill had been a great help. Jill helped June with the flowers and landscaping. It looked beautiful. Barb has been by Shirley's side all the way through. The art centre looked amazing.

The morning of the opening both Shirley and June were up early. Jacque arrived, still checking on last minute things. Heather and Jenny came to see if they could be of any help. Dave had gone for a walk. He had no idea this was such a beautiful area.

The only person yet to arrive was Gary. He was driving and had got held up at the crossing, but was only one hour away now. Bill and Mary were booked in at the hotel, and so were coming with Gladys and Frank. Mary phoned to say she was so excited and said she would see them soon.

Shirley had spoken to Alex who was unable to come; things were still not good between him and Linda.

The caterers were putting the finishing touches to the buffet. One of the local wineries was supplying all the wine. Barb had arranged for the principle from the art college to do the official opening along with the mayor and many of the councillors, who would also be in attendance.

Michael and Jenny were about the same age. They got on so well. They looked so smart, with Jenny in her new dress and Michael with his shirt and tie. All the businesses owners in the area had been invited. "And so we should get a good turnout," said June.

Everyone was now starting to arrive. Shirley and June both looked very elegant as they greeted the guests. Shirley was so relieved to see Gary pull up in the courtyard. He quickly went into the house and got washed and changed.

Alex was not able to get there, but he did send Shirley some red roses and wished her luck and said she was to phone him tomorrow to tell him all about it. Shirley and June were so pleased to see Mary and Bill arrive with Gladys and Frank.

The local paper sent along a reporter to interview Shirley and June as well as a photographer for photos to go into the paper.

Everyone was arriving and, before long, the art centre was full. They were so pleased to see so many of the artists they had met in the market turn up. The caterers were serving wine to everyone as they arrived.

The principle from the college gave a speech, saying how lucky the area was that Shirley and June decided to come on a holiday to France, that they fell in love with the area, and then opened this beautiful art centre. Then he asked everyone to raise their glasses to Shirley and June and officially opened *Petit Bijou* art centre.

Shirley got up and thanked everyone for coming. She also thanked Jacque for all his vision in turning an old barn into such a spectacular art centre. "June and I are completely overwhelmed. Thank you all so much."

The evening could not have gone better. Jacque and Gary were so proud of the way the art centre turned out. Heather and Dave could not believe what Shirley and June had achieved. Heather gave her mum a big hug. "And to think I said you were having a midlife crisis when you told me you were going to France on holiday," she said and laughed.

Bill, Mary, Frank and Gladys were getting on so well. Mind you, June suspected the wine had something to do with that. Michael and Jenny were also having a great time. Heather and Barb said: "I think they will sleep well tonight."

Everyone was leaving, but Shirley kept getting many contacts from artists. The principle said he would be coming over for a meeting with Shirley about organizing some lectures. Barb had also been talking about putting a program together.

Shirley said she wanted to arrange a meeting with Barb, Jill and Gary about what would be the next step. June was promoting the rental accommodation, which was getting busy. Jacque was helping her with that side of things.

When everyone had gone, Shirley, June, Gary and Jacque sat on the patio (their favourite place) where they finally had time to have something to eat and a glass of wine. Gary said, "That was the best night ever. I can see myself moving here."

Shirley went over to Gary and gave him a big hug. "That is the icing on the cake. We need you here, given that I can see the centre being very busy."

Dave, Heather and Jenny were leaving at lunch time. Dave was a guy that said little, but still he came over to Shirley and June to say how impressed he was to see what they had achieved. "We'll be coming back to visit as soon as we get the opportunity. Jenny will want to come and see her new friend Michael. That's all she can talk about."

They were calling to see John and Jill on their way home. Their ferry crossing was not until evening, and so there was plenty of time. June and Shirley saw them off and thanked them for coming to support them.

Mary and Bill had decided to stay a few more days so they could spend some time exploring the area. They were talking to the owners of the winery that supplied all the wine, who then invited them to come and visit their winery.

Shirley phoned Alex to tell him all about the opening as he wanted to know all the details. He was very disappointed he had not been able to make the opening. "When you have two children and a wife that wants everything, it's hard." John got very upset with his situation but, as he said to Shirley on more than one occasion, it would never change. Shirley knew that he gives into her all the time. We cannot interfere, she thought.

Shirley phoned Jill and Barb and thanked them both for all their help. She told them that they could not have pulled this off without their support. "We wanted to set up a meeting with you both. Let me know when you're available." She told them that Gary and Jacque would be at the meeting.

By the end of the day a date was set for the meeting. June said she would prepare a lunch and that they would meet on the patio. Shirley told them to come with any ideas they might have.

June had everything ready. The lunch was delicious. As they got started, Shirley said she had an idea that she wanted to run by them, but she made it clear it was only an idea at this stage.

"So, after going through all the artists we've been in contact with, I'd like to suggest that Barb, helped by Jill, should head the pottery and stained glass classes, and that Gary and myself can head the art, sketching and painting. June, with Jacque's help, can keep the rental accommodation up and running. Well, those are my ideas. What does everyone else think?"

Barb said she thought that sounded good. "I love working with Jill."

"We have the two rooms in the barn, and each room is big enough to hold a work shop," Shirley added. Jill was very enthusiastic. "I'm excited to get started," she said.

"If we had a big event we could always open up the partition wall between the two rooms," said Jacque. "I know that Eric the principle from the college wanted to speak to Shirley about organising lectures. That would require the two rooms opening into one large room."

Gary was very quiet. Shirley asked him what he was thinking.

"All I know is I want to be involved in this venture from the beginning, and so I guess you can count me in. I would like nothing better than to head the art side of things with Shirley. It may mean I'll have to travel back to Brookdale for a while until I get things in order."

They got all the information sorted out. Anything for art would go to Gary. Pottery and stained glass would go to Barb and Jill. Shirley said: "We should contact all the artists to keep them up to date with what we're thinking of doing."

They were just finishing when Mary and Bill arrived. They brought with them a copy of the local paper. It had a feature in it of the opening of *Petit Bijou* art centre. "We have been to the local market this morning and everyone is talking about it. By the way, if we lived here we would be so fat. The local bread and cheese is delicious."

They all looked at the paper. The write up and photos were excellent. This was the exposure we were hoping for. Eric had given a glowing report on the art centre and pointed out that they would be holding lectures from distinguished artists.

June and Shirley told Mary and Bill about the meeting and asked what they thought. Bill said: "I think you two have everything under control." Bill turned to Gary and said: "So you will also be moving to France?"

"Well, I've to work on a few things first, but that seems to be the idea."

Mary smiled at Shirley but said nothing.

Jill left as her and John were going out for supper. Shirley suggested that they all go out for supper. June said she would call the restaurant in the winery and book a table. The table was booked, allowing enough time for everyone to freshen up.

The restaurant was busy. They gave them a table overlooking the vineyards. The owner came across to see them and to congratulate Shirley and June on the opening of *Petit Bijou* "Everyone is talking about it," he said. "You must drop us some information as we want to help in any way we can. The more people come to the centre, the more wine we sell, and so it works both ways."

The meal was outstanding and so was the local red wine. Bill bought some to take home with him. Mary said she could get used to this life. Everyone got on so well. Jacque said he was sorry the barn conversion had come to an end. June quickly told him he was still needed. At this, Mary and Shirley winked at one another.

The next day Bill and Mary called in to say goodbye as they were on their way home. June and Shirley told them to come back whenever they had time. Mary said: "You may regret saying that."

Just as they left, the phone rang. It was Eric. He wanted to know when he could come and meet with them. He said he had a few suggestions he wanted to run by them. Shirley arranged a time, but she wanted Gary, Barb and Jill to be at the meeting, so she would get back to him to confirm.

After checking with everyone the meeting was set.

June could not believe how busy the rental accommodation would keep her. Jacque and June were inseparable. They were together all the time. Jacque was a very gentle man; but loved to fuss around June. His wife died many years ago and he had kept himself to himself ever since. They never had children, and so he was very much on his own.

June was on her own, too, and so they made a nice couple and were enjoying one another's company. They would go off to the market and return with enough bread, fruit, and cheese to feed an army. Gary was always teasing June, and she would get so embarrassed.

The meeting with Eric went very well. He gave Gary a good contact who was well- known in the art world and would be pleased to come give a talk on local artists in France. He also gave Barb two contacts, one on local pottery and one on stained glass. The contact for the stained glass was an artist who did windows in many churches throughout France. He was very talented. Barb said she would call both contacts tomorrow, and Gary also said he would be calling the artist about booking him to come and give a talk.

Shirley and June thanked Eric for the wonderful write-up in the paper he did on the opening of the art centre. He quickly said it was well deserved. "This is going to be popular in the art world. I wanted to ask that, when you're ready, if you could come and give a talk in the college to let all the students know what will be available. We have many budding artists in the college."

Both Gary and Barb were happy to do that. Gary said: "You will have to give us a bit of time to feel our feet as we want to get it right. We don't want to be rushed and make the wrong decisions." Eric agreed with Gary.

Before Eric left, he wanted them to know that he would help them in any way he could. Gary thanked Eric again and said they would be in touch.

After Eric left, Shirley said she had a thought and would like to run it by everyone. She started to tell them her idea. "What if we contact all the artists we know of, and then advertise in the paper for other artists to come and show their artwork. We could do all the advertising and they would pay a fee to be in the art show. The object of having the art show would be to find out what we want to focus on. Then we can see about offering monthly lectures. We could approach schools and, of course, go to the college as Eric suggested."

They all thought this was a great idea. She said: "Our main focus when coming to France was to help all artists."

June followed by saying that she would be standing back from the art centre as she wanted to concentrate on the letting accommodate.

Shirley thought, 'that works, but I don't want you to feel left out.'

Jill and Barb were going to work on the advertisement for the paper. Shirley also asked them to work on a flyer. "I'll take them to all the hotels and wineries in the area. Before we go any further, let's fix a date for the art show.

It was agreed they needed three weeks to get everything ready. Gary suggested they run the art show for one week to see how it went, given there are so many holiday makers around that would surely love to come to the centre.

Next morning over breakfast Shirley said to June: "I really think things will happen now. I'll give Eric a phone call and find out when Gary and I can go to the college and talk to the students. Then we'll phone the schools to see if they are interested in getting involved."

June was busy as she had guests leaving and new guests arriving. "Jacque is coming over later and I want to run a couple of ideas by him."

"Jacque is such a nice man. I can see he makes you happy," Shirley said.

June blushed but had to agree. She really liked him and missed him when he was not around.

Gary walked into the kitchen as Shirley was cleaning. "Sit down and I'll make some coffee," she said.

"Shirley, that was a great idea of yours to hold an art show. I still want you to be involved, but I don't want to pressure you in any way."

"You're not pressuring me in any way. All I know is I want to be where ever you are." Shirley was taken by surprise. "That is the nicest thing anyone has ever said to me."

Gary went over to Shirley and held her in his arms. "I think I fell in love with you the first day you came to my art class. What I love about you, Shirley, is that you don't know how pretty and charming you are. You're always thinking of everyone else first, and you're a very talented artist in your own right. I want you to do some sketches for this art show, and I won't take no for an answer."

"Okay, okay," Shirley laughed. "Now, we have lots to do today, but let's have lunch out, just the two of us."

Gary said, "That's the best idea you have had today." And they both laughed.

"Oh, and Gary can you phone Eric and see when we can meet with the students to let them know about the art show. Then I'll call the schools to see if they are interested."

Shirley had the biggest smile on her face when June popped back into the kitchen. "Have I missed something?" she asked.

Gary winked at Shirley as he went into the office to make his phone call to Eric

"You will have to update me later," June said. "And I want to know everything, remember."

Gary and Shirley left for the meeting at the school, hoping it would go well. Gary's French was better than Shirley's, and so they agreed he would do most of the talking. The meeting went very well. The teacher thought it was a good idea to get the children involved. Gary proposed one area to be designated to the children. "If you could let us know what ideas you could come up with, that'd be wonderful," he added.

Gary then suggested that they would like to invite the children up to the art centre. "I want them to feel comfortable," he said.

The teacher agreed. "I'll discuss this with the other teachers and let you know when we can come. Shirley suggested the children bring a packed lunch with them. "We'll supply the drinks to make it more of an outing. It's not a large school, and so I think it would be good to bring everyone."

Gary thanked the teacher for wanting to get involved. "I think the children will really enjoy it. This is such a beautiful area and artists come here from all over the world to paint, and so we want to make the centre well known in the art world."

As they left, Shirley and Gary thanked the teacher for her time and said they looked forward to hearing from her. Gary said he would work on a program for the children, and that it would be interesting.

As they got back in the car, Gary said, "Now I'm taking you for a nice lunch. Not sure where, so let's drive and see where we end up."

"That sounds perfect to me," said Shirley.

They come across a small village up in the mountains with a few shops and a delightful little restaurant/winery. As they got out of the car, the smell coming from the restaurant was divine, and so in they went.

It was quite dark inside, but the waiter invited them to follow him. He took them up some old stairs to a roof terrace. It was not large, and there was only one table left on the roof terrace. This was a popular place. Shirley noticed the white linen tablecloths and napkins. It was the most beautiful restaurant she had ever been in. Gary leaned over to her and kissed her on the cheek and said: "This will be our secret restaurant."

They ordered the local wine. The food was amazing. They got talking to the waiter, who was the owner's son. The family had owned the place for centuries. They told him about the *Petit Bijou* art centre. He was very interested and said he wanted them to meet his mother and father. He told them they did not speak much English, but they would manage.

They were a lovely couple. They talked for ages. Shirley told Marcel (the waiter) to bring them to see the art centre. "We would love to show you all around."

Gary told Marcel to make sure he brought some business cards so they could recommend his restaurant.

Back in the car, Shirley said, "What a wonderful day, and very successful."

Gary said, "We now have to put our heads together to arrange a program for the school children. Michael, Barb's son, will be coming, as I'm sure he goes to this school. He will be pleased, as he loves coming to the centre."

As they pulled into the courtyard, they noticed June showing a couple around who had booked one of the *gites*. Jill and June had outdone themselves with all the hanging baskets overflowing with flowers.

Shirley went over to June and said she was making some tea. "So come and have some when you're finished with the guests." Gary went to his *gite* to freshen up and said he would be across shortly.

Shirley made the tea, and then called Barb and Jill to let them know how the meeting went with the school. She told them that Gary was working on a program, and then they'd all go over it together. Both Jill and Barb thought it was a good idea. Barb said: "We also need to go over the final details for the upcoming art show."

Gary had a message from Eric at the college. He said he would like them to come the following afternoon if that worked for them. Gary asked Shirley if she could make it. If so, he would phone Eric and set the meeting up. Shirley said, "It works, so set it up."

June came in for a cup of tea and wanted to know about their day. June said Jacque had just left as he had a few things to do at home. Jacque has lived in the same house for many years and it was a work in progress with always something going wrong that needed to be fixed.

After Gary had his tea, he said he was going to work on a program for the children and would see them in the morning. He came over to Shirley and kissed her goodnight. June did not say a word until he left. "Now, I want to know what is going on between you and Gary."

Just as they both sat down, Barb called with a date for the meeting to go over the details for the art show. She had spoken to Jill and arranged the meeting. "Perfect," said Shirley, and she thanked Barb for setting it up. "I'll tell Gary and June and also Jacque, as he may want to come."

June sat down and said, "Now can we talk? We have to catch up."

Shirley said she would make some fresh tea as she thought this would be a long chat. By the time June settled herself on her favourite chair the tea was ready.

Shirley told June she had always admired Gary. He was so talented and so easy to talk to. "Over the months I started to get quite attached to him. It was not until we moved to France that I realise how much I was missing him. But I had no idea he was feeling the same. As we started to work on ideas for the art show, the thought of Gary not being here brought things to a head. Gary made the first move, and then everything fell into place. We went to the school and were very well received. Then we decided to go for a drive and lunch somewhere. We found the most amazing restaurant up in the mountains. We sat and talked and talked about everything and anything. I did not know much about his personal life before. Gary had a girlfriend who he lived with for many years, but he said that in the end it was like a brother and sister relationship. They met at Art College, and so they just stayed together. He hears from her from time to time as they parted on good terms. She married, but it did not last. Now she lives on her own, which works better for her as she is a bit of a loner. Gary has been on his own ever since, and so he said there is nothing keeping him in the UK. He owns his own house, which he has lived in for years, but if he comes to join us in France he will sell. He told me he has never felt so alive and he is excited to be involved." Shirley then asked June what she thought about Gary coming to join them; the last thing Shirley wanted was to upset June.

June was delighted for Shirley. "I've got to agree with you, Gary is so talented and such a nice person."

"We're not rushing anything. We'll concentrate on the art show as well as the school children's tour and go from there."

June said she was so happy for Shirley. "When you're ready you must call Mary. She will be so happy for you."

Shirley then turned to June and said, "So what about you and Jacque?"

June said she calls him her gentle giant. "We're enjoying one another's company. He loves to be involved with what we're doing in the art centre. Jacque is a great help to me in helping with the holidaymakers. He gives them so much information as he has lived in this area all his life. He likes nothing better than to go to the farmers market with me. We come back with way too much food, but as I say, it all looks so good and tastes even better."

Shirley smiled. "When we next phone Mary she will not believe what we're up to. And to think she was the one with the exciting life."

June said she enjoyed their girly night. "We'll do this again soon."

Next morning Gary came into the kitchen where Shirley and June were having breakfast. Shirley said, "You always come when food is on the table."

He laughed and said he had a few ideas for the children's tour and suggested they go over the details later.

CHAPTER THIRTEEN

First Art Show

JUNE SET OUT the chairs in the art centre, ready for the meeting, with notepaper for everyone. Barb and Jill arrived together as they lived near one another. Jacque had been helping June, and so he was ready. And then Gary came with Shirley.

Shirley said: "We'll start with the school children's tour first. Gary said he wanted to get the children involved, and so I suggested an art competition. We could do it in three age groups."

Gary asked Barb what were the ages of the children.

"They go from five years to ten years, so three groups would work."

Shirley suggested that the winner from each group would have their artwork framed and put on the wall of the art centre along with their name. They all thought that was a good idea. "But I think we need to have a prize for the winner," Shirley said.

Gary asked Barb to come up with ideas for the prize. "You're more in touch with the children, having Michael at the school."

Barb agreed to come up with something and get back to them. Shirley looked over at June. "The children will be bringing a packed lunch so, June, can you get drinks for the children to have with their lunch?"

"Yes, I can do that. Jacque said he would set the tables and chairs out ready for the children."

Jill said she would help June with the drinks or anything else she might need. Jill asked how many children they could expect. Shirley said the teacher would let her know. Barb said, "It is only a small school, so we'll be able to cope."

Gary suggested Shirley ask what time they would be coming and what time they would leave. "As the children are younger, I think it would be better to have colouring pencils, not paint," Barb put in.

"That's a good point," said Shirley. "Then we must make sure we have plenty of paper and colouring pencils.

Now they moved on to the art show. Barb said she had contacted everyone on the list. "We'll charge per table for each artist. They will be able to sell their artwork. Jill had a sample of the flyers for the show and also a copy of the advertisement ready to go in the paper. I want you all to read through them carefully so there are no mistakes, because once they are printed it will be too late. Also check the dates as this is to be a four-day show."

Gary asked Jacque if he would help him tomorrow to plan out the room. "We need to see how many artists we can accommodate." Jacque was happy to do that.

Gary looked at Shirley and said he wanted to see some of her sketches in the art show.

"I do have some sketches that need finishing," she admitted. "Barb, remember to bring your stained glass pieces, as they are beautiful and will sell."

Jill said she would go around to all the hotels, bed & breakfast and wineries in the area with flyers. Shirley told her to take John and make a day of it. "I'll give Gladys some flyers to give to her guests," she added. "June and Jill will be in charge of refreshments.

They will go to La Maison Bakery, our favourite local baker, and put in an order."

Jill told June to let her know when she wanted to do that. "I think we should not leave it too late to get the order in. We'll leave that in your capable hands," Jill told June.

They all agreed that the meeting went well. "We now have to get busy and make the children's tour and the art show a success," Shirley said.

Eric called with a date for Shirley and Gary to go to the college the following week. Jacque and Gary were busy all the next day working on a plan for the art show. "We have to make sure there is plenty of room for the artists and for the public. We can't have everyone on top of one another," Jacque said.

The art centre was looking good and very much an art centre now. Shirley and Gary went to the college where they gave a talk to the art students, which was well received by everyone. Gary's French was better than Shirley's, and so he did most of the talking. They gave out flyers and invited them to come to the art show. Eric was a great help to Shirley and Gary.

The teacher that headed the art students asked if his students could take charge of the children's area at the art show, but said that he would be overseeing them. "This would be a great help to the students," he said. "As most of his students want to teach art one way or another."

Both Shirley and Gary thought this was a great idea; they wanted to get everyone as involved as possible.

Gary said they could work out a program. He pointed out he would provide prizes for the top three, one for each age group. "I'll leave the age groups for you to work out and we can judge on the final day," he told the teacher. "I also told the children that we would frame their work and hang in in the art centre."

Gary then suggested they come to the centre to see the area they have to work in. Eric was very pleased and thanked Gary and Shirley for helping the students in this way.

The days leading up to the art show was crazy busy. Jacque and Gary started putting the tables up ready for the artists. June and Jill were doing the refreshments. Jill had made flower arrangements for all the tables in the refreshment area.

The day before the show, artists started to arrive with their artwork. Barb brought her stained glass pieces, which were outstanding. Gladys came over to see how things were going. She was so impressed. She told them many of her guests at the hotel were coming. June and Jill shouted hello to Gladys as they went off to the local nursery to pick up extra planters to go at the entrance to the art centre.

Gladys said she would see them tomorrow.

The artwork that was being put on display was so original and eye-catching. One of the displays featured patchwork quilts. Shirley and Gary stood in the doorway and could hardly believe what they were seeing.

The couple who had brought the quilts had come the furthest and were staying in one of the *gites*. June had welcomed them before she left with Jill. The quilts were gorgeous. Behind every quilt there was a story. Shirley and Gary were helping to carry the boxes in with the quilts. Jacque was helping to hang them on the wall.

The students from the college came along with their teacher. Bob had been busy all day. The children's area looked amazing—so colourful. Eric came to check the children's area. Bob and Eric were very pleased with what the students had come up with.

By the end of the afternoon the art centre looked like a magical place. Shirley realised they had not eaten, and so she went to got pizzas from the best pizzeria in town. Gary said with a smile: "That was the best idea you've had all day."

Gary was so impressed with the quality of the artist's work. It was so professional and so inspiring. Jacque had set up security camera and lights at the art centre. He said they should not leave anything to chance.

The artists were all excited for the art show to start. Everyone said it was so well organised.

Heather phoned to wish them good luck and that she was so sorry she was unable to come to their first art show. John arrived as they were all sitting down to have the pizza and a glass of wine, and so he pulled up a chair and joined the party. Jill could not wait to show him what they had done. June said she was going to make coffee, and so Jill took John across to see the art show.

John was totally speechless. "This is amazing. I had no idea there were so many artists with this standard of workmanship. It is so professional."

Jill took him to see the children's corner. They had put up screens, and so it was like a little room. She pointed out Barb's stained glass and his mother's sketches.

June was just about to serve the coffee and dessert when John and Jill came back from looking at the art centre. John went straight over to Shirley and June to say how proud he was of them both. Also he told Shirley how much he liked her sketches. "I think this is going to be a very successful art show."

"The art show opens at ten sharp," Shirley said. "And so I would like everyone here by eight or eight thirty in the morning, no later. The artists will be coming at nine. Eric from the college and the mayor will be doing the opening at ten."

June said, "I won't sleep tonight. I'm so excited."

"Now June," Jacque said. "You need a good night's sleep as it will be very busy tomorrow."

Shirley told Gary that if he wanted breakfast, be in the kitchen by 7:30. "And that goes for anyone else that wants breakfast!"

John smiled at his mum and said that they would not be late. He also said he had taken a few days off work to help during the art show.

June and Shirley were up bright and early. The sun was shining. Gary arrived followed by Jacque. June and Shirley were putting out fresh croissants and selection of jams and cheese along with tea or coffee. By 8:00 AM John and Jill arrived, followed by Barb and Tom. Barb's mother was bringing Michael a little later.

June went with Jill to make sure they were ready, as they were in charge of catering. The local bakery was arriving at 8:30. Before long, the place was hectic. The artists were arriving and busy doing last minute touches to their artwork.

Shirley asked John to help Jacque with any last minute things that needed doing. Shirley and Gary were checking everyone as they came in. Gary brought a beautiful book for everyone to sign and make comments for future art shows. Shirley thanked him.

The students arrived. They were getting excited to meet the first children. Gary went over to speak to them. His French was better than Shirley's. Mind you, they liked to speak English. The baker delivered the pastries and told Jill and June that if they ran out give them a call and they would bring more.

The florist came in and asked for June and Shirley. Mary and Tom had sent them a basket of beautiful yellow roses. The card said: *Wishing you all the best on this your first of many art shows, love Mary and Tom xxx.* "We'll get a table and have them at the entrance to welcome everyone," June suggested. "And we'll phone Mary later."

The local paper was coming to take photos of the grand opening. Just before 10:00 the mayor arrived with Eric. John came over to Gary and his mum and said, "We have crowds outside. Jacque and I are making sure the parking goes smoothly."

The young man who came from the paper took lots photos, and then the doors were opened. Shirley and Gary were busy greeting everyone and taking the money as they came in.

Tom was helping Barb with her stained glass, which was getting a lot of interest. Barb's mother brought Michael, who went straight over to the children's corner. Everyone was having a great time. The mayor come over to Gary and Shirley and congratulated them on a job well done. Shirley thanked the mayor, as getting the grant was a great help in making it all happen.

"June is over doing the refreshments," Shirley said. "She is my partner and she would also like to meet you. I'll go and see her right now."

People came from all over the world, as far away as Australia. They had many couples from England who had homes in France. All the artists—from the young lady who made jewellery using beautiful gem stones, to the two young men making unusual pottery—were experiencing strong sales The couple with the quilts were also doing very well. People were intrigued with the stories that came with each quilt.

Then there were the artists with their artwork. Some were water-colour artists and some were oil artists. One lady made all kind of bags out of old sweaters. She boiled the old sweaters until she had felt, and then made the most amazing bags. She was an older lady and had been making her bags for years. She said the art centre was the best thing that had come to this area in years. She wanted to know more about Shirley and June and how they came up with the idea to open the art centre. "I want to sit down and talk to you at the end of the show," she said.

Shirley agreed but said she had to go and help Gary with people coming in.

The show was busy all day. Jacque was taking groups around the building and showing them what the barn was like before work started. He had made a book and had taken photos throughout the renovations. He was being asked for a copy, and so he was taking information of interested people when he had more copies of the book.

The children were having a great time, making all sorts of things with the students and also getting their faces painted. Michael had his face painted so that he looked like a lion.

The young man from the paper grouped some of the children together and was taking their photos.

June and Jill were also busy all day and had put the order into the bakery ready for the next day. The industrial dishwasher Jacque had installed had been well used and a great help.

Gladys and Frank came later in the day. Frank was not very artsy and was more interested in talking to Jacque about the barn and the renovations. Gladys was busy buying one of the quilts and hearing all about the stories that went with each quilt. She was also fascinated with the lady selling the bags and purses.

Gladys later came over to Shirley and said she had seen the lady doing the bags and purses before but could not remember where. "I have her card. Her name is Celia Bury," Shirley said. "What an interesting lady!"

Shirley told Gladys that she wanted to sit down with June and her at the end of the show as she was interested in finding out how they came to France to open the art centre. Gladys went to find Frank, but said she would be back tomorrow or the next day.

Gary was astounded to hear where people had come from. He was getting them all to write in the book so he would be able to form a register for future art shows.

It was getting to the end of the first day and everyone was making their way out to their cars all carrying their purchases. June and Jill had sold out. They phoned the bakery back to make the order larger for tomorrow.

The last people were leaving and the artists were getting their stands restocked for tomorrow. Shirley went around to everyone to see if they were happy with how the first day went. Many were going to have to bring more stock, as they did not expect to sell so much. So you could say it was a success.

The students had cleaned the children's area ready for tomorrow. They told Gary it had been a great day and that is was very enjoyable meeting people from all over the world.

Tom and Barb were there, along with a very tired Michael. Tom said: "I think he will be asleep as soon as we get in the car." Michael said sleepily that he would be coming back tomorrow.

Barb had sold quite a few of her stained glass pieces, and so she would be busy when she got home, getting ready for tomorrow.

John and Jill left soon after. John was going home to phone Heather and Alex to let them know what a great success the first day had been.

As soon as the last artist left, Jacque locked up and went across the house where Shirley, June and Gary were sitting in the kitchen. Gary said he had booked a table at the restaurant in the local winery just up the road. "So get yourselves ready and we'll go."

Shirley said that was the best suggestion. "I don't think I could face cooking supper tonight."

Gary had brought the book into the kitchen and was looking through everyone's comments. They were all positive. He also had a section where they could put their suggestions. One of the main suggestion was to ask if they would be putting on any lectures or having any workshops in the future.

I think we could talk about this over supper and get everyone's ideas. Shirley thought that was a good idea. "But I must go and get ready for supper. Before we go I need to phone Mary to thank them for the beautiful flowers and also to let her know how the first day was such a success."

Within no time, everyone was ready. Jacque said he wanted to check that the centre was locked then they could go. June told Gary and Jacque: "We could not do this without your support." Shirley agreed. "We had no idea the amount of work that was involved in putting an art show."

Gary looked at Jacque and said, "Well, it is so nice to know we're needed."

They arrived at the restaurant. Their table was ready for them. It was overlooking the vineyards. They ordered some wine and then looked at the menu. Shirley asked what the special was. It sounded so good, so they all went with the special. Everyone in the restaurant was talking about the art show. Many had been today, and many were coming tomorrow. One couple came over to as they were leaving and said, "What a beautiful art centre, and it was so nice to see you had involved the children. There was something for everyone."

Another group said they had bought a stained glass window and also one of Celia's designer bags and were busy congratulating Shirley and June on their vision to open the centre.

June smiled at Shirley. "This is what it must be like when you're famous."

Jacque said. "Don't let it go to your heads. We have a lot of work to do in the next two days."

The wine arrived so Gary made a toast to the first of many art shows at the *Petit Bijou* Art Centre.

As they were enjoying the wine, Gary asked what they thought about future lectures or workshops. Shirley thought arranging lectures was a good idea. "What about speaking to Eric at the college? He may have some contacts for us to consider. Barb also has contacts in stained glass and that is very popular, I gather, just from speaking to people today."

Shirley said she would be talking to Celia Bury, the lady who had the bags and purses. "I've a feeling there is more to her than we know. The couple with the quilts are interesting as they have a story that goes with every quilt they make. That fascinates me. Also they are from different areas of France. I'll ask them if they do lectures and see what they say."

Jacque said when he was doing the tour of the renovations of old barn and showing everyone the photos he had taken and they all wanted a copy of his book. "And so I think we should look at getting a book printed."

Gary thought that was a very good idea from a business prospect.

They were all pleased to see the food arriving; it looked divine. "Now, no more business let's enjoy our meal before it gets cold," Shirley said. The rest of the evening was fun, with many people coming over to them talking about the art show.

Driving home from the restaurant, Gary said he was looking forward to the next few days and in meeting such interesting people from all over the world.

As Shirley went into the kitchen she saw there was a message on the phone. The message was from Gladys, who wanted Shirley to phone her when she got in. June thought it was a bit late to be phoning Gladys, but Shirley said, "She is always up late, and so I'll try her as we won't have time in the morning."

When Gladys answered the phone she wanted to talk to Shirley about Celia Bury. Gladys told Shirley she thought she knew her but could not remember how she could know her. After talking to Frank about her, she decided to look through some of her old photos, and then it came to her. "I went to art college after leaving school and there in the middle of the box of old photos was a photo of my final year and, to my surprise, Celia was in the photo. Her name then was Celia Turner. We were never close friends, but we all hung out together as you do in college."

Gladys did remember she was very talented and very bohemian in her outlook. "If I remember, she went on to one of the top fashion houses in London, and I never heard anything about her again. I did interior design but was not in the same league as Celia. I'll come back to the art show tomorrow and bring the photo with me as I would like to chat to her and have a catch up."

Shirley thought that was a good idea. "I look forward to seeing you tomorrow," she said as she hung up the phone.

Jacque and Gary had both left, and so June and Shirley were having a cup of tea before going to bed. Shirley told June what Gladys had told her. We'll have to wait until tomorrow to hear how it goes.

June said to Shirley how lucky they were to have Jacque and Gary. "You know, we could not manage without them, as they are so good." Shirley said Gary would have to go back home next week. "Quite honestly, I'll miss him so much."

"Have you told him how you feel? If not, you need to tell him before he leaves."

June said then that Jacque has gotten so many job contacts since doing the barn conversion. Everyone had been so impressed with his standard of workmanship. It was top quality. Old barns were being rapidly bought up for holiday homes but needed renovating and converting into living accommodation.

Jacque had lived in this area all his life, which helped. He was also had good men that worked for him. If ever they needed anything to do with the council, he knew everyone. He was very well respected. They all seemed to be his friend, or at the least, school mates.

CHAPTER FOURTEEN

Old College Friend

THE MORNING ARRIVED. Shirley and June were sitting in their kitchen with the sun streaming in, enjoying tea, toast, and fruit. "Just think. We get to do it all over again. Are you ready?" June asked. "I hope we get a good turnout like yesterday." Shirley was optimistic it was going to be good.

Before long everyone started to arrive. Jill was busy in the refreshment area, sorting out the bakery order. She looked at June and said, "Do you think we'll sell all this?"

June smiled and replied, "Yes, if not, we have to eat them all!"

The day was as busy as yesterday. Jacque shook his head and said to Gary, "Where are all these people coming from? This is a small rural area." That was the last Jacque and Gary spoke all day. Jacque was doing tours and Gary was taking peoples details and entrance fees as they came in.

The students were having so much fun with the children. It was so nice to hear the children laughing. Michael had his face painted again. Today he was a monkey. He was playing along with all the other children, which made Tom and Barb happy.

Gladys came later in the day. She had brought the photo to show Celia. Celia was busy with a customer, and so Gladys went to see June and Jill to get a cup of tea and one of their pastries. They had had another busy day with not much left. Jill was telling Gladys they would need some more of her business cards for tomorrow. Jill had been talking to an interesting couple from Germany who come to France every year to tour around. They are horticulturists and visited the Monet Gardens most years, although they also liked to visit the wineries in the area to stock up on wine.

They had been talking to June and booked one of the *gites* for later in the year for a month.

Gladys was talking to Jill about Celia, the lady selling the bags. Jill quickly said she had bought one and had her eye on another. She was thrilled to see the photo Gladys had. "That is so cool," she cried.

The show was coming to an end, and so Gladys went across to see Celia. As she approached Celia, all her college years came flooding back. She got the photo out and handed it to Celia, who looked at it with a tear in her eye. Then she looked up as Gladys said hello and introduced herself. "When I saw you yesterday I thought I should know you, and so last night I went through some old photos and found this photo." Gladys could see that Celia had great sadness in her eyes, but they were kind eyes.

Celia said she would love to sit down and talk some more. They hugged, and then Celia said, "It was so nice to see you."

Gladys explained where her hotel was and invited Celia to come for supper. Celia had rented a small apartment in the village, and so was delighted to go for supper with Gladys. Celia seemed to come to life after meeting up with Gladys. Gladys said she would not hold her up as everyone was closing up their stands and getting ready for the next day.

Gladys said goodbye to Shirley and June and told them about her having supper with Celia later. Shirley said, "how exciting. I can't wait to hear how it all goes."

Gladys told Frank about Celia. He was pleased for both of them. Gladys said, "I think we'll eat on our private patio, and that way we'll be away from the hotel guests."

Frank agreed. "Why don't you go and speak to the chef to get the meal sorted out. I'll arrange to have one of his chicken salads and a bottle of local wine.

Gladys was ready when Celia arrived. She looked just as Gladys remembered her. Her long, flowing skirt was in shades of blue and lilac. Her top was green shot with gold thread and was completed by a pink silk scarf. Only Celia could pull these colours off.

"You look amazing," said Gladys; she had not lost her style of dress at all.

Gladys introduced her to Frank, and then he had to go. Gladys said she had been given the night off as she smiled at Frank.

They went out onto the patio with its beautiful views onto their private rose garden. "You're so lucky to live in such an amazing place," Celia said. "Have you been in France many years?" Gladys said they had been in France about fifteen years and just loved it. The language was the hardest, she admitted, "But when you live here it comes naturally after a while. Now, let me get you a glass of wine. I've arranged a chicken salad. I hope that works for you."

"That sounds like music to my ears," Celia said.

They looked at a few more photos that Gladys had found in the box. "The last I remember about you, Celia, was that you went to join a big fashion house in London. We were all very envious."

Celia took a sip of her wine and said: "How long do you have?" Celia proceeded, "I joined the fashion house in London, which was so amazing. That was where I met Craig. He was the editor. We had a great time. We partied with the in crowd. We travelled all over the world with the fashion industry from Hong Kong, to Paris, New York and London. We then found out I was pregnant, and so we got married. Life was good. We had a small flat in London. Craig was still travelling all over the world. I was home with our daughter, which I did enjoy, but I missed Craig so much. We then had another daughter. They were beautiful, the light of our lives. And then we moved to a house still in London. When the girls were starting school I thought I would go back to work, but Craig was against it. I could not understand why. Then one day I dropped the girls off at school and went to the fashion house to see how everyone was. I was surprised, as everything had changed. I walked into Craig's office to find him having it off with some girl. To say they were taken aback was putting it mildly."

Gladys said, "You don't have to tell me all this."

Celia said she wanted to. "Craig said it would never happen again," she continued. "But we were never the same. I could never trust him again. When our oldest daughter was ten she got knocked over by a drunk driver and three days later she died. Craig went out and got drunk and was not sober again. He could not handle the grief. I did try, as we had Kim, our other daughter, and she needed us more than ever. I went back to work in the fashion house. They were very good to me and I was pleased to have a job. But getting over the death of your child is something else. Kim and I became very close as we helped one another. She was a good girl. Then three years later, after I had not seen or heard from Craig at all, the police knocked on my front door to say Craig had been sleeping rough and had died of hypothermia as we were having very cold weather at that time.

"I went to identify him. It was the hardest thing I've ever had to do. It was like looking at a stranger. That was when we moved out of London. I had the chance to move to France to work for a small design company. We bought a small house and did it up. You know me; I was always a bit of a hippy and a back-to-nature girl. Kim loved it and did very well. She is now married with a daughter and they live not far from me. She is very good to me. We have been through a lot. I started designing bags and that keeps me busy. Now I want to know about you. I can see you have done very well for yourself. This is an amazing hotel."

Gladys cleared the dishes and said she would be back in a minute with coffee and dessert. She came back with the best dessert Celia had ever had. "You have spoilt me tonight. I could get used to this."

Gladys asked Celia if she would like to take a walk around the grounds. "That sounds good to me."

At the end of the evening, Gladys said she would like to keep in touch if Celia agreed. Celia said she would like nothing better. "I think this will be the start of a re-kindled friendship," she said. They went to find Frank before Celia left.

Frank told Celia that she was welcome any time. Celia asked Gladys if she had kept in touch with anyone else from college. Gladys did keep in touch when she first left college, but she had gone to work for a company that was very demanding, and so she lost touch.

When Celia left, Gladys phoned Shirley and told her all about Celia. They both agreed not to talk about her life unless she brought it up. "I think she has had a hard time, but now she seems happy to be in France and living near her daughter and her family. I'll tell June and we hope to see you before the show ends. We have two more days. I think we'll be ready for a rest, although we're having the best time ever."

The following morning, June and Shirley sat in the kitchen having breakfast. Shirley and June were talking about Celia. "I think she is a very private person," June said. "And so apart from Gary and Jacque we should keep this to ourselves."

As always, Gary arrived as soon as food went on the table. Jacque followed soon after.

Before long everyone arrived and was busy getting ready to open. Shirley had a few phone calls to return and so she went off into the office. As soon as John arrived he went to help Jacque with a few things that needed attention outside.

"We have some coach trips arriving today from hotels in the area," Gary said to Shirley and June. "And so I think it will be busy.

I just hope they don't all come at the same time." Gary said Jill had the bakery order all under control so they would be ready.

Little Michael was patiently waiting for the students to start. Barb told him he could not go to the stand until they were ready. One of the young students came across and asked if Michael would like to help in the children's area. Barb told the young student, "Don't let him get in the way." Michael had the biggest grin and off he went.

The show was busy. As soon as Shirley had chance she went across to see Celia, who had just done another sale. She looked up when she saw Shirley. "By the end of tomorrow I'll be out of stock. I'm having the best time ever." She told Shirley about her evening with Gladys and what a wonderful hotel they had. "I was treated like a queen. It was so nice catching up with an old college student. Seeing your advertisement in the paper about your art show has changed my life. I had lost a lot of my confidence but coming here and meeting up with Gladys has been the best thing. I phoned Kim my daughter last night and she was so thrilled for me."

On the next stand to Celia there was a gentleman who did wood-turning and made the most original bowls and walking sticks and many other objects. He had taken a shine to Celia and was always going to fetch her a tea or coffee. He smiled at Shirley as he came with her cup of coffee and one of the fresh pastries.

"I could get used to this with living on my own for so many years. You forget what it is like to have someone wait on you. As soon as I get home, I'll be so busy making more bags and purses for the next show."

Shirley had to go as Gary was calling her. "I'll see you later," she said. "Did Gladys say she was coming today? I know she wanted to order more quilts, and so she will be coming, but it may be later as they are busy in the hotel today."

Gary was busy and needed help. The first coach had just arrived. Shirley was taking the money and Gary was taking their details. Eric and the art teacher came to check on the students. They wanted to make sure they had not run out of paper, paints, etc., Shirley told them the students were a great hit, as people could leave their children with the students while they looked around.

Jacque came in for something to drink and eat as he had not stopped all day. He told June he was getting so many job offers. "I'll have to be thinking of employing more builders if all these jobs go ahead. I'm so enjoying myself. I've never thought of myself as a people person."

June told him to sit down and take a breath.

Two more coaches arrived during the afternoon, and so it kept everyone busy. Gladys came in and went straight over to see Celia, who was pleased to see her. Shirley could see Celia introducing Gladys to Rene, the man with the wood. It was so nice to see Celia smiling. She looked so sad on the first day but now she looked alive.

Gladys had found more information about their college days to show Celia. Celia told Gladys she had phoned Kim and told her about meeting Celia. "She can't wait to meet you, and so we'll get something planned."

"That sounds good to me," Celia said with a board smile.

Gladys then went to order two more quilts. "I don't need them today, so keep your stock. You can send them to me."

The couple said they had many orders to mail out. "This has been a good show for us and we have met such interesting people."

Gary had just had a message from two more hotels to say they could expect two more coach trips tomorrow as he was telling everyone in the show. The one trip today was from Britain. "You can imagine their surprise to find out Shirley and June were from Britain.

I don't think June will need to ever advertise her accommodation again as she has given out so many business cards and taken so many bookings. She will need to order more as soon as possible before she runs out."

Tom was getting a bit concerned about Michael, and so he told Barb he was going to see how he was doing and take him for something to eat. As he went to the children's corner there was Michael with his face painted. Today he was cat, and he was in the middle helping the students sort out the paints. Tom asked him if he would like to come and get something to eat. Reluctantly he agreed.

He told the young student he would not be long. They told him not to worry, come back when you're ready. Tom took him to the refreshment area and sat him down while he had a sandwich and juice. Jill and June came over to see him. He told them all about the students and what they were doing. As soon as he had finished he turned to Tom and said, "Come on, Dad, I've to go."

Tom took a sandwich and coffee for him and Barb back to the stand. He was laughing as he was telling Barb. "I hope he is this keen when it is time for him to get a job!"

Barb had another good day and would have to bring more stock for the last day tomorrow.

As the day was coming to an end, Gary and Shirley were checking that everything was in order for the last day tomorrow. Shirley said she was going to order pizza to be delivered for supper. She was going to ask Celia if she would like to join them. Gary thought that was a good idea, as they wanted her to come and give a lecture on her experience in the fashion industry.

Celia was delighted to join them for supper. Shirley said: "We're having pizza, salad, and a glass of wine."

"After a busy day, I'll be happy with anything as long as I don't have to cook it."

June and Jill were closing up and were getting ready for the last day. They got on so well together. John went over to Jill, as he was tired and ready to go home. Tom collected Michael from the children's area. Barb had the stand closed up and everything was in place for the final day tomorrow.

Celia went across to the patio to join everyone. They were having a glass of wine. The pizza had been delivered and June had made the salad. Gary was asking Celia how her sales had been so far. She just about had enough bags and purses left for the final day.

During the evening Shirley asked Celia if she would be interested in coming and giving a lecture of her experience in the fashion industry and about the work she did. Gladys said. "You were always ahead in your fashion outlook and very talented."

"Well, I think Gladys is being very kind. But I do, and always have, loved fashion."

"We would provide you with accommodation and, of course, a fee for doing the lecture," June said.

"I would be honoured to come and thank you for asking me. I've been a bit out of circulation lately, but this show and meeting Gladys has done my confidence a world of good."

Shirley said, "We also thought about asking the couple with the quilts to see if they would also be interested. We like the idea that they are very French and how each quilt has a story."

Celia thought that was a great idea. "Also I think your friend Barb should do a lecture with her stained glass. She is an amazing artist and so talented. I just loved talking to her. She has so many unique ideas."

Gary was making notes. "We'll be having a meeting after the show finishes tomorrow to work on some dates. We have to make sure we offer something at least every month. There are so many talented artists in France. I had no idea."

Jacque raised his hand. "We have to work on the book about how you two ladies came to France and started the art centre."

June said Jill would be good to do that as she worked in that line back in Britain.

Shirley told June to ask Jill if she would be interested. "She is my daughter-in-law so it would be better coming from you."

"I'll ask her tomorrow and let you know."

Celia thanked everyone and said, "Goodnight, I'll see you all tomorrow. I'll be sad to see it coming to an end. Everyone I've spoken to says the same."

Jacque went to check on everything, making sure everywhere was locked up for the night. June said she would go with him as she had been inside all day.

While Shirley was cleaning up, Gary told her that he had to go back to Britain next week. "I've made my decision. This is where I want to be, here with you."

Shirley was thrilled to hear him say that. "I don't want you to go back, but if I know you're coming back, I can accept that."

"I've to get things in order and I need to sell my house. I was going to keep it, but I've no desire to go back, and so I may as well sell it. John was asking me only the other day if I was going to make this my permanent home. I thought I would speak to John tomorrow to let him know what my thoughts are if that is all right with you."

Shirley went over to him and gave him a big hug. "I could not imagine my life without you. Gary then turned to her and told her again how much he loved her. "You and June have done so much. Can you believe you own your own art centre?"

Shirley said, "Pinch me."

As Gary left to go back to his *gite* June came in. Jacque had just gone home. Shirley made her and June a cup of tea. As they sat there, she told June that Gary was going next week but coming back for good. He had to sell his house and had a few things to get in order. "They will have to find someone else to run the art classes in Brookdale," Shirley said. "Now, June, I want to ask you if you mind if Gary was here all the time."

"I would be delighted. We need him and I know he makes you happy."

"Hmm, I could ask you the same thing about Jacque." Shirley smiled at June as they drank their tea before they went to bed.

Everyone was early for the last day of the show. Before long, it was time to open and cars were already lined up. For the last day all the students were in attendance and, of course, Michael was helping. They loved him. First he was getting his face painted. Today he wanted to be a tiger. As soon as they finished, he went straight over to show his mum and dad to get their approval.

Shirley went over to say good morning to Celia. She looked so happy and was talking to Rene on the stand next to her. She was

WHEN DREAMS BECOME REALITY

going over to Gladys's after the show finished before she drove home tomorrow.

It was a steady flow all day. Midafternoon they had two coach tours stop by. The one was from Britain and the other from Germany. The one young lady selling her jewellery was especially busy. She had never sold so much at a show. Her jewellery was very different. She incorporated local gemstones. She polished the stones to bring out the colours. They were quite beautiful.

Shirley told Gary to put her name down regarding getting her to do a lecture in the future. "We want to encourage all age groups. I noticed the students were going to her stand and taking her drinks."

Gary thought it would be a good idea to have all the artist come and have a glass of wine and refreshments after they closed tonight. Shirley said she would go and get June or Jill to order some pastries from the bakery to be delivered later.

Shirley went around to every stall holder and asked them to stay for refreshments after closing. They were all happy to do that and, of course, the students were always ready to party. Eric and the teacher came later in the day. Even the mayor came back.

The last vehicles were driving out of the parking lot, and so everyone was starting to pack away. Shirley told them when they were ready to make their way to the refreshment area. Jill and June had it all set out: fresh coffee, tea and wine, and the newly-delivered pastries.

They were all relaxed and enjoying the refreshments. Shirley and June thanked everyone for making the first of many art shows a success. She announced they would be having lectures and workshops in the near future. "We're also putting a book together as to how this art centre came about."

The mayor and Eric stood up and thanked Shirley and June as the show had been a big success, and he thanked them for involving the students. They really had a ball. One of the students also wanted to thank Michael, as he had been there every day. Tom and Barb were so proud of Michael, standing there with the students.

"Now," said June. "We have all these pastries, so please come and enjoy them."

Jacque did not need to be asked twice. He had been busy outside all day. June made him a coffee just the way he liked it. "I could get used to this," he said as everyone laughed.

As soon as they had finished, everyone started packing up as many had a long way to go. Shirley went across to the couple doing the quilts and asked them if they would be interested in giving a lecture on the quilts and how they come up with the stories. She told them the same as she told Celia. "We would provide accommodation in one of the *gites*. Also, we would pay you a fee."

They jumped at it and agreed that as long as they were available they would love to come back and give a lecture on their beloved quilts. "We're having a meeting in the next few days to sort things out and I'll phone you," said Shirley.

They said they had so many orders to put together and mail out. "We're not used to being this busy. Mind you, we're not complaining."

As the last artists left, June said she was going to phone Gladys to see if she has a table for four available for tonight in the restaurant at the hotel. They all agreed. "So go and make the phone call," said Jacque.

Gladys booked them in; all they had to do was get themselves ready. As they arrived at the hotel, Gladys came out to greet them. She took them through to the restaurant and told them to enjoy their meal. "Frank and I'll come and see you before you go," she promised.

During the meal they went through the last four days. Gary said he would be booking a crossing on the boat tomorrow. "I want to drive as I need to bring things back with me, so I can get a lot in the car."

Shirley asked him how long he would be going for.

"I'm not sure how long it will take me. I've already told them in the community offices that I'll not be doing any more teaching for their evening classes. Also, I've contacted an estate agent who will be coming to meet me as soon as I get back to get my house on the market. The agent I spoke to told me my house should sell quickly as there is little on the market at the moment. But I do have a lot of sorting out to do. I've been in the house for many years and have collected a lot of stuff and junk."

June said, "We'll miss you, but we're so pleased you want to come and live in France with us. I know Shirley has never been happier."

Gary kissed Shirley and said he would be back as soon as he could. "I don't really want to leave, but things have to be done."

The rest of the evening was very enjoyable—good food and a nice bottle of wine. Frank came to ask them to join them for coffee on their private patio at the back of the hotel. Gladys was telling them more about Celia and how they planned to keep in touch.

Shirley told Gladys that Celia had agreed to come and do a lecture in the art centre. "We just have to work on dates. Frank told us you have been extra busy because of the art show and I know the village has been busy. I would say it was very successful for everyone in the area."

Driving back in the car, June said she was going to have a lazy day tomorrow. Jacque said he had a list of people he needed to call that wanted jobs done.

Next morning Gary came into the kitchen where Shirley and June were having breakfast. He had arranged a crossing on the boat for the evening, and so he would be leaving at lunch time. June phoned Jill, who was thrilled to be asked about putting a book together on the art centre. "I'm going to speak to Jacque later and arrange a time so we can sit down and go over things. Jacque has so many photos that can be used."

Shirley was helping Gary get ready for his journey. Gary had spoken to John and told him what he was going to do, and also how much he thought of Shirley. "I told John I would never hurt you, and I would always make you happy."

Shirley asked, "What did John say?"

"He was happy for us both, as everyone could see we cared for one another."

June had already rented the *gite* out that Gary had been staying in, and so she was busy getting that cleaned with fresh sheets and towels. After Gary left, Jacque arrived a little later. He had phoned everyone he needed to and now had a list of jobs to go and see. June told him Jill would work with him on the book. "And so just let her know when you have time to get together to get started."

Shirley was pleased to receive a phone call from Heather to see how thing went. "I've a surprise for you," Heather said. "Dave has a week off next week, and so we thought we would come to see you if that is all right. I've not told Jenny yet. I wanted to speak to you first."

"We would love to see you. Are you driving or flying down?"

"We're going to drive as Dave has some business go do on the way. I've spoken to John and he said the show was a great success."

"It was. I'll tell you all about it when you get here. Gary has left to go back to Britain. I'll also tell you about that when we see you next week."

No sooner had she put the phone down when Alex called to see how the show went. Alex told Shirley about the children, which was so nice to hear. Shirley told Alex that Heather was coming down next week.

CHAPTER FIFTEEN

Shirley and Gary

As soon as Gary arrived back in Brookdale he phoned Shirley. He had had a good crossing with no hold-ups, but the traffic was busy, and so he was pleased to finally get home. After he put the phone down, he took a look around the house and thought to himself, 'I've a lot of work to do in getting the house ready to sell.'

As he went from room to room, he could not believe he had so many books and stuff. He kept thinking about what Shirley said, 'one room at a time' and then there was the garage and garden shed. He decided he would get a good night's sleep then make a start in the morning.

The following morning he went and found stacks of boxes, and then he sorted each room. There would be one box to go to charity and one box to keep. Junk went in black plastic bags. It took him a while to get started, but when he did, it went very well. It was evident there was more for charity and more junk than he imagined. He had a three-bedroom house with two bathrooms upstairs, and so it was a large house. As he carried the boxes downstairs he felt a good sense of achievement.

He phoned Shirley to let her know how he had got on. She was very impressed. "Just keep it going and it will be done in no time," she assured him.

They chatted for a while, and then he said he had to get on. "The quicker I get this done, the quicker I can come back to France."

He put all the boxes for charity into the garage. The black bags with the junk went into his car and were taken to the local dump. At the end of the first day he was pleased with the progress he had made.

On his way back from taking the junk he went to see the estate agent and arranged for someone to come and give him a valuation on the house. "I've to get the ball rolling if I'm to get the house on the market," he told the agent. He wanted the agent to give him a couple of days before they came to see the house. He also had a few other things to attend to, and so with all that done it could be said that he had a good day.

It took him four days to get things sorted out in the house. He had a gardener that took care of his garden, and so he called him to tell him where he was going so that he would carry on doing the garden until the house was sold. To his surprise, the gardener was interested in buying the house. "My wife and I've always loved your house. Could we come and look around it first?"

The gardener and his wife came that evening and loved it. "As soon as you have a price, let us know as we're very interested. We wouldn't have to sell our house first as my wife has had some money left to her, and so we'll move as quickly as you want us to." As they left, Gary could not believe his luck.

Gary phoned Shirley straight away as he was in shock. She was thrilled. "You will be back in France before you know it, Gary." They chatted for a while. Shirley told Gary that Heather and the family were coming next week.

The agent came back after looking around his house and gave him a selling price. Gary had told him about the gardener wanting to buy the house. "If the sale does not work out, phone me." And then he wished Gary luck with the sale.

Gary spoke to his lawyer, and so they set things in place. He then spoke to the gardener, who came around that evening with his wife to discuss the house. Before long the sale was agreed and then Gary gave him his lawyer's information.

It was agreed they could have the house in four weeks. That would give Gary time to organize movers for the things he wanted to take to France and to clear the house. The gardener told Gary he could leave the garden shed as it was. "Just take what you want to take with you."

Over the course of the next two weeks Gary did not stop. Every day he went to bed exhausted but feeling satisfied that he was one step nearer. He phoned Shirley every night. Gary told her he missed her so much and she told him she missed him as well.

Shirley kept Gary up to date with what was happening. She said they were waiting for Gary to return before organizing the lectures. "I'll be back in two weeks. I've arranged everything with the moving company." He told Shirley he had done better than he thought he would with the sale of his house. "I also have a few ideas when I get back that I want to run by you all."

Shirley laughed. "Should I be alarmed?"

"No, it's all good, but I want to talk it over with you first."

The sale went as planned. The movers put all the items he wanted into a container, ready for shipping to France. He did have a lot of his artwork, and so the movers took extra care when they packed them. The paperwork was finalized and Gary was ready to go back to France. He could not wait. Everyone asked about Shirley and June and sent them their good wishes.

Gary went to hand the keys in at the lawyer's office ready for the new owners. He went around to see the new owners to wish them good luck when they moved into his house. He was then ready to set off on his journey back to France. Shirley spoke to him in the morning to make sure he had not changed his mind about moving to France. He assured Shirley there were no second thoughts. He could not wait to be back in France.

The journey went well. He would be with Shirley within two hours from when he got off the boat.

As he pulled into the driveway of the house, Shirley came out to welcome him back. They hugged one another. He was very tired but so pleased to be back in France. The container with his things had already arrived. She told Gary there was no hurry on the container, "Just phone them when you have emptied it," she suggested.

They went into the house. June was getting supper ready. "Jacque is joining us, and so we can all catch-up on what has been happening here and in Britain." By the time Gary emptied his car and freshened up Jacque arrived for supper.

Shirley had set the table on the patio. Jacque opened the wine and June started to serve the supper. Gary told them about selling his house and how lucky he was that his gardener had wanted to buy it. "I've only brought a few pieces of furniture. The rest is books and my artwork.

Now, I've an idea, but I would like to discuss it with Shirley first and see what she thinks. To be honest, I got a better price for my house, which surprised me."

Shirley was anxious to find out what his plans were.

The rest of the evening was spent catching up. Shirley had a good visit with Heather, Dave, and Penny. Jacque told Gary about all the jobs he was looking at since the art show. June said Jill had been working with Jacque on putting the book together. It was nearly ready to be published. Jill was so organised, they all agreed.

Gary asked Shirley to book a table at their favourite restaurant up in the mountains. "I'll book it for lunchtime tomorrow."

Gary said, "That sounds perfect."

June looked at Jacque and smiled.

When the meal was over, Gary said he was going to have an early night, as he was very tired by now; it had been a long day. June told him his *gite* was ready for him. It was the same one he had before. "If you need anything else let me know," June said.

He said good night and he would see Shirley in the morning.

Jacque left soon after, and then June and Shirley sat in the kitchen. Shirley was wondering what Gary was thinking of doing. She asked June if she had any ideas. As soon as they had cleared away, Shirley said she was ready for bed and said good night to June.

Next morning Shirley booked a table for lunch at the winery. Gary came in. He was feeling much better after a good night's sleep. "I only have a few things to do this morning," Gary said, and added he was going to open the container, as he wanted to get his artwork out. They decided that Gary could put his artwork and books in the art centre. There was a spare area in the loft he could use. Jacque would build him some book shelves for his books. "He will be back later this afternoon, so tell him what you require," Shirley said.

Gary and Shirley set of for lunch. Gary told Shirley she looked beautiful. Shirley was beginning to take care of her appearance these days. She had a regular appointment with Michelle at the new hairdressers in the village. "You don't look so bad yourself," she teased

It would take them a while to get to the winery, and so they allowed plenty of time. They chatted about everything in the car, but Gary mentioned nothing about the idea he had. They arrived at the winery and made their way to the restaurant. Good job they had booked as it was already getting busy. The table was perfect and Gary ordered some wine while they looked at the menu.

They gave their order and the waiter poured the wine. As Shirley picked up her glass Gary said he wanted to talk to her first. Gary told Shirley he was in love with her. "I know I've told you before, but being away back in Britain made me realise how much truly I love you."

He pulled out a box from his pocket and opened it. As he opened it, he asked Shirley if she would do him the honour of becoming his wife. Shirley was so taken aback. She looked at him and then at the most beautiful ring she had ever seen. Gary waited, and then said with a big grin: "It is customary for you to answer."

Shirley said she would be honoured to be his wife and could not be happier. "Oh, this is such a shock. I was not expecting this at all."

He put the ring on her finger and kissed her just as the waiter came back with their meal. He was first to congratulate them. The owners came to congratulate them as they remembered them from before. Everyone in the restaurant was so pleased for them.

"Now I'm expected to eat my lunch! I'm too excited."

"Let's eat, and then we can talk as I've not told you about my idea yet."

"You mean there's more to talk about?"

The meal was as delicious as the last time they were here. After they had their meal, Gary asked if they could go out on the patio for their coffee. Out on the patio overlooking the vineyards, a slight breeze blew. Gary told Shirley his idea. "I want to see if I could buy a piece of land to the one side of the art centre then build more rental accommodation. The art centre is going to grow and we need to offer more rental accommodation. I would like Jacque to be involved as he is the perfect person to do the building. We could even build a house for us if you like. I don't think it will be long until June and Jacque get together. They could have the house you're in now. What do you think? I won't do it if you're not happy."

Shirley thought it was a great idea. "We'll discuss it with June and Jacque as they have to be in agreement. And I do agree that June and Jacque are very fond of one another."

On the way home they chatted nonstop. "I've got to phone the children as soon as I get home to tell them the news," Shirley said as she looked at the ring on her finger. "I wonder what June and Jacque will say?"

"I think they'll be very happy for us," Gary said.

As they got out of the car they found June busy watering the plants. Jacque was fixing a door. Shirley called June and told her to get Jacque. "We'll meet you on the patio." June said she would be there as soon as she finished the watering.

Gary had a bottle of wine and Shirley got the best glasses out. They were sitting on the patio when June and Jacque arrived. "What have you two been up to?" asked June. Gary poured the wine and gave June and Jacque a glass. They all had a glass in hand when Gary said. "We have an announcement to make. I asked Shirley if she would become my wife and she said yes." At that, Shirley proudly showed off her ring.

June could not contain herself. "This is the best news. I'm so happy for you both." Jacque also was pleased. He went over to Shirley and gave her a big hug and then hugged Gary.

While they were drinking and laughing, Gary told them of his idea about buying some more land to expand the rental accommodation. "I just want you all to think about this idea for the future. Jacque, I would want you to do the building of the extra accommodation. Also, Shirley and I may want to build our own house. What do you think? I know these are only ideas, and we would have to first see if we can buy the land, and then see if we can get planning permission."

Jacque said, "There should be no problem in buying the land as I know the family that owns all the land next to the art centre. They will be happy to think it is going to help the community, as that is very important to them."

Shirley said she had to go and phone John, Alex, and Heather. "I don't know what they will think of the news. Wish me luck. I'll phone Mary and Tom tomorrow."

Jacque and Gary did not waste time and started planning. "How much land will we need for what we're looking to build?" Gary wondered.

"Tomorrow I'll go and take a look at the land. That will be a start," Jacque said.

"This is so exciting," said June and turned to Gary. "When are you and Shirley thinking of getting married."

"I'll be leaving that up to Shirley," Gary said. "Whatever she wants works for me."

"Jill called by today about the book," June said. "She should have a draft for us to look over in the next two days. She has a few more details on the construction that she needs to add in a few areas. She's doing a great job. We have a list of people that want one as soon as she has it finished."

When Shirley came back onto the patio, Jacque and Gary had paper out and were already started sketching out ideas. Jacque was a very good architect and very creative when he got going. Even June was putting some ideas forward, as she knew what worked in the rentals they had now. She also knew what did not work. Shirley came back. Gary was interested to hear if the family were happy with the news.

"They were all delighted to hear the news," Shirley said. "They wanted to make sure I was happy and they like Gary very much."

Gary said: "We should have a meeting about organizing the lectures. Could we sit down tomorrow to make a start?"

Shirley went and phoned Jill and Barb to see if they were available tomorrow. They were, and so Shirley set a meeting for 2:00 PM.

Jacque said he would not be able to make the meeting but that June could fill him in later. Gary asked Jacque if he could get him information on who owned the land they were talking about.

Gary asked Jacque to go with him to the centre. "I've put my books and artwork into that spare room in the loft area. I want you to build me some book shelves when you get time."

"Let's go and have a look," Jacque said.

"The problem is, I've so many books and I want to keep them all!"

Shirley and June looked at the drawings that Jacque and Gary had started. They were looking good so far. "We have to think how many rental properties they are thinking of," June said.

Shirley said she did not think it had been decided.

"I think if we had an extra four, that should be enough. I would prefer them to be of a higher standard, so, yes, four would be enough. Then we can upgrade the ones we have so they are all to the same standard. We want to attract good artists, and so we want good quality accommodation."

"I agree," said Shirley. "I would get Jill to help when it comes to the interior décor as she has great ideas."

First job for Shirley this morning was to phone Mary and tell her the news. Mary could not believe it. "Wait till I tell Bill. I'm so thrilled for you both. I knew there was a spark between you two when I came to that first art class. I'll phone you back tomorrow," said Mary.

Jill and Barb arrived for the meeting. Shirley remembered that she had not told Barb about her and Gary. Barb was so happy. She said they were made for one another. Shirley flashed her ring for Jill and Barb to see. "I feel like a teenager. Do people our age get engaged?"

"Of course they do," said Jill. "I'm so pleased for you both."

Barb had an agenda for the meeting and gave them all one so that they did not miss anything out.

"We have four artists on our list for lectures," Jill said. "And so we need to work out the dates for the lectures. Barb, you can have first choice and we'll work from there."

The meeting went as planned. After they had gone through the list, Gary then wanted to talk about having regular exhibitions. He suggested they categorize so they could have a pottery exhibition, and then a jewellery exhibition and so on. "We have so many talented artists as we found out when we held the art show," he said. He then went on to tell Jill and Barb about his plan to buy extra land and build more rental accommodation. "Also we want to build another building so we can have a separated area to concentrate on photography. I was speaking to one of the professors from the college. He would come and give us ideas as to what would be needed."

Everyone was in favour of learning more about Gary's idea, but he said, "These are only early suggestions as we have to speak to the landowner first. I would welcome any suggestions you have."

Jill gave everyone a copy of the finished book. "Jacque and I've worked hard on this, and so I hope you're happy with what we have achieved."

Shirley was first to give her approval. She had only flicked through the pages and looked forward to reading it later.

Jill said she would like everyone to read through it and let her know in two or three days, then she can place an order. June had read most of it but seeing it in print gave her a sense of achievement. Shirley smiled as she looked at the front cover: *Petit Bijou, Art Centre.* "I love it."

After the meeting Jacque and Gary went into the office to make a phone call to the owner of the land to see if they would agree to sell. Jacque had been making inquiries. He was hopeful, but until they asked they did not want to get their hopes up.

Jill and Barb left, both with jobs to follow up on. Shirley and June went into the kitchen. June asked Shirley when she was thinking of getting married. "I know this may sound odd, but this has happened so quickly that we haven't even talked about a wedding."

"I think we'll wait to hear if Gary is able to buy the land that he is looking at. I'm not sure we need a separate house. I would not mind living over the photography centre, as it will be a large enough area for us. We would get an architect to plan something out for us. Mind you, I think Jacque could plan something for us, as he is so creative."

June thought that was a good idea. "Jacque would love to do the planning. By the way, June, how are things with you and Jacque? Are you serious about one another?"

"Well, you know, Jacque, the strong silent type. We care about one another very much. We see one another every day and he also phones me two or three times a day, and so I would say we're serious."

Shirley was smiling. "Just think, we could have a double wedding."

June proceeded to make coffee as Jacque and Gary came into the kitchen. "Well, you both have a smile on your face," Gary said, "So I hope that means good news. Let's sit down and have coffee. We have a meeting tomorrow morning with the owner so between now and tomorrow. We have to have some kind of a plan to show him what we would want to build, and so we had better get started."

Shirley told Gary that she would be happy to live above the photography centre as long as it could be large enough.

"That's a great idea. What do you think, Jacque? Could we make that work?"

Jacque thought it would be a lot less expensive. "I could design whatever you wanted. You would have plenty of room. We would just have to make sure there are no height restrictions. We'll take our coffee across to the art centre, as there is more room to work over there. We have to get as much information as possible down on the plan. Also, we'll have to allow plenty of room for parking. That will be a big concern when we go for planning permission."

Shirley asked June what she thought about her and Gary living over the photography studio. She thought it was a good idea.

"I would like room for the family to come and stay with us, though," Shirley added.

June pointed out that she would be in the main house. "There would be plenty of room for them to stay with me. I don't have family to come and stay. I look upon your family as my family, and so they would be very welcome."

Later in the evening Jacque and Gary came back over to the house with their ideas all planned out, hoping to go over them with June and Shirley.

June cleared the kitchen table as Jacque and Gary explained the plan. "We're going to see if we can buy enough land to build the main building, which will be large enough for living accommodation above." Jacque explained the living area to Shirley. She was very impressed, as it would give her and Gary plenty of room.

Jacque then explained the four rental accommodations to June. "They are larger than the ones we have now." June looked at them closely and liked what she saw. I want to make sure the bathrooms are large enough, as I do get comments saying the bathrooms we have now are a little on the small size."

Jacque arrived early the next morning to go over any last requests on the plans before they went to the meeting. Gary had a couple of questions, but apart from that everyone was happy. Shirley and June wished them luck as they left for the meeting.

Jill came by to say the order for the books would be delivered next week. "I'm going to go into the office and go through the list of people who placed orders. Then I want to update our website to say the book will be available in a week's time with pricing and information on the book. Barb has given me the dates she has booked for the upcoming lectures. I've information on each of the lectures, so if people want to book in advance we would welcome that."

Shirley said, "That is a great idea as it would give us a better idea about how many people would attend."

Gary and Jacque arrived back later in the day. Luc who owned the land took them for lunch. He was very happy to sell some of his land. Also, he thought what they wanted to do would be good for the area and was happy to be able to help. He had arranged for the area they were interested in to be pegged out so they could get it valued.

Jacque invited him to come and see what they had done so far; he would come tomorrow morning. Shirley said she would prepare a light lunch. Gary went over to see how Jill was getting on in the office. The rest of the day he spent in the art centre sorting out his paintings and books.

Chapter Sixteen

New Plans

Luc arrived. Jacque and Gary took him on a tour of the art centre. He was very impressed at what had been done to the old barn. He knew the previous owners, and so he knew exactly the condition it was in before they started. Gary went and got him a copy of the book, showing in great detail the before and after photos.

Luc was now waiting to hear back with the valuation. He said he should hear in a day or two. "But as soon as I hear, I'll let you know." Gary said that they would like to start the process moving as soon as possible. Luc said he could be of help with that as he had contacts in the planning department and in the council offices.

After touring around everywhere, they made their way to the patio where Shirley and June had been busy preparing lunch. They were looking forward to meeting Luc.

Lunch went very well. Jacque and Luc were both from the area, and so they chatted and reminisced about old times and how the area had changed over the years. Jacque was always so quiet. It was nice to see him open up about the area he loved so much.

Luc was interested in hearing about how Shirley and June had come to France. His English was very good. He could see they were very close friends.

Luc brought up a good point about their book. He asked if they were also going to have a French version. Gary said they had not thought about it. "But I think we should."

Luc pointed out that local people were interested in what happened in the area, but that not all of them could read English. "I think you should consider it, as you will get a lot of support from the locals. And the last thing you want is to upset anyone."

When Luc had left, Shirley said Luc has a good point. "I think we should have a French version as well as an English one." June agreed with Shirley. "I'll phone Jill and see what she can do."

Jacque also said that, by having the book in French as well as English, local people would accept them a lot more. "We want to be able to sell the book all over France; it will be good marketing. There are many areas where they only speak French."

Shirley said, "This is still a learning process for all of us."

When June spoke to Jill she totally agreed. She had never thought of it. She said she would go to see the publisher and arrange to have the book in French and English. "Also, I'll make a note on the website to say the book will be in French and English." Jill added that she would also let Barb know.

The next few days were busy with bookings for the upcoming lectures. Also orders for the book, as many wanted to read the book in French. Jill warned there would be a small delay for the French version of the book.

Gary was starting to get concerned. He wanted to hear from Luc. Jacque reassured him not to worry, "Things don't happen quickly out in France."

Just then the phone rang; it was Luc. He wanted to set up a meeting with them. They agreed to meet him later that day. Luc said he would come to the house for a meeting.

Gary was a little nervous. Shirley told him not to worry it would all be good. He kissed her, and then said, "You're the sensible one." She just smiled.

Jacque and Gary were ready when Luc arrived. The price he wanted for the land was acceptable to Gary. Actually, he thought he was very fair. Luc had also been to see the planning department in the council, and there would be no problem as long as they had plenty of parking.

The council stipulated to Luc that cars would not be allowed to park on the main road, as this was a country area. Gary and Jacque agreed.

Luc said he would go to his lawyer's office and Gary would need to get a lawyer also. Jacque said Gary could use his lawyer, as it was a different one from Luc's. "We'll make an appointment in the morning to get the ball rolling," Luc said. "We'll exchange lawyer information as soon as I've spoken to my lawyer."

Luc told Gary and Jacque he would have the boundary marked out showing the area of land that they were buying. "As we're in France, we should toast this with a nice bottle of wine," Luc concluded.

Shirley and June came in to have a glass of wine with them. June told Luc they had decided to have the book printed in French and English. "We should have thought of that in the beginning!"

Jacque had been so busy since the art show. He was employing more men to keep up. He said to Gary: "We should go over the plans, because when we go to the council for permits we need to know exactly what we're building. We can do small changes, but the main area needs to be correct."

The four of them went over the plans, making a few changes here and there. Shirley was very happy with the living area above the photography studio. June was also very happy with the rental accommodation. "When Jill has finished the interior design the rooms will be spectacular," she said.

Jacque went with Gary to the lawyer's office, as his French was better than Gary's. This was very important, and he did not want to miss anything.

June and Shirley were waiting to hear that everything went well at the lawyer's when the phone rang. Shirley went to answer it. She was pleased to hear Mary on the other end of the line. She just come off the phone with Gladys and had booked a week's holiday for her and Bill. Shirley was thrilled and wanted to know when they were coming.

"We'll be there next week and are looking forward to spending some time with you both," Mary said.

Shirley told Mary about the first lecture that was taking place next week. "The lady's name is Celia. She makes the most incredible bags and purses. Celia came to the art show and was a great success, and so she is coming to give a lecture on how she makes the bags. The most amazing thing is, she went to art college with Gladys, who lost touch when she went to join a fashion house in London. We have so much to catch up on. We want to know all about you, Bill and Polly."

Mary said, "We're not bringing Polly. She'll stay with Liz next door. We're driving so we have the car. We want to do some exploring while we're there."

"Lovely, let us know as soon as you arrive at the hotel and have a safe journey."

June was looking forward to seeing Mary and Bill. It seemed ages since she last them. "I'll put two tickets aside for them for Celia's lecture. I think I'll phone Gladys to see if she wants a ticket."

Shirley went to get the mail, as it had just been delivered. There was a letter addressed to Shirley and June!

They both sat in the kitchen and opened the letter:

Dear Shirley and June,

I hope you're both well and enjoying life in France. Mary and Bill were up visiting Clive and Amy so they came into the cafe. I can't tell you how proud I am of you both. Mary brought in photos she had taken of your 'Art Studio.' You have both excelled and come to life since moving to France. The area you live in is outstanding. Now I can understand why you moved.

The day Mary and Bill came into the cafe there was a group of ladies from thegolf club. You should have seen their faces when they saw Mary with Bill.

I was so proud of her. She went across to them and introduced them to Bill. As you know Bill is the perfect gentleman. It made my day.

I also have some news to tell you both. Our daughter who lives up in Scotland has not been well lately and, as you know, she has three children.

We have been travelling back and forward a lot in the last few months so we have decided to move nearer to her. That way we can then help out more.

You remember Jackie? She worked for me for many years. Well, she will be taking over the cafe.

So you could say I'm "retiring"

We have bought a bungalow and sold our house, and so all being well we should be moving within the next month.

I'll send you a letter as soon as we get settled. Please keep in touch as I want to know what you two are up to. You're such an inspiration to us all.

Thinking of you.

Love Molly xxx

Shirley said she thought she had Molly's phone number. "I'll look for it and call her before she leaves for Scotland. We must keep in touch."

It was later in the afternoon when Gary and Jacque came back. Everything went as planned. The lawyer said it would only take about six weeks to get all the paperwork together. They went for lunch with Luc where he introduced Gary and Jacque to two friends from the planning office, and so they joined them. They were so helpful. Jacque was asking many questions about permits, and if they thought there would be any problem in what they wanted to do.

Gary said we now have to wait. "If the lawyer can get it done earlier, he will let us know. I've the money in the bank in Britain, and so I'm going to contact them as I may transfer the money to a bank in France."

June said the tickets sales were going well for all the upcoming lectures. She told Jacque and Gary that Mary and Bill would be here for Celia's lecture. "We're also getting orders for the book. Jill has been so busy. Before long she may need someone to help her, as I'm so busy with the rentals."

The phone rang and Shirley went to answer it. She was a long time. June said she hoped it was not bad news. Shirley came back into the kitchen. She looked surprised. Gary asked her if it was bad news. She shook her head and smiled broadly. "Not at all. A lady bought one of my sketches at the art show and wanted to know if she could commission me to come and sketch their chateau. They have been looking for someone to sketch it, as they don't want a painting. I've asked for some pictures of the chateau first, and then I'll phone her. So she will be emailing me pictures later today. She was impressed with my attention to detail. The chateau is about two hours away from here. I think I would enjoy the challenge."

They were all thrilled for her. "This is a great honour! I know you can do it," June said.

Gary asked when they wanted her to start, cautioning, "Give yourself plenty of time."

"I'm going to wait to see pictures first and go from there. I'm quite excited. I've never been commissioned to sketch anything."

Within no time the pictures came through on email. Shirley said, "Heavens, who lives in a place like this. It's fantastic." She printed the pictures and took them to show everyone.

Jacque said he recognised the chateau. "I think it belongs to the retired French prime minister. This is a great honour, Shirley."

"Gary, you will definitely have to come with me," Shirley said.

June asked her if she remembered any of the people who bought her sketches at the show, but she couldn't. Shirley then went into the office to make the call, as she wanted to be able to talk in private.

She came back with all the information and arranged a day to go and see the chateau. Jacque knew where it was, and so he explained it to Gary.

"Oh, and I have take a book on the art centre with me as they want to buy one," Shirley added.

Jacque had to go as he was in the middle of a big conversion and he wanted to go and check to see how his workmen were getting on. He had very reliable workmen. They had worked for Jacque for many years. Gary said Jacque had been a great help to him when he was with Luc at the lawyer's. He knows so many people in the area.

Barb and Jill were coming to get the room ready for Celia's lecture, and so it would be a busy day. "We also have to think what comes after the lectures," June said.

Gary suggested that they organise a series of exhibitions starting the week after the lectures finish. "Let's talk it over tomorrow with Jill and Barb. They always have good ideas."

Shirley phoned Heather, as she wanted to tell her about being asked to sketch the chateau, She did not tell her who owned the chateau. Heather was so pleased for her mum. They chatted for quite a while. She promised to let her know what the chateau was like. Heather told her to take plenty of photos. "It sounds amazing," she sighed.

As soon as they arrived, Shirley told Barb and Jill about being commissioned to sketch the chateau. Barb knew straight away who Chateau Frontenac belonged to when she heard the address. "This is so exciting for you. I'm pleased your work is being recognised, and that you're being appreciated for how talented you are."

Gary went across to the office where Barb and Jill were discussing organising exhibitions that would follow straight after the lectures. Between the phone and emails to answer, they were busy all morning in the office.

June was also busy with guests leaving and the next guests arriving. She now had a local lady helping her. Between washing the bedding and towels, not to mention the cleaning, it was too much for one person. Shirley had gone to do some shopping. She loved to go to the fruit and vegetable market. She always came back loaded with fresh produce. The bread was so good. There is nothing like a French market. June said, "We'll be eating well tonight. I hope she goes to the shop that sells the cheese and the stuffed olives. They make them all themselves. The flavours are so good."

It was late when Gary, Jill, and Barb finally closed the office. Shirley arrived back from shopping and was preparing supper. June had gone to have a shower and get ready for supper.

Barb was so pleased the way the tickets were going for all the upcoming lectures. Jill was concentrating on the book sales and updating the website. She was working on a brochure on all the upcoming exhibitions that would go to all the information centres, wineries, hotels and bed and breakfasts in the area. Jill was also contacting all her contacts in Britain. "We want everyone to know about us. Gary is putting some information on the new photography studio. I know it is early days, but we want to wet everyone's appetite."

After Jill left, Gary said, "We're lucky to have Jill. She is so driven and has so many good ideas, and she is so professional in her marketing skills."

John told Shirley he has never seen her so passionate about anything. "She just loves the centre and meeting all the artists."

Shirley and June were so excited to see Mary and Bill. June said she was going to book the spa for them to have some girly time. The spa was part of a hotel and had a very good reputation. Shirley said to book a table for them to have lunch. "I'll speak to Gary and he can do something with Bill that day."

The next few days were busy. Shirley was getting her sketchpad and pencils ready for the meeting at the chateau. Gary was checking that his camera was in tiptop condition with plenty of film. Shirley was wondering what size sketch they were thinking of. She could not wait. Gary thought it would be quite large, but told Shirley to be patient.

Today was the day. Shirley was up and ready early. Gary put everything into the car. June came to wish her luck and enjoy the day. It would take them a while to get there, and so they allowed plenty of time. Shirley did not want to be late.

The scenery was astounding. Gary stopped the car a few times to admire the landscape. He said he would like to come back some time to paint at this location. He took many photos. Shirley was getting impatient, but Gary pointed out they were a bit early and he was killing time. As they drove through the country roads they glimpsed their first view of the chateau. It took Shirley's breath away. "Where do I start? It's quite magnificent. The photos don't do it justice. Could you imagine living in a place like that? Now, Yvette, the owner, said she would meet us at the front entrance."

Gary grinned and said, "I'm so pleased I washed the car."

As soon as Shirley saw Yvette she recognised her. She was a petite, middle-aged lady, beautifully dressed, with silver-white hair. Shirley remembered her from the show as she had the sort of beauty that turned heads. Gary could not take his eyes off her.

Yvette was very friendly and took them on a tour all around the chateau. She wanted Shirley to capture the architectural detail on the front of the chateau. Yvette told Gary and Shirley she wanted the sketch as a gift for her husband. "He has talked about having a sketch done of the chateau for years but never got around to it."

The chateau had been in her husband's family for years. She then went on to say her husband was in hospital after having a stroke a week ago. "We have one son. He also knows how much this would mean to his father."

"I'll do my best to capture all the architectural details you talked about. I have to say this is the most amazing chateau I've ever seen."

Yvette congratulated Shirley and Gary for the work that has gone into creating the art centre. "This area has a wealth of artists, and now they have somewhere to show their work," she said. Shirley said Gary would like to take some photos for her to study first. "If that's all right with you."

"Please feel free to do whatever you require," Yvette said. "My husband is expected to be in the hospital a few weeks, so please feel free to come and spend as much time as you like until he comes home. I do want this to be a complete surprise for him. Please come on to the terrace when you're ready. I have some refreshments being prepared for us. I'll then be leaving for the hospital."

Gary and Shirley carried on taking photos and making notes. "I wonder what size sketch Yvette is thinking about?" Shirley mused. "It needs to be quite large so I can capture all the details."

Yvette also asked Shirley to give her an approximate price. Gary suggested they wait until Shirley knew the size.

They made their way to the terrace. The terrace looked onto manicured gardens. When Yvette saw them coming she called the maid to bring out the refreshments. Shirley whispered to Gary, "This is like living in a fairy tale. They chatted for a while, and then Yvette said she would have to leave. Shirley had all the information she needed today. "I'll study the photos we have taken today, and also the photos you sent me, then I'll be back to start my sketch."

Yvette was so pleased. "I can't wait to tell our son. I know he will be as excited as I am. You can come whenever you want. I've told the gardeners and the house staff about the sketch but they are sworn to secrecy. All our staff has been with us for so many years. They are all like family, and so they know what this means to us."

Before they left Shirley gave Yvette a copy of their book. She also told her about the upcoming lectures she may like to attend.

Gary and Shirley got into the car and headed home. "Wait till we tell June and Jacque about this." Shirley was pleased that Yvette wanted the sketch to be large. "I'm so excited to get started. Can you get the photos developed as soon as possible?"

"Of course," Gary said as he dropped Shirley off at the house. He then went to get the photos developed. June and Jill heard the car. They rushed out. They wanted to know all about her meeting. Shirley could not stop talking about the chateau and could not wait to get started. Shirley had a few reservations about doing the sketch, as this was a long-time wish for Yvette's husband.

"We know they'll not be disappointed," June assured her. "While you're doing the sketch we'll help with the house. To be honest, we should employ a cleaner to help out."

"After thinking about it, I think employing someone to help around the house is a good idea," Shirley said.

"I'll take care of that," Jill said. "Leave it to me. You just have to let me know when you need help."

June suggested each morning Monday to Friday.

"If you need more you can extend the hours," Jill said.

"That sounds good to me," June and Shirley chorused.

June said she would ask Jacque if he knew of anyone who may be interested. "He knows so many people in the area." Jill asked June to phone her later after she had spoken to Jacque.

June and Shirley started preparing supper. "I hope Gary was able to get the photos developed, I can't wait to see them," Shirley said.

June asked if she could come to see the chateau.

"I don't see why not. You could come with me next time I go if you like. Yvette has let everyone who works there know what I'm doing. You'll just love it."

Gary came back as June was setting the table for supper. Jacque was not joining them for supper but would call by later. He had so much going on at the moment, and so he was working around the clock. Gary was able to get the photos of the chateau developed. "We can look at them during supper. We got some very good shots. I think you will be happy with them," he said to Shirley.

They had just finished supper when Jacque arrived. He wanted to hear all about Shirley and Gary's day at Chateau Frontenac. "Come and look at the photos that Gary took. They're very impressive," June said.

Shirley wanted to check if she had everything she needed to make a start on the sketch. "I would like to start doing rough sketches tomorrow while everything is fresh in my mind."

June asked Jacque if he knew anyone that would be interested in helping Shirley with the running of the house. He thought for a moment then said, "I think I have just the person. Leave it with me and I'll let you know. I'm doing a small job for a lady who lives nearby. Her husband passed away a few months ago. She was telling me she needed to get a job to get her out of the house. I'll ask her tomorrow when I go back to finish off the job I'm doing for her."

Shirley was busy getting her studio ready. She put all the photos on the one wall. "Until I started to set it up," she told Gary, "I didn't realise how much I missed my artwork."

"If you need anything, make me a list and I'll go and get it tomorrow. There's an excellent artist shop in High Street."

Next morning Shirley was in her studio bright and early. Everyone worked differently Shirley did many sample sketches. She was happy the way it was coming. The photos were a great help. She worked all day, just coming out for meals. June was in charge of cooking until they got some help in the house.

She was very pleased when Jacque said the lady he spoke about helping out was interested. Shirley had to phone her. She would then come and meet with Shirley. Her name was Annie. "You will both like her. She is a little nervous, as she has not worked for many years. She nursed her husband for four years before he passed away. Her English is very good as her husband was British but had lived in France for many years."

Shirley phoned her straight away and set up a time for her to come and meet June and her. She sounded very nice on the phone, and so June and Shirley looked forward to seeing her.

When Annie arrived, Shirley and June were there to greet her. Shirley had set a tray with pastries and coffee in the kitchen. They took to her straight away. She was a quiet-spoken lady. It did not take her long to warm to Shirley and June. She was amazed with what they had achieved with the old barn. Annie told them she knew the people who lived here before. "If they could only see it now," she exclaimed. Annie lived about fifteen minutes away and was happy to come whenever they needed her.

It was agreed. Annie would work mornings Monday to Friday. She was happy with that. "I'm so pleased Jacque thought of me. That was very kind of him. I've been feeling very lonely lately. This is just what I needed." As she left she was smiling.

June phoned Jill to let her know that they now had employed Annie to help with the running of the house. June told Jill how nice she was and that she would love her. Gary had been busy all day in the office. Jill had the day off. Also, he was still sorting through the boxes with his books in. He could not get over how many books he had. Shirley suggested the ones he did not want they could take to the charity shop. He quickly said, "But I want them all."

Annie arrived next morning as they were having breakfast. Shirley poured her a coffee. They introduced Annie to Gary. They chatted for a while, and then he left as he had so many things to do in the office.

CHAPTER SEVENTEEN

Visit to the Chateau

SHIRLEY ASKED JUNE if she wanted to come with her to the chateau, as she wanted the check a few things out. June could not wait. "I'll make sure Jill and Gary are here to cover for us."

They set off. Shirley had all the sketches she had been working on. "I did call Yvette to let her know we're coming. She may not be there, but I like to let her know."

They arrived. June was speechless. "Wow, this is something else," she finally managed to say.

Shirley set herself up in the grounds in front of the chateau and started to work. June knew not to disturb Shirley when she was sketching, as she liked to be quiet. June had brought a book and found the perfect spot under a tree. 'This is bliss,' she thought to herself.

At lunch time, June went to the car and took out the picnic she had made along with a rug so that Shirley could take a break. They sat and enjoyed their picnic lunch. "This is the perfect setting," June said and then asked if she knew how long Yvette's husband would be in hospital.

"I don't think even Yvette knows that yet," Shirley said.

After lunch Shirley said she wanted to carry on with the sketch. "I still can't believe I've been asked to do this," she said.

June cleared away and put everything back in the car. Just then, she saw a young lady walking towards her. She asked if they would like to come and have tea on the terrace before they left. June could not wait, but she knew she could not disturb Shirley. Eventually, Shirley started packing her things away, and so June told her they had been invited to have tea on the terrace. So off they went. As they walked around the rear of the chateau, June's mouth dropped open.

"Close your mouth, June, and act casual."

The young lady came out. It was the same young lady that Shirley saw before. She brought a pot of tea and a selection of pastries. They were the best that June had ever tasted. Shirley chatted so casually to the young lady. "You know, Shirley, you fit right in here," said June.

Soon it was time to get back in the car and head for home. June said she felt she had been on a mini vacation and thanked Shirley for letting her come along. "You can come next time if you like and then you can meet Yvette. She is a lovely lady and dresses beautifully. I think you would like her."

Annie had settled in so well; they all felt they had known her all their lives. She was always happy and willing to lend a hand to everyone. Jill had taken her under her wing and brought flowers for her one day to say thank-you from everyone.

"Mary and Bill will be arriving tomorrow. Gladys said she would phone us as soon as they arrive," Shirley said. "I'm so looking forward to seeing them and especially spending time with Mary. It's so long since the three of us had a good chat."

Gary came in and said he was going to the lawyer's tomorrow to sign the paperwork on the land. "I need to see Jacque. Let me know as soon as he comes over."

Shirley gave him a hug and kissed him. "I'm so pleased for you, and I love you so much."

After supper Gary wanted to discuss the sketch with her. She refused to show anyone else until it was complete. As Gary looked at the sketch. He did not say a word. He just kept staring at it. Shirley was getting concerned, then he looked at her and said, "This is your best work yet. I'm so proud of you."

They were in the studio until late discussing the finer details. Shirley was not sure about the shading, and so Gary was giving her some advice, but he wanted it all to be her work. "I think I needed to be reassured on a few details, but this is the first and last time you will see it until it is complete."

Gary said he understood. Gary then set off to meet with the lawyer to sign all the paperwork and hand over the money. He had arranged to meet Jacque later to go to the council to apply for the building permit. Jacque had already phoned his friend in the council to give him the heads up that the application form was coming in.

Gladys phoned to say Bill and Mary had arrived and would be over to see them later. There was so much going on as Celia was also coming tomorrow to start getting ready to give her lecture.

Bill and Mary were joining them for supper. June was putting the finishing touches on the table and the food. Gary had got the wine ready. He had Bill's favourite red wine.

Bill and Mary arrived as June was putting the food on the table. "It is so nice to see you all," Mary cried. "First of all, we want to see Shirley's ring." They congratulated Gary and Shirley. Mary loved her ring. "You're one lucky lady," Mary said.

"No," said Gary. "I'm the lucky one."

They chatted all through supper. Bill was anxious for Gary and Jacque to show him the building plans. They went to see the land outside as it was marked out, and then it was over to the office to go through the plans.

Mary, Shirley and June had a good catch-up. Mary told them that Amy and Clive were expecting a baby. They were all so thrilled. "I've never seen Clive so happy," Mary said. "Susan said he has become very domesticated since he has been with Amy. Bill and I are so happy. I can't believe my luck. We have so many friends."

She then showed us some photos of Polly. "I walk with Liz every morning. She has been such a good friend to me. Mary asked Shirley when she and Gary were thinking of getting married.

"We have not given it a thought yet," Shirley said.

Shirley showed Mary the letter they had received from Molly, June said, "I am proud of the way you reacted in the cafe with the ladies from the golf club, Mary."

June told Mary about the sketch Shirley was doing of the chateau. Mary was thrilled for Shirley. Shirley told Mary that she has tickets put aside for them to attend Celia's lecture. "She is so interesting and very talented," Shirley said. "Gladys is coming, too. She went to art college with Celia, but they lost touch. Then she turns up here at the art show. It really is a small world."   By the time Bill had come back with Gary and Jacque. It was getting dark.

"Well, what do you think of our plans?" asked June.

"I think they're amazing. We have had a very long day, and so I think we had better go now," Mary said.

"The next two days will be crazy getting everything ready for the lecture, but then we're going to treat ourselves to a spa treatment followed by lunch," June said.

Gary said to Bill, "I think you're with me that day. Unless you want to go to the spa?" Bill quickly said, "I'll be glad to spend the day with you, Gary."

Bill said they would not see them tomorrow, as they were going to do a bit of sightseeing in the area. "We thought we would check out a couple of wineries," he added.

Annie arrived a little earlier as she knew it was going to get crazy. Jill picked up flowers so she could make everywhere look nice. Celia arrived midmorning. She was organized as to how she wanted to set up for her lecture. She brought plenty of stock, as she had been asked if there would be bags and purses for sale.

Jacque was busy putting signs up, and also making sure there was plenty of seating. This was the first lecture and everyone wanted it to be a success. Eric phoned from the college to see if they needed any help on the day as his students would love to come and help. Gary said they would welcome some help with the parking. "If you don't have someone showing everyone where to park, they park all over the place."

Eric phoned back to say he had six students coming to help. "If you need more, please let me know. I'm coming to the lecture along with some of the teachers." Gary told Eric he would like to show him the building plan that had gone in for permit. Eric said he would love to see them when he had time.

Barb was helping Celia with her display. Celia was feeling a bit nervous. Barb was reassuring her, as her display looked beautiful. Celia was telling Barb she had received so many orders since the art show. Money had been a worry for Celia, but things were on the up and up now.

Gary came around at the end of the day to make sure everyone was ready. He came over to Celia and congratulated her on all the work she had put into her display. She told Gary how helpful Barb had been to her.

Annie was going about her normal routine while they were having breakfast, and then she asked if she would be able to attend Celia's lecture. Shirley said, "Yes, you can come and sit with me. June and Jill do the refreshments, so they will be busy."

The lecture was due to start at 2:00. By noon the students arrived, getting ready to help in the parking lot. In no time, cars started to arrive. Celia was putting the final touches to her stand. She looked lovely in her flowing pink and orange skirt and large silver hoops earrings.

By 2:00 the centre was full. Every seat was taken. Bill, Mary and Gladys had arrived together. Gary and Shirley got up and welcomed everyone. Gary went on to say this was the first of many lectures. He encouraged everyone to take a list of upcoming events at the end of the lecture. Shirley then spoke about Celia and gave a short biography. She then introduced Celia.

The lecture could not have gone better. Although Celia was nervous to begin with, as soon as she got into her stride she was great. At the end, she opened the room up for questions. Everyone was so interested and the questions came one on top the other.

Gary and Shirley came across to thank her for a very interesting lecture. Shirley told everyone that Celia was selling her bags and purses. "So please feel free to come and chat to Celia," she added. They also announced that refreshments were now available.

Mary and Bill went across to meet Celia and to say how much they had enjoyed her lecture. Bill congratulated her on the quality of her work. He went on to say he had a shop in Clifton on the south coast in Britain and would like to discuss selling her bags and purses.

"Are you busy right now? We're staying in the area, and so could we meet either later today. Or would tomorrow be better for you?" Bill asked.

Celia suggested he come back later when it was less busy, "Then we'll have more time to talk." They went off to get some refreshments.

June and Jill were so pleased that Annie was helping. Annie was having a ball. She loved dealing with the people. She was an asset as she was from the area and recognised many of the people there.

Jacque came in for a cup of tea and was surprised to find that Annie served him. She thanked Jacque so much for getting her this job. He said, "I only gave Shirley your name. You did the rest. I'm pleased you're enjoying working here."

June took some refreshments across for Celia. She was still busy with people. Gladys was also helping Celia with her sales. She was nearly sold out. Mary had bought two bags. She just loved them.

Gary went over to talk to Shirley. "If all the lectures are as busy as this we'll need to get more help. We're running around like headless chickens."

"I agree, let's discuss it later."

Bill met with Celia later to work out an order. He told Celia about his shop in Clifton. He explained that most of his customers were seasonal, but he still had a good local following. Mary helped him with the order, as she would know more about what people would like to buy. Celia arranged to ship the order to Bill. Mary also asked if Celia could include some brochures about herself, as her method in making the bags was so interesting. Celia agreed. She said she had been thinking about a brochure for some time. "This has given me the push I needed," she said.

It was quite late by the time everyone left. It always took a while to clear away. Gary said to June and Jacque that they needed to sit down before the next lecture to discuss getting more staff. June said, "Without Annie's help with serving the refreshments, Jill and I would have been in trouble. Everyone comes at the same time."

Jacque could not praise the students enough. They were great. "We'll get them to come next time to help with the parking. They even helped me take down the signs and put them away."

Shirley and June were looking forward to their girls' day out at the spa with Mary. Gary was also looking forward to spending the day with Bill. Shirley asked what they were going to do. "First," Gary said. "He wants to see the plans for the new building, and then we're going to take in a couple of wineries in the area. You don't have to worry about us. You girls can enjoy yourselves at the spa and whatever else you have in mind."

Bill and Mary arrived in plenty of time. She was anxious for her girls' day out. Mary was still saying how much they had enjoyed Celia's lecture and how talented she was. Annie asked them if they wanted a coffee, as Shirley and June were still getting ready. "That sounds like a good idea," June said, and Shirley agreed.

They arrived at the spa. It was set in the most beautiful grounds. "It reminds me of a medieval castle," Mary said. "Everywhere in France is like out of a fairy tale." As they entered the reception, a young lady came to escort them to the spa.

The smell that was wafting from the spa was intoxicating. First they were taken into a room and given white gowns to put on, and then they were told to come into the lounge area where their masseuse would be waiting for them.

They entered the lounge to find three, beautiful young ladies waiting for them. They introduced themselves and explained what treatment they would be having today. "You will be starting with a massage, followed by a warm, towel-wrap to relax. Then a facial. That will be followed by a light lunch on the terrace overlooking the rose garden. After lunch, you will be having a manicure and then you will finish up with a pedicure."

They all went off in different rooms. "We'll meet up again on the terrace," said Shirley.

By the time they were on the terrace they were so relaxed. Mary said she felt like a film star. "This is the best experience in a spa I've ever had!"

June said, "That warm towel-wrap was so good I nearly fell asleep."

Shirley agreed.

The terrace overlooked the rose garden where the gardeners were tending the roses. There were arches covered with yellow roses cascading over one another. In the distance the lavender fields swayed in the gentle breeze.

Lunch was beautiful served with a selection of herbal teas, fruit drinks, fruit, and delicate pastries. "Now, all we have to do is decide what colour to have our nails painted," Shirley said.

There were other small groups of ladies spoiling themselves, giving the place had a festive atmosphere.

"June, now tell me all about Jacque. Are you going to surprise us all and marry first?" Mary asked.

June looked a bit sheepish. "I don't know what you mean. Jacque and I are very good friends, but I do have to say I couldn't imagine not having him around. I feel I can talk about anything and every-thing with him."

Shirley said, "Well, you know what they say: you have to watch the quiet ones."

"Now, that's enough about me," June said, changing the subject. "Shirley, when are you and Gary getting married? Have you decided yet?"

"No, we have not decided yet, but when we do I'll let you both know first."

It was soon time to go and get their manicure and pedicure. Another young lady came to see if they were ready, and so off they went. The room had luxurious seats that they just fell into. Soft music played; they could not help feeling relaxed.

When they had finished, Shirley went to pay the bill. She said this in on *Petit Bijou*. "We deserve it. They were all given a gift. It was a silk pouch with samples of all the creams and lotions they had used on them. They were thrilled, as it had been a memorable experience. Shirley left a few of her brochures, which they were pleased to display.

They went for a stroll through the rose garden before we finally left. Next stop was to do a bit of shopping. They never had time to shop as they were always rushing to get back. There were many small, individual shops that they all loved. One always found the neatest things in these shops.

Shirley had booked them a table at the hotel to end the perfect day. They had talked and talked all day, and so they were ready for a nice meal and a bottle of wine. The meal was just perfect, but now it was time to head for home.

They arrived back. Jacque, Gary and Bill had also been out for supper and by the look of them, more than one bottle of wine had been consumed. June said she would make them all coffee and then promised to tell them all about their day.

Bill said he loved the plans. Jacque and Gary had done a great job of planning it all out, he said. "We went to two magnificent wineries. The architectural design was incredible. I've been taking photos all day," he told Mary.

Mary then went on to talk about the spa they went to. "I've been to many spas before, but this one was outstanding. We were made to feel like film stars. And just take a look at our manicures and pedicures."

June said, "We were even wrapped in warm towels to help us relax."

Jill had been working all day in the office. "We have had good feedback from the first lecture," she said. "The reporter from the local paper came back to check that he had all his information correct as he has an article going in this week's paper."

As they drank their coffee, they all agreed it was the end of a perfect day.

Gary had a message come through on his computer telling him of an exhibition that was being held at one of the large art galleries in Paris. It was an exhibition of the great artists of France. As he was reading it he thought that Shirley may like to go with him.

After breakfast he asked Shirley to come to the office as he had something to show her. As he read it out, he asked Shirley if she would like to take a trip to Paris to see the exhibition. "I think it would be great exposure for what we're doing, but mainly it's a wonderful opportunity for us."

She thought for a moment, and then said, "Why not? We're always working, and it would be nice for us to get away together. I've always wanted to visit Paris. It's one of the most romantic cities in the world. I'll speak to June just to make sure she has plenty of help while we're away. I feel giddy with excitement. Me going to Paris? Can you believe it?"

Gary held her in his arms and said, "I want to show you the world if I can."

"Well, let's just start with Paris."

June was thrilled for her. "We have to work out when you will be going. As long as we're all here for the lectures that are booked, it's no problem." They got the calendar out and a date was set. Gary said he would work on getting the trip organised.

Gary received a message about the permits he had applied for. There were a few questions that needed a bit more clarification. Gary phoned Jacque to see if he was available to be at the meeting with him. Jacque said he would meet him there, as he was just finishing up a meeting with his builders.

They went into the planning office, hoping it was going to be good news. The meeting went very well. Gary was given a form to fill in. It turned out he could get another small grant for the photography studio but not for the letting accommodation. "The next council meeting is the following week. Now, as long as we have no objections from anyone your permits will be passed," the secretary said.

Jacque and Gary both said they would be attending the meeting. "If there are any questions or concerns we can address them immediately," Gary said.

Driving home, Gary said he could not wait to get started. "I'm getting impatient now. I would like the studio to be built first."

Jacque said that would work. Gary then told Jacque about the Paris trip with Shirley. "I have to finalize all the travel details now."

Bill and Mary were at the house when they got back. Shirley could not stop talking about her Paris trip. Mary said, "It sounds so romantic. I've always wanted to go to Paris."

She looked at Bill. He chuckled. "That's a subtle hint if ever I heard one. I'll make a note."

Bill and Mary were driving home tomorrow, and so they were all going out for a meal to on their last evening. "It has been a wonderful trip. We have so enjoyed it, meeting new people and of course catching up on all your news," Mary told Jacque and Gary. "You know you're all welcome to come a stay with us in Clifton. We would love to have you."

Jacque said he had never been to Britain. This coming from Jacque, who said little, surprised them all. June said, "Well, what about a short trip then?"

"Sounds good to me," said Jacque.

June looked at Mary and said, "Leave this with me, and I'll let you know when we're coming." She smiled at Jacque. "If Gary and Shirley are going to Paris, I think we deserve a trip as well."

Bill and Mary went back to the hotel to finish their packing, as they were making an early start in the morning. They agreed to meet for supper at 6:00 at a small restaurant they had been recommended. Gary was busy getting the Paris trip planned. He wanted to purchase tickets to the art gallery ahead of time.

He booked a small hotel in Paris in a good location for sightseeing. He wanted this to be a memorable trip for Shirley. He was all afternoon in the office doing it. Eventuality he came out and said it was all booked.

The restaurant did not disappoint. "Why does everything taste and sound romantic in France?" Mary said to her friends. "We have so enjoyed our holiday. We're so pleased you came to live in France."

"You do know we'll be back," said Bill.

Gary was not saying much about the trip to Paris, only that it was all arranged. "I'm sure Shirley will be out shopping before we go. She always says she has nothing to wear."

"Well, if you insist. June you will have to come and help me."

Bill and Mary did not come back for coffee as they wanted an early night. Because of the early crossing they wanted to allow plenty of time to get to the dock. They promised to phone as soon as they got home. June said she would let them know when her and George were coming for a visit.

Next morning Jacque came by to say he had been to get the forms for his passport. June could not believe it as he had never been anywhere. He had not travelled in France, never mind to Britain. She thought it was wonderful to see him so interested. He even went to the library and got some travel books.

Shirley was laughing to herself as she smiled at Gary. "I think he thinks he is off around the world. He was telling Annie all about it as soon as she came in. He is so excited." Shirley added that she would be in her studio most of the day working on her sketch."

June told Annie if she needed anything she was not to disturb Shirley but to ask her. Annie was a delight to have around. She was always singing to herself. They had seen a big change in her since she started working. It got her out of the house, and gave her purpose, they agreed.

Barb was starting to prepare, for she was doing the next lecture on her stained glass. She had been busy at home making stained-glass window panels, as they were the most popular. She was also working on smaller items and making samples showing the different stages up to completion.

Gary was telling Jill and Barb all about the trip to Paris. Barb knew one of the artists who had his work in the exhibition. She was very jealous, as she knew he did not do many exhibitions. "I'll want to know all about it when you get back."

Gary said they were going after her lecture. "It is very important that we're all here when we put the lectures on," he said.

Gary asked Jill and Barb to put some thought into getting more people to help when they had lectures or future exhibitions. "We should have a meeting later in the week to discuss it," he suggested.

Jill agreed. She said, "If we did not have Annie to help us last time, June and I would have struggled."

The rest of the week was busy, with everyone catching up. June's holiday lets were going very well, but keeping her very busy. Now that she had help with the changeover of guests and general cleaning it went much more smoothly. And she was now all up to date with her paperwork.

The council sent Gary a message about the council meeting that would be discussing the permits. Gary replied and said they would be attending the meeting. Jacque rearranged his work schedule to be at the meeting with Gary.

Finally, the day of the meeting. Gary and Jacque looked so smart in their suit and ties. June and Shirley hardly recognised them. "We want to make the best impression we can," said Gary.

After arriving at the council offices, they went into the correct room. They were number nine on the agenda list. Jacque said, "We could be here quite a while, so make yourself comfortable."

To their surprise, it did not take long. They were next. The gentleman read out all the permit details. They talked about it between the councillors, and then they voted. There were no objections. They did say that they would have to wait to see if they would get the small grant.

"But we got all the permits we asked for, and so we could now go ahead with the building," Gary reported later.

They knew Jacque, and so they knew he understood the rules with getting the inspector out at certain stages of the build. Gary phoned Shirley as soon as they got outside to tell her the good news. She would tell June.

CHAPTER EIGHTEEN

Trip to Paris

Bill and Mary arrived back in Clifton after a wonderful holiday. Mary was very anxious to go and pick Polly up from Liz. She told Bill she really had missed her. He also had missed her. She was so much part of their family now.

Mary so enjoyed her life in Clifton. Liz had been a great help to her. They enjoyed doing so much together. Apart from walking the dogs every morning they had also joined the church, which opened up so many doors.

Once a month they helped with arranging the flowers in the church, which had got them involved with doing weddings and various other events. Bill had been a member of the gardening club in Clifton for many years now. Mary and Liz were also members. Liz's husband Fred was not really interested in joining. He said it was not his thing, but he told Liz to go with Mary and enjoy herself.

Bill's order from Celia arrived, and so Mary went down to the shop to help him check it all and do a display of the bags and purses. Celia had also sent some very nice brochures packed with information on her work.

Mary arranged a display in the shop window. By the end of the day Bill had sold quite a few, and so decided to phone Celia for a second order. They were so unique. Mary phoned Liz to come and see them before they sold out.

Susan was a regular visitor with Emma. Bill had built the most amazing house for her in the garden, and also a swing. He just loved to see them coming to visit. Clive and Amy were so happy together and were about to become parents.

Back in France the tickets were selling very well for Barb's lecture on stained glass. *Petit Bijou* was going from strength to strength. They had extra help this time, so that things would run more smoothly. Also Annie wanted to help Jill and June with the refreshments.

Gary and Jacque were very busy getting everything set up so the construction could get started. Gary went along to the college to meet with the tutor of the photography class. He wanted the students to be as involved as much as they wanted, and so a meeting with the students was set up.

At the meeting the students were so interested. Gary took the plans along, as he wanted their suggestions. They had some very good ideas as to what the would need. Gary told them this photography studio was for their use; he wanted to encourage them as much as possible.

"I'll be keeping you all informed as the construction commences, and you will all be encouraged to come to site. I'll have hard hats for you to use. I cannot stress enough that this is for your use. We want it to help in your education."

Eric came in to thank Gary for what he was doing for the students. "I know they all appreciate so much," he said. As he left, he told them not to forget the upcoming lecture.

As Gary arrived home he was pleasantly surprised to see Jacque with the architect, pegging out the studio. "He said the digger will be breaking ground tomorrow, so get your camera ready," Jacque said.

"I'll go and tell Shirley and June the good news," Gary replied

"This is so exciting," said Shirley. "Not only are you starting the studio, but you're starting our new home. I just can't wait. I'll phone Heather and Alex tonight as they want to be kept up to date with the progress."

Gary asked Shirley if she had all her shopping done for the trip to Paris. "I have a few things, but I need one more outfit. You know what they say: when in Paris you have to fit in."

"Well, don't leave it until the last minute. You know you don't like rushing."

Shirley laughed. "I think you know me better that I know myself."

June told Jill, as she was still in the office that they were breaking ground and to make sure she told John. "If he has time, I know Shirley would love to see him here. We'll both be here taking photos."

When June, Shirley, and Gary were having supper, Shirley said she found Heather very pre-occupied. "I hope there's nothing wrong. Gary told her not to worry."

"I'm sure you just caught her at a bad time," Gary said.

June agreed. "If there were a problem, she would have told you. She tells you everything. Now, we have to go and get your last items for your trip. It all has to be done before the lecture."

Gary agreed as we left the next day. They decided to go the next day, as soon as they had seen the start of the studio.

Next day was crazy. Annie was as busy as always. She just got on with things as soon as she arrived. Jill and John arrived then Barb, Tom, and his son Michael arrived. Michael was thrilled to see the big digger arrive. He went out with Gary and never left his side.

It was exciting for everyone, given they had been talking about it for so long and now it really was happening. As soon as the ground was broken, June left with Shirley to finish off her shopping. Gary told them again: "Don't come back until you have finished."

The rest of the day was nonstop. Workmen arrived. Jacque had it all under control. He was so organised and professional.

Later in the day all sorts of building material arrived. Little Michael, complete with his own hard hat, was in the thick of it all day and loving every minute of it. Tom had to leave, but there was no way Michael would leave, and so Gary said he would take him home later.

By the time Shirley and June arrived home it really did look like a building site. Gary could see lots of bags. "So I guess you have finished shopping."

June said, "We have it all and more than she needed."

Gary said he was going to take Michael home and would be back later. Michael looked exhausted and covered in mud. "Hmm, I hope your mother won't be upset with us," Gary joked.

Michael was nearly asleep by the time they arrived at his house. Barb came out to get him. He was telling her all about his day. He was so proud to have his own hard hat. "Gary said I got to wear it every time I go to the building site. Safety doesn't take a holiday," he said sagely.

That evening over supper Jacque and Gary planned out what was going to happen tomorrow in the building department. Shirley and June checked that they would be ready for Barb's lecture. They did learn a lot from the first lecture. The main thing was they did not have enough helpers, and so this time they were more prepared.

Jacque said he had spoken to the same group of students that helped with the parking; they were happy to come again. The young people were a breath of fresh air, they all agreed. Nothing was too much trouble for them, and they were so helpful with the public.

Gary asked Shirley if they were going to have a fashion show to see all her new clothes she had bought for the trip.

"No, Gary. It's a surprise for our trip!" Shirley said.

June said he would not be disappointed. "So wait until you're in Paris."

"Now I'm intrigued," said Gary as he smiled at Shirley.

The workers were on site early. "I think we'll have to get used to this," said Annie. It was only a few days until Barb's lecture so work was underway to set the room up. Barb was getting her area organized. She needed more room than Celia did, as some of her stained-glass pieces were large.

Barb had attended the stained glass evening classes at the community centre. So many of them were coming to support her lecture. She was looking forward to showing them around after the lecture had finished. Tom was a great support for her and, of course, Michael would be coming.

Barb said, "Don't be surprised if he turns up complete with a hard hat. He never takes it off." They all loved Michael. He was always so happy.

Jill was doing the flowers and making sure they had everything ordered for the refreshments. Jill, June, and Annie had become a great team. Jacque was always checking that Annie was all right. He could not believe the change in her since she had started work here.

Shirley and Gary had to make sure their cases were packed the day before the lecture as they were catching the early train to Paris the day after the lecture. Gary said he needed to go out for a while but would not be long. Shirley asked if he would like her to go with him. He quickly said, "No, you stay here. I won't be long."

The night before the lecture everything was ready. The room looked amazing, as always. Jill had outdone herself with the flowers. The colours complemented the stained glass display that Barb had done. This was Barb's first lecture, and so she was a little nervous. Tom was great, and reassured her that all would go well.

The lecture went great, with not a hiccup. It was so much better with extra help on hand. Barb had nothing to worry about. She was so professional. Every seat was taken in the room. Tom was helping her with her sales afterwards. Everyone wanted to chat to her. Michael was with June helping, or eating the refreshments, no one was sure which. Annie had taken quite a shine to Michael and Michael to her.

Shirley and Gary greeted people when they arrived and thanked them when they left. The feedback was encouraging. Gary was telling everyone about the new photography studio that was being built.

The next lecture was to be on the quilts, the ones with a story behind every one. Jill had made posters that had been put up on the notice board and around the room. They were already selling tickets. "I think it is going to be another popular lecture," Jill mused.

By the time everyone had left it was late. Shirley said she must get to bed or she would not be ready for morning. Everyone was wishing her and Gary a good trip and could not wait to hear all about it on their return.

Gary had arranged a taxi to pick them up to take them to the train station. Shirley was ready in good time. June was there to see them off and wished them a great time.

The train journey was very pleasant. It had been a time since Shirley had travelled by train. The scenery was very enjoyable. They went through villages after village. Gary said he forgot how relaxing it was not to be driving. The train got busier the nearer to Paris they got. Shirley was so excited. "I hope we have time to do some sightseeing. I don't want to miss a thing."

"Don't worry, we have plenty of time. The hotel we're staying in is very central. When we get there we'll check into the hotel then do some exploring and have a meal," Gary said.

The train's loud speaker blared out that Paris was the next stop and to make sure to take all luggage as they disembarked. The platform was packed with people rushing to catch trains. The atmosphere was infectious.

Shirley was hanging onto Gary so as not to get lost. "As soon as we get outside we'll get a taxi which will take us to our hotel," Gary assured her.

There were plenty of taxies and everyone was so helpful. They got into the taxi and Gary gave the address of the hotel to the driver. Within no time they were outside the hotel. Shirley said, "I thought you said a small hotel. This looks large to me." The foyer of the hotel was so luxurious. The furniture and drapes were so elegant. A porter came over to them and took them up to their room. "I feel very important," said Shirley. "I'm so pleased I bought all new clothes."

The porter flung open the door to their room. It was like an apartment with a bedroom, a lounge, and with the most luxurious bathroom Shirley had ever seen.

When the porter left, Gary asked cheekily, "Well, do you like it? Is it up to your standard?"

"Gary, this is amazing. I've never in my life stayed in a place like this. Come to think of it, I've never seen a suite like this. I've only read about them in magazines."

He held her in his arms and kissed her like she had never been kissed before. "I want you to remember this trip for the rest of your life."

"I will," said Shirley.

"I thought we would freshen up, and then start exploring. I'll make us coffee while you relax and unpack first."

Shirley came out of the bathroom, exclaiming: "We even have matching bathrobes and slippers."

Their first evening in Paris was just magical. They found a small restaurant. It was full of charm and atmosphere. "This is exactly how I imagined Paris would be," said Shirley. "Just wait till I tell June about this." After supper they walked some more, then decided to make their way back to the hotel and have a nightcap to end the day.

Gary had ordered breakfast in the room the next morning. They were enjoying the fresh croissants with a selection of jams and fresh fruit with coffee when there was a knock on the door. Gary asked Shirley if she could answer it.

She opened the door. In came John, Alex, and Heather. "What on earth are you all doing here?"

Gary came over to Shirley. "Well, you agreed to marry me, and so I thought, what about getting married in Paris? It is the most romantic city in the world, and I wanted to make it special for you."

Heather said, "Well, we're waiting. Mum, what do you say? We're staying in the hotel."

"But I have to say our rooms are not like this one," Alex put in.

Shirley hugged them all. "So, what have you all planned?" she asked.

Heather told her she had flowers arriving later, and that Gary has done the rest.

John could not believe he managed to pull it off. "I think we all need some fresh coffee and then we should go over the day."

Gary phoned and requested coffee for five in their room. As the coffee arrived, Gary started to tell everyone the day's plan. "We're getting married at noon in the hotel, and then we'll have a light lunch. After lunch, I'm sure Shirley will want to phone June and Mary. I've booked us a dinner cruise on the River Seine later."

Heather said, "I don't know about you, Mum, but I can't wait for the day to begin."

Shirley asked Gary if he had a ring. "Yes, I have a ring. That was what I was picking up the other day when I said you couldn't come with me."

Shirley then looked at Heather. "And to think I was worried about you as you seemed so off hand with me on the phone the last time I spoke to you. When did you all arrive?"

"John arrived just before you did, but Alex and I arrived earlier. We had an early flight."

Heather then wanted to know what her Mum was going to wear.

"Well, I thought we were going to a very important dinner with an artist friend of Gary's, and so I did buy a nice outfit that will be perfect."

Gary kissed her. "The flowers I ordered for you is a small bouquet of cream roses, as I thought they would go with whatever you're wearing."

"Oh, Gary, you really have blown me away," Shirley cried. "I can see you're not to be underestimated. Well, we had better get moving."

At that, Alex, John and Heather left to go and get themselves ready.

"The bouquet will be delivered at eleven thirty, so you have nothing to worry about," Gary assured Shirley.

By the time the flowers arrived Shirley and Gary were both ready. Shirley's blush-coloured dress with a light jacket matched the cream roses perfectly.

Gary told Shirley she looked beautiful.

"Well, you don't look so bad yourself," she said and looped her arm in his.

They walked into the lounge and found John, Alex and Heather waiting for them. Alex was first to say how beautiful Shirley looked, followed by John and Heather. Gary also complimented Heather. She looked stunning and the boys so handsome.

The small service was perfect. Soft music played the whole way through the ceremony. The hotel did am amazing job. Nothing was left out. After the service they took photos, and then made their way into the restaurant where they were given the best table. The decor was stunning. Heather was in awe of it. She snapped photos of everything.

Gary ordered champagne and toasted his new bride. He also thanked John, Alex and Heather for helping pull this off. Shirley asked John if Jill knew about all this. "Of course she did but was sworn to secrecy. She wanted to tell June so badly but didn't."

The meal did not disappoint. It was not too heavy as they were going on the river cruise later. They drank and chatted. It had been so long since they were able to do this. Alex brought them all up to date about the children. He did seem happier than the last time Shirley saw him.

Shirley said she wanted to freshen up and to phone June and Mary. John said he wanted to phone Jill. "She will want to know how it all went."

They then all agreed to meet in the foyer of the hotel when everyone was ready.

Shirley phoned June to tell her first. She was so surprised she started to cry with emotion. She was so happy for them both. "Wait till I tell Jacque!" June then told her to enjoy the river cruise and she sent both of them her love.

Next she phoned Mary. She also started to cry. "Gary has set the bar very high. I don't think Bill or Jacque can top that." Mary added that they were the perfect couple. That made Shirley so happy.

They met in the foyer before setting off, as planned. Gary suggested they get a taxi to take them to board the river cruise. The taxi took them through Paris to see some of the sights. They then went for a walk along the river to take in more of the sights before it was time to get on the boat.

The river cruise was out of this world. Heather and Shirley were busy taking photos and the guys were getting on so well. Gary had no family, and so it was nice that the boys were becoming his friends. During the cruise they went into the dining room and had a champagne supper.

"This is so romantic," Heather sighed.

John said, "Jill would love to do this. Gary, you have thought of everything."

Alex told his mother: "Gary is a keeper, and so look after him."

Shirley replied that she intended to look after him very well indeed. "He is so good to me."

The evening was the end of a perfect day. Cruising down the River Seine, drinking champagne. "This has been the kind of day that you read about but don't ever think will happen to you," said Shirley.

Alex and Heather had their flight booked for lunchtime the next day and John's flight was mid-afternoon. Gary and Shirley were going to the art exhibition. Also they wanted to visit a couple of art galleries while in Paris.

Back at the hotel they had a nightcap and agreed to meet for breakfast in the morning. Gary and Shirley thanked them all for making the journey and making the day so perfect. "It would not have been the same without you three," she added.

Shirley and Gary spent the night in one another's arms. Shirley said she had never felt more loved. Gary told her he loved her so much, and they would now start the rest of their lives together. They promised one another they would have no secrets and to talk openly to one another about everything and anything always.

They all had breakfast. Gary and Shirley were leaving first as they wanted to get to the exhibition, and it would take them a while to get there. Heather said she would phone her mum next week. "And, Mum, remember one thing: be happy." She hugged her, and then she hugged Gary.

John and Alex shook Gary's hand and said, "Welcome to the family." And then they hugged their mum and told her that they loved her very much.

The exhibition was inspiring. Gary was in awe of the artwork on display. Shirley had never been to a big exhibition like this. She made notes and was mesmerized by some of the attention to detail. She could not get enough of one painting in particular. Gary came over to her and asked her if she was going to stare at the painting all day. "It is so breathtaking," Shirley said. "The more you look at it the more you see."

As they were leaving the exhibition, Gary recognised a man standing by the door. He introduced himself to the man, who by now was looking very closely at Gary. It suddenly came to him who he was. "Stuart, I haven't seen you since we left university."

Stuart now realized who Gary was and shook his hand and said, "How nice it is to see you."

Gary introduced Shirley to Stuart. It seemed strange to be introduced as Gary's wife. Gary asked Stuart what he was doing in Paris. "I've lived and worked in Paris for many years. I help in putting these exhibitions together. I have my own work on display at another gallery."

Stuart asked how long they were staying in Paris, as he would like to meet up for lunch if they had time. "I would like to take you to my gallery to see my work."

Gary said they would love to do that. "We're here for a few days as this is our honeymoon. We got married yesterday."

Stuart grinned and congratulated them both. He then gave them the address of the gallery that was showing his work and they agreed to all meet up tomorrow. "I'll arrange for someone to cover for me here tomorrow so we can spend some time catching up," Stuart promised.

The rest of the day was spent sightseeing around the city. There was so much to see. They went to see the Eiffel Tower. It was such a thrill. Shirley said she never thought she would be standing by the Eiffel Tower, especially with a new husband. Gary just squeezed her hand lovingly. "I feel the same. We're so lucky, don't you think?"

As they sat drinking coffee at one of the many street cafes, Shirley said she could sit here all day. "I just love people watching. They are so interesting."

By the time they got back to their hotel they were both exhausted. Gary was telling Shirley about Stuart. "He was always a bit of a loner but a great guy and a very good artist. I'm not surprised he has ended up in Paris helping to organise big art exhibitions."

They met up with Stuart the following day at the gallery that was showing his work. It was a larger gallery than what they expected. Everyone that was coming into the gallery was excited that Stuart was there. He left Gary and Shirley to look around, as he was busy answering questions from customers.

They were very impressed with his artwork. One section Shirley was particularly interested in was his sketch work. They were still looking at his sketching when Stuart caught up with them. Gary told Stuart about Shirley's work, and she went on to tell him about the chateau she had been commissioned sketch.

Stuart took them to lunch. There Gary told Stuart all about their art centre. He was very interested. To their surprise, he wanted to come and visit it. Also he wanted to know all about the chateau that Shirley was sketching. Stuart was very well known in the Paris art world. People often came up to him to shake his hand.

Before they finished lunch, Shirley gave Stuart information on the art centre and told him to phone and let them know when he wanted to come and visit. "I'll phone you in a week's time to time and arrange a visit. I want to see this Chateau Frontenac you're sketching. I'm most intrigued."

Gary shook his hand and said, "It has been a pleasure meeting up again. We look forward to hearing from you again."

The rest of the time in Paris was spent sightseeing and just enjoying one another's company. On their last evening they went on a horse-drawn carriage ride. There was a chill in the air, but they were given a warm blanket, and so they were like two toasties.

They just had time for breakfast before catching the train to take them home. Shirley hugged Gary and told him this had been the most romantic trip she had ever had. She could not believe he had organized everything from start to finish.

He looked at Shirley and said he loved her so much and that they now had a new life together to look forward to.

On the train journey home, Gary wondered how the building was going. "I hope Jacque has been able to get on with it."

It was so relaxing travelling on the train. Shirley loved it. When they arrived home, June was so excited to see them and wanted to know all about the trip from start to finish. Jacque congratulated them both and told Gary he was a dark horse. "How did you manage to keep the wedding a secret from all of us?"

June said, "Jill was busting to tell me, but she promised John she would not say a word."

June added that she had arranged a celebration in the art centre as they missed the wedding.

"That is so nice of you," Shirley said. "But I hope you have not gone to too much trouble. June said it was no trouble at all as she winked at Gary.

Jacque was anxious to show Gary how the building was coming on. When he looked at what Jacque had managed to accomplish he was amazed. "My men have really worked hard while you were away to get to this stage. We'll be having the roof trusses that are to delivered next week, and so we have still got quite a lot to do before then."

Shirley and June were busy catching up. Shirley said she would be getting all Gary's clothes out of the *gite* he had been staying in and into the house. "I'm so looking forward to us having our own place above the photography studio and, just think, you will have the house all to yourself, June."

It was so lovely for the four of them to have supper together. Shirley warned she would be a Paris bore. "I loved it so much. I still can't believe all the things we did. The river cruise down the Seine, the Eiffel Tower, and the horse-drawn carriage ride. I'll never forget any of it."

CHAPTER NINETEEN

Stuart Comes to Visit

JUNE HAD THE celebration all organised with the help of Jill and Annie. Jill and Barb had decorated the art centre, and it looked magical. Shirley had no idea what they had done as she was not allowed to go near the art centre.

On the day of the celebration everyone was there. Caterers took care of the buffet and served drinks. When Shirley and Gary arrived, they could not believe what they had done with the art centre.

Hundreds of tiny lights glittered all around the room. The flowers were all in shades of lemon and white. Soft jazz played.

Then the surprise guests started to arrive. Bill and Mary came with Gladys and Frank, followed by Heather, Jenny, and Dave. Eric came from the college with a group of students. The owners of the winery that Gary and Shirley went on their first dinner out together came. Even Celia came to wish them well.

The children, Michael and Jenny played all afternoon. They were so pleased to see one another. Many neighbours from the area came to congratulate Gary and Shirley. Everything went according to plan. The food was delicious and there were plenty of drinks for everyone.

Shirley was thrilled to see Jenny and, of course, to have Mary and Bill make the journey as they had only just gone back. They got a flight and had to leave tomorrow as Bill was busy at the shop, but he would not have missed this day, that was for certain.

Heather, Dave, and Jenny were staying for a few days before they drove back. John did a toast to the happy couple and again welcomed Gary to the family. Gary then spoke to thank everyone for coming and, of course, for everyone helping June to pull this off.

Shirley enjoyed spending some time with Jenny and Heather. Dave was very interested in the new photography studio. He spent most of his time with Gary and Jacque. He loved design and construction.

Annie took to Jenny straightaway. She followed Annie everywhere and wanted to help. Annie said she would have to give her half of her wages at this rate. Jill was busy as they had another lecture coming up. This time it was on the quilts. Again tickets were going well.

They had quite a few groups of ladies coming from different villages around the area. What interested them was that there was a story behind every quilt. Jill had put a write-up in the local paper, which turned out to be very successful.

Dave, Heather, and Jenny went off on their own the next day, and so Shirley went into her studio to work on her sketch. She phoned Yvette to see how she was and to see if they had any idea when her husband would be home. Yvette said her husband was not progressing as well as they had hoped, and so she still no idea when he would be home.

Shirley was very happy the way the sketch was progressing, but she realized she wanted to go back and check out a few details. She knew June would love to come to see the chateau again, so as soon as Heather and the family left, they would take a trip to the chateau.

Gary and Jacque were busy over at the construction site. It was coming on so well. They were just starting on the roof. It looked huge. Gary was going over the final plans on their living accommodation with Shirley when Heather when the family came back.

Dave was so interested in looking at the plans. "I think we should build a new house. Heather, what do you think?"

"I've never given it a thought. We have lived in our house all our married life. I think I would be sad to leave it."

Dave asked her to give it some thought. "We could look for a parcel of land to see if it is possible."

Heather and Dave had the car packed up and ready to start the journey home. Jenny started to cry, as she wanted to stay. They promised her they would come back when her Nan and Gary were ready to move into their new home. She was happy with that. Annie and everyone was out to wave them off. Heather said she would phone as soon as they arrived home.

The lecture was only a few days away, and so it was busy. Jill had local people coming to pick up their tickets. Jo and Sally were the two ladies that did the quilts. They were arriving the next day. June had their accommodation ready for them, as they wanted to stay three nights. It took quite a while to hang the quilts, and Jacque and Gary would be helping them.

Shirley asked June if she would like to go with her to the chateau after the lecture. She quickly accepted. Shirley told her that she would meet Yvette. "I need to ask her a couple of questions on the architectural detail."

The day before a lecture was always crazy. The quilts were looking outstanding. Jill had prepared a brochure to hand out that contained so much information. Quilting was a very popular craft in many areas of France. Jill had been getting many messages asking about the area that Jo and Sally came from.

Gladys phoned to ask Jill to keep her two tickets as Celia was coming with her to the lecture. Gladys had already bought quite a few quilts and her guests wanted to know where they could buy the quilts, and so she wanted to make sure she could have a few brochures.

People started to arrive on the day of the lecture early to get a good seat in the room. The students were getting on with the parking. Jacque just left them to it. They even had a bus full of ladies that came from one of the villages nearby.

It did not take long before the room was full. Gary introduced Jo and Sally.

Sally started by giving a little history into quilting in France: "Quilts were often made by thrifty housewives who pieced leftover fabric together in elaborate patchwork quilts. Album quilts, however, are quilts to which every member of a community contributed as a gift for a departing mayor or pastor. Often quilts were the prize in a raffle or for a worthy cause. Quilting in France dates back to approximately the 17th century."

Jo went on to say, "Here in our region, a group of quilters decided to go one step further and they came up with their idea of adding a short story with every quilt."

Jo and Sally made the lecture so interesting and welcomed questions. They clearly liked to have interaction from the audience in the room.

Gary got up at the end and thanked Jo and Sally and everyone for coming. The refreshments were going well. Annie was chatting to everyone. Gary was getting lots of questions on what the new building was all about. There seemed to be a lot of interest when he said it was going to be a photography studio.

One man was standing at the back of the room. When he could see Gary was free, he went over to him. He introduced himself, explaining that he owned a photography company that sold cameras and anything connected with photography. He wanted to invite Gary to come and see what he stocked, as he could buy any equipment he needed from him. Also he told Gary that if he could be of any help, he was to call him.

Gary set up a day and time to go and see his business. "I'll give you a good deal on whatever equipment you buy," the man promised. "As a photography studio is so needed. We have nothing in the area where photographers can meet up." Gary thanked him and said he looked forward to meeting him.

The next afternoon Shirley and June went to the chateau. They were meeting with Yvette at 2:00 PM, and so they did not want to be late, as she then went to the hospital later in the afternoon to visit her husband. When they arrived, Yvette had tea ready for them on the terrace as usual. Shirley introduced Yvette to June.

Shirley wanted Yvette to come with her to the front of the chateau because on the one side of the roof she had noticed a piece had broken off. "My question is, do you want me to sketch it as it is? Or do you want me to sketch it complete?"

Yvette thought about it for a moment, and then said she would like to speak to her son, and then she would phone Shirley. Yvette then looked at Shirley and said: "I cannot believe you noticed that, because I had no idea there was a tile broken on the roof."

Shirley explained, "That's why I take many photos to study before I start my sketch and, well, it is part of the decorative trim. That was how I noticed it."

Yvette left for the hospital as Shirley made her way back to the terrace where June was enjoying herself. The young lady then made them another pot of tea and told them not to hurry but relax and enjoy the views.

When Shirley and June arrived back, Gary was sitting in the kitchen looking far away. Shirley asked him if he was feeling all right.

He looked at Shirley and said he was not sure.

"Whatever is the matter? Has there been an accident?"

June also asked if Jacque was all right.

"There has been no accident, but I've just received a phone call to say I have a son." Shirley stared at him. "You have a son? Now let's take it one step at a time. Who phoned?"

"His name is Henry and he just found out that I'm his father."

"Did he say who his mother was?" June asked.

"No, no. He just said his mother had died." Gary said, then added. "You know I lived with Gwen for a number of years, but we just grew apart so we parted years ago. Well, Gwen would never tell Henry who his father was, and she never told me she was pregnant when we parted. In the last few years she had been battling cancer and as she was dying she told Henry that I was his father. Since her death he has been trying to find me. He lives in London. He wants to meet me. I've told him I would like to meet him also, but it is such a shock. I said I'll phone him in the morning. I can't get my head around this."

June poured Gary a brandy. "Now drink this. You're in shock."

As Gary was drinking the brandy, Jacque walked into the kitchen. He took one look at Gary and asked if there was a problem. Gary turned to Jacque and said, "I've just found out I've a son. He just called to tell me."

Jacque looked as shocked as Gary. His first reaction was, "Are you sure?"

Gary went on to explain. "I'll phone him in the morning and go from there."

During supper, Gary asked Shirley how she got on at the chateau. "Did you get answers to the concerns you had?"

"Yvette said she wanted to speak to her son then get back to me."

June piped in that they had tea on the terrace. "Whenever I go there, it is like walking into another life."

Jo and Sally were very pleased with the reaction they got at the lecture. The one group of ladies belonging to a quilting group were very interested. The main thing that set them apart from other quilters was that every quilt came with story. They took many orders and wanted to be kept up to date when they did another craft show. Annie put an order in for a quilt. She had a niece getting married soon, and she thought it would make a great wedding present.

Next morning after breakfast Gary went into the office to phone Henry. They had a nice chat about everything. Henry was easy to talk to. Turned out, Henry had married two years ago. His wife's name was Carol. He was an accountant and worked for a large accounting company in London. They had a small flat in London. Carol worked in a lawyer's office, and so their flat worked well for them until they decided to have children.

Henry told Gary that Gwen never married, but that she had a full life. She had a great circle of friends. When she became ill she would not tell anyone at first, but after a while she needed her friends around her. "I asked her many times who my father was," Henry explained to Gary. "But she always said I was wanted and loved by her and that had to be enough. It was in her last few days that she thought I should know. But what she did say was that you were the love of her life but you could not live together. Also she told me that if I did find you, I had to make sure I told you that you're not to feel any guilt whatsoever, as it was her choice never to tell you."

Gary told Henry that he would like to meet him and Carol. "I got married two weeks ago to a wonderful lady called Shirley who would also love to meet you both."

Henry said they were still clearing his mum's house and finishing off with all the paperwork. "Let's keep in touch over the phone for a while, then when I'm ready I would love you and Shirley to come over to London and stay with Carol and I."

Gary said he would like that. "Please feel free to phone any time. I'll always be here for you."

When Gary came back into the house, Shirley said she had made coffee. "Let's take it out onto the patio or would you like to take a walk?"

"Let's just sit here," Gary said.

Shirley was feeling anxious, so she just let Gary talk. He told her all about Henry and said when he was ready they should both go to London to meet Henry and his wife Carol. "He sounded like a very nice young man. I still can't believe I have a son."

Everyone was so busy. Jill had the next lecture to think about and was busy getting the advertising material ready for printing.

She was always so organized and never missed a deadline. June was busy with letting accommodation. She was confident that when they had the extra letting accommodation they would be easily filled. Annie was running the house like clockwork. Shirley told her one day she did not know how they had all managed without her.

The photography studio was taking shape. It now had the roof on and the inside work was underway. The inspectors had been to check it out before Jacque and his workmen could move on to the next stage. Jacque was always a bit nervous when he knew they were coming. His workmen were very professional. Gary could not understand why he got nervous. But that was Jacque.

Gary was pleased when he had a phone call from Stuart. He was going to be in the area the following week and would love to stop by and visit them. Gary invited him to stay a few days if he had time. He quickly said he would make time. "Shirley will be so pleased to see you again," Gary said.

As soon as Gary told Shirley that Stuart was coming she said she wanted to do the finishing touches to the sketch. "It may not be complete, but I want to spend some time on it. I hope Yvette's son phones me soon so I can complete the roof details. And I would like to take Stuart out to the chateau and introduce him to Yvette. She would love to meet him."

Gary told Shirley he would come as well. "We could make a day of it and stop at a winery for lunch."

Yvette phoned Shirley to say her son would like her to sketch the roof as it was. Shirley had taken many photos, and so she could get on with it. She thought they had made the right decision. The sketch was looking really good. Shirley was looking forward to Stuart's opinion on her work.

She would let no one see it. Even Gary was not allowed to see the original. He had seen some of her many samples, but that was it. She had spent many hours in her studio, lost in her work.

The day before Stuart was due to arrive, she felt a bit nervous. 'I hope he thinks I've done the chateau justice,' she thought. Shirley

WHEN DREAMS BECOME REALITY

was in her studio from early morning till late in the evening. Annie took her something to eat and drink before she went home.

Stuart arrived late morning. Gary took him to see June as she had his *gite* ready for him. They then went into the house for coffee and a light lunch that Annie had prepared for them. Gary was so proud to show him around the art studio and the future photography studio. Gary introduced Stuart to Jacque who was busy working, as always. Stuart congratulated Jacque on the standard of his work. "I can see you're very passionate about your work. This is truly a wonderful place for artists. All I can say is I'm so pleased Shirley and June took that trip to France."

Shirley was busy in her studio. She was looking forward to seeing him again. As they opened the door, Shirley greeted Stuart. He could not take his eyes off her work all around the room. "How long have you been sketching like this?"

Gary said, "She came to my classes a few years ago. Until then she had never sketched or painted a thing. She just wanted something to do."

"I always loved to sketch but never had the time," Shirley put in. "I had three children and a husband to look after."

Shirley told Stuart she had loved it from the time she picked up a pencil and a piece of charcoal. "I was so surprised when Gary told me to enter six sketches into the art exhibition in Brookdale at the end of the first year. Gary told me to price each sketch and, to my complete amazement, I sold every one."

Stuart was still studying her artwork. "You're very talented, and I don't say that often. I would like to see what you're working on at the moment."

Shirley had the large sketch on the easel that was covered with a white sheet. "I've never worked on such a large piece before," she said. As she took the sheet off the sketch, Stuart and Gary stared at it for a long time, not saying anything.

"Well, what do you both think?" Shirley had photos of the chateau pinned on a large board on the wall. Stuart looked at the photos then back to the sketch. "I can't believe you're so modest. This work is incredible. You're one gifted lady. I would be honoured if you would come to my gallery in Paris and put on an exhibition. I've not seen sketches of this standard, ever."

Gary smiled proudly. "I've been telling her how good she is for so long."

Shirley asked Stuart if he would like to drive out to the chateau tomorrow. "Yvette would like to meet you. I think you will find it very interesting. As I told you, Yvette's husband has had a stroke and is in hospital, and so this sketch is a surprise for him when he comes home."

"Shirley, you do realise this is a masterpiece. And I would, again, like this to be shown in your exhibition in Paris. We would take great care of it as I have high security in the gallery."

Gary left Stuart and Shirley together in her studio; he had to go to the office. Shirley found Stuart so interesting. He gave her lots of advice, though he said she did not need it.

Shirley phoned Yvette and said she was bringing Stuart to meet her tomorrow. Shirley had told Yvette all about Stuart and his gallery in Paris. Yvette was pleased that he had time to visit the chateau. "We'll see you late morning," Shirley said.

Yvette quickly said she wanted to serve them lunch.

Shirley covered her sketch as they went into the main house. She told Stuart she had many more sketches all around the house, some big, some quite small.

"Well, what are we waiting for? Let's go and see what you have."

They walked into the house. Stuart could not believe his eyes. "Your work is everywhere."

"Shall I let you roam all around the house? I'll come and find you when we're ready to eat."

Stuart said he was in heaven. "I don't think you understand just how talented you are." Gary came into the kitchen to see if supper was ready. "Where is Stuart?" he asked.

"He is checking out my sketches all over the house. Could you go and find him? We have set the table for supper out on the patio. They say we could have a good sunset."

June went to get Jacque so they could eat. Gary and Stuart were having a glass of wine on the patio. The others joined them. The evening could not have been better. Shirley asked Stuart if he had checked out the sketches. I've just been talking to Gary. I want to catalogue all of them for the exhibition in Paris.

June queried: "What exhibition in Paris?"

Stuart said how impressed he was by Shirley's work. "And I want to put on an exhibition in my gallery in Paris. We can discuss a date that works for me and that allows Shirley time to prepare. I don't want you to feel rushed in any way."

The evening was so relaxing. Jacque told Stuart all the plans they had for the photography studio. In fact, he went to get the plans to show him. June and Shirley cleared away, made coffee, by which time the guys were still talking.

Stuart got up to leave, but before he left he said he was so pleased Gary had come over to him in Paris. Shirley told Stuart to come over to the main house in the morning for breakfast. "We'll leave for the chateau about eleven."

The journey to the chateau was so picturesque. The road meandered through lavender fields. Stuart was so amazed with the area. "I've lived in France many years, but I've never seen scenery like this."

Gary said, "You wait until you get to the chateau. It will blow your mind."

They turned the final corner and saw the chateau in the distance. Gary stopped the car so Stuart could get out to take in the views over the landscape. Chateau Frontenac stood proud on its own surrounded by vineyards. All Stuart could say was, "Wow!"

Gary entered the code to open the gates. They drove up to the front door as Yvette came out to greet them. Shirley introduced Stuart to Yvette. To their surprise Yvette knew Stuart's gallery in

Paris. "I did a bit of research before you arrived. When Shirley said your name, it rang a bell. I've been to your gallery with my husband many times."

They entered the chateau. Stuart could not believe his eyes. There in the hall hung one of his paintings.

"We bought this painting many years ago," Yvette explained. "Since then we have bought another four of your paintings and put them through our home. We love your artwork. I feel so honoured you have come to our home."

They made their way through to the terrace where lunch was set out ready for them. "Please make yourselves comfortable. I'll just go and tell them we're ready to eat," Yvette said.

Stuart looked at Gary and said, "I'm in heaven. Take a look at this terrace. It is straight out of a high-end magazine."

Yvette came back followed by the beautifully dressed young lady who had served them wine, and then lunch arrived. Shirley told Yvette that she would be ready to deliver her sketch next week. "I do hope you're going to like it."

Stuart quickly told Yvette he had seen the sketch and that it was breathtaking. "You and you husband will not be disappointed."

"I already have a couple of Shirley's sketches. She is too modest. She is a very talented artist."

Stuart asked if Yvette came to Paris much.

She said they went as often as possible. She went on to tell them that they had an apartment in the centre of Paris. "As soon as my husband is well enough we'll be going. We plan on staying a few months."

After lunch Yvette, as always, went to the hospital to visit her husband, but she told them to take their time. "Shirley will take you on a stroll around the grounds. Do go down to the lily ponds. The lilies are at their best right now."

Shirley thanked Yvette for lunch and said she would be back next week with the sketch.

As they wandered around the grounds, Stuart took photos. "This is an amazing place. You're so lucky to have met Yvette at the art show. She has really taken to you, Shirley."

Gary was so proud of Shirley. She had gained so much confidence since coming to France.

The lily ponds were awash with colour. Stuart said he often went to Monet's gardens. "The lily ponds there are my favourite, but these lily ponds are as good, if not better." The gardeners were busy tending the flower beds, not a weed was to be found.

The rose beds were in groups of white roses, yellow roses, pink roses and red roses. As you walked from one rose bed to another you went under arches covered in roses. It was mesmerizing in its beauty and form.

On the way back, Stuart said he had had an amazing day. "You live in a beautiful part of France. When we get back I want to discuss again about you coming to my gallery to present your work."

Shirley said she would need to know how many pieces of artwork would be needed so she could allow myself enough time.

Arriving back at the house, Gary told them he needed to go and see Jacque and find out how things had gone today. Stuart and Shirley went into her studio to discuss the exhibition. He wanted Shirley to sketch some of the old buildings in the area. "Also, I think you should sketch the art centre."

Stuart gave her so much confidence. She still was having a hard time thinking about having her own exhibition in Paris.

That evening she phoned Heather to tell her about Stuart and what he wanted her to do. "Wow, to think my mother has her own exhibition in Paris. Wait till I tell Dave. We're so proud of you, Mum. You never stop amazing us. I feel like a shrinking violet beside you."

Stuart left early the next morning as he had a meeting at a gallery on his way back to Paris. Shirley had her work cut out to get ready for the exhibition. Gary was taking her out later to look around for suitable buildings to sketch. Jacque had suggested to Gary two churches that would work just fine.

They set out after lunch. The car was piled high with camera, pads and pencils as Shirley liked to make rough sketches first before she started the main sketch. It was a beautiful day, but it was a little overcast, which was better for taking photos.

As they were driving through the countryside they came across a field with the most beautiful group of horses. Immediately, Shirley asked Gary to stop. They leapt out of the car. While Gary took photos, Shirley started sketching. The horses looked so majestic. And, apart from the swish of their tails, they were motionless.

Shirley had never sketched horses or any animals, but she could not resist them. There was a slight breeze blowing, which added to the overall look. Gary took many photos from all angles, as the chance of the horses being in the same pose again was very slim.

Back in the car they headed to see the first of two churches Jacque told them about. The first church was in the middle of a village that was surrounded by old stone cottages. They parked the car. It was a very small church but perfect for sketching. Again Gary took photos and Shirley sketched. There was an archway covered with roses at the entrance to the path that lead them to the door of the church.

The door was open, so in they went. The ladies from the village were doing the flowers and cleaning the church. Shirley wanted Gary to take photos of the stained-glass windows. The colours were so deep and rich. Outside the church they walked around, and then Shirley found the perfect location to sketch the church.

After a while they were again back in the car. Gary stopped a few times to take photos. This was truly a pretty village. Now they were on their way to the second church. As they left the village, Shirley spotted a field of lavender.

Stuart had suggested she do two or three sketches of the lavender fields. Lavender fields were a firm favourite whenever they were in exhibitions. "They always sell first," he told her.

Gary found a good spot to stop. Shirley got her seat and started sketching while Gary took photos once again.

The next church was not too far away. It was even smaller but so charming. As they approached it, they could see it had been a bit neglected over the years.

They parked the car and walked towards the iron gates. Gary proceeded to open the gates, as he did he saw a group of men working on the grounds. He went over to them and found out in his broken French that the local people were cleaning up the grounds.

Apparently the church had not been used for many years, and so it was nice to see it starting to come alive again. The one man spoke English and offered to take them inside the church. As they entered the church they were overwhelmed with the most peaceful feeling. Everything was how it had been left many years ago.

Shirley said she was an artist and would like to sketch it. The man was interested and asked Shirley if she would phone him when the sketch was finished. Gary took the information down, and then they carried on looking around the church and taking photos.

It was soon time for them to head for home as the light was starting to go down. Gary planned to get the photos developed as soon as possible. Shirley was happy with all the sketches she had. This will keep me going for quite a while, she thought.

June was preparing supper when Shirley walked into the kitchen. Gary went straight to see how the building was going. Shirley told June they had enough to do all the sketches for the exhibition. "All I have to do now is get started."

June said Yvette phoned and wanted Shirley to phone her that evening if possible. "I'll do it right now so I don't forget."

Yvette answered straight away. She sounded excited. Shirley asked her if everything was all right. Yvette told her that her husband would be coming home at the end of next week. "So if you could come with the sketch early next week that would be good."

Shirley was happy with that. She only had a few finishing details to do, and then it was ready. Yvette wanted her husband to be involved with the framing of the sketch. "He has a very keen eye and knows what he wants," she explained.

Over supper Jacque told them he was happy with the progress on the building. "We'll be concentrating on your apartment first, and so I think you could start looking at kitchen cabinets, bathroom cabinets and flooring, etcetera," he told Shirley.

Shirley said she would phone Jill tomorrow as she will be helping her with all the interior décor.

Gary was getting very excited. He said he would have to start thinking about what would be needed for the photography studio. Jill has been in the office all day. The tickets were now being sold for the next lecture, which was Pat with her jewellery.

Pat was a local girl, and so it would surely be a sell-out. Her jewellery was very different and appealed more to the arty or younger crowd. She had won many awards for her designs. She used coloured gemstones of all kinds.

As soon as supper was over, Shirley went into her studio. "I want to get the sketch completed for Yvette," she said to herself. She asked Gary if he could you come with her on Monday morning to deliver it. Gary told her that was not a problem. "If you need me to do anything else let me know."

"Just make sure that nothing is in your car so we can get the sketch in."

"No problem. The seats go down to give plenty of room."

Shirley thanked Jacque for suggesting the two churches. "They were both perfect and very different." Jacque told her that he once lived in a cottage near the small church. "That village has not changed in centuries. It is run by the community. They have no crime at all. It is known as a sleepy village," he said.

CHAPTER TWENTY

Gary and Shirley's New Home

Sunday night Shirley asked everyone if they would like to see the sketch before she took it to Yvette in the morning. Gary brought it into the art centre for them to see it, as there was more room. She had it covered until everyone was there. Even Annie came to see it.

When she uncovered it, no one said a word. They just stared at it. The sketch was three feet by three feet, so it was large.

Barb was first to speak. She thought it was wonderful. "No wonder Stuart wants to put on an exhibition of your work."

She had never done such a large sketch with so much detail. Had it been smaller she would have lost a lot of detail, they agreed.

They all loved it. Gary told her that Yvette and her husband were going to love it also. "Yvette has agreed that I can have it on loan to put into my exhibition in Paris," Stuart said. Gary took a photo of it with Shirley standing by it. She could not believe it was finally finished.

Next morning Jacque helped Gary to get the sketch into the car before setting off for the Chateau. Gary drove very carefully, but given the way Shirley had the sketch wrapped up in towels and blankets, it was not moving anywhere.

Yvette was waiting for them. She could not wait to see the sketch. She called one of her handy men to come and help Gary get the sketch out of the car. They went into the conservatory to unwrap the sketch. Shirley asked Yvette to stand back so she would get the best view of the sketch as she took the final sheet off the sketch.

Shirley unwrapped the sketch. Yvette was speechless. And then she started to cry, saying her husband and son would be overwhelmed. She could not take her eyes of it. "You have captured so many intricate details. This is the icing on the cake today. I'm going to pick Andre up in a little while and when he sees this he will be thrilled."

Shirley was so pleased she liked it, and Gary was proud of her, as he always was.

Yvette asked them to cover it up with the sheet as her son would be coming later and she wanted them both to see it at the same time. Shirley gave Yvette the date of her exhibition in Paris and to check and then asked if she would still be allowed to put the sketch of the chateau in the exhibition.

Yvette said she wanted to talk about the exhibition in Paris. "Would you and Gary like to use our apartment in Paris while you're there?"

Gary looked at Shirley and quickly said, "Yes, please, if you're sure. We'll go for the opening and stay a few days. The exhibition runs for four weeks. So, as we said, we'll go for the opening, stay for few days, and then go back at the end of the exhibition."

"Good. I'll phone you tomorrow to let you know the reaction I get from my husband and son."

Shirley said she looked forward to her call.

"Oh, and I think Andre will want to meet you sometime if that works for you."

Shirley said she would look forward to meeting him.

Back at home Gary was on the phone to Henry. They were speaking every other day. It was so nice to hear Gary talking about him, Shirley thought. Henry told Gary that Gwen wrote him a letter before she died, which he would give him when they went to London to visit.

They seemed to have much in common. Although Henry was an accountant he was also interested in the art world. He said they would both be going to Paris to see Shirley's exhibition.

Jill took Shirley and Gary to look at kitchens, flooring, and paint colours. They had so much fun, but it was so overwhelming. Good job Jill was helping them. She had samples all over the kitchen when June came in. Shirley also wanted June's opinion.

They had a deadline to get the kitchen ordered and time was running out. "I think we have finally settled on a style of cabinets we want," Shirley said.

Gary said that as long as Shirley liked it, it was fine by him. Jill told Gary he was the perfect man. "Hah! Don't say that. It will go to his head." Shirley said and laughed.

The windows were now installed. It looked so much bigger than Shirley and June first believed. When June and Shirley were on their own, Shirley asked June how things were going between her and Jacque. June told Shirley, "We're almost like an old married couple. Jacque is very set in his ways and, of course, very French."

"Do you think he will move in with you when Gary and I move into our new apartment?"

"To be honest, he never says anything about it."

"Would you like Gary to bring it up? The house is very big for you on your own."

"Well, I don't think it will hurt, but I don't want Jacque to think I'm asking him to move in with me."

"I'll speak to Gary later, so leave it to me. You make such a nice couple."

"Well, Jacque is not romantic at all. One day he said we were like a pair of leather gloves. We fit together and get better with age."

Shirley smiled but June was not amused.

The following morning Yvette phoned to say Andre and her son were delighted with the sketch. "He has not moved from it. He said the longer you look at it, the more you see in it. We have the framer coming this afternoon to give us some ideas. Would you have time to come this afternoon? I know it's short notice, but we would really appreciate it if you had the time."

"I can come, but I'll have to check to see if Gary is available. What time are you thinking of?"

"Well, around two thirty if possible."

"I'll see you later. If Gary can't come, I'll bring June for company on the drive. As you know, she would love to come and would enjoy an afternoon out."

As soon as she put the phone down she went to find Gary, who was in the office with Jill. He said he had an appointment with the some of the students who were helping in setting up the photography studio. "I have to get things ordered as they take weeks to be delivered."

"No problem. I'll go and find June to see if she wants to come."

Jill asked if she could come as well.

"Sounds good to me. I'll go and see June then come back and tell you what time we're going."

Jill was so excited. "I can't wait to see the chateau," she cried.

Shirley said she would love it. "We'll leave about twelve thirty to allow plenty of time." June was thrilled. She told Jill to bring her camera.

They arrived at the grand entrance to the chateau. Jill was in love. "Wow, what a place."

June told Jill she would love Yvette. "Andre her husband has only just come out of hospital, and so I'm not sure how he is doing."

Yvette came out to welcome them. Shirley introduced Jill to Yvette, and then they followed Yvette into the conservatory. The sketch was in the same place where Gary had put it. Yvette's husband was so pleased to meet Shirley. He was an older man in a pinstriped suit. He started asking her all kinds of questions as to how she had managed to bring the chateau to life in a sketch. "It is such a special and intriguing style," he said. "And so very lovely."

Shirley thanked him for his comments. She said she was so pleased he liked it. "Chateau Frontenac is so beautiful. It was an honour to be asked to sketch it."

Just then the man arrived with frame samples. Even he was taken aback by the sketch. "That's really something. I see lots of art work—water colours, oils and sketches, but this is in a league of its own."

They spent time looking at all the different samples. Eventually, a frame was selected. Andre went for a lie down and the framer left. "There is tea on the terrace for you ladies. I'll join you shortly. Shirley take June and Jill on to the terrace."

Jill turned to Shirley, "They just love you."

"Wait till you see the terrace, you will love it," June said.

The terrace was decorated in royal blue. White cushions adorned all the chairs. The couches were the kind one sinks into like a warm bath. Heavy wrought-iron lanterns hung from the ceiling; matching wall sconces surrounded the terrace. In the middle was a magnificent, heavy table with a white lace tablecloth. On it sat tea and pastries.

As they sat and enjoyed tea and pastries, Jill took photos of the terrace. "Wait till I show this to John." Jill was all into the design and this was at the top.

On the way home in the car, Shirley told them that when they went to Paris for the opening of the exhibition that they were staying in Yvette's apartment. Jill and June were so jealous. "Can you imagine what the apartment in Paris will be like," Jill mused.

The next few weeks were busy. Jill finalized all the details for the jewellery lecture, which was a sell-out. Shirley was busy between doing selections for the apartment and working on her upcoming exhibition in Paris. June was swamped with the letting accommodation and keeping all the paperwork in order,

Jacque, along with his workmen, was doing a great job on the new studio. He also worked with Jill, as they had now putting a program together for art centre. There was so much going on.

Shirley did not get too involved in the jewellery lecture, as she was concentrating on her exhibition. She was on the phone to Stuart quite a lot. He was so helpful to her. She got sketches ready and packed them in special packing bags ready to go into containers. Gary and Shirley would be going to Paris to help unpack the sketches before the exhibition opened. But there was still plenty of time until then.

The kitchen was being installed the same week as the lecture. This was not the best plan but once it was delivered it couldn't be sent back. It was looking so nice. Shirley was getting excited to see it all coming together. Gary was more interested in planning his studio; it had been so long since he did any painting, but he was eager to get started again.

Shirley decided she wanted to include a few of her water-colour paintings in the exhibition, and so she phoned Stuart to see what he thought. He was happy to add the watercolours. "I think we could do a feature in the brochure. It's always good to show the diversity of an artist when they are putting on their first exhibition." He told Shirley they were getting lots of inquirers at the gallery about her exhibition. "We've not had an exhibition on an artist who mainly does sketching. The exhibition will run for four weeks."

Jill finished off putting a brochure together for the Paris exhibition. "We want to promote the *Petit Bijou* Art Centre as much as possible," she said. She had also ordered more of the book that told the full story on converting the old barn into the art centre.

Pat was busy setting up for her lecture. She was a breath of fresh air. Before she started, she put on her music, which was so relaxing and calmed everyone down. Even June and Jill were humming to the music. Annie came in and asked what the beautiful smell was, because along with the music she was burning scented candles that smelt of fresh berries. Her display was not that large but very unique. She used rare gemstones in many pieces of her jewellery.

Barb arrived to help and, of course, Michael came with her. He always wanted to involved. He made straight for the refreshments where June put him to work. Barb was very taken with Pat and her approach to her artwork. Her work was so different.

Before long the centre was full. It was a much younger crowd. Pat was a local girl, and so they had come to support her. She had graduated from a university in France. Many of the young girls were fans of her jewellery. She gave a very informative lecture and proved that she knew her subject very well.

At the end of her lecture, a lady sitting at the side of the room put her hand up and asked if she could say a few words. It turned out she was Pat's tutor in university. She had heard she was giving a lecture today and wanted to attend. She went on to congratulate her on a very professional lecture. She told everyone that Pat was a very talented young lady.

As always, Gary spoke and thanked Pat and everyone for coming and giving their support to the art centre. He also announced that Shirley had her first exhibition in Paris, and that it would be running for four weeks.

Pat was very pleased with the way everything went. She had sold much of her jewellery. June came across to her with some refreshments. Barb helped Pat with her sales. Barb told her she should also be selling the candles. Everyone was commenting on the beautiful fragrance and the soft music that was still playing.

This was the third lecture, and they were still learning, said Barb. Michael was busy helping Annie in the kitchen. She made him have some juice and whatever he wanted to eat, so he was happy.

Shirley took Barb and Jill to see the apartment, as the painters were painting now. They loved the kitchen and the design. The apartment had a French 'shabby chic' look. Barb had not seen it at all, and so she was amazed at the size. Shirley told Barb, "Without Jill helping me, this would not have looked like this. I just can't visualize anything. Jill is so gifted in putting it all together. Gary and I are just thrilled. We hope to be moving in within the next two weeks. Once the painters have finished, it is just the rest of the flooring to be finished. I can't wait."

"How is June going to manage in the house all on her own?" asked Jill. "Do you think Jacque will moving in?"

"To be honest, I really don't know," said Shirley. "But I don't like the idea of June being on her own. It is a large house, as you know."

As they sat down to supper, Gary remarked that he was so pleased with Pat's lecture. He said how nice it was of her tutor to come and say a few words. They were doing a feature on her in next week's local paper. Pat was so excited. She had quite a few family and friends that came to support her.

When supper was finished, Gary went to phone Henry. June said, "It is so nice for Gary to have a son. When do you think you will go to London to meet Henry and Carol?"

"We'll go as soon as Henry has finished selling his mother's house," Shirley told her.

Jacque wanted to check on a few things with the building, and so he left. Shirley and June cleared away the dishes and then made a pot of tea. As they sat by the table drinking tea, Shirley asked June how things were going with Jacque and if she thought he would be moving in with her.

June seemed a bit quiet. "The problem with Jacque is that he is so shy and finds it hard to show his feelings." She looked at Shirley and said, "Do you think it would be too forward of me if I asked him if he would like to move in with me?"

Shirley thought about it for a while, and then said she thought it would be a good idea. "At least you'll know where you stand."

"I'll wait until you and Gary have moved into your new apartment and I'm living on my own. If he has not said anything to me after two weeks of me being on my own, I'll ask him."

As always, Shirley was in her studio early as she still had quite a bit to do; she wanted to get it finished before they moved into the apartment. By lunch time she came to find Gary as she wanted his advice on all the artwork before they got packed, ready to go to Paris.

Gary looked at each one, and then they packed it. The moving company had brought all the packing material. By supper time they had only done a few, and so after supper it was back to the studio. It was after midnight by the time they finished.

Gary was so pleased with the quality of Shirley's work. Shirley phoned Stuart to say the artwork was now complete and ready to go. She told Stuart the movers would be packing the sketch of the chateau. They were going to phone Yvette and arrange it.

Finally, Gary and Shirley's moving in day was here. Annie was helping Shirley do the last cleaning in the apartment. The drapes were being hung along with the window blinds. Shirley was so excited. Jill was on hand to organize all the furniture. She knew exactly where everything was going.

Annie kept saying she had never seen such a beautiful home. She was making sure everyone had their shoes off. Gary looked at Shirley and said he was pleased he did not have to live with Anne. By the end of the day it was complete; everything was in its place. Jacque came in with June to take a look. They both said how well it had turned out.

John came with the big bunch of flowers and a bottle of wine for Gary and his mum. Gary found the glasses as John opened the wine. John wanted everyone to raise their glasses and toast Gary and his mum in their new home. "I know you will both be very happy here, and so I want to wish you many happy years together, and good luck, Mum, with the exhibition in Paris."

John turned to Jill and said she had outdone herself in the décor of the apartment, and everyone agreed. Jacque asked June if she needed him to help rearrange the furniture in the house now that Shirley had moved hers out.

June said she was going to ask Jill to come and help re-organize the house and also if it needed to be painted. Jill said she would come and work with June, but there was no hurry. Jill told June she had a few ideas to make it her home now.

Jacque said it was a big house for one person. "I know Shirley's studio is in the house, but it is still a big house."

Shirley and June smiled at one another but said nothing.

When everyone had gone, Gary hugged Shirley and asked her if she was happy. She told him she was over the moon. "We have so much to look forward to—my exhibition, then the opening of the photography studio, and also the full program in the art centre."

The next day, Gary was in his room all day sorting his artwork and putting the books on the book shelves. He told Shirley he was excited to be able to get back to painting again, as it had been a long time. He suggested to Shirley that he may consider giving art lessons and what did she think.

Shirley thought it was a great idea. "Why not wait until after the exhibition and the opening of the photography studio?"

"That sounds like a plan. We do have so much to look forward to and not forgetting we're going to meet 'my son' Henry with his wife Carol."

Mary phoned to ask how the move went. "Let me know when you're ready for a visitor ha! ha!" Mary said she was going to send Shirley and June photos of her new grandson, Max. "He is growing so fast. Clive and Amy make such a nice couple. They had been down to see them for the weekend with the baby," she reported. "You know Bill, now he is planning to build a fort in the garden for Max to play in. He said Emma has her little house in the garden, and so Max needs a fort. As I told him, he can't even sit up yet so you have plenty of time."

Shirley went across to see June to see how she was doing after her first night on her own. She went into the kitchen and found Jacque sitting there, having his breakfast. He quickly got up and told June he would see her later.

Annie was not working today. June asked Shirley if she would like a coffee. She accepted. Shirley asked June what was going on.

"Well, Jacque is not as slow as we first thought. We're now living together."

They drank their coffee and June told Shirley she was going with Jacque later to his house to see if there was anything he wants to bring here. "Well, our Jacque is a dark horse. Did you have any idea he had this in mind?"

June chuckled. "I had no idea at all. We just came across to the house and he just said he wanted to be with me and did not like the thought of me on my own in this house, and so he stayed. All I'll say is we had a fantastic night together. So don't ask me any more questions. He did not think he could be so happy."

"June, I'm so thrilled for you both. Just think, we have now all found our Prince Charming."

"Jacque told me that I could have all new furniture if I like, as he has the money to do it. But you know me, I get attached to things. Although, I want to speak to Jill to give the place a facelift."

Shirley could not stop smiling at June. "You look like a cat that has just got the cream."

"I know I could not be happier. Jacque is going to tell Gary, but please don't tease him."

Shirley went back across to her apartment where she phoned Mary. Mary answered the phone. Shirley said, "You will never guess what I have to tell you."

"Well, don't keep me in suspense."

"June and Jacque have moved in together!"

Mary was thrilled but not surprised. "They make a nice couple. Jacque is so laid back and very quiet, but you can see he adores June."

Later that afternoon, Jacque took June to his house, which was located on the other side of the village. It was a nice stone cottage. It had not had anything done to it for a good many years. It lacked a woman's touch, and the furniture was all very old, but June told Jacque he could bring whatever he wanted to.

Jacque turned to June and, in his thick French accent, said she was being kind, as it all needed to be dumped. "I just want to sell the place."

"Can I suggest we speak to Jill. She will give us ideas on painting throughout, and then staging the house to sell."

"That sounds like a good plan. I knew you were a smart lady." And he smiled at her.

Jill had left by the time they got home so June said she would speak to her tomorrow. Jacque said he would like to get it done as soon as possible. June had to go to the office to reply to a booking that had come in this morning.

CHAPTER TWENTY ONE

Exhibition in Paris

HENRY PHONED GARY to say that finally things had settled with his mother's estate. It had taken so long. "Carol and I would like to invite you both to come to London for a long weekend."

Gary was thrilled. "I'll speak to Shirley, just to check she is available this weekend."

Shirley spoke to June to see if she could manage if they went to London for the weekend. June said she would be fine. "Jill and Annie will help me if I get busy."

Shirley told June that Gary was very nervous about meeting Henry. "He feels very guilty that he was not around while he was growing up. I think he just needs to meet him."

Shirley told Gary to make the travel arrangements for the weekend. "It has come at the perfect time before we get ready to go to Paris. Our lives are so busy. We never get time to get bored. By the way, how are things coming along with the new studio?"

"The group of students from the college that are involved with setting up the photography studio are so helpful. We're so lucky to have them. We're now working on the lighting, which I'm finding out is one of the most important aspects of the studio. Jacque has set up a meeting for everyone involved in the lighting, painting and design to get together, that way we're all on the same page. Eric from the college asked if he could come with the students to the meeting. Gary also had a representative from the firm that is supplying the photography equipment.

The meeting went very well. Jacque and Gary were taking notes. Eric and the students knew exactly what was needed in the lighting department. The electrician was so accommodating. He just wanted to get it right. They decided to change one area to make it more interesting, and the painter involved the students so as to get the best paint colours. Also, we have to make sure that all the paint is a matte finish, according to one of the students. At the end of the meeting, Gary thanked everyone for taking the time to come. He said we want to get it right so we have to work together. Jacque said the next time we meet will be when it is completed, unless we have any questions before then," June finished, nearly breathless

.

That evening, as Gary and Shirley were relaxing in their living room, Shirley asked Gary if he was ready for the weekend trip to London. He said he was so ready and excited. "I just hope Henry is not disappointed with me."

"There's no way he will be disappointed in you, so put that out of your mind. He is a very lucky man to have you as a father. We how have to get to know them both. I have a small gift for them to hang in their apartment."

"Let me see what you have."

Shirley brought out a framed photo of Gary outside the art centre on the day they opened.

"When did you take that? I've never seen it before! I took many photos, but this one is special so I framed it for Henry."

Gary thanked Shirley. "That is such a thoughtful thing for you to do.

"I also have a gift for Carol," Shirley added.

They had a flight booked that took them into London. Henry and Carol were meeting them at the airport. As the plane landed, Gary was feeling a little nervous, and so Shirley took his hand and gave it a squeeze and told him everything would be fine.

They collected their bags and made their way to the arrival area. Gary had a photo of Henry and Henry had a photo of Gary so they could find one another. The arrival area was full, with people waving arms and greeting one another, some with flowers and balloons, some with banners. Then Gary spotted Henry and Carol.

It was very emotional. Shirley could not get over how much Henry looked like Gary, only younger, of course. They all hugged one another for what seemed like ages. Carol was so pretty, and she could not stop crying. Henry said his car was in the parking area, and so they made their way outside. Gary did not leave Henry's side.

It did not take long to get to their apartment. Carol was so pleased to have them come and stay. They arrived at the apartment and Henry got the case out of the car as Carol went on ahead to open the door. It was a beautiful apartment. Not that big, but they had it furnished so nicely.

Carol showed Shirley their room and told them to make themselves at home. There was something about the apartment that made them feel so welcome and at ease with one another straightaway. Carol made coffee. "When you have unpacked, please come into the living room," she said.

Henry told Gary he had many photos to show him, "So please ask as many questions as you want, and I'll do my best to answer them."

Shirley got on with Carol from the beginning. She got out their wedding photos. Shirley could see from the wedding photos that Gwen was not well, and that was two years ago. Henry said his mother had cancer for about three years, but it was only in the last year that it progressed rapidly. She had a very good support group of friends to help her. She only went into the hospital in the last week before she died. "It got to the stage that it was impossible to look after her at home, but I'll say she did not suffer at the end," Henry said. "Mum talked about you a lot in the last few months of her life and really wanted me to contact you, but not until she had died. Mum told me how much she loved you, but that you could not live together. You were her one and only love. She always wanted me to know that I was not a mistake, and that I was conceived out of love."

Gary asked if he had lots of friends growing up and if his mum had lots of help.

"Our house growing up was always full of love, laughter and warmth," Henry assured him.

Gary and Shirley were enjoying looking at photos with Henry and Carol and reminiscing through Henry's childhood.

Then Henry gave Gary a letter from Gwen. "You don't have to open it now. If you want to open it in private we understand."

Gary stared at the envelope. "No, I would like to open here with the most important people in my life. We have no more secrets from this day on."

Shirley leaned over and kissed him on the cheek and told him she was so proud of him.

Carol said she would make some more fresh coffee as she thought they would all need it. Gary opened the letter. It read:

My dearest Gary,

First of all I don't want you to be upset with me in any way. When I found out I was pregnant we had already decided to go our separate ways. I know if I had got in touch with you, you would have come back and would have wanted to do the honourable thing. I could not have lived with myself. I had good friends and they always were there for me. Henry was the most perfect baby (I know all mothers say that but he was perfect).

I had a job that I was able to work around a baby's schedule. Henry was always good in school and worked hard. I think you could say he got that from you as I was a little on the lazy side. Henry will have been going through the baby box by the time you read this. It is packed full of his growing up. I made sure he never suffered being brought up by a single mother. He is a well-brought-up young man and I know you will be very proud of him as I've always been. Then we come to Carol. Well, what can I say? Again, I know I'm biased, but you have to agree she is quite special. She makes Henry happy and looks after him so well. I think they will have a wonderful life together. You have to promise me one thing, when they have children you have to be the best granddad ever.

I never married as no one measured up to you. I do hope you have been able to find someone to make you happy. If you did find someone, I know she would be a very special lady and lucky to have you.

Fondest memories

Gwen
xxx

Gary pressed his forehead. "I think I need a drink. Do you have anything stronger that coffee?"

Henry said. "We have a bottle of brandy for emergencies. I think this is the emergency right now."

There was not a dry eye. Shirley and Carol were both crying. Gary and Henry were trying to put on a brave face, but it was not working.

As they went through the box they had more tears and lots of laughter. Henry turned to Gary and said, "I feel that Mum is with us tonight."

Carol agreed. She turned to Shirley and told her she would have loved Gwen.

Henry suggested they go out for a walk and get a meal. There are some nice restaurants in this area of London. So they all freshened up and out they went.

During the meal they were very interested in hearing all about the art centre as well as about Shirley's upcoming exhibition in Paris. "Why not come for the opening?" Shirley said. "We have been given an apartment to use in Paris, so you can stay with us."

They considered for all of five seconds, then said yes. The rest of the stay in London could not have gone better. Gary and Henry had so many things in common. The next day Shirley and Carol went off shopping to give Gary and Henry time together.

Soon it was time for Gary and Shirley to head for the airport. They had had such a wonderful time. As they were leaving, Carol said to Shirley that Henry was so happy and loved Gary so much. Shirley replied, "And I can tell you that Gary loves Henry. We'll be seeing lots of one another in the future."

It was hard for Gary to leave Henry, but they would be seeing one another in Paris for the opening of Shirley's exhibition. Shirley thanked them both for making them so welcome.

They arrived back in France and picked up their car and were soon on their way home. Shirley phoned June to let her know they would be home in about one hour's time. June was looking forward to hearing all about the trip.

Jacque and June were sitting in the kitchen when they arrived. June called them in to have some coffee before they went to their apartment to unpack. Gary told them that they had had a wonderful trip. "Henry and Carol made us so welcome," he said. "Gwen did an amazing job of bringing him up. He has great values. We both loved Carol. She had the apartment so beautifully decorated. When we unpack, we'll show you some photos that Henry gave me."

Shirley also said that Gwen had written a letter for Gary, a letter that had them all in tears. "She really was an amazing lady, and you could tell she had loved Gary so much. Now, Henry and Carol are coming to the opening day of the exhibition so you will be able to meet then."

"That reminds me," June said. "Stuart phoned. He wants to speak to you as soon as you get back."

Shirley said she would go and phone him.

Stuart wanted Shirley to make sure she brought all the sample sketches she did when sketching the chateau. She could not quite understand why, and then he went on to tell her that he was doing a feature on the chateau. "I want to show what goes into doing a sketch on such a large and important piece."

As soon as Shirley had unpacked she went to her studio and started to sort through her sample sketches. Some of them had writing on them, and so she asked Gary to come and help her. Gary suggested they take them all, and then Stuart and he could see which ones he wanted to display. "Remember, he has been putting on exhibitions for famous artists for many years."   Next day, Shirley put them all together in one box ready for the journey to Paris. Jill and Gary were busy in the office most of the day. They were busy with artists who wanted to come and display their work in the next exhibition in the art centre.

Shirley went to find June. She found her in the house sorting out furniture. She had persuaded Jacque to bring a few pieces furniture, as this was going to be his house as well as hers. Shirley looked at the furniture. Although it was old, there were some beautiful pieces. "I'm not sure I like Jacque's furniture," June admitted. "He is so happy to be moving in here that I can't hurt his feeling, so I'll just have to get used to his stuff."

June said that Jill was helping get Jacque's house ready to sell. "I think we need to paint it throughout as it needs to be freshened up. We have been doing the garden while you have been away, and I've to say it looks better already. We have donated so much stuff, but I've to say most of it needs to be dumped. Jacque has been a bit of a hoarder, not that I could tell him that."

Shirley agreed she should keep that to herself.

"We want to get it up for sale as soon as possible, and then I would like this house painted to make it mine and Jacque's house," June finished.

Gladys called in to see them on her way back to the hotel. It was nice for them to sit down and have a catch up. Shirley gave Gladys the dates of her exhibition in Paris. "Do you think you and Frank will be able to get away and come?"

"I don't think we'll both be able to come, but Celia and I will be coming."

Gladys told them that Celia had been so busy ever since she did that lecture on her bags. "She always says she has so much to thank you two for."

"Bill has reordered, as the bags sell very quickly. They are so popular. He has customers coming back for more," Shirley said.

The moving company was coming the following week to pack all the artwork for the exhibition. Shirley was going through it one more time to make sure she had not forgotten anything. She told Gary she was sending everything, and then Stuart could pick out what he wanted to use.

Jacque's house was looking really lovely now that it had a fresh coat of paint. The agent was very impressed at how quickly they had done the work. Jacque had the advantage of getting his workmen in to do the work. "It should be on the market for sale by the following week," the agent said.

The moving van arrived. They were a very professional company. Stuart had worked with them many times, and so they were used to moving valuable artwork. They had finished by mid-afternoon, and so now they were going to the chateau to pick up the sketch from there. Shirley phoned Yvette to say they would be with her shortly.

Gary could see that Shirley was nervous about seeing all her work packed in one van. He assured her that all was good and not to worry. "Yvette will phone as soon as they have left."

Gary and Shirley were leaving for Paris the next day, as they wanted to be there when the artwork was unloaded. Shirley spent the rest of the day and evening packing for her and Gary's trip to Paris. Yvette had given them all the details on the apartment in Paris. Shirley said to Gary, "It sounds very grand. We'll now find out how the other half lives."

Gary had arranged to phone Henry when they arrived at the apartment.

The next day, Shirley and Gary set off for Paris. June and Jacque came to see them off along with Annie, who wished Shirley good luck. Shirley was a bundle of nerves. "I've packed so many clothes as I couldn't decide what I'll want to wear."

June gave her one final hug and told her not to worry.

They had a good journey, though the traffic was crazy busy getting into Paris. Eventually, they found the apartment. Gary looked at Shirley. "Could you check the address?"

"Yes, this is correct," she said.

They got out of the car. A doorman in brass buttoned uniform came over to them to help with their bags. He then asked for their car keys, as he would park the car for them. Inside the main foyer they were escorted to the lift that took them to the apartment. The apartment was furnished in creams with a splash of pale bluish-grey. It was large, with three bedrooms and two bathrooms. The kitchen was out of a magazine. The living room was to die for. "We're going to enjoy staying here," Shirley stated.

They phoned Stuart to say they had arrived. He asked them for the address of the apartment so he could give them directions on how to get to the gallery. When Gary gave Stuart the address. He did not answer for a minute, and then he asked: "Is that Yvette's apartment?"

Gary said yes.

"Hah! All I can say is she must like you two. That is the most prestigious address in Paris."

Gary said he had never been in such luxurious apartment in his life.

"Well, make the most of it and enjoy every minute you're there. The gallery is only a short taxi ride away, and so I'll see you both tomorrow."

After they had freshened up, they went down to the main foyer to pick up their car keys. They then went for a walk and stopped in a small restaurant, had a meal, but then went back to the apartment as they had a busy day ahead of them.

When they arrived at the gallery, Stuart was there. The van had arrived and was about to be unloaded. Everything was being unloaded and put into the one big hall to be checked. The curator of the gallery had it all under control. The staff was taking great care unpacking each piece.

Everyone was so nice to Gary and Shirley. They made them so welcome. You could see how respected Stuart was. The staff just loved him. When everything was unpacked and checked, Stuart and the curator came up with a master plan, which they started to go through with the staff.

Gary and Shirley had never experienced anything like this. Shirley was amazed as she watched everyone getting on with their part in the overall plan. The one hall Stuart called 'the star of the exhibition.' He had the area zoned for the sketch of the chateau with all the sample sketches.

Stuart had taken photos of the chateau, which had been enlarged and mounted on boards with all the samples next to them. The main sketch had pride of place on the same wall. Shirley could not wait to see that area completed. She had brought some of her watercolours that she had made when she and June went to the Monet gardens. Some were of the lily ponds. Others were of other areas throughout the gardens. Stuart had not seen them, and so she said, "If you don't want to use them, I'll not be offended."

Stuart looked at them and then called the curator over to look at them. They both agreed they were very good and would be in the exhibition. Gary was having a ball helping the staff. They were giving him so many tips as to the correct way to show artwork.

It was getting late in the day so Stuart said, "That's enough for today. We'll carry on tomorrow."

Stuart wanted to take Gary and Shirley to supper. He knew the perfect restaurant where all the local artists hang out, plus a few characters.

The restaurant was well worth the visit. It was full of artists and characters and the food was excellent. Stuart and Gary were talking away, and so Shirley started a conversation with a young girl sitting on her own on the table next to them. She was telling Shirley she was a student at one of the universities and was studying art and design. She was not sure which she wanted to settle on.

Shirley told her about her exhibition and the name of the gallery. The girl was instantly impressed. She loved that gallery. They always have great exhibitions. She had been to quite a few. Shirley introduced her to Gary and Stuart. She explained that Stuart owned the gallery. Stuart instantly gave her a pass to come and see Shirley's exhibition. He told her she would not be disappointed. Just then Stuart, Gary, and Shirley's food arrived and the young lady left.

That night they slept so well in the luxury of the apartment. Gary said he could really get used to this way of life. They got ready to leave, allowing themselves enough time to go and get breakfast in one of the small cafes nearby. Fresh coffee and fresh pastries. What could be better?

When they arrived at the gallery they found that it was taking shape. Stuart called them to come and look at the star attraction. Gary and Shirley were taken aback when they first saw the sketch of the chateau mounted on the wall. The photos and the write-up Stuart had done really told the story.

"Yvette and Andre are going to be so proud of their chateau and to see it in an exhibition," Stuart said. "It has come alive. This is going to be the talking point of the exhibition. Now came and see what we're thinking of for your watercolours. The one room had pastel colours on the walls with good lighting, so we're going to mount your watercolours in here."

Shirley agreed this was the perfect room.

"You're getting rave reviews on the watercolours from the curator and, believe me, he knows his artwork."

The rest of the day was busy. Gary was helping the staff and Stuart was on the phone most of the day. A young lady came in to say they were putting up the posters outside and that they are very eye-catching.

Shirley and Gary, along with some of the staff, went outside to see the posters. Shirley looked up to see her name and photo on the poster. She was taken aback. "Well, you can't miss it, can you?"

Gary thought it looked great and quickly took photos. "I'll send them to June, Henry Heather, and Mary. I want everyone to see you."

There was only one day before the opening. Stuart said he would not be at the gallery the next day, but that he would be here for the opening. Shirley and Gary decided to go to the same restaurant as they went to with Stuart the night before, but that they would not stay long as they wanted to have an early night to get ready for the opening.

Shirley was up bright and early. Gary went out to buy coffee and pastries and brought them back to the apartment. When they were ready, they set off for the gallery. Henry and Carol would be going straight to the gallery.

Heather and Dave had arrived and were staying in a hotel close to the gallery with John, Jill, June, Jacque, Mary, and Bill. So they were meeting us at the gallery later. They had all phoned Shirley to wish her well and good luck.

Shirley was a little sad that Alex was unable to come.

Stuart was at the gallery along with a few of his friends. He was doing a few last minute things before they opened the doors. Gary and Shirley had one last walk around. Gary asked Shirley if she was happy with how her work was displayed. "I'm over the moon. He makes me look so good! I just hope everyone likes it."

The staff in the foyer and throughout the gallery were dressed all in black. The curator came and opened the doors. Henry and

Carol were first in. They hugged Shirley and said they had no idea she was so famous. Shirley laughed. Everyone was asked to sign the book as they came in.

Gary suggested Henry and Carol stroll through the gallery and that they would catch up with them later.

There was a steady flow of people, and then Shirley spotted all the familiar faces coming in together. She was so pleased to see them all. They all commented on the poster above the door. John said he had never been so proud in all his life. "To think my mother has her own exhibition in Paris," he mused.

Gary had gone off to find Henry and Carol, and so Shirley walked around with everyone.

The young man from the front desk in the foyer came to find Shirley and said there was a group of people in the foyer that were asking for her and Gary. Gary had just gone to the foyer so they were waiting for her, he reported.

Shirley walked around the corner to the front foyer. She heard all the clapping. Then stopped, shocked. She suddenly realized it was her old art class from Brookdale. Gary was in the middle of them clapping. "What a wonderful surprise! How did you know about the exhibition?" Shirley asked.

They all said she had her husband to blame. Mary heard all the commotion, and so came to join the party with Bill. "When Gary told us you were having your own exhibition in Paris we started putting a trip together so we could all be with you on this special day," Mary said.

Shirley, with a tear in her eye, thanked them very much for coming and hoped they enjoyed the exhibition.

Stuart had a small reception in the main hall. Everyone gathered for a glass of wine to toast the artist. Stuart said a few words about meeting up with Gary again and spoke all about Shirley and June's art centre. Shirley called June up to join her.

Stuart cleared his throat. "These two ladies had the mindset to open this wonderful art centre called *Petit Bijou* and it has been a great success." Stuart then went on to talk about Shirley and her sketching and how she had been commissioned to sketch this magnificent chateau. "I had the privilege to go to the chateau with Shirley and meet the owner when I went to stay with Gary and Shirley. Now, I recommend you go to the main hall there you will find the star—in my opinion—of the exhibition as well as her watercolours which, by the way, she just handed these to me at the last minute. To fill in empty spaces, as she put it. This is a very talented lady and, to my surprise she was not even aware of it. And so, I would like you all to raise your glasses with me to Shirley. This is the first of many exhibitions. Paris is lucky to have her."

They all raised their glasses to Shirley.

"Now, please, everyone go and enjoy her work. As you leave, there are cards for you to fill in, as we do like to have your comments. By the way, Shirley and June have a book out, which is on sale in the foyer. It is all about their art centre."

The opening could not have gone better. Shirley, June, and Mary enjoyed catching up with all their old friends from Brookdale. Gary was introducing Henry and Carol to all their friends. The art work except for the chateau was for sale, although if anyone wanted to buy, they could not have it until the end of the exhibition, and the exhibition ran for one month.

Bill bought Mary one of Shirley's watercolours. She was so pleased with it. Heather was enjoying telling everyone that Shirley was her mother. The one sketch that was getting rave reviews was the one of the horses in the fields, but they were all good.

By the end of the day Shirley was exhausted. Stuart was very pleased with the turn-out for a first day. "Now go and enjoy your family and friends and I'll see you both tomorrow."

They all went out for a meal together and had a wonderful evening. Everyone loved Henry and Carol. They said good night, and that they were all going back the next day because of work, but Henry and Carol were staying a while longer. Gary told Henry and Carol: "Wait till you see the apartment. It is quite special."

They arrived at the apartment building. The door man opened the door for them with a flourish. Henry looked at Carol, who was taking photos in the foyer. Henry told her not to keep taking photos. "Wait till there is nobody around. Gary said we can take photos in the morning. Wait till you see the apartment."

Gary opened the door. They walked in. Henry and Carol stared. They could not believe their eyes. "This one room is bigger that our apartment in London," Carol said.

Shirley took them to their room. "Now make yourselves comfortable, and then come and have coffee."

They all changed so they could relax and get ready for tomorrow. They chatted about the day. Shirley could not get over her friends from Brookdale, and how they had come all this way just for her.

Gary said, "As soon as I told them they all agreed it gave them a reason to come to Paris."

Shirley said they told her they were staying three days in Paris, and so they had lots planned. They were so supportive. June had more time with them than she did.

"I've never signed my name so many times," Shirley said.

Carol congratulated her on all the artwork. "We just loved them all. Also, we were so proud to say we're family."

Shirley smiled her thanks. "Now, remember, Carol, you're only here for two more days so you don't have to be at the gallery all the time. There is so much to see in Paris. Gary suggested we should meet at the end of the day for a meal."

Henry thought that was a great idea. "We do have a few things we would like to see while we're here."

CHAPTER TWENTY TWO

Henry and Carol

THE EXHIBITION WAS getting rave reviews. They had not had an exhibition which was mainly all sketches before. A reporter came to interview Shirley. She was very nervous but Stuart talked her through it. Although she was full of nerves, she came across so confident. Gary and Stuart said she was a natural. The book sales were excellent, and so Gary phoned Jill to send more as soon as possible.

Shirley phoned Yvette to let her know how it was going, and that the chateau was a great success. "When you come I think you and Andre will be very happy the way Stuart and the curator have displayed it."

Yvette replied that she could not wait to see the whole exhibition.

That evening Gary and Shirley took Henry and Carol to their favourite restaurant, the one where all the local artists hang out. Henry and Carol had had a wonderful day sightseeing around Paris. Carol was in awe. "I'm so pleased you invited us to come and join you both."

They entered the restaurant. Who should be there studying in the corner but the young lady they met on their first visit to the restaurant. They got seated, and then Shirley went across to say hello to the young lady. To Shirley's surprise, she was reading the paper with Shirley's photo and interview.

"You're quite a celebrity, you know. There is a group of us coming from the university tomorrow. Will you be there?"

"We'll be there, but please ask for me as I would love to meet your friends."

"The one teacher went to the first day," the girl continued. "He was very impressed. He wants us to see, as he put it, the star of the show."

She gave Shirley her name and said she looked forward to seeing her at the exhibition tomorrow. Shirley went back to join the others, who were waiting to order supper. Shirley told Gary the young ladies name was Louise and that she, along with her friends from the university, were coming to the gallery tomorrow.

Henry loved the restaurant. It had great atmosphere. Gary told him that Stuart brought them there and that they loved the atmosphere, too.

Carol added, "I just love nothing better than people watching. I've become very nosy since arriving in Paris."

The next day Henry and Carol were off to do more sightseeing. Carol had taken so many photos in the apartment. Henry said, "I even think she has taken a photo of the bathroom, and then she told me we needed to redecorate their apartment when we get home!"

The gallery was busy, as people had seen the report in the paper. In middle of the morning, Louise and her friends came in. Louise introduced her friends to Gary and Shirley. The lady in the front foyer gave them all the information on the exhibition.

Shirley told them to take their time and tour the exhibition. "If any of you have any questions, please come and find me."

The one student had a camera, but Shirley told them all taking photos was strictly forbidden in the gallery. Louise thanked her and said they were all looking forward to seeing the exhibition.

Shirley noticed she had missed a call on her phone. When she checked she saw it was from Alex asking her to phone her when she had time. She found Gary talking to a group of people looking at her watercolours. When he saw Shirley he could see she was concerned about something, and so he excused himself.

He asked Shirley if she was all right. Shirley explained she had missed a call from Alex and so she needed to phone him as soon as possible. "Come on, I'll come with you to Stuart's office and you can phone Alex from there."

Stuart was in his office, and so Gary asked if Shirley could phone her son. "No problem," he said as he got up and left her to do it in private.

Shirley dialled his number. He answered almost immediately. Alex sounded stressed, and so she quickly asked if everything was all right. "Mum, I just wanted to talk to you. I've left Linda. I just can't take it any longer."

Linda had never been very friendly towards Shirley or to anyone in the family. Alex could never give her enough; she always wanted more. They had the two children but kept them away from the rest of the family. When Jim, Alex's dad died, she wanted nothing more to do with Shirley and the family. Shirley just gave up trying in the end.

Alex explained that things had gone from bad to worse. The final straw was when she wanted to move her 'girlfriend' in to live with us. She told Alex he could carry on living with them, but she wanted to be with her girlfriend and that she never really loved him. "To make matters worse she's brainwashed the children and now they don't speak to me. I've got myself a small flat about five miles away from them. She wants to divorce me and has already been to the lawyer, so I'm meeting with my lawyer tomorrow. So sorry I missed the opening of your exhibition," Alex continued. "I would have loved to have been there for you."

Shirley said she would support him in whatever he wanted to do. "The last thing I want is for you to be unhappy. Have you spoken to John?"

Alex was quiet. He said he would phone John.

"When you have spoken to your lawyer, why don't you come and stay with us. We would love to have you."

"You know, Mum. I think I'll do that if you're sure."

"That's settled then. We're only in Paris another two days, and then we return home so we expect you as soon as you have met with your lawyer. I'll phone June tomorrow, and so if you arrive before we get back she will take good care of you. You know June. She loves to have someone to mother."

They chatted a little while longer. Alex sounded more relaxed at the end of the conversation.

Shirley told Gary she would explain about Alex when they got back to the apartment; she did not want to discuss it in the gallery. Gary was so enjoying talking to everyone in the gallery. He said he had picked up so many great ideas for their art centre.

Shirley went back into the gallery. Louise was looking for her. She asked if Shirley could come to the hall where the chateau sketch was as her friends had a few questions. When Shirley got there, they were all studying the sketches with great interest.

Shirley said, "I believe you have a few questions for me?"

One student asked how she got started on doing a sketch on such a grand chateau.

"Well, I like to study it first. And then I take loads of photos. It takes longer in the beginning, but everyone works differently. As you can see, I do many sample sketches. These are just a sample of all the samples I did. I put all the photos up on a board then started sketching. I did go back many times to see the chateau at different times of the day to get the correct lighting. There are so many architectural details on a magnificent building like this. It was so challenging but a great achievement."

Louise thanked Shirley for taking the time to explain her technique to them. Shirley told them to make sure they filled in the forms at the front desk. "We do want your feedback, and thank you all for coming. Also, good luck to you all and remember, never give up, as I was a late bloomer."

Gary and Shirley were talking to people in the gallery. Everyone was so interested to hear how Shirley got started in the art world. Shirley told everyone: "You're never too old to take on a new hobby." Because that was what she did.

Stuart came to see them as he was leaving to attend a meeting. He would see them tomorrow before they leave for home, he said. He said the exhibition was getting a good report from everyone. "I want to have a meeting with you both tomorrow when you come in. I have a few ideas I would like to run by you."

Tonight was Henry and Carol's last evening in Paris, and so Gary booked a meal on the boat cruise down the River Seine. It was a surprise for Henry and Carol. Back at the apartment Henry and Carol were having a rest after their full day of sightseeing.

Gary told them to be ready as soon as they could as they were all going on the River Seine Cruise, and would be having a meal as they cruised.

Carol jumped up and down. "Just when you think it can't get any better!" she cried.

Shirley and Gary were showered and changed in no time. Shirley did manage to tell Gary about Alex while they were getting ready.

He was so sorry to hear about Alex. He never really knew Linda, and had only heard about her from John and Heather. He was pleased that Shirley had invited him to come and stay with them. "It will give him breathing space to decide what he wants to do," Gary said sadly.

The evening cruise could not have gone better. It was such a romantic cruise and the food was sublime. They chatted about the wonderful trip and Henry thanked Gary and Shirley so much for including them in their special time.

Henry and Carol quickly packed when they got back to the apartment. They were setting off by 8:00 AM the following morning, and so they had to make sure everything was packed the night before.

Gary and Shirley hugged Henry and Carol with heavy hearts, even though they had all had such a good time. Gary told them that they are very welcome to come and visit whenever they had time off.

Henry said they look forward to visiting them as soon as they got some more time off work. Shirley said, "All you have to do is phone us. We love you both so much."

When they had left, Gary and Shirley started to get ready for their last day at the gallery. Shirley wanted to phone Heather about Alex before leaving. Heather was not surprised, but she was surprised to hear she had a girlfriend. "I've nothing against gays, as we have friends that are gay and I've the greatest respect for them. It's just that Linda has led Alex through a dog's life for years. I think this is the best thing that could have happened, and I'm so pleased he has agreed to come and stay with you for a while. Let me know when he is coming and I might be able to come and visit with Jenny."

Shirley thought that would be a great idea.

Heather said she had seen the report in the Paris newspaper about the exhibition. "We're so proud of you, but after seeing your work we were not surprised."

When Gary and Shirley arrived at the gallery, Stuart was already there and working in his office. "No wonder he never married as he is married to the art world," Shirley observed.

The lady on the front desk asked them if they could go to Stuart's office when you were ready.

Gary knocked on the door of the office. Stuart called them in. He ordered coffee and asked them to sit down. He went on to say that the exhibition had excelled his expectations. "This is the first time I've put an exhibition on that, with the exception of a few watercolours, was all sketches. The comments we have been getting are that the public wants more of these exhibitions. Now, this is what I would like you to do: concentrate on the old vineyards, churches, chateaus, or any heritage buildings you can find. There are plenty to choose from in France. Even bridges and landscapes. Anything that appeals to you."

Shirley was thrilled as this was right up her street. Gary thought it was a great idea. "My question is, this will take time, so do you have a time we need to work towards?"

Stuart said he would work with Shirley. "I do not want to put her under any pressure at all. We could have fewer sketches, but I would like to present them in the way we did the chateau in this exhibition to include the photos and your sample sketches. That is what people liked. That way there is a construction plan leading up to the final sketch."

Shirley wanted to thank Stuart for giving her an opportunity of a lifetime. "I feel very honoured," she said.

She told Stuart that Yvette and Andre were coming to Paris the following week and would be coming to the gallery to view the exhibition. Straightaway he said: "They must ask for me as I want to escort them around the gallery personally."

Gary said they would love that.

They enjoyed the rest of the day meeting people in the gallery. Before they left they went around to every member of staff and thanked them. They also told them they would be back during the last week of the exhibition.

The last evening was supper in their favourite restaurant. They were well known by now, and so everyone chatted to them. Shirley was disappointed that Louise was not there that night. They told her they were going home the next day but would be back in a few weeks and that they would hopefully see her then.

They were packed and ready to leave by 8:00 AM, as Gary wanted to get through Paris before it got too busy. On their journey, Gary did a detour through small towns. They came across some beautiful building that he thought Shirley could use in her next exhibition.

It took them ages to get home, but at least they had collected many photos for Shirley to look through in her own time. The countryside in France was not to be underestimated. One could spend a lifetime driving around these roads and never tire of them.

When they arrived home, they were pleasantly surprised to find Alex had just arrived. He looked very drawn and in need of a complete rest. He was so pleased to see his mum. Shirley hugged him and told him he could stay as long as he wanted to.

She took him over to their apartment. He thought it was amazing. "Look at all the rooms you have. This is great."

Gary came in to welcome him and said June had prepared a meal, which would be ready in thirty minutes.

Shirley told him he was their guest. "And so come and see the guest room. Jill has been helping me with all the décor. She did a great job. I always thought she had a good eye for design." Shirley then asked Alex if he had spoken to John.

He said, yes, and that he had been very supportive.

"Well, I want you to relax and make yourself at home and please don't push yourself. I can't wait to see what Gary and Jacque are building. They will love telling you all about it over supper."

June was pleased to see Shirley and Gary back. She missed Shirley, and Jacque missed Gary. Also Gary had missed a home-cooked meal, although they went out to some amazing restaurants, they agreed it was not the same.

Jacque got Gary up-to-date on the photography studio. He also told Alex all about it. Jacque said, "As soon as we have finished supper we'll go and do a tour."

Shirley smiled at June and said and, "We can catch up on what-ever else has been going on while we have been away."

June told Gary that Jill and Barb have been very busy booking artists for the next art show. She would be coming in tomorrow to get them up to date. They also wanted to discuss having a workshop with potters. "They have some good ideas that I think you will like," June said.

After supper Jacque could not wait to take Alex and Gary to the studio. "They have done a lot of work," June said. "I think Gary will be amazed at the progress they have made."

They walked into the studio. Gary was shocked. They had done so much. The electrical work had been completed. All the trim and doors had been installed, and the painters were just finishing off.

Alex was taken back as to the size and the design of the whole studio. "Gary and Jacque, you have thought of everything."

Gary had told Alex that they had had a lot of help from the students from the art college. They are so knowledgeable and, as I said, a great help."

Gary tried the lighting out now that the walls had been painted. "This is a photographer's dream," said Alex. "I had always liked photography, but I don't know that much about it."

Gary thought they would be ready to start installing the equipment that was ordered. "The painters have to finish off inside. Then it is all outside work. We have been working with a sign writer that did the work on the art centre, so they have come up with a very neat logo for the studio. Jill and Barb have had a big input on the exterior, and so I'm sure we'll not be disappointed."

Alex looked much better when he got up the next morning. Amazing what a good night's sleep could do. Shirley asked him what he wanted to do. He said he would like to help with the studio as long as he was not in anyone's way.

Straight away Gary told Alex they would love to have another pair of hands to help. Gary took Alex under his wing. "We'll go and check with the sign writer, and also with the company who we're buying the equipment from. So, as soon as we have finished breakfast we'll be off."

"Sounds good to me," said Alex.

Shirley phoned Yvette to thank her so much for letting them use their apartment in Paris. She told Shirley they would be setting off the next day to go to Paris and were so looking forward to visiting the exhibition. "It will do us both good to get away. We have many friends in Paris, and so there will be a group of us going to the exhibition."

"Stuart is looking forward to showing you around. He is very proud of his gallery, and so he should be. You will also meet the curator. He is such a nice man and so knowledgeable and very interesting to talk to. We're going back during the last week of the exhibition so we're there on the final day."

"Well, remember you must stay at the apartment."

"Thank you so much. We felt very privileged to stay in such a magnificent apartment."

Yvette went on to say they had bought the apartment off a family member when they got themselves in debt many years ago. Then they wanted to buy it back years later, but there was no way. "We struggled when we first bought it, but it was worth it in the end," she confided.

Heather phoned to ask how Alex was. "He looks so much better today," Shirley said. "He went off with Gary and I've not seen them since."

"All I hope is that he does not go back to Linda, as you know I never liked her, but she was Alex's choice."

"It is early days," Shirley said. "But I don't think he will go back. If Linda had a boyfriend it might be different, but because she has moved her girlfriend in, there is no chance. We have to support him and respect his decision, and so please be careful what you say to him."

It was late in the afternoon before Gary and Alex returned. They had accomplished so much and Gary was feeling very pleased with himself. Alex said he had had the best day for a very long time. "I don't feel stressed at all."

They had a quick coffee then went off to find Jacque, who was busy helping to do all the final touches before the equipment was installed. The painters had made great progress. It was looking very impressive.

Jill had been speaking to the landscapers to go over their plans and asking when would they be able to start. She was pleased to report the landscapers would be there as soon as they phoned them. All the plants and trees that were ordered had arrived.

Jill told Gary, "We need a meeting about the art centre. Barb and I have things we need to discuss with you and Shirley."

Gary said he would check with Shirley. "What about tomorrow? Does that work with the both of you?"

Jill agreed that would be good.

At the meeting, Jill and Barb told Gary and Shirley they would like to organize a workshop with a potter. "He approached us and asked if he could do a workshop in the art centre," Jill said. "We have been to see him in his studio, and he is very professional. His work is first class. He was a teacher but now works at home organising small workshops, but he was interesting in doing a workshop in our art centre."

"And he has attended everything we have put on since we have been open. To be honest, he would be a great asset to the art centre," Barb put in.

Both Gary and Shirley thought it was a great idea. "When were you thinking of?" asked Shirley.

"We were thinking of arranging it as soon as possible, before we open the photography studio," Jill said.

"If you think you can organise it in the next two week, then go ahead," Shirley said, all smiles.

Barb and Jill said they would get on to it straightaway. "I'll go and phone Bob, the potter, to see if that is allowing him enough time," Barb said.

Bob was pleased to get a phone call from Barb and said he would love to do it. Jill asked him if it was possible for him to come out to the centre so they could sit down and discuss all the details. Bob agreed to come out later that day.

When Bob arrived, Jill and Barb wanted to introduce him to Gary and Shirley before they went into the centre. Shirley and Gary welcomed Bob, and then told Jill and Barb that if they need them to come and find us. "We won't be far away."

They went into the office in the art centre. Jill was taking notes, ready to put a notice in the paper. Bob said he would like to do two days with ten people on each day. "I find if you have too many, nothing gets accomplished. I'll bring everything I need."

They had a good meeting and went over everything. Jill had all the information. Bob said he would come the day before to bring everything he needed. Barb told him if he wanted to come back before then just come as there was always someone here.

Everything was going so well leading up to the opening of the photography studio. Gary was getting lots of inquiries, but he had no idea there were so many photographers. The sign company had put up the sign and it looked so good. *Photography Studio*. Alex and Gary just stared at it, bursting with great pride.

Before long, Jacque, Annie, Shirley, Jill and Barb were all staring at it. Jill informed them that the landscapers were coming the next day, which would bring it all together.

Gary said all the equipment would be delivered tomorrow, ready to be installed the following day.

Shirley asked about the furniture. "Has anyone checked to see when that is being delivered?"

Gary said he would phone them. They had told him everything he wanted was in stock so it should not be a problem, he said.

When Shirley went back into her studio she noticed there was a missed call from Stuart, and so she phoned him. He wanted her to ship more books, as they only had a few left. Stuart told Shirley that Yvette and Andre, along with a group of friends, had been to the gallery. "They were so proud of the way we had displayed the sketch of the chateau," he said. "Yvette had tears in her eyes as she looked at Andre's face looking at the sketch. Also all the photos and sample sketches you did … well, it really has been the star of the exhibition. When you come back before the end of the exhibition I think you will be shocked at the amount of sales we have done."

Shirley told Stuart they would be back to have the last two days in the exhibition before it closed. She also told Stuart about all the photos she and Gary took on their way home. "I'm looking forward to getting started!"

Stuart asked her to bring the photos with her when they came back to Paris.

Shirley, Gary, and Alex were enjoying their supper when the phone rang. Gary answered. It was Linda. She wanted to speak to Alex. Gary handed Alex the phone. Shirley and Gary got up so Alex could speak in private. He stopped them and told them to stay. "I have no secrets."

They could hear Linda shouting on the phone and telling Alex to get back home as she was now on her own. Alex stopped her and said he had been to his lawyer and she would be hearing from him in due course. Linda was saying she was sorry. He stopped her again and said it was over, and that he had never felt so relaxed

He inquired about the children, but she quickly said they did not want to speak to him again.

Alex took a deep breath. "I'm going to put the phone down now so there will be no need for you to phone me again."

Gary then got up and said: "I think this is the time when we all should have a brandy."

Shirley asked Alex if he was all right. He turned to his mum and said, "Never better. You're the greatest mother ever. You never judge, but are always there when we need you."

Gary poured the brandy and toasted Alex. Gary told him he was very proud of him. "I'm going to need a manager for the photography studio in time as I think it will be very busy, and I want to get on and get the other rental accommodation built."

Shirley looked at Gary and said, "I'm going to also need you to help me with my new career. I've spoken to Stuart and we have to take the photos we took on our way home with us when we go back to Paris."

CHAPTER TWENTY THREE

Photography Studio Opens

THE LANDSCAPERS ARRIVED in force. There were vans, trees, bushes, and workmen in abundance. Jill was in the thick of it. She had her plan, and so she knew exactly where every plant was to go. John came to see Alex while all this was going on.

Alex was inside with Gary and Jacque, but was so pleased to see John. John wanted to take Alex out to lunch and have a chat away from everyone. Shirley was delighted to see her boys getting together.

Alex quickly changed out of his work clothes. From experience he knew John always went to nice restaurants. It was a long time since they had had time together. Like the rest of the family, John never had much time for Linda.

They arrived at a winery where they served food out on the terrace. John said he had never been to this restaurant, but it came highly recommended. It had great atmosphere, also it was full of locals, which was always a good sign. They were taken to a table out on the terrace where they ordered drinks while they looked at the menu.

Lunch was ordered, and so they sat back and enjoyed their drinks. John asked Alex how things were going. "I'm not here to pry, but I want to give you my support in any way I can."

Alex told John all about what had happened and that Linda phoned him to say she was now sorry and her girlfriend had moved out and wanted him to come home.

"Please, don't tell me you're going back to her."

"Absolutely not. I think she did me a favour, to be honest. I just needed a push. She certainly did that. I do miss the children, but she has brainwashed them, and they won't speak to me."

"I'm so proud of you, because it could not have been an easy decision to walk away from the children. I was never a fan of Linda because of the way she spoke to you."

"I went to see my lawyer before I came out to stay with mum and Gary as I want a legal separation to begin with. He will be sending paperwork to Linda that she has to sign. I think that is how it goes. I did move into a small flat before I moved here, and so I now have to decide if I want to go back to live there. Gary is a great guy," Alex continued. "Mum is so lucky to have found him. He's offered me a job to manage the photography studio when it opens. I've taken leave from work for a few weeks, just to give me time to think things through. What do you think I should do? I'm open to any suggestion you can throw my way."

"First of all, you have to make your own decisions in the end. But to me, you seem like the Alex I used to know. You look as though a weight has been lifted off your shoulders. What does Mum say?"

"She says the same as you. I feel so lucky to have you all to support me when I need it most." Alex added that he couldn't get over how Jill had settled into life in France and how she just loved working at the art centre.

"Yes, Jill has just excelled since we came to live in France, Mum and Gary adore her. She runs the place."

The rest of the lunch was great, as they just enjoyed catching up, but as they left the restaurant John said: "We have to keep in touch more."

Alex asked John if he missed anything about Britain.

He looked at Alex and said: "Not one thing."

When they arrived back, the landscapers were busy doing an amazing job. Jill and Gary were in the thick of it. John said to Alex: "Just look at her. She's having a ball."

She spotted John and Alex and came over to them. "I hope you two boys had a nice lunch. It is so nice to have you here with us, Alex. Please, say you're going to stay. Gary needs you. Mind you, there's no pressure." She wandered off then.

Gary asked John and Alex to come and see the furniture and equipment in the studio. Alex had great pleasure showing John around. "It's amazing, don't you think?" John said.

Gary said to John quietly that he had offered Alex the job to manage the studio. "He has a lot of decisions to make, but I'm quite confident he will make the right ones."

John asked where Jacque was. Gary said he and June had gone over to Jacque's house as the agent now had an offer on it. "That did not take long to sell," John observed.

"Well, Jill worked with Jacque to get it ready for sale. It looked as pretty as a picture by the time she had finished with it," Gary said.

Jill told John he was going to see his mum. Gary said she was in her studio, working on her next project. When John went into her studio he saw that Shirley had photos all over the place. She then told him what Stuart wanted her to work on. He thought it was a great opportunity.

Now that they were on our own, John sat down to talk about Alex. "I hope he sticks to what he is saying at the moment and does not change his mind. Linda is bad news, but at the end of the day it has to be Alex's decision. If he does go back, she will do this again and I think he knows that. He was telling me that Gary offered him the job to manage the new studio, which I think he would be good at. He has great respect for Gary and really does appreciate his offer.

Shirley told John that they are going back to Paris next week as the exhibition closed at the end of next week. Stuart had told them there have been quite a few sales, but he would not tell how many. "It has been a very popular exhibition," Shirley added. "As the numbers had been up from previous exhibitions, which was good to hear. Oh, and Yvette phoned to say we can stay at their apartment whenever we're in Paris. We may ask Alex if he would like to come with us. Do you think it would be a good idea for him to come?"

John thought it would be good for him. "He needs to be kept busy. I'll ask him tonight, that gives him time to think about it."

John hugged his mum as he left. "I'll go and see if Jill is ready, but when I saw her she was busy with the landscapers."

Shirley just smiled. "Well, you know Jill. We would be lost without her."

"I just don't want her doing too much."

"Don't worry about her. She is loving it. This is her world."

Shirley heard June come in. "I want to know if Jacque accepted the offer on his house," Shirley said.

June told Shirley that Jacque did accept the offer on the house. "We just have to wait for all the papers to be signed. Hopefully it will be completed in about four weeks."

June said the buyers were a nice young couple, and so Jacque asked them if they needed any of the furniture. "They did, so now we don't have to clear it out. They were thrilled, as I don't think they have much. They could not get over the fact that the house had been redecorated inside and outside. Jacque was happy. He did not want to sell it to someone who was going to demolish it, as it had been his home for many years. He is quite a softy, I know, though he does not say much."

Shirley told June about John taking Alex out for lunch. "It's wonderful to see them spending time together. Have you been to see all the landscaping around the studio? They have done a wonderful job so far. They will be back tomorrow to finish off."

That night, when Gary and Shirley were in the apartment with Alex having supper, Shirley asked Alex if he would like to come to Paris with them. He asked how long they would be in Paris.

"Well, I would think about four days, but it might only be three days."

He said he would like to see her exhibition, as everyone said it was amazing.

Gary said, "You don't have to tell us now. Think about it, and then let us know. We have an apartment we can use so we don't need to book the hotel."

"Let me sleep on it," Alex said, "And I'll let you know tomorrow." He added that he really enjoyed having lunch with John. "I forgot how well we got on together."

The phone rang. It was Heather. "She wants to know how you are," Shirley said.

Alex laughed. "I had no idea I was so popular."

Shirley handed the phone to Alex so they could have a chat. Then he gave the phone back to Shirley. Heather could not believe the difference. "He sounds so upbeat," she said.

Shirley said, "We have asked him to come to Paris with us next week. I want to be there for the last two days of the exhibition. He is thinking about it at the moment."

For the next few days they were busy finishing the studio. Gary asked the students who had been helping with the design to come and check it out. Bob had been meeting with Barb and working out the plan for his workshop.

Jill came in to say that the information went onto the website and in the paper, and that already they were getting inquiries. "Some people have already booked, and so I don't think there will be problem filling the rest of the places."

Bob was taking photos. He wanted to print his own brochures to give out to everyone that came. Barb liked his approach. Some of his old students may come, not to take part, just to listen.

Alex decided he would like to come to Paris. Gary told him he was very pleased. "You will get to meet Stuart, who I'm sure you will get on with very well. When you see your mum's work you will be so proud. She is so well-thought of by all the staff."

It was soon time to get packed for the trip to Paris. Gary said he liked to make an early start, as the traffic was so heavy the nearer you get to Paris. "We like to stop on the way so we get to enjoy the countryside on our journey."

Alex was so looking forward to the trip. "I hear the apartment is not too shabby."

"Oh, just wait till you see it," Gary said. "Henry and Carol would not have minded if we had spent the whole time in the apartment."

Gary had been speaking to Henry. They had such a nice, relaxed relationship. It just came natural. Mind you, when he told them that they were off to Paris again they were not so happy. They wanted to go, too!

They set off early, as planned. The journey was very enjoyable. The countryside was breathtaking. They stopped in a small town that had a country market. Lunch consisted of fresh bread rolls, butter, and a selection of local cheeses and fresh coffee.

Alex looked at Shirley and said he was so pleased he had decided to come on this trip to Paris. "If I'm in France much longer I'll have to buy all new clothes. I mean, larger clothes."

Gary wanted to get back on the road. At the market, Shirley bought enough food to feed an army.

In no time they were on the outskirts of Paris. The traffic was crazy. Gary did well to remember the road that took them straight to the apartment.

They arrived at the apartment and the doorman promptly came out to help with the cases, and then he took the keys and arranged for someone to park the car. Alex looked at Gary. "You said it was in a very prestigious area. But this is something else."

Inside the apartment building Alex could not believe his eyes. The doorman took them to the lift while Gary was chatted to him. He told him it was nice to see him again, and then introduced Alex to him.

As they entered the apartment, Shirley said to Alex. "I don't think you will be disappointed. It is beautifully decorated and the height of luxury."

It did not take them long to get freshened up. "We thought we would go for a walk to stretch our legs after being in the car most of the day," Shirley said.

"Sounds good to me," said Alex. "I'm ready when you are."

Walking around the streets in Paris was always exciting as there was so much to see. They walked and walked. Alex was taking photos of the buildings. "I love the architectural detail on old buildings. Sometimes I think we have lost all our creativity over the years in Britain."

Gary agreed with him. "To think how many years these building have been here, and yet they look better with age."

Next morning they were ready to go to the gallery. Shirley could not wait to show Alex her work. She had all the photos in a carrying case to show Stuart. "To think these are the final two days of the exhibition," said Gary.

The staff at the gallery were all so pleased to welcome Shirley. They all shook her hand and congratulated her on such a successful exhibition.

Alex whispered to Gary, "I had no idea she was so well regarded in the art world. I have shivers up my arm. I'm so proud of her. And to think she is my mother! John and Heather told me it was an amazing exhibition, but I was not expecting this welcome."

There were quite a few people already in the gallery and as soon as they saw Shirley they wanted her autograph. Gary told Shirley he would take Alex around the gallery, as she was going to find Stuart.

As they walked around the gallery, Alex was in sheer amazement. "This totally fantastic!" he cried. They stopped in the area where Shirley's sketches of the horses in the field were hanging. A couple was looking at it with their friends. Apparently they had bought two of the sketches. The older lady said they had bought them for their granddaughter, who had just graduated and just loved horses.

The older man with her said, "We were hoping to meet Shirley the artist and have her sign them, but I don't think we'll be lucky."

Gary interrupted them and told them that Shirley had just arrived. "If you wait here, I'll go and look for her so you can meet her."

"Do you know her?" the lady asked.

Gary very proudly said: "She is my wife and this is her son."

Gary left them talking to Alex and went to find her. She was with Stuart, going over the photos. When he explained that Shirley had fans waiting, Shirley told Stuart she would be back shortly. Stuart grinned and said he would come as well.

They found Alex in deep conversation. As soon as the couple saw Shirley, they rushed to meet her. Shirley spoke to them for quite a while. She introduced Stuart to them. She arranged to sign the back of the sketch and took all the details about their granddaughter.

Shirley then introduced Alex to Stuart. Stuart told Alex he had a very talented mother. "Mind you, we have trouble convincing her how talented she is."

Shirley said they had better get back to Stuart's office and carry on going through the photos. "As I don't want to take up all your time."

Gary carried on walking around the gallery. Finally they arrived at the star of the exhibition. "What a great way to display the chateau." Alex was blown away with all the detail Shirley had managed to capture.

Gary said, "The more you look at it, the more you discover. Look at the roof line. Shirley even managed to capture the one area where the roof tile was broken. She went back so many times before she was happy with it Andre and Yvette, who own the chateau, also own the apartment we're staying in. Andre was the French President for many years before he had his stroke. This sketch was commissioned by Yvette as a gift for Andre when he came home from hospital. They were thrilled with it and took to your mum straightaway, and so they told her whenever she is in Paris she must use their apartment."

Alex enjoyed himself immensely with talking to the staff, who were so knowledgeable about Shirley's work. He also met the curator who, along with Stuart, had put the exhibition together. Stuart called Gary to come and look at the photos that he had selected. Shirley was happy with the ones he had chosen. "We'll go home the same way and take more photos of all the buildings you selected."

Shirley asked Stuart how many of the sketches had been sold. Stuart got out a book with all the sketches listed to do a final check. "I hope you're ready for this. With the exception of six, all are sold."

Shirley looked at Gary in disbelief.

"As tomorrow is the last day," Stuart said. "I want to know if you agree for us to put sold on the all the sketches that are sold. Because I think we'll sell the final six tomorrow."

Shirley said she had no objections. She turned to Gary and asked him what he thought. "I agree with Shirley."

Stuart tapped his chin. "When you work on the next exhibition I think you should put in a few sketches of horses. They always sell from past experience." Stuart then turned to Alex and asked him what he thought about the exhibition.

"To be honest, I'm blown away by the talent she has."

They left the gallery at the end of the day and decide to take Alex to their favourite restaurant. They entered the restaurant Alex straight away said, "What a great place!"

"We like it as it is full of artists and the atmosphere is great," Shirley said. "Plus the food is so good."

They found a table and sat down and ordered drinks as they looked at the menu. Shirley looked around to see Louise sitting in the corner with her head in her book, as always. Shirley went across to see her. She was so pleased to see Shirley again.

Shirley asked her if she had eaten. She said no, but she had ordered.

"Well, would you like to join us? You can tell us what you have been up to since we last met."

"I don't want to intrude, but it would be nice to catch up,"

"That settles it. Tell the waitress you have moved tables."

Gary hugged Louise and introduced her to Alex as they all sat down. Louise asked how long they would be staying in Paris. Shirley told Louise the exhibition closes tomorrow. "And so we'll be here two more days." Louise said her exhibition had been so inspirational to everyone in the university. "We have been back twice."

They had a nice meal, and then Gary, Shirley and Alex left as they wanted to go for a walk and Louise was meeting her friends.

After a walk around they made their way back to the apartment. Alex said he was so pleased he had decided to come. Shirley said Stuart enjoyed meeting Andre and Yvette again. "They would like all the sample sketches, and so he asked me to think about it."

Gary said, "So what do you think?"

Well, I would like to make a gift of them."

"That sounds like a nice idea. Can you believe that today is the final day of the exhibition?"

"Do you think it will be busy on the last day?" Alex asked.

"Well, I'm not sure," said Shirley. "What do you think, Gary?"

"I think it will be busy this morning, but by the middle of the afternoon I bet it will quiet."

They got to the gallery just at opening time. To their amazement it was busy. They went to check if the 'sold' signs were on the sold sketches and, of course, they were. Many people had come back for one final look. The books were selling. Alex was helping out as people were coming in.

Gary said to Shirley that he thought Alex had really enjoyed himself. It was a steady flow then lunch time. "I think people were coming in their lunch break," Gary said. Before long four of the last six sketches had sold, so now they only had two available.

Stuart came by towards the end of the day. He was sorry he had not been able to come in earlier, but he had been to another gallery for a meeting. Then a young man came in. He seemed to be a little stressed. "My wife told me to come in early as she wanted two of the sketches, and I knew they were still available yesterday as she checked the gallery website."

The one young man at the entrance went with him to find the sketches he wanted. To his delight they were still available. He told them his wife was suffering from cancer, but was very positive and doing well. She so wanted those sketches.

Alex asked him if he could wait while he went and found Shirley. "She would like to meet you," he said. A young lady dealt with the sale as Alex went to find his mum.

Shirley was speaking to a couple, but she could see Alex wanted to speak to her. She excused herself. Alex explained about the young man and the two last sketches.

Shirley walked in and Alex introduced the young man to Shirley. She said she was sorry to hear about his wife. "If you give me her name, I'll send her a message on the back of the sketch."

The young man was delighted. "This will make her day."

Shirley wished her well in her recovery.

Soon it was time to close the doors. Stuart gathered all the staff and his curator into the one room. He had organized light refreshments and wine. "Now has everyone got a glass of wine, as I want to make a toast," he began. "Thank you all so much for making this a very successful exhibition. Also I would like to thank Shirley for bringing her work to Paris. I think this will be the first of many exhibitions she will be putting on. Also, I want to thank Gary for being there at Shirley's side throughout the exhibition."

They chatted with everyone and had some wine and refreshments before it was time to go. Stuart said they would take care packing the sketch of the chateau. Shirley told them to include the sample sketches in the crate at the same time.

"We could take the sketches with us in the car," Gary said.

"Sounds like a plan," said Stuart.

Gary asked about all the sold sketches. The curator said they would take care of that. Gary then thanked everyone for making them feel so welcome. "As this was Shirley's first exhibition and it was in Paris she was very nervous, but you all put her at ease from day one."

They had said their goodbyes and were on their way back to the apartment. Alex was carrying Shirley's bag. "What about getting ourselves freshened up and going and having a meal?" he asked.

Shirley said she thought that was a great idea.

Gary found a nice little restaurant, and so they relaxed with a good bottle of wine and good food. What could be better? The restaurant was packed.

"Where do all these people come from?" Alex mused, and then said: "I want to thank you both for giving me such a great few days. This I'll never forget."

As always, Gary wanted to get an early start to the journey home. Shirley had a list of areas she wanted to stop at to take photos. The traffic was crazy until they got to the outskirts of Paris, then it slowed down a little. Alex said to Gary he was glad he was driving and not him.

Before long they got to the first town they wanted to stop in to take photos. "We can take lots as you don't want to have to drive back here any time soon," Gary said.

Soon, Gary was taking photos of churches, buildings, chateaus, and wineries. Between stopping for photos and food, they didn't get home until after dark. June was waiting to welcome them with hot supper. "Go and put your bags in your apartment, and then come and eat."

"It was nice to go away, but you can't beat the company of great friends and a home- cooked meal," said Gary.

During the meal they caught up with all the news at home and in Paris.

Alex said, "Mum is treated like a rock star in Paris."

"Don't say that, there will be no living with her," Gary teased. "Tomorrow we have to see where we are as to when we arrange the opening of the photography studio."

"I think you will be thrilled with the progress," Jacque said. "See you in the morning."

Gary was up bright and early, and so was Alex. They could not wait to go and check everything out. Shirley was a little more subdued this morning. "I think I'm going to have a lazy day if nobody minds."

"You take your time, Mum. Take the day off."

They went across to the studio. The first thing they noticed was the landscaping. It was amazing. The trees looked so mature, one would think they had been there for years. The sign was up and all the painting was completed. It looked so good. Because of the exterior building material they used it looked like it had been there for years.

"This is exactly how I envisaged it," Gary said. "Jacque, you have done an amazing job. I could not be more pleased. Now, come and see the inside. Everyone has been working so hard over the last few days, but it has paid off."

Jacque opened the door. "Now don't come in until I call you. Stay there."

Jacque went in and put the lights on. All the light fixtures were installed. "Okay, come on in. Welcome to your photography studio!"

Gary and Alex walked inside. The studio took their breath away. The lighting, along with the colour on the walls, was fantastic. There were many different areas, as suggested by the company that set up studios for professional photographers.

Alex said he was going to get his mum to come and see it. "She will be as thrilled as we are." He returned with Shirley and June. They were overwhelmed at what had been achieved. Shirley thought Jacque had done a truly outstanding job on the building of the studio.

As they all walked around inside, Shirley asked Gary, "When are you thinking of opening the studio?"

"I'll be working with Jill tomorrow to get the opening advertisement ready to go into the paper. Then we're ready to go. I have a professional photographer who is interested in doing classes every week if we're interested. Alex what do you think about that?"

Alex was getting more interested now. He had said to Gary earlier that he was interested in taking on the job of managing the studio. "I think we should phone the guy and get him to come over and meet with us as soon as possible."

"Well, can you phone him tomorrow and set up a time? Now, if we could get everything in place I see no reason why we can't open in two weeks. Let's work towards that date. It is better to have a date in mind, or we'll keep putting it off."

June said Jill went home early today. She said she was feeling unwell. She thought she had a cold coming on, but said she would see them tomorrow. Shirley asked if she thought she should phone her tonight.

"No, I would leave her to have a good night's sleep," June said.

Back in the apartment, Shirley asked Alex if he was serious about taking on the job of managing the studio. "We don't want to put any pressure on you but, on the other hand, we would love you to be part of our venture."

"I'm very interested. When I was with you and Gary in Paris and could see what you're achieving, I had never felt more alive and excited."

"That is so good to hear. I can see the real Alex, and I've not seen him for a very long time. You know, Alex, we're only on the earth once and we have got to make the most of it. I remember when June and I booked a holiday to France. Our friends thought we had lost our minds. And then when we came back with the idea of moving to France! Wow. Then when they found out we were going to open an art centre and have rental accommodation? Well, they shook their heads and said it would never happen. Then when I had my own exhibition in Paris and everyone was there! What an experience. I did not know, but Gary had been in touch with all those friends and they came to the opening day, so you can imagine my surprise. They were shocked to see how well June and I had done. Also, I married Gary and June lives with Jacque."

Alex asked what their reaction was.

"They congratulated me and June, and then apologized for ever doubting us. I must say June and I loved every minute of the apology. Gary enjoyed it as much as we did, if not more.

So you see, Alex, sometimes things happen to you to make you open your eyes and see what else is out there for you."

"Well, I want to be part of it. I phoned John and we discussed it at great lengths, and so the decision is made. I'm moving to France and taking the job. I'll have to go and pack up my apartment, which won't take long as I have no furniture. It will depend on the opening of the studio when I go."

Gary came in, and so they told him that Alex wanted to take the job when he was ready.

The next morning Gary went to see Jill. She did come in and looked a bit under the weather. They worked on putting a notice together about the photography studio opening and to welcome people to come to the opening to look around. "We'll work on opening in two weeks. And we have the pottery workshop next week, which is all booked up."

Alex phoned the professional photographer who was interested in giving classes. Alex arranged for him to come that afternoon to look around. He was very keen to be involved. Alex then went to find Gary to confirm the appointment.

Shirley phoned Heather to let her know about the opening as she and Dave wanted to come. She was so pleased to hear that Alex was staying in France.

"You will see a big difference in him when you see him," Shirley said. "He is so happy and just loves Gary."

The next two weeks were busy, what with everything getting set up for the grand opening. Shirley has started on her sketches and paintings for the next exhibition, but she had plenty of time. The pottery workshop was a great success. Everyone was asking when the next one was going to be, as they wanted to come again.

By now it was two days till the grand opening. The students from the university were ready. Pierre, the professional photographer, was ready. The good thing was that the students all looked up to Pierre as he used to teach at the university.

Annie was going to be helping with serving refreshments with June, who was more than ready. Heather, Dave and Penny arrived and were so thrilled to see Alex. Henry and Carol also arrived. Gary was so thrilled that they were able to get extra time off work.

The grand opening was to be at 2:00. Everyone was ready and excited to cut the ribbon by the front door. Jill had arranged for the photographer from the paper to come and take photos.

They were all ready. Gary said a few words and welcomed family and friends for making the journey to join them on this special day.

He introduced Alex as the manager of the photography studio. "And I would like him to join me in cutting the ribbon."

Alex looked so proud to be asked. The ribbon was cut. Everyone enjoyed looking around. Gary also introduced Pierre, the professional photographer. "You can ask him any questions you might have," Gary told the crowd.

When everyone had gone, the family and close friends all got together on the patio of June's house. June and Shirley made coffee and tea. There was more wine and nibbles. Michael and Jenny were having a great time playing together.

Then John got up. "I would like to say something. Jill and I have some very special news. We're expecting a baby."

Everyone went wild. Shirley was excited. Jill had thought she could not get pregnant. "This is the best news ever!" Shirley cried. "I wonder where we'll go from here !!!"

About the Author

ANNE BEEDLES WAS born and raised in Welshpool, Mid Wales, UK. Married to Roger moved to live in Ludlow England where she opened her own hairdressing Salon.

Moved to live in Swansea South Wales, where she started her career in Real Estate. Immigrated to Canada in 1997 where she continued working in Real Estate. In 2017 she retired to follow her life long ambition to start writing.

Anne and Roger have two children and five grandchildren.